Fate Accompli

The Water Nymph Gospels, Book 1

Keith R. Fentonmiller

Fate Accompli

Keith R. Fentonmiller

Ellysian Press

www.ellysianpress.com

Fate Accompli
© Copyright Keith R. Fentonmiller. All rights reserved.

Print ISBN: 978-1-941637-74-6
First Edition, 2021

Editor: Maer Wilson
Cover Art: M Joseph Murphy
Painting on cover: Harpsichord, Claude Jacquet, 1652, The John and Mable Ringling Museum of Art, Sarasota, Florida. Photo of inside harpsichord lid courtesy of Heidi Taylor, Associate Registrar of Loans/Acquisitions

DEDICATION

For Bay, whose fighting spirit inspires me

CHAPTER

ONE

Livorno, Grand Duchy of Tuscany, 1573

Enzo burst into the shop and darted around the display table of mitre hats and brimless caps. He breezed past his father, ignoring his greeting. Not to be rude. Something was muddling the connection between his mind and his mouth. This had happened before, after he'd unwittingly felted wool from a sheep that had rollicked through a patch of deadly nightshade. The delirious Enzo proceeded to regale baffled customers with what, in his mind, was the lyric poetry of Sappho, but which emerged from his lips as incoherent bleats and baas. Present circumstances differed in one key respect: Enzo could not blame a hallucinogenic sheep.

He parted the heavy curtain and strode into the cutting room. The black velvet drape swung closed behind him. He gripped his chest to calm his palpitating heart, to no effect. He stretched the collar of his chemise to ease his constricted breathing, also to no effect. It was as though an invisible hand was pounding on his sternum and squeezing his windpipe – well, two invisible hands, he supposed.

Enzo paced the plank floor and pulled at his unkempt hair. Only one person could rescue him from the encroaching madness: the coachman. The coachman was the miniature doppelganger who lived inside his mind – the homunculus who, dressed in a driver's livery, controlled his host's every thought and action.

He rapped his knuckles on his forehead.

Where the hell are you, man?

He knocked on his pate again, harder. Knuckle-shaped contusions sprouted on his brow.

Why do you shirk your duties?

Had the coachman fallen asleep on his perch? Had he gone on a bender? Was he carousing with tiny coach-women? Was he frequenting a tiny tavern where groups of tiny coachmen groused about the people they animated?

Enzo's rage turned to concern. Maybe his coachman was in distress. Maybe he'd encountered an unexpected bump in the road. Maybe he was languishing in a ditch, exposed to the elements, at the mercy of tiny highway robbers.

Enzo groaned. Knees weakening, he leaned against the cabinet of hat blocks for support.

Calm yourself, Enzo.

He closed his eyes, took a breath, and exhaled.

Get out of your head. The coachman can fend for himself. Think about your hands. Think about your work.

The tightness in Enzo's throat and chest relented. His heartbeat settled into a steady rhythm. He was himself again.

There. That's better.

Enzo opened his eyes and declared to absolutely no one, "Let's get to work!"

Enzo spied a square of burgundy felt on the cutting table. It was badly wrinkled. He strode past Hermes' portrait and entered the kitchen. He filled the flatiron with hot coals from the stove, then returned to the cutting room and pressed it into the fabric. An invisible cloud of heat buffeted his cheeks, carrying with it a gamy, animalistic odor that roiled his guts. He lifted the iron from the felt and instantly the odor vanished, and the nausea abated. When he reapplied the iron, the odor and nausea returned with a vengeance. He set the iron on end and dabbed his clammy brow with a sleeve.

He assumed the hot iron had liberated putrid particles trapped in the fabric. Occasionally, a drunken sailor vomited on the crates of rabbit pelts transiting from the Levant. But when Enzo sniffed the swatch, he detected nothing foul. He glanced toward the kitchen and recalled his mother had made candles that morning. Perhaps she'd dripped tallow on the coals. He opened the iron's coal chamber and inhaled. He didn't smell even a hint of rendered animal fat.

For Fate's sake, I'm not imagining it . . . or am I?

Indeed, he was. He recalled the odor from a dream he'd had shortly before awakening. In it, Enzo was standing over the tiny coachman, who lay dead in a muddy ditch, his livery tattered, soiled, and sun-faded. He'd been dead for days and reeked of decomposition. His face, or what used to be a face, was raw and featureless – no nose, eye sockets teeming with fly larvae, mandible stretched into the semblance of a horrified scream. Enzo knelt and ran his fingers along a deep, narrow impression in the coachman's thighs. He traced the impression to a line in the mud that ran to a hawthorn tree, where the carriage lay in shambles. The coachman, Enzo deduced, had been run over by his own carriage. What's worse, this accident had happened before. It had happened to the tiny coachman's father and grandfather, just as it would happen to his son and grandson. It was an unbreakable chain of accidents.

A primal rage surged inside Enzo. He pounded his fist on the cutting table and locked his flaming eyes on the ceiling.

"Listen well, Fate . . . or Moira . . . or whatever name you call yourself these days! I am leaving, and you cannot stop me. I shall cobble shoes or sow fields or lay bricks – anything but make hats. Mark my words. The only way I shall return to this hat shop is inside a coffin."

If Fate or Moira or whatever-name had marked Enzo's words, she might have annotated them with a word of her own: hollow.

* * *

Two years later, Enzo shambled back through the hat shop's front door very much alive, though his ragged condition suggested he might have been cohabitating with the dead all that time. His aghast parents ushered him to a chair by the oven. His mother handed him a pewter cup of warm bone broth, while his father draped a wool blanket around his shoulders. After regaining some vigor, Enzo recounted his ordeal.

He'd gone to Florence and established himself as a cobbler. He spent his saved-up florins to buy hammers, awls, leather, a shoe stand, and to lease a hovel in the shadow of the Palazzo Pitti. In the first week, lightning struck the shop not once, not twice, but thrice. That final strike collapsed the roof. Still, Enzo counted himself lucky for having taken out insurance on his wares. Unfortunately, the policy offered no protection from a fourth bolt, which struck him directly and rendered him as hairless as the day he was born. Although the thick black ringlets covering his scalp grew back as before, the follicles on his pubis, under his arms, and over his eye sockets returned white and bristly. The jolt also damaged the nerves in his left foot, inducing partial lameness and an unsettling sensation that he likened to a fish in his shoe. A grouper, by his estimation.

From there, Enzo took a job with an industrial weaving operation. He didn't last a day. Although his weaving technique was flawless, the warp threads snapped every time he threw the shuttle across the loom – indeed, across *any* of the ten looms he subsequently tried.

On a tip from a tavern-keeper, Enzo hopped a donkey cart to the Florentine countryside, where an elderly couple hired him to farm cabbage and eggplant for a share of the profits. Days were grueling under the hot sun, and nights were restless in the stifling lean-to in which he slept. Despite his diligent watering, weeding, and tending, the cabbage succumbed to locusts and the eggplant to a fungal parasite. Nevertheless, Enzo was heartened when the landlords accepted the bad news with grace. The woman waved off the apology, explaining that Enzo could not be responsible for what the Almighty God had willed. The man asked Enzo to pray with them. Five minutes of the old man's monotonous reading from the Book of Job drifted into slurred mutterings and an interminable silent meditation. When Enzo began swaying involuntarily and feared his legs might give out, he opened his eyes only to discover the couple slumped over the dining table, hand in hand, their feeble hearts having gone the way of the ill-fated cabbage and eggplant.

After that, Enzo laid bricks for two churches, a water mill, and a warehouse along the Arno River. Well, he tried anyway. Violent winds, subsiding ground, and lightning strikes wrought havoc on every foundation and wall he'd had a hand in. His employers took notice, and the masonry guild eventually circulated a flier warning its members about the itinerant bricklayer with "the fat nose and pig-hair eyebrows." A shame, yet Enzo found some solace in the sketch of his likeness, which accorded him the strong chin he'd secretly longed for.

Although Enzo had no employment prospects and nary a florin in his purse, he didn't despair. To his astonishment, he seemed incapable of despair. Whenever he'd contemplate taking a blade to his jugular or slinging a noosed rope over a rafter, something joyful would pop into his head and muddle the morbid fantasy. It was usually a little thing, like eating figs with caciocavallo cheese, bathing in cold springs on hot days, singing bawdy villanelle in the taverns, and dancing – yes, dancing, notwithstanding his chronic case of "floppy fish foot." He was especially adept at the Galliard, which involved quick, intricate steps and the ability to leap high in the air and execute one-foot landings.

And, of course, Enzo had to admit that millinery also brought him joy. His heart ached when he recalled trading Dante and Boccaccio quotes with his mother, while he and his father crafted linen coifs, velvet capotains, and conical hennin hats. He'd forsaken those sweet moments for a futile quest to liberate himself from Fate. But he'd deluded himself. That kind of freedom was a heartless abstraction. So what if he couldn't choose his destiny? He liked making hats, and he loved his parents. Leaving the hat shop because Fate demanded he stay wasn't an act of courage; it was petulance.

To be sure, Enzo couldn't rule out the possibility that Fate had implanted a love for millinery and his parents in his mind. After all, these sentiments eventually led him back to the hat shop. But Enzo refused to believe that Nature was cynical enough to endow humanity with self-awareness only to deprive them of choice in all matters. There had to be one sentiment over which he, and he alone, had exclusive dominion, and he realized what it was. Although Fate might control his destiny and nearly every choice he made along the way, she had no say whatsoever about his attitude toward that destiny. He could freely choose to embrace his fate, to love that fate, to follow the creed of *amor fati*. This freedom was proprietary and inalienable.

Enzo's epiphany triggered a fit of crazed, exhilarated

laughter. As his guffaws died down, he swore he heard faint sounds in his mind. If he wasn't mistaken, they were tiny footsteps. They were the sounds of a coachman climbing to his perch, taking the reins, and hollering, "Giddyap!"

* * *

Three decades later, Enzo sat in the chair by the tall cabinet of hat blocks, hunched over a blur of metal and fiber. While his fingers recognized the needle and thread, his aged eyes had to take it on faith because he was too cheap to invest in corrective lenses.

Stasi was standing at the cutting table, a mere five feet away. His eyes were young and clear. Stasi easily could've threaded the needle for his father, but Enzo was too proud to seek assistance, and Stasi knew not to offer it, for the gesture would only invite a reproachful scowl followed by a dubious aphorism like "Myopia is no match for a healthy dose of willpower" or "The man who cannot bend his eyeballs to his will is no man at all." Not that Stasi was focused on his father right then. He couldn't focus on anything. His mind was moving too fast. No, it wasn't the speed of his thoughts. It was their direction. They were spiraling. They were a vortex, and he was trapped in the empty center. He grabbed the scissors.

Enzo began to hum while rhythmically tensing and relaxing his brow. His fluffy white eyebrows merged and separated, over and over, like indecisive clouds. At length, he poked the thread toward the needle's eye, or, from his perspective, toward the vague center of an amorphous, semi-reflective blob. He missed.

Stasi tightened his grip on the shears.

Enzo threw himself back in the chair, hard. "Damn my old man eyes!"

Stasi released an animalistic groan and threw the

scissors on the cutting table. The clatter made Enzo flinch, interrupting his fit. He gaped at his son. *What's gotten into the boy?* Stasi was quaking, building to another paroxysm.

Stasi raised a defiant fist and began shouting at the ceiling. "Mark my words. I am finished with hats!"

Enzo nodded with resignation.

Stasi kicked the cutting table. The table collided into the wall and jostled the portrait of Hermes. The portrait swiveled on its nail and knocked into the tall cabinet, where Bronte was perched. All at once, the cat's one eye popped open, his tail shot upright, and he launched himself into the ether. Even by feline standards, Bronte's landing was remarkably quiet. This wasn't due to the cat's innate grace but his pendulous gut, which had absorbed the impact. Bronte raced across the floor, belly swinging to and fro, tail fur flared like a bottle brush, and darted behind the drape separating the cutting room from the store front.

Poor boy, Enzo thought. *He's wasting his breath.*

"Strike me down with a lightning bolt," Stasi fumed. "Infect me with plague. Drown me in the Ligurian Sea." His eyes were wild, his smile a mixture of lunacy and desperation. "I do not fear death. I welcome it, for when I finally cross the veil into Death's domain, I shall carry your wretched curse with me. Ha ha!"

Enzo set the needle and thread on the cutting table. He stood and rested a hand on Stasi's shoulder. His warm touch told Stasi in that visceral language spoken by fathers and sons, *I know your anguish.* Enzo did the only thing a cursed father can do for a cursed son. He embraced him.

Enzo broke off the hug, lest he dissolve into tears. Stasi nodded. Enzo went to the kitchen and returned with two cups of wine, handing one to Stasi.

Enzo raised his cup. "To you and your upcoming journey . . . and to him, of course."

"Who's 'him'?" Stasi asked.

"How quickly you forget our traditions," Enzo gently admonished. "It's the fourth Friday of the month."

"Right," Stasi said dubiously. He shook his head. "Do you think there's any chance he will show up in our lifetimes?"

"Only Fate can answer that question, my boy. Drink up."

Enzo downed his wine, but Stasi brought the cup to his lips and hesitated.

"Something I've often wondered, Father – if it's all up to Fate, why do we bother with the libation?"

"I don't know if it's *all* up to Fate. Maybe Fate has given him some say into the when and where of his appearances. Our ancestors clearly thought the ritual would get his attention."

"It's been twelve centuries. Clearly, they were wrong."

"So far. Anyway, we do not drink just for him. We drink to celebrate our twelve centuries of perseverance. We drink to us."

Stasi downed his wine, all the while maintaining a skeptical gaze on his father.

Enzo gestured with his head toward the stairway. "Pack your things, then we'll have to tell Mother. She's known this day might come, and yet . . ." His voice cracked with emotion.

"I'll gather my things, Father."

Quickly, Stasi set down the cup and headed to the stairs. Enzo cleared his throat and then straightened the portrait of Hermes. He scanned the room, bereft until he caught sight of the inchoate needlework on the cutting table. He picked up the needle and thread, squinted his eyes, and got back to the business of making hats.

* * *

Fate Accompli

Maria lay awake, drumming her fingers on the pillow in synchronicity with the raindrops pelting the ceramic roof tiles. She kicked off the blanket and rolled away from Enzo, both resentful and envious of her husband's snoring. She slipped a gown over her camicia and went downstairs.

She prepared a bowl of Monticellan wheat dough and set it near the wood stove to rise. As she sat and waited, a cloying sensation crept into her chest. She had a name for this odd sensation, which felt like a vortex inside her heart – the "goodbye feeling." She'd first experienced it on the sad day that Stasi no longer found her oven mitt puppet shows amusing. The second occurrence came after she'd returned home from a week in Pisa and saw a gawkish, teenaged Stasi in his same old doublet and jerkin, which, to her shock, he'd clearly outgrown. The third goodbye feeling had come upon her the morning Stasi stumbled home, reeking of a prostitute's sickly lavender perfume. Enzo had prearranged the liaison, justifying the gift as a traditional rite of passage for Petasos men. Maria refused to speak to Enzo for a week. It took her a month to look him in the face without shaking her head reprovingly.

Those prior goodbye feelings had been triggered by Stasi's metaphorical departures from one stage of maturity to another. This time, however, was different. Stasi was actually leaving home, and if things went as planned, he wouldn't return. She'd been able to endure her boy's steady ascendance toward manhood because he'd remained under her roof, albeit transformed. Come the next day, he would be gone. The prospect of having to endure that kind of goodbye – a real, enduring goodbye – terrified her.

Maria swallowed the lump in her throat and opened her copy of the Purgatorio. She flipped to the part when Dante entered Peter's Gate. She read until Dante reached the sixth terrace. Retrieving the bowl of leavened dough, she molded it into three loaves.

She stared into the fire as the bread baked. When the loaves were done, she set them on the table. She pressed a finger into the dark brown crusts, liberating wisps of steam tinged with herbal notes. Satisfied with the crusts' firmness, she wrapped a loaf in waxed cotton and slipped it into Stasi's leather satchel by the front door.

"What are you doing?" Enzo asked from the steps.

Maria gave a start. She felt like a thief caught in the act, which she most definitely was not. She was the precise opposite. Thieves didn't *give* things away. She was irked by Enzo's purportedly innocuous question, which was really an accusation.

"Providing sustenance for my son," she answered defiantly.

Enzo became agitated. "You know the rule, Maria. We cannot aid Stasi's departure. Do you want to bring Fate's wrath on our heads?"

"Don't get your codpiece in a twist, Enzo. It's a loaf of bread. Stasi has eaten hundreds of them under this roof."

"Precisely. *Under this roof.* You've packed the loaf in his satchel. He will eat it on the road, under the open sky, after he has left the hat shop."

Maria knew Enzo was right. "You and your inane family curse," she said with exasperation. "Why did I ever marry you?"

Enzo wrapped his arms around her, pleased by his wife's contrition. "Because of my Apollonian good looks."

She playfully resisted. "Ha! You are short and squat. And that giant nose of yours? When you turn your head to the south, everyone in Pisa has to duck. And those eyebrows – oof! I could scour the skillets with them."

Enzo smiled furtively. "The same hair grows on my nether regions. Come. Let us scour each other."

He pulled her close. She swatted his chest.

"You're a pig!"

Undeterred, he kissed her neck. "You're just a font of compliments this morning."

"Stop. You know how that tickles."

He kissed her cheek, then her lips. He pressed her into the table and leaned his pudgy body into hers until she relented and kissed him back. With one hand, she swiped away a lock of fallen hair. With the other, she grabbed hold of Enzo's right buttock.

"Well, I'm all packed up," Stasi announced as he entered the kitchen. He stopped short. "God's Blood! Can't you two wait until I've left?"

Maria wriggled from the gap between Enzo and the table. She adjusted her chemise.

"Your father and I were sorting out a disagreement, and things, well, things got out of hand," she said.

"Disagreement about what?" Stasi asked.

"Your mother's bread," Enzo said. "She snuck a loaf into your satchel."

"I didn't sneak anything," Maria protested. "I placed it on top of your breeches."

"Be that as it may," Enzo said to Stasi, "had you not discovered the bread until later, Fate might have punished us for aiding your departure." He opened the satchel, pulled out the wrapped bread, and offered it to his son. "Take a bite."

Stasi's eyebrows rose quizzically. "Right now?"

"Right now," Enzo insisted. "You must start eating it here or else leave it behind."

Stasi accepted the loaf. He peeled back the canvas and bit off the tip of the loaf, revealing a yellow interior. "Delicious, Mother," he said with a full mouth. "Best you've ever made."

Maria seized him in a tight hug. Caught by surprise, Stasi momentarily gagged on the half-chewed bolus.

"Careful, my love," Enzo warned. "Don't kill the boy

before he gets started."

She released her son, sniffling, and backed away.

Enzo patted Stasi's shoulder and looked upward. "The roof leaked last night. Soaked my pillow. I must tend to the repair."

"Father, let me take care of it," Stasi said. "With your bad foot—"

Enzo waved him away. "Bah! I've made scores of repairs with this lame foot. I'm more concerned about my heart."

"Your heart, Father?"

Enzo looked squarely at Stasi. "It will break in two if you do not leave us forthwith."

Enzo moved to Maria and took her hand.

Maria wiped her tears. "Your father is right, Anastasi," she said softly. "Let us not delay this awful business any longer."

Maria had invoked Stasi's full name. She hadn't done that since boyhood. The name sounded formal and aloof coming from her lips.

Stasi nodded and headed toward the front door. He picked up the satchel and turned to say a final farewell, expecting to see his rheumy-eyed parents. But they'd moved on in that brief interlude. Enzo was fishing through the closet for a trowel. Maria was feeding logs into the oven. Stasi felt like a ghost at his own funeral. He'd been given last rites. It was time for the afterlife.

* * *

The cloudless morning sky glowed with oranges and pinks. The night rains had cleansed the accumulated donkey dung and human waste from the streets, and a generous breeze blowing inland from the Ligurian Sea was keeping the hinterland's swamp gasses at bay. The breeze passed over the large shipment of ginger and cloves stored in the port's warehouses, carrying piquant aromas into town. Stasi inhaled the sweet air, which infused him with optimism. Maybe, just maybe, Fate was smiling on him.

He contemplated which way to go. He could've turned right, toward Pisa and Florence, or left, toward the sea. His father had turned right and failed miserably. Left, it was. He sauntered past homes and shops adorned with frescoes of harvests, silk markets, corsair raids, and the celestial spheres. He negotiated the spades and shovels of Muslim slaves and Florentine prisoners who were digging a massive ditch into the old earthen road. Farther on, Christian peasants poured in rubble, compacted it, and covered it with a mixture of coarse aggregate and concrete. Soon, Livorno would have proper roads, just like a proper Tuscan city.

Only a year earlier, Livorno had been a swampy hamlet of a few hundred tradesmen, peasants, sailors, smiths, coopers, and Jewish coral merchants. To get there, inland travelers had to cross hectares of foul-smelling marshes, a breeding ground for the notorious "Livorno Fever." And they wouldn't have found much upon arrival: a modest fortress, warehouses, an arsenal for shipbuilding and repairs, and an underground grain silo. But then Grand Duke Francesco announced a bold plan to build canals and a grid of roads to suit a future population of ten thousand souls. Following an ostentatious ceremony with fireworks and a celestial-themed basse danse, Bishop Alessandro de' Medici uttered a blessing, and the Grand Duke spoke what was to become Livorno's new motto: "*Diversis gentibus una*" – out of many peoples, one.

The roads remained a work in progress. However, the Construction Office had completed several big projects, including a dike connecting the mainland with the lighthouse and another pier connecting the lighthouse to the Old Fortress. The Navicelli Channel had been widened for boats to reach the Arno River at Pisa. Livorno was slowly becoming the main transit point for commerce between Tuscany, Iberia, and the Levant. Its population was poised to explode, which meant the demand for hats was set to explode as well. Stasi hoped Enzo would be able to handle the extra work. Perhaps he'd finally invest in a monocle or a pince-nez.

Stasi tore off an enormous hunk of bread and stuffed it in his mouth. He ruminated over the ships he might board. The one bound for England? For Holland? For the Levant? He was leery of settling in a land where he didn't speak the language, where his inability to communicate except through hand gestures and grunts would relegate him to brute, manual labor. Better to remain on the Italian peninsula, he decided. He would take a ship to Naples or Messina, where he could finagle an apprenticeship with a trading house. He figured an office job better fit his family's social station, which hovered between tradesmen and merchant cl—

Stasi couldn't breathe. He felt as though a stone had lodged against his uvula and was blocking his airway. He brought his hands to his throat. A gaggle of laborers on a water break gaped at the staggering, red-faced young man. A burly Moor dropped the dipper in the tureen and rushed over to the floundering Stasi. He got behind him, hugged his belly with interlocked hands, and gave a mighty squeeze. Stasi heaved, ejecting a round bolus from his throat that struck the wall of a nearby wine shop with an incongruous pinging sound. As Stasi bent over, hands on knees, to catch his breath, the curious Moor picked the wad from the dirt, shook off the bread residue, and wiped what remained against his stocking. It was a ring.

The Moor laughed heartily. He asked if Stasi was a djinn, for only djinns produced gold from their bellies. Stasi shot him a perplexed glance. What was the man talking about? Unsteadily, he stood and came over to investigate what appeared to be a woman's golden posy ring in the Moor's palm. Stasi picked up the ring and held it to the sky. Letters were engraved on the inside: "A-M-O-R F---." A bready paste obscured the letters following the F. He cleaned the ring's inside with his finger, revealing the letters "A-T-I."

AMOR FATI. God's Blood!

His parents' wedding bands bore that very inscription. Could this ring be his mother's? Might the ring have slipped from her finger when she was kneading the dough? It had happened before, but she'd always found it before baking. The ring in the bread must have been accidental. His mother knew well the consequences of providing anything of value that he might sell or exchange for shelter or transportation. Fate, however, wouldn't see it that way.

Stasi sprinted home with the ring squeezed tightly in his fist. It wasn't far, and when he got there, he spotted Enzo limping across the low-grade rooftop. He shouted to his father, warning him to stop moving in a panicked voice. The startled Enzo wheeled around, catching his lame foot on the edge of a roof tile. He lost his balance and stumbled into the two buckets of patching mortar. He reflexively spread his arms for stability, which helped his balance but did nothing to halt his forward progress. Momentum carried him over the roof's edge. With his arms extended, it appeared he'd taken a running leap in a foolish attempt to fly. He crashed onto the muddy street with a grotesque cracking sound.

Maria rushed out the front door, asking no one in particular what the commotion was all about. She stopped cold at Enzo's twisted corpse. She looked up and saw Stasi. She was flummoxed. Enzo was supposed to be on the roof, and Stasi had left home. They were not in their proper places. She had to be dreaming, she told herself. But she saw the wedding band in Stasi's open palm. She felt her own naked finger and understood she wasn't dreaming. She was living a nightmare. Everyone was where they were fated to be.

"What have I done?" she moaned.

Those would be Maria's final words. For five days and nights, she sat in the kitchen in a cocoon of despondence. She didn't speak. She didn't cry. She refused all food and drink. She didn't budge from the chair, not even to attend her husband's funeral. All she did was stare fixedly at the mouth of the cold oven. Stasi read her the Decameron and short stories by Franco Sacchetti, and performed oven mitt puppet shows, but nothing could alter her stone-faced demeanor or pry her hollow gaze from the oven. He poured broth in her mouth. She didn't swallow, and the brown liquid cascaded down her chin and saturated her chemise. Stasi bathed her and changed her until the fourth day, when he could no longer articulate her stiffened limbs or open her locked jaw. When a fog descended behind her eyes, he pressed his ear to her chest. He could no longer discern distinct heartbeats, just a meek whooshing sound. At dawn of the fifth day, he set off for the hill overlooking the sea and dug his second grave of the week.

CHAPTER

TWO

Tartarus, 1600 B.C.E.

The night-sky curtain was a quilt of fabrics – part grain weave to refract the starlight and swell the lunar disc, part diagonal twill for a dynamic, twisting impression over the open plains and steppes, and part shimmery satin weave to augment the crisp winter night. Moira set down the shuttle, stepped back from the loom, and considered what story to stitch onto the ink-black fabric. She'd tired of her "go-to" myths about creation, heroic battles, and star-crossed love. She wanted to break the shackles of the tried and true. An escape story, then.

Hand-stitching demanded Moira's undivided attention. She cranked a valve on the wall-mounted horn, muting the brassy din of the Clarion Calls. She threaded a needle with yarn and began knitting a series of abstract symbols – logograms – that would recount the tale of a mortal who'd slaughtered a minotaur and found his way out of the labyrinth by following a string he'd tied to the entrance. It wasn't an easy story to relay in fabric. The logogram for "minotaur" consisted of manifold layers and intricate knots, making the final step – a stitch through the logogram's fat heart – arduous.

Moira pressed the needle until her knuckles whitened, but she might as well have been sewing into a lead ingot. She leaned in with her shoulder, which did nothing. Only after putting her entire body into it did the needlepoint advance, and only in miniscule, begrudging increments. She gasped and grunted, gathering and regathering her determination. Her vocalizations evolved into a sustained moan whose volume rose in lockstep with the quaking of her muscles and reddening of her face. She took a deep breath, and her moan yawned into a bellicose howl – a weaver's war cry, if there ever was such a thing. The stubborn knot, however, refused to give ground. Moira was losing the battle. She was nearly out of air, her visual field narrowing to a cone, knees buckling.

It's now or never, she exhorted herself. *Show the fabric who's master.*

With a final, desperate push, the needle burst through the knot like a knife through watered-down ambrosia. Moira, however, had neglected to prepare for the sudden absence of resistance. She blundered forward and face-planted on the curtain.

After pausing to collect herself, she wearily peeled herself off the loom. She had six more minotaur logograms to stitch. Maybe an escape story hadn't been the wisest choice.

A puff of frigid air set her neck hairs on end. She had a visitor, probably her neighbor, Eros. The fat cherub never passed up an opportunity to brag about shooting his golden arrows to induce love and leaden arrows to provoke disgust. Worse, he couldn't utter more than two sentences without tittering like a coquettish old woman. The key with Eros was to cut him off before he got on a roll.

Moira turned abruptly. "I'm sorry, Eros. I really don't

have—"

She fell into stunned silence. The shadowy figure lurking at the cave mouth was definitely not Eros. He was taller than the infant-sized love god, not to mention Moira's visitor was fully clothed. He – *no, she* – had her arms folded, hands tucked into the opposite sleeves of a flowing black robe. Her face was veiled, except for her onyx-black eyes and severe, S-shaped eyebrows.

"Mother?"

Nyx ambled toward her daughter. The combination of short, soundless steps and a floor-sweeping hem gave the impression of a ghost floating across the floor. Nyx unfolded her arms and ran a spindly index finger along the loom's iron frame.

"The loom is different," Nyx commented in a grim, affectless voice.

"I made modifications," Moira said – a gross understatement. The loom was far more complex than the upright, warp-weighted loom she'd inherited from Nyx. Moira had commissioned a metalsmith to create scores of prototype looms, ultimately settling on a horizontal model mounted to four tall posts.

As Nyx scrutinized the curtain in progress, Moira rocked heel-toe, trying to anticipate what her mother might be thinking. It was impossible to tell behind that veil of hers. Rumor was, Nyx's face was so beautiful even the slightest glimpse induced madness. Moira sometimes wondered if her mother had fabricated the myth to conceal a plain, or even an ugly, face. Such myths were easy to perpetuate. Gods were always taken more by what they wished a thing to be than what it actually was.

Nyx straightened her spine. She raised her chin and pulled her shoulders back, projecting a militant air. Her pupils reflected the oil lamp's flickering flames, conjuring an image of twin beacons on a dark shore. All at once, Moira felt a glimmer of hope.

Look there, she observed with a frisson of excitement. *Creases have formed at the corners of Mother's eyes, and her veil bulges along the jawline. Are these not the signs of swelling maternal pride? Mother is going to compliment me, the first in twenty-four-hundred years! Even one kind word passing her lips (does she have lips?) would set my spirit soaring. What word will she say? Impressive? Amazing? Ingenious?*

"Frippery," Nyx declared.

"I beg your pardon," said the deflated Moira.

"Frippery," Nyx repeated. "Your elaborate weaves and patterns, these strange symbols, serve no purpose."

Something in Nyx's left hand glinted – a pickaxe with a highly-polished head of blue-gray lead. Not a scratch on it.

Moira peeled her glance from the pickaxe and asked, "But . . . but don't you find the curtain beautiful?"

Nyx squeezed the pickaxe's oaken handle. "Beauty is irrelevant. The night-sky curtain's sole function is to block sunlight from striking Earth. Your embellishments are a waste of time and effort."

"I've never missed a deadline," Moira proffered in her defense. "I've always delivered the curtain well ahead of schedule."

"That is not the point. With this loom, I could produce ten curtains in the time it takes you to make one."

"But your curtains were—"

"My curtains were what?" Nyx interjected.

So many adjectives to choose from: dull, uninspired, tired, hackneyed. Moira regarded her mother. The shade cast by her heavy brow had snuffed out the flames in her pupils. *Better change the subject.*

"Well?" Nyx pressed.

"Forgive me, Mother," Moira said, feigning forgetfulness. "I seem to have lost the thread." Her eyes darted to the pickaxe. "What's that in your hand?"

"Ah, yes," Nyx said, recalling the purpose of her visit. "This is for you. For the next phase of your career."

"Next phase?"

"Day and Light have come of age. They will be moving on."

Day and Light were Nyx's children. Nyx had been working two jobs when her brother, Erebus, had gotten her in the family way. She'd weave a night-sky curtain half the day and pull that curtain around the world the other half. Despite being Nyx's partner in curtain-pulling and the father of her children, Erebus had flatly refused to share in her "woman's work." Erebus was a cad, but Moira was indebted to him. That cad was the reason she worked the loom.

"How wonderful," Moira remarked in an affected congratulatory tone. "You and Erebus will be empty cavers. A chance to rekindle the old flame . . . unless, of course, you two plan to have more children."

Moira wished she hadn't said anything about old flames and children, which inspired unwelcome thoughts about parental copulation.

Do they have a sex life? If her veil dislodges during coitus, would her ruinously-beautiful face destroy him? They must take precautions – extra-strong binding for the veil, a blindfold for him, copious lubrication to minimize bodily turbulence, a rear-entry position, etc.

"I plan to return to work," said Nyx.

"Good for you, Mother. What work will you do?"

"I shall weave, of course."

Moira's smile faltered. "That's . . . that's . . . Weaving, you say. Hmmm." *Find a positive spin, Moira, and hope to Hades it's true.* "Well, that makes sense. Tartarus' population is growing. There is a shortage of high-quality robes and peplos, and there's not a single place to get a good hat."

"I shall be weaving night-sky curtains again."

"You—?" Moira choked on her words. "But . . . but I weave night-sky curtains. You gave the job to me, remember?"

"A temporary assignment while I was preoccupied with the children."

"You never said it was temporary."

"Nor did I say it *wasn't*," Nyx said reprovingly.

"What will I do?"

"As you say, Tartarus is more populous, as are the other spheres. The demand for refined metals is especially high in Othrys and Hades. You will work in the mines."

Moira released an explosive guffaw at the absurd suggestion. But no, Moira realized. Born of the infinite nothingness underlying reality, Nyx was incapable of a jest.

Moira was bereft. "I don't know the first thing about mining."

"Your brothers will teach you. Strife, Pain, and Doom have eons of experience."

"Are Day and Light going to the mines with me?"

"Don't be silly. They are too bright for this darksome realm. Their destinies lie in the outer spheres."

"Perhaps mine does as well."

Nyx shook her head. "I am a creature of the dark. Therefore, so are you."

"Why is that?"

"Because I made you from a piece of myself."

That was true. Moira was fatherless. Nyx had spawned her asexually by pinching off a piece of her divine essence. Moira didn't know which piece, but she wouldn't have been surprised to learn Nyx had harvested her from a gnarled pinky toe, an intestinal polyp, or worse – a dandruff flake or a glob of snot.

"Why must biology determine my destiny?" Moira

pleaded.

"It doesn't have to." But any hope Moira might have gleaned from her mother's concession was promptly dashed when Nyx added, "But that is my wish."

Moira sat on the loom's bench seat and buried her head in her hands.

Nyx approached Moira and hovered over her for a moment. She spoke in a more encouraging tone, which, for her, was somewhere between wretched and gloomy. "This is a tremendous opportunity, Moira. You should be delighted."

"If you say so," Moira muttered to the floor.

"If you prove even half as proficient with the pickaxe as you have with the loom, you will soar through the ranks." The glory in Nyx's voice rose as she recounted Moira's future career path. "Picker Apprentice, Picker Second Class, Picker First Class, Foreman, Picker in Chief, Assistant to the Head Smelter. Then one day, Head Smelter!"

Moira looked up, horrified. "I'll have to smelt heads?"

"No, head *of* the smelters. You'll be the first goddess to hold such a high-profile position in the realm of man's work."

"You speak so enthusiastically, Mother. Perhaps that honor should be yours."

Nyx raised the pickaxe to shoulder height. Moira recoiled, fearing her mother was about to mine a chunk from her skull.

"Rise," Nyx commanded.

Reluctantly, Moira stood. Nyx lowered the pickaxe slowly and with great solemnity.

"Take it," said Nyx.

Moira hesitated.

"Take it," Nyx repeated, this time sternly.

Moira gripped the handle. When Nyx let go, the leaden tool wrenched Moira's shoulder and thudded on the floor.

"You have until the winter solstice to strengthen your

muscles."

"The solstice is but thirty revolutions away," Moira remonstrated.

"Practically an eternity in divine time." Nyx pointed behind Moira and added, "Hand me the curtain off the loom, and then I shall leave you to it."

"Wait," Moira said, flustered. She turned toward the loom. "The curtain is unfinished. I just started weaving the story."

Nyx extended her hand and made a beckoning motion. Moira was frozen with disbelief.

"Hand it to me," Nyx commanded.

Moira picked up a shears and brought the blades to the outermost warp thread. She snipped one thread, paused, then snipped another. At this rate, it would've taken her an eon to finish the task.

"Stop dallying, Daughter!"

Frustrated, Nyx swiped the shears from Moira and sliced the remaining warp threads with two quick sweeps of her arm. She threw the bulky curtain over her shoulder and departed, seemingly taking all the cave's air with her.

Moira collapsed on the loom's bench seat and broke into tears. Thirty days hence, her fingers would no longer know the feel of warp and weft, only the pound, pound, pound of fracturing ore. That couldn't be her destiny. She'd sooner snuff out her own existence than give up the loom. So be it. In thirty days, she'd climb the rickety stairs to the mouth of Tartarus, walk to the edge of Chaos, and take the irrevocable leap into the sea of nothingness. Until then, she would weave every spare moment.

Moira shot a weary glance at the empty loom. She needed to remove the warp-thread remnants and restring new threads. Her limbs were heavy with languor. Thanks to Nyx's visit, Moira had missed lunch. She picked up a golden thimble, cranked open a tiny spigot on the wall, and collected her allotment of the precious, claret-colored fluid. Strange. Usually, the fluid filled the thimble halfway. Today, it rose to the rim. Was there a problem with the inter-sphere plumbing? Had the heavens increased the daily ration? Moira shrugged and downed the distilled human faith and licked the thimble clean.

The double-allotment of faith ignited an inner fire. Her reinvigorated hands and arms trembled with potential energy, their way of saying, "Work! Work! Work!" She switched on the wall-mounted horn, and the Clarion Calls flooded the cave.

The Clarion Calls Network was the divine system for mass communication. The system relied on three bugling giants to blast out messages encoded in musical phrases. Although the Network's primary purpose was to broadcast warnings about pending disasters and leadership changes, the gigantic trio freelanced in between calamities and coups. For a small fee – a few drops of human faith – the trio would disseminate advertisements across the spheres. The ads ranged from offers to sell custom spells, curses, and magical implements, to "help wanted" postings for experienced ferrymen to transport mortal souls into Hades, to personals like "TSM seeking VW to KMS" (tentacled sea monster seeking voracious whirlpool to kill mortal sailors). Moira, however, wasn't interested in the ads' content so much as their melodies, which complemented the rhythmic clanking and knocking of her loom work.

After restringing the warp, Moira pulled yarn from the bobbin and tied it to the shuttle. She threw the shuttle across the gap in the threads and caught it in her opposite hand. Twice, she pulled down the comb-like batten and tamped the row of yarn in place, producing a metallic *clink clunk, clink clunk* sound.

One row down; a million more to go.

Back and forth she wove, falling into a rhythm of:

Throw. *Clink clunk, clink clunk.* Throw. *Clink clunk, clink clunk.* Meanwhile, the giants were playing the usual Clarion-Call dross: "for sale" notices for timeshares in Atlantis, tinted cyclops monocles, overripe apples of discord, gorgon hair clips. All of a sudden there was a new, intriguing melody. It shook Moira to the core. She stopped weaving and listened intently. The description was terse but elegant. "WANTED, WEAVER. Obedient. Able to work an eternity without breaks. Location: Heavenly Sphere, Mount Othrys. All new management! An equal opportunity employer."

Moira's skin prickled with electricity. Rumor was, the heavens were a cornucopia of colors, teeming with light and life. She imagined weaving with a color other than Tartarian black – splashy hues like Gaia green, underworld umber, and minotaur maroon. She envied the lucky soul who'd land that job.

Moira was struck with an idea, an idea she hadn't considered until her mother's unannounced visit. The idea was so obvious, so simple and right, it ricocheted through her brain, demanding to be noticed.

Why not me?

Why not me?

Why not me?

Why not, indeed. Moira assumed this weaver would report to Cronus. He had just overthrown his father, Uranus, and tossed his testicles in the sea. That gave Moira pause. Was paternal castration a harbinger of Cronus' fraught management style? Would Moira be able to concentrate on the loom if she was constantly on guard for severed genitalia whizzing overhead? Then again, her days on the iron loom were numbered. Thirty, to be precise. The occasional soaring testicle was a minor nuisance compared to the daily dust and dankness of a Tartarian mine.

Moira got to work on a cover letter and a curriculum vitae. Instead of writing her application longhand on parchment, she weaved the relevant information into two small tapestries using the tactile alphabet familiar to all gods. She lamented the brevity of her résumé, which was barely longer than her one-sentence cover letter. But what could she do? She'd only ever held the one job her mother had given her. She hoped her body of work on the night sky would put assumptions of nepotism to bed, even though those assumptions were wholly warranted.

Moira decided to hand-deliver her application to Mount Othrys, hoping the personal touch would give her an edge over other applicants. The question was how to get to the heavens. The most powerful gods – the Titans – could cross realms at will, as could Eros, by firing a golden arrow skyward. But those self-important bigwigs didn't offer ride-sharing services. Divine hoi polloi had two options for traversing the spheres: the free option (a stairway) and the expensive option (a gryphon ride). The stairway was as poorly maintained as it was treacherous. Many a frugal immortal had fallen through and vanished into the great void, never to be heard from again. A long-promised, cross-realm elevator for the masses hadn't come to fruition. The Titans blamed repeated construction delays on the gryphons. The winged beasts held a monopoly on intersphere travel and delivery services and were employing frivolous procedural maneuvers to gum up the permitting process.

A gryphon ride it shall be.

Moira completed the rest of her preparations in two nights. Freed of artistic constraints, she was able to manufacture thirty days of basic night-sky curtains. She was defying her mother's wishes, but at least she'd be professional about her defiance, if that was possible. She knitted a tasteful gryphon-sized neck scarf. She would present the scarf to her beastly conductor as her fare for the ride to Mount Othrys.

With the scarf in one hand and two small tapestries in the other, Moira set off for Tartarus' industrial section, located on the banks of the fiery Phlegethon River. Originating in Hades, the Phlegethon's flammable waters burned with a violet color due to the riverbed's high concentration of potassium salts. An artificial sluiceway splintered from the main flow to feed massive crushers and furnaces smelting galena and electrum into lead, silver, and gold ingots. Farther ahead, the channel's burbling flames illuminated a basalt sculpture of an elm tree. There, a creature was perched on a bough, a hybrid of lion and eagle: a gryphon.

Moira's throat tightened when she realized she had no idea how gryphons communicated. How would she tell the beast where to take her? She also worried she'd made a huge mistake with the scarf. With its abundant fur and feathers, a gryphon would seem to have no use for a scarf. Indeed, a scarf might be dangerous. The material could flap in the beast's face or get stuck in a wing.

If only I'd knitted socks. You never go wrong with socks. Well, too late now.

Moira bent her head in supplication and extended her arms, over which she'd draped the scarf. She spoke in a low, solemn tone. "Noble beast, singer of the eternal note, crosser of realms, I humbly request passage."

The gryphon squawked, leapt off the bough, and landed with a dusty thud. The ground trembled under Moira's feet. She suppressed her alarm and didn't move a muscle. She figured there were three possibilities. The beast would (1), accept the scarf and whisk her to Mount Othrys, (2), scoff at the scarf and fly away without her, or (3), scoff at the scarf, snap off her head, and *then* fly away without her. She peered up and was relieved to see the beast had lowered its head. She wrapped the scarf around its neck and tied the material in a bow to keep it from flapping in the wind. The gryphon squawked and lay flat on the charcoal gray sand. It folded its wings and extended its neck.

Moira was uncertain what came next. "Am I meant to . . . climb up?"

The gryphon squawked again, this time with an edge of impatience.

"Oh. I . . . uh . . . very well."

She gripped the gryphon's thick lion fur and scaled an arm with the grace of a drunken cyclops. Inch by effortful inch, she elevated herself until she managed to plant a foot on the edge of a wing and hoist herself the rest of the way. She kicked her leg ungracefully across the gryphon's back and positioned herself into the saddle. She slid in front of the wings and grabbed hold of the pommel. She was a mess. Stray hairs poked from her hair band and draped over her nose and mouth. She blew the hairs from her face, only to have them resettle on her skin. Her himation was in a twist, as well. She readjusted the robe – no easy task, given she was sitting on the gathered fabric – and stuffed the annoying stray hairs behind her headband. Perspiring and panting, she settled on the mount and was ready to go.

Thirty seconds later, they'd gone nowhere. The gryphon remained prostrate.

Silly Moira, she told herself. *The beast cannot very well read my mind. I must tell the creature I wish to go to Mount Othrys.*

"Please take me to—"

All at once, the gryphon raised itself into a crouch and bounded into the air. Moira's neck snapped backward from the sudden acceleration. Had she not grabbed the pommel with her free hand, she would have tumbled head over sandals.

Evidently, gryphons can read minds.

The thrust of the launch tapered off at a hundred yards. The gryphon unfurled its wings and began flapping with slow, powerful strokes. The beast carried her higher and higher, following a gentle, coiling trajectory to an uncertain elevation.

After Moira's stomach settled, she mustered the courage to gaze down at the sunless abyss. The smelters and the Phlegethon bathed the barren moonscape in grimy illumination. She could just make out the scores of tree- and flower-shaped basalt sculptures designed to lend a semblance of fecundity to the infertile realm. The ersatz flora receded from view and disappeared into the darkness. She saw only the fiery river coursing down the abyss' wall like molten lead spilling from a massive ladle.

After an hour at full flap, the gryphon emerged from the abyss' gaping maw. Moira was awestruck as she regarded Tartarus from above. A vast stone well embedded in the nothingness of Chaos, Tartarus was the mother of all chasms. Moira felt the exhilaration and panic of an escaped prisoner. She willed the gryphon to fly faster. Repeatedly, she glanced over her shoulder, in part to convince herself of her freedom, in part to reassure herself that gargantuan arms weren't about to yank her back into that hopeless black bottom. But her anxiety was for naught. Tartarus shrunk to a distant speck and eventually winked out altogether.

Moira was immersed in the blackness of Chaos and the warmth of the infernal Phlegethon River raging beneath her. She gave an internal sigh and allowed the tension to drain away. She didn't feel as desperate now. She figured if Cronus didn't give her the job, she'd settle on a remote Earthen island, weave tapestries by day, and sleep under her mother's sterile skies. She was going to be just fine. She snuggled her cheek into the gryphon's fur and closed her eyes. The rhythmic flapping lulled her into slumber.

CHAPTER

THREE

Livorno, Grand Duchy of Tuscany, 1578

Stasi returned from the goldsmith, who'd agreed to care for Bronte, and double-checked his satchel. He'd packed light, having decided to make a clean break from the hat shop. He would abandon the unsold inventory of caps and hats as well as a cutting room filled with bolts of wool and silk, tanned leather hides, threads of different colors and gauges, needles, thimbles, pins, shears, and hat blocks. He could've sold these things off, but that process would've taken weeks, and he didn't want to stay in Livorno any longer than he had to. He emptied his father's bank account at the local branch of the Medici Bank. He also scrounged up the Spanish reals and florins at the bottom of drawers and clothing chests. He discovered a small fortune knotted up in Enzo's old codpiece. Evidently, Enzo's confidence in the security of the Medici Bank was not absolute. Banks could fail, but history hadn't recorded a single run on codpieces.

Stasi packed two of Maria's things – the Decameron and an ebony wood hairbrush. He had always admired the brush's handle, which was inset with a swirl of mother of pearl surrounding a black diamond "pupil."

None of Enzo's things held sentimental value. Nevertheless, there were two things he was obliged to take. The items hadn't belonged to Enzo in the strictly legal sense. He'd been their bailor and steward, just as Stasi's grandfather had been, and so on back through generations of Petasos men. One item was a large gold coin bearing the likeness of Hermes. The coin was valuable, owing to its weight and purity, but otherwise indistinguishable from myriad other gold coins bearing masculine faces. The second item was not at all as ostentatious as the first. Indeed, by all appearances, it was prosaic, its ostensible purpose as pedestrian as sturdy shoes. But to those in the know – and there were very few of those – the item was tangible evidence of miracles.

Stasi unmounted the portrait and propped it on the cutting table. The nook the portrait had concealed was a crude hole about a foot in diameter. Stasi reached in, grabbed the coin, and stuck it in the satchel. He reached back in, farther this time, until his fingertips sensed the object's fleshiness and preternatural heat. He handled it like a soiled undergarment. In one swift motion, he yanked it from the nook, stuffed it in the satchel, and buckled the flap. He hurried through the front of the shop, fixating on the door to avoid noticing the hutch to his left, where his mother had stored the jar of Monticellan wheat.

He closed the shutters. He crossed the street, turned, and gave his childhood home one last look. There was the oaken door whose squeaky hinges Enzo had charged him with lubricating at age five – his very first chore. There was the three-foot-high cairn stacked left of the door and the small marble phallus mounted on the right doorpost. Every so often, a Jew would spot the phallus from afar and mistake it for a mezuzah. Although the phallus contained no holy biblical words, it did convey a divine message. It was a symbolic invitation to Hermes, which, for twelve centuries, had gone unanswered.

Stasi scanned the fresco on the façade and broke into a smile. He'd been six years old the day Maria seized his hand, marched to Livorno's Construction Office, and demanded that the chief architect overseeing the town's beautification efforts remove the freshly-painted fresco. She argued that the scene of the lascivious Apollo chasing a nude water nymph through the Olympian woods made her home resemble a brothel. She unconsciously tightened her grip on Stasi's hand and added that the sill of her child's bedroom window was now resting squarely on a nipple the size of a dinner plate. The chief architect's right eye twitched. Perhaps it was a coincidence, or perhaps the word nipple, or the notion of a dinner-plate-sized nipple, had discomfited him. Regardless, he grumbled something about "artistic integrity" and "the Grand Duke's master plan." But his feeble defenses were no match for Maria's deathly stare. He agreed to alter the fresco so it would depict the nymph transforming into a laurel tree, thereby avoiding the suggestion of an impending rape. He'd also instruct the artist to obscure the nipple with a strategically placed "dinner plate." He quickly corrected himself, having meant to say "tree branch" in lieu of "dinner plate." Satisfied, Maria thanked the chief architect and relaxed her vice-like grip on Stasi's hand. Oh, what Stasi wouldn't have given to relive that pain!

Stasi did a double-take at the roofline. He'd been so distracted by his parents' demise, he'd forgotten about his father's incomplete patching job. The toppled buckets of mortar had solidified in place, the upper bucket oozing mortar into the lower, and the lower oozing onto the eave. The accidental sculpture was the embodiment of motion without movement, which sounded absurd, but Stasi knew such things were possible. He had proof in his satchel.

Stasi felt a deep kinship with the Port of Livorno, as if the place was his godchild. He'd attended the shallow harbor's rebirth into a beacon of international commerce and culture. He'd embraced the Grand Duke's bold vision of Livorno as a cosmopolitan city of ten thousand souls. Stasi's faith in this future had empowered him. Although he was fated to make hats in Livorno, the port was a great consolation: it promised to bring the world to him. A mere whiff of the saltwater air would make his heart swell with hope. But that ended when a breeze redolent of sailor's sweat and rotting fish blew in. He realized there had been another death in Livorno. Hope. Its invisible corpse was lying on the quay, rotting in the sun. Stasi's heart, if not his nose, was telling him what his unconscious mind already had resolved: it was time to move on. He would go to the port, pay his respects to his godchild, and vanish into the wind.

Stasi strolled far out on the quay and set down his satchel. Descrying no one about, he opened the flap and retrieved the floppy black sunhat. The scaly leather was warm, even though the morning was cool, and the sun hadn't heated the satchel. This was no surprise. He donned the hat and adjusted the brim so it didn't hang over his eyes. The fit was tight at first, but the material relaxed and conformed to his skull. This, too, was no surprise. He regarded the Medicean galleys and the English and Dutch trading ships in the harbor. He wouldn't board a ship to leave Livorno. Nor would he mount a horse, take a carriage, or walk. He wouldn't move a muscle. Motion without movement was his mode of travel.

He paced while contemplating his destination. He desired a distant place where he wouldn't face an insurmountable language barrier. Only one location fit the bill, the place he'd dreamed of ever since his mother made her first loaf of bread with Monticellan wheat. It would be easy to get there. All he had to do was exhale all his breath, imagine Monticello, and think, *Take me there.* He closed his eyes, inhaled, and thought of Monticello. He exhaled and got as far as *Take me—*, when he realized he wasn't holding the satchel. Anything he wasn't holding at the time of the wish wouldn't make the journey. His eyes popped open, and he turned toward where he'd left the satchel, just a few paces down the quay. The satchel was gone.

Ten paces beyond that spot was a lanky man in a yellow mariner's cap squatting beside an open satchel – *Stasi's* open satchel – and rummaging inside. The thief was dressed in baggy breeches stained a deep red from tar-based waterproofing, suggesting he was a sailor or, more specifically, a pirate, given he'd absconded with Stasi's satchel. The pirate tossed undergarments, shirts, and shoes asunder, and removed the ebony hairbrush. Outraged, Stasi strode toward him. The scoundrel stood and turned halfway, exposing his profile. Stasi halted, befuddled. The pirate's face had a delicate bone structure. His skin was white and creamy, as though it hadn't seen a day in the sun. Stasi couldn't fathom how such a virginal face could sprout one whisker, let alone the thick black horseshoe mustache dangling below his nose. The pirate removed his knitted cap and raked his fingers through his matted coif. Stasi was aghast. The pirate intended to defile Maria's hairbrush.

"How now!" Stasi shouted. "Don't you dare touch that brush to your disgusting mop!"

The pirate loosened his compressed hair, spilling streams of wavy blond hair to his shoulders. Stasi gaped as the pirate calmly turned toward him. The rapscallion was unperturbed, even though Stasi had at least five inches and fifty pounds on him. The pirate regarded Stasi gravely. Each second that passed, Stasi grew more anxious. Yes, the thief was slight, but his stature wouldn't matter if he were to thrust a cutlass into Stasi's kidney. Even a straight fistfight was risky. The sum total of Stasi's combat experience amounted to wrestling Bronte to the floor for bimonthly claw trimmings. Half the time, Bronte escaped his clutches untrimmed.

As Stasi fretted, the pirate twitched his nose in an exaggerated fashion. His horseshoe mustache swung right and left to such an absurd degree that Stasi forgot about his trepidations and laughed. The pirate then peeled the mustache from his face, triggering a percussive "Ha!" from Stasi's throat. To his astonished delight, the pirate was a she, and a beautiful she at that. Her smile blossomed like a field of white poppies.

"Tell me, Madonna," Stasi asked with bemusement, "is it your practice to rifle through a gentleman's belongings?"

"You obviously have an overinflated sense of your social standing," she retorted in a serious tone. "You clearly are not a gentleman. At best, a merchant."

"Even a merchant is higher in the social order than a lawless pirate."

She flicked her wrist in the air. "The social order can kiss my arse."

The coarse language from such a refined face fascinated Stasi. Her nose was small and slightly down-turned. Her high, round cheekbones created two mountainous peaks over which mirthful eyes peered in playful contempt. Due to her large bosom and small frame, she stood with shoulders back, lending her a haughty, unattainable air. Stasi was eager to play whatever game she was up to.

He raised his eyebrows. "Pray tell, Madonna. Which arse cheek should the social order kiss?"

"It was a figure of speech, not a request."

"Oh, I beg your pardon, Madonna."

She admitted a tiny smile. "Granted."

"May I ask, though, had it been a request, which cheek

might you have preferred?"

"I don't engage in hypotheticals. I live for the here and now, what's real at the moment. Hypotheticals are frivolous. No, worse than frivolous. They are the opiate of the hopeless."

Stasi blinked slowly. He had no idea what she was talking about, but the way she spoke her nonsense enthralled him.

She regarded him askance. "Lucky for you, I'm feeling magnanimous. Answer me one question, and I shall answer your hypothetical."

Stasi rubbed his hands together. "Oooh. Is it a riddle?"

"Only for me." The woman handed the hairbrush to him. "How do you explain this?"

Stasi looked puzzled. "It is called a hairbrush. We landlubbers use it to make ourselves resemble civilized people."

"I know what it is, you knave," she said with exasperation. "What interests me is the vortex on the handle and, specifically, the black diamond at its center. The nothingness."

"Nothingness? You could demand more than a few florins for that diamond."

"I speak not of its value in coinage but in symbolism."

Stasi tilted his head.

She sighed. "What I mean is this. The vortex cannot be a vortex without the empty center, just as a mouth cannot be a mouth without a void between the lips. Nothing and everything are hopelessly entangled, you see?"

Stasi plucked a blonde strand from the bristles. "Speaking of entangled."

"Methinks you were not listening."

"I was listening. I've never thought of the swirl as meaning anything. It's pretty, that's all. The sky is pretty, but ask me the sky's meaning? That's nonsense."

"Many a sailor would beg to differ."

Stasi dropped his playful tone. "If you had desired to inspect my satchel, you might have asked me."

"You were lost in thought. A sad thought, by my estimation."

Stasi blanched. Was his grief so obvious?

"Well, purloining my satchel didn't exactly buck up my spirits. Plus, it was risky on your part. I could've summoned the bargello to arrest you."

She shook her head. "I knew you wouldn't."

"How?"

"By the cut of your jib," she answered in the voice of an old salt.

Stasi scrunched his forehead. "The cut of my . . . *what?*"

"The cut of your jib." She stroked Stasi's cheek and said warmly, "You have a very kind face."

"Thank you," Stasi said with a dry throat. "I also admire your jibs."

"It's 'jib,'" she corrected with a wink. "Singular."

Embarrassed, Stasi glanced away, assiduously avoiding the pale blur of her bosom and focusing on the lighthouse.

She took his hand and studied it like a naturalist studies a butterfly.

"Rather clammy," she remarked.

Stasi cleared his throat.

She tested the flexibility of his knuckles and wrists and palpated the muscles of his forearm. Tingles of electricity shot up to his shoulder and banked hard toward his thumping heart.

"Good, strong fingers," she observed in the detached tone of the meticulous slave merchant. "Nimble. Calloused fingertips. Do not tell me. You must be a sculptor."

"A hatter."

"I was close," she said with triumph. "You make sculpture for the head."

He laughed. "A sculptor for the head? Preposterous."

"What is felt and silk but the hatter's marble and clay? Both sculptors and hatters are addressed as 'Maestro,' are they not?"

Stasi twisted his mouth and considered her point. "I . . . I suppose I am something of a sculptor."

"You bet your britches you are, Maestro!"

Stasi was tickled but also melancholy. All those years spent with Enzo in the cutting room, and not once had he fancied himself an artist. Had Enzo thought that way? He'd never know.

He took her hand, bowed, and introduced himself. "Maestro Anastasi Petasos, at your service. My intimates call me Stasi."

"Bianca de Leòn," she answered back.

"Your family are Spaniards?"

"Fifty years ago, we were. We might still be, had a coral competitor not accused my grandparents of being crypto-Jews."

"Were they crypto-Jews?"

"Does that matter to you?" she shot back.

He shook his head. "Not in the least. Just curious."

Bianca smiled but didn't answer the question. She touched the brim of Stasi's sunhat and ran her fingers along the crown. "What strange leather," she said dreamily. "It's scaly like a bird's, yet soft as silk. And warm, like a dog's belly."

Stasi had forgotten he was wearing the ancient Greek sunhat. Mortified, he quickly removed it and tucked it behind him.

"It's a silly old thing. Impractical as a sunhat. But it's been in the family so long I can't bear to . . ." He trailed off.

Bianca held out her yellow cap. "Do you know this cap circumnavigated the world with Magellan and Elcano? I bet you can't say anything as remarkable about your hat."

"No . . . well . . . no."

"This cap was my Great-Aunt Esmeralda's."

Stasi was dubious. "Your great-aunt was aboard the Victoria? I hadn't heard of any women on that voyage."

"Well, there was one. Esmeralda disguised her sex. Apparently, it wasn't difficult for her. She was a large-boned woman with a lantern jaw and a husky voice. Went by Antonio."

"I am pleased you do not take after her."

"Why would you say such a thing?" Bianca said sharply.

Stasi rocked back on his heels and said defensively, "Do not be affronted. I refer only to the cut of your jib. You clearly favor Esmeralda in spirit."

The clarification placated Bianca. Her flare of anger dissipated, and she changed the subject.

"When do you leave, Stasi?"

"Leave?"

"You are here at the port," she said didactically. "You have a packed bag. I assume you are traveling today."

"Right," he erupted. "Of course. Yes, I am setting off."

"To gather material for your hats, no doubt."

"No. Well, maybe. It's more for leisure."

"I envy you."

She locked eyes with him. There was a pause. She seemed to be searching for something. Whatever it was, was difficult to get to, maybe even impossible.

"This is going to sound rather forward," Stasi said, his voice squeaking on the word forward. "It is rather forward. Of that, I am certain. But – oh hell – perhaps you can venture with me."

Her eyes turned rheumy. "I would love nothing more than to venture with you," she said in a voice devoid of irony. "Alas, I must remain close to Livorno." She rested a hand over her heart.

"That is too bad. Are you quite sure?"

"Quite. Best I not waylay you any further," she said grimly. She knelt and began folding and repacking Stasi's things. She forced a smile and said in a cheery tone, "I shall put back your things, carry the satchel to your ship, and see you off. Will that be adequate recompense for my crime?"

"Let me think. No, I would have to say it is totally inadequate. If you recall, I answered your question about the hairbrush. Therefore, you must tell me which arse cheek you would have the social order kiss."

"Very well. The right one. It's the less flattering of the two, at least it was the last time I saw its reflection."

She stood and stepped close to him. She locked another searching gaze on him and stroked his lips with her finger in the same languid way she'd stroked the sunhat.

"Your lips are chapped," she said. "They won't survive the salt sea air."

She retrieved a tin from a small purse at her waist, removed the lid, and rubbed two fingers in a circular pattern over a golden yellow substance inside. She applied the sweet wax to Stasi's lips with the same circular motion. He could hear her breathing. Her lips were so close to his. He wanted to kiss them. He was going to kiss them, but she stepped back, closed the tin, and stuck it back in her purse. She returned to the satchel.

"I will pack the rest and then see you off."

As she repacked the remaining items, Bianca revealed she was the daughter of coral merchants. "We moved from Pisa not long ago. My father believed it advantageous to be close to the ships that traffic in his coral. Also, he got tired of paying bribes to the Pisan Customs Office."

"Where is your family's shop?"

"Near the glass factory."

Stasi nodded with recognition. "I believe I passed by your shop months ago. Men were carrying things inside. I recall an exquisite nautilus shell, cut in half, revealing the many chambers. I'd never seen such a shell, nor did I know what it was until I heard a tall, bearded man in black garb order the laborer to 'take care with the nautilus shell,' calling him an oaf for good measure."

"That was my father. He's very protective of that shell. Esmeralda acquired it in Timor."

"Do you sell coral with your father, or are you a full-time pirate?"

"The coral business is dreadfully boring. I made it plain to my father that I'd assist only half the day in the shop. The other half was for dressing in costume."

"As a pirate?"

"As a pirate, coachman, stevedore, notary, priest, ditch digger."

"All men's occupations."

"Men are freer than women. They need not marry or bear children. They can be pirates, priests, or magistrates. Unless she's an Esmeralda, a woman cannot travel alone, not very far anyway."

"Perhaps you just need the right travel companion. One who can show you a land where a woman can be anything she wants."

Bianca's white poppy smile bloomed for the second time. "Do you really think there is such a place?"

"I don't know. But if there is, I'll find it."

Her smile shriveled. "It matters not. I'll never leave Livorno."

"Why not?"

"It's easier if I show you."

Bianca glanced left and right, then began unbuttoning the top of her thigh-length blouse.

"Wait," Stasi said urgently. "What are you doing?"

"Answering your question."

"But—"

Bianca unfastened three buttons. The canvas flopped

43

open, revealing the skin above her left areola. Stasi felt an explosion of heat in each ear. He turned his head this way and that. He looked everywhere but in front of him until settling on the lighthouse.

"Is this something you should show me here . . . in the open?" he asked, voice-rising.

"Don't be such a ninny. There is no one about." She pulled Stasi's chin toward her chest. "Stop looking out there."

His gaze brushed over her face, her long smooth neck, down the V of parting canvas, before coming to rest on her partially-exposed breast. Her chest was emblazoned with five concentric blue circles.

"What is that? A tattoo?"

"I was born with a hole in my heart. My physician uses heated cups to draw my heart flesh into itself. He believes it helps close the hole. As you can see, the treatment has left me deformed."

"Well, it's an exquisite deformity. Botticelli would've painted your bosom had he been as fortunate as I to see it."

Bianca blushed.

Stasi cleared his throat. "Does this treatment work?"

She refastened her buttons.

"Some days, I believe it does. Some days, not. On the days I believe, I feel better. My physician says I could either live a long life or drop dead tomorrow. The heart is an unpredictable organ. This is why I cannot venture far from Pisa, where my physician resides."

Stasi's spirits flagged. Such a cruel twist of fate – to bury both his parents in the same week, only to fall instantly in love with a woman he might end up burying in a day or two.

"Do you believe in fate?" she asked hopefully.

"I have no choice but to believe," he said somberly.

"I didn't believe until this very moment. The similarity

of the swirls on your hairbrush and my chest is beyond coincidence. Something – God, Fate, the West Wind, I don't know – has brought us to the same spot." Her smile faltered. She seemed about to erupt into tears. "A cruel something. Our time is fleeting. You are leaving. Most likely, I will be residing with the worms upon your return. My feeble heart demands I bid you farewell."

As she turned away, Stasi said, "To hell with your heart, Bianca."

She turned around. "I beg your pardon."

"Who knows how long any of us shall live? Why, I could be run down by a carriage tomorrow or struck with the plague the next. Lightning could strike me down right here, right now. Still, I would count myself blessed because . . . because I've just met the most remarkable pirate in the world. If that's what Fate intends, then I say, 'Amor Fati.' All I ask is you say it with me."

Tears welled in Bianca's eyes. "Amor Fati," she answered.

"Good," Stasi said, as though concluding a bargain. "I'm glad we've got that settled."

Bianca turned and pointed to a triple-masted ship. "Is that your ship there? The caravel? She's headed to Africa, I believe."

"I'm not going to Africa."

"Ah. Then, the carrack over there. It's a Levant ship, headed for Marseilles."

"I'm not going to France either."

"There are only two ships departing Livorno today, Maestro. You have either missed your ship, or you have mistaken the day of departure."

"I fear you are correct, Madonna."

"What shall you do?"

"I shall head home. Perhaps my ship will arrive later." He extended his elbow to her. "Would you care to see my hat shop?"

"The hat shop," echoed Bianca with wonderment. She took Stasi's elbow. "Yes, I shall wait with you at the shop until your ship arrives. I hope that is no imposition."

"Not at all."

"What if your ship doesn't come by day's end?"

"Then I shall make up a bed for you."

She eyed him lasciviously.

"In a separate room," he added with affected piety. "I have a reputation to maintain."

They began strolling down the quay.

"Tomorrow, I plan to dress as a stable boy," she said matter-of-factly. "If your ship has not come in by the morn, we shall have to stop by the coral shop and gather some items. My father and mother will be there. They will have questions for you."

"And I will provide answers. Real answers, mind you, not the hypothetical variety."

She squeezed herself tight against Stasi. His mind began racing through their immediate future – a brief engagement, a wedding ceremony, and the marital bed. She looked at him with a puckish smile, exuding both affection and a benign wickedness. What occupied her mind at that moment? Love at first sight? The miracle of entangled destinies?

"I have been thinking," Bianca said at length.

"Tell me, Madonna."

"Should I survive to the day after tomorrow, I shall dress as a fish monger."

* * *

Bianca arose from Stasi's bed in the morning and asked, "Do you think your ship has come in?"

Stasi shook his head, said, "No, not today," and pulled

her back on the bed.

The next morning, Bianca rose from Stasi's bed, and they repeated this exchange. Days stretched into weeks, and weeks into months, and they engaged in the same call and response. It was their mantra, spoken whether Bianca awoke as a first mate, an apothecary, or the Grand Duke of Tuscany. They spoke those words in lieu of vows on their wedding day. They spoke them when Stasi handed a swaddled newborn to her five years later. They spoke them through her bouts of sickness, deviating from their script only once.

On that day, Bianca asked in a hoarse voice, "Do you think your ship has come in?"

"Yes, my love," Stasi answered. He kissed her cold purple lips and pulled the blanket to her chin. "I have booked passage for two."

Bianca's smile blossomed and immediately deflated. "Stasi, you fool!" she chided him.

"What is wrong, my love?"

She shot a glance to the corner of the bedroom. "You forgot about Andolosia."

Stasi glanced over his shoulder at his son seated on the stool. The bleary-eyed eight-year-old was tying bits of wire into a complex geometric shape. With a fixed scowl, crinkled brow, and baggy eyes, he manifested the facial undulations of a tired scholar or stern magistrate, not a child. The apocalyptic nightmare had deprived him of sleep and preoccupied his waking thoughts. That monstrous nautilus. Its smothering tentacles. The deluge. The end of everything.

Bianca released a long, rattling sigh.

"A careless oversight, Madonna," Stasi said. Abruptly, he turned his head and added, "I shall purchase another tick—"

As soon as Stasi caught sight of his wife, he guffawed at the horseshoe mustache pasted to her upper lip. Her solemn expression made the image all the more hilarious. Stasi quickly realized, however, that it was easy for someone in her condition to keep a straight face.

He wept all evening, of course, but never for long. Every so often, an insistent, insuppressible laugh would escape his throat and stab a knife into the heart of his grief.

CHAPTER

FOUR

Oblivion, 1600 B.C.E.

Moira shot awake. Her mouth felt like a clogged hairbrush, the consequence of sleeping slack-jawed on a gryphon instead of a proper pillow. She raked the fur from her tongue and gaped at the blazing, moon-like sphere dead ahead. It was Oblivion, bathed in the Phlegethon's raging, purple fire.

We shall burn to a crisp!

The beast's lungs expanded like titanic bellows and unleashed a booming, brassy howl. Goosebumps cascaded to Moira's toes. An exquisite tickle blossomed in her center and radiated heat to her extremities. She was in awe. According to divine lore, an identical sound had spawned the universe's creation, which was why the gods described the gryphon's call, like the perpetual hum of the River Oceanus, as "the eternal note" or "the note that began it all." Although a gryphon's call could not create a universe, it was powerful enough to tear a rent in the present one. The fiery curtain parted before Moira, and they soared through the fissure, which sealed behind them with an explosive "Pop!"

Oblivion's sky was bright enough for Moira to appreciate the gryphon's glorious plumage. Silken indigo feathers carpeted the beast from its curved yellow beak to its broad shoulders, while golden-orange fur coated the rest of its body and tail up to the fluffy, indigo tip. Below Moira lay a vast desert of gray-sand plains, gorges, and an enormous sandstone mesa. As best she could tell, there were no animals or bodies of water, not a single plant or tree, not even the fake variety. Perhaps that was why the air had no discernible scent. Oblivion appeared to be as lifeless as Tartarus.

The gryphon loosed a call, opening another rent, and they entered Hades. The persimmon sky was brighter than Oblivion's and dappled with colorful clouds – honey-yellow puffs, mustard streaks, and goldenrod wisps. Unlike the sterile atmosphere in Oblivion, the air here was pungent, simultaneously sweet and putrid, punctuated with notes of ginkgo pollen, rotting pomegranates, smelting copper, and asphodel flowers. Rivers streaked across a quilt of fields and meadows, some barren, others lush and forested. The largest river, Styx, flowed in an improbable seven-armed spiral. Beyond Styx were the underworld's eastern outskirts and the River Oceanus. That was where they were headed.

The gryphon climbed, leveled off, and dove toward the humming river. They plummeted like a leaden arrow. Wind ripped away Moira's headband, and her hair exploded into a fluttering black tempest. The rush of air into her screaming mouth ballooned her wobbling cheeks. Tears leached sideways from her eyeballs and instantly evaporated on her temples. As they barreled toward Oceanus, the river's hum intensified like an approaching swarm of bees. She braced for impact, tensing every muscle, squeezing her eyes shut, and tucking her tongue well behind her teeth.

But when no splash came and she sensed her cheeks deflating and the gryphon leveling off, she tentatively opened her eyes. She blinked rapidly to rehydrate them. She closed her lips and willed herself to salivate and moisten her leathery tongue.

How odd.

They were flying under the clear blue, Earthen sky. She glanced over her shoulder, expecting to see Oceanus rapidly receding from view. Instead, there was only alpine landscape. The great river was invisible on its Earthen side. She looked forward and saw they were approaching Mount Othrys, though this was the Earthen Mount Othrys, not its heavenly counterpart.

Another gryphon call exposed the second loop of Oceanus' figure-eight shape, the loop that separated Earth from the heavens. After passing through the rent, the gryphon ascended a thousand feet. At the apogee, the beast tucked its wings, girded its neck, and broke into yet another dive. Now indoctrinated into the peculiarities of intersphere travel, Moira didn't panic about her imminent collision with the river. Indeed, instead of a violent splash, the river greeted her with a warm purple flash and a peaceful silence.

Moira was disoriented. Their flight trajectory had spontaneously shifted from downward to level. Also, they seemed to have emerged in a blinding snowstorm. No, not snow, she realized. Although she'd hadn't experienced the stuff firsthand, she'd heard snow fell in cold flakes. This was coarse powder, and it wasn't cold. A zephyr was kicking up pollen from the copious pellitory plants blanketing the mountain. Moira swatted the pollen from her face and spat it from her mouth, to little effect. Mercifully, the pollen thinned as they ascended and abated entirely by the time they reached the summit of Othrys' heavenly twin.

The gryphon alighted beside a rectangular building of rough-hewn cypress, stone, and thatch. A copper cylinder – *A pipe?* Moira wondered – projected from the roof hundreds of yards into the sky. The pipe joined a massive copper bowl more than five hundred feet in diameter. A billowy, wine-red cloud was raining into the bowl, making a steady, metallic patter.

The gryphon lowered its head and waited for Moira to disembark. She didn't. She was too absorbed in the fascinating red cloud. The gryphon sighed. Ten seconds later, it sighed again. Still, Moira hadn't budged. Nor did she get the hint to dismount after the beast grumbled and wriggled its body. The gryphon squawked, listed, and dumped its passenger unceremoniously onto the dirt. Moira had arrived.

Moira was on her hands and knees, thoroughly discombobulated, as if she'd fallen out of bed in the midst of a deep sleep. She shook her head and gathered her bearings. The résumé and cover letter had escaped her clutches in the tumult. She fished them from the dirt and was smoothing them out when someone in blue, curly-tipped shoes approached. She regarded the diminutive creature standing over her. He was dressed in crisp, blue velvet overalls and sported an imperial-style mustache, beard, and bushy eyebrows. Recalling stories about the "lesser creatures" who populated the heavens, Moira deduced he was a tree-elf.

Without even the pretense of chivalry, the tree-elf grasped Moira's elbow and hoisted her upright. The jostle caught her unawares, and the tapestries slipped from her hand yet again.

"Wait," Moira said, reaching toward the ground. "My tapestries."

"You won't need those," the tree-elf said curtly while tugging her in the opposite direction.

Moira tried resisting, but the tree-elf's dwarfish stature belied a hulking strength. Given the ease with which he dragged Moira toward the building, she might as well have been an empty robe. He kicked open the door and shoved her inside.

"Welcome to Cronus' palace," he said brusquely and slammed the door in her face.

The ruffled Moira smoothed her wrinkled robe and peeled the perspiration-soaked fabric clinging to her buttocks and groin. She patted the pollen from her shoulders and chest, which made dusty plumes that triggered a coughing fit. She gingerly touched her tender cheeks, which felt like burlap after her tumultuous travels through wind, fire, and the expanse of Chaos.

My face must look like a sunbaked satchel.

Moira knotted her windblown hair into a bun and scanned the room. Wall-mounted oil lamps illuminated the interior with dim, flickering light. The red silk rugs on the hard-packed dirt floor exuded a peculiar vibrancy. Their fibers rippled to and fro like water lapping on a beach. More strangely, the fibers were multiplying. The rugs were enlarging before her eyes. The unadorned walls exhibited the same motility and growth. The cypress beams pulsated and rippled, as did the mortared stone between the beams.

Moira sauntered past a rectangular table riddled with knots, splits, and cracks, and surrounded by twelve decrepit wooden chairs. The chairs were different heights and patently crooked. Like the rugs and the walls, they were in transition. Short legs were growing, while long legs were shrinking. The splintery timber comprising the table and chairs was smoothing out, as if ghost-carpenters armed with hand planes were swarming the furniture and shaving the uneven spots.

Beyond the table was a burbling red pond surrounded by a short stone wall. The copper pipe descended from the ceiling into the pool's depths.

Could it be?

Moira studied the viscous, red fluid in the pool. She sniffed and detected the unmistakable coppery scent.

Yes, it is! Pure human faith!

Fate Accompli

This pool fed an intersphere plumbing network that delivered human faith to spigots in every god's bedchamber. Moira fantasized about diving in the pool and gulping it dry. *How powerful I'd become! More potent than Cronus!* She promptly banished the blasphemous notion from her mind.

Curious. A pyramidal clump of black strands was floating on the pond's surface. A long-handled tool with a wide, fan-shaped head of fine mesh was propped against the stone wall. It was a skimmer like the one Moira had used in Tartarus to collect congealed Chaos fibers from Black Pond. Disentangled threads dangled on a nearby drying rack.

"Ahem. Are you Moira?" inquired a thin voice from the room's far end.

In the dimness, Moira spied a male figure sitting on a bema.

"I am," she answered. "Lord Cronus?"

Cronus raised his hand in a beckoning motion. Moira took the gesture as an affirmative response and approached the bema.

Cronus was not at all what she had expected. For such an important god, he was short, no taller than she, by her estimation. And what there was of him was unimpressive. His head was bald, save for meager tufts of iron-gray hair on the sides. His body lacked the burnished undulations of well-defined chest and arm muscles. Pasty white skin clung to his frame like a wet bedsheet and gathered into a flabby paunch. His throne, meanwhile, possessed all the majesty of a prop from an itinerant theatrical troupe. It was a high-backed chair of rough-hewn cypress, legs crooked and of varying heights. The chair's gaudy arms were studded haphazardly with emeralds, rubies, and gold nuggets.

"My lord," Moira said with a bow of her head.

"I fear my valet was a bit rough with you," Cronus said apologetically. He held a scythe in his right hand. Fastidiously, he picked a flake of crusted blood off the blade.

"Ahem. Ahem," he continued. "The palace construction disrupted his slumber, and he would not stop shouting. I would have smitten him on the spot, but Mother Gaia insists we maintain good relations with the lesser creatures. Hee. Hee. The only way for a tree-elf to fall back asleep is to have him perform a good deed. I asked him to welcome you and show you inside – in retrospect, not an ideal task for the surly fellow. Ahem. Hee hee."

Cronus' "hee hee" didn't sound like laughter or an expression of irony, more like a nervous tic or a symptom of dyspepsia.

Moira bowed again. "Your sentiment was most thoughtful, my lord." She raised her head and added, "My application materials are outside. With your permission, I shall fetch them."

"Do not bother," he said without affect.

Moira's heart sunk. Had he already filled the position?

Cronus shifted restlessly in his throne and fidgeted with his ill-fitting toga. "Ahem," he uttered. "Moira, I – that is, Mother Gaia and I – are leading the Titans in a different direction – ahem – a different direction than my forefather." Cronus picked another scab from the scythe, held it to the light of the wall sconce. "Uranus was a fool," he said to the scab. "He refused to accept – ahem – refused to accept we gods are products of the human imagination and therefore require mortal faith to thrive. He was content to exist as an abstraction, a fanciful idea in the mortal mind – hee hee – as tenuous and impermanent as a wisp of steam. Ahem."

The incessant hee-hees and ahems were driving Moira mad. Cronus inserted them willy-nilly, following no syntactical or metrical logic. Back in Tartarus, Moira used to imagine loud electrical discharges from the Phlegethon River whenever Nyx offered her unsolicited weaving advice. Moira adapted this strategy to Cronus by reinterpreting each ahem and hee-hee as an innocuous wind gust. It proved an imperfect strategy, but at least Moira would emerge from their conversation with her sanity intact . . . mostly intact.

Cronus flicked away the scab and stared at Moira with his narrow-set eyes and conical nose. Moira wondered if Cronus had created the shrew in his image.

"To be great and powerful," he continued, "we gods must dirty our hands with mortal business and earn their faith. Do you not agree?"

Moira didn't harbor an opinion but presumed the prudent course was to agree. "I . . . That makes the utmost sense."

Cronus adjusted his toga, cleared his throat, hee-hee'd, readjusted his toga, started to clear his throat again, fell silent, hee-hee'd once more, and gestured over Moira's shoulder.

"Behind you, on the drying rack, is an untapped source of faith," he said.

Moira ambled to the rack and inspected the strands. Unlike Chaos thread, these strands varied in thickness and emitted a sharp, sweet musk that set her nose hairs on end. She sneezed. She rubbed her nose to eviscerate the tickle and grazed a strand with her fingertips. It was warm and gave off a tingly magnetism. It felt . . . *alive*.

"Is this thread?" Moira asked with fascination.

"*Destiny* Thread."

"I've never heard of Destiny Thread."

"Neither had we. We long assumed these strands were useless detritus. For eons, we skimmed them right off the faith pool and tossed them away. Three days ago, we learned what fools we'd been. Ahem."

"What happened three days ago, my lord?"

"We threw a surprise birthday party for Mother Gaia. Ahem. What a disaster. My sister Theia overindulged on mead, as she is wont to do. Slurring her words. Fondling the servant-sprites. Abominable. Gaia told Theia she should grow up and take a husband. Theia's response? She belched in her mother's face, climbed on the table and announced she would never marry, lest she turn into a stodgy fossil like her mother. Drunkenly, she stumbled into a bowl of ambrosia, slipped off the table, and crashed into Hyperion. Hee hee. Gaia was so furious, she abandoned her own celebration. I'd like to say the scene was atypical, but family dinners in the Titan house are often drama-filled.

"Mother Gaia was still upset in the morning. Hee – ahem. I suggested a distraction, perhaps build a new mountain or carve a canyon. But Mother said terraforming in her state of mind was a bad idea. She was liable to trigger a massive earthquake in a populated area. So I proposed she take up a hobby."

"Mother Gaia has hobbies?" Moira asked.

"Now she does. Just the one. Knitting. With no yarn handy, she skimmed the strands from the faith pool, spun them into yarn, and knitted a purse. She intended to present it to Theia as a peace offering. Hee hee. As Mother knitted, she cogitated over Theia's future and had a vision: Theia would take a Titan husband in the very near future. Mother laid the finished purse next to Theia's slumbering face. Wouldn't you know, that very afternoon, Theia and Hyperion announced their nuptials. Ahem – hee. The turnabout was miraculous, even by divine standards. Mother has always possessed the gift of prognostication, but never before had she manifested the power to dictate the future."

Cronus reached inside his robe and extracted a black purse. "Look sharp!" He tossed the purse to Moira, who bobbled it twice before securing it. She rubbed her fingers along the mishmash of fabrics while examining the purse from different angles.

Cronus went on. "The weave is sloppy, which is unsurprising. Mother Gaia raises mountains, carves gorges, and pushes glaciers across plains – all by hand. The toils have rendered her fingers thick, brutish, and calloused. But the quality of the craftsmanship is not what interests me."

"What does interest you, my lord?"

"You tell me, Moira."

She looked up. "I don't know what to look for."

"Look first, then you'll know."

Moira crinkled her brow. It seemed utterly backward to embark on a search with no object in mind. Still, she saw no option but to play along. She focused on the bottom of the purse. As she rubbed the jumble of patterns, she made a face of intense concentration, as if trying to discern a distant sound. All at once, her searching expression turned to awe.

"I take it you've found it," Cronus said with building excitement.

"Astounding!" she declared. "These twists and nubs form a pattern like none I've ever felt. It fills me with warmth, a sense of connection."

"Keep going. What else do you sense?"

"Meaning. Not literal meaning. More like music. I can't explain it, but somehow I know – through intuition, I suppose – that the warmth is Hyperion, patron of the sun, and the sense of connection is his impending marriage to Theia. It's madness."

"A madness we all share," Cronus rejoined. "By dint of Mother Gaia's accidental design, the purse brought about the very future she had wished for. This is no mere parlor trick. This is a discovery on par with Creation. I believe we can exploit Destiny Thread to accumulate an ocean of human faith."

"How so, my lord?"

"If humans believe the gods determine their fates, they—ahem—they will assume we care about their paltry lives, and that assumption will lead them to one inevitable conclusion: 'To be happy, I must curry favor with the gods.

This will ensure a favorable fate or prevent an unfavorable one. I must pray to them. I must drink wine in their honor. I must sacrifice beasts and spill blood for them.'"

Moira nodded approvingly. "Ingenious."

"The difficulty is in the execution. Mother tried her hand at more textiles. She crafted bags, pouches, cloths, and other notions, all the while attempting to invest meaning in her patterns. Her craftsmanship was poor and uninspired, and thus, her ability to determine mortal fates was rudimentary at best. Oh, she could make humans fall in love, but only a third of the time. She could induce pregnancies, but more often than not the offspring would diverge wildly from their intended paths, ending up slaves instead of kings, paupers instead of princes, or vice versa. I realized if we Titans hope to assert even a modicum of control over human fates, we must employ an expert weaver, someone capable of fashioning complex textiles that mirror the complexity, variety, and richness of a human life, with only black thread at her disposal. That someone is you, Moira. Hee hee."

Moira bowed her head deferentially. "I am most honored, my lord, but it is one thing to make a night sky. It is quite another to weave a fate. If Mother Gaia is incapable, how can I . . ." Overcome with modesty, she stopped herself and raised her head. "Perhaps you have already interviewed someone with this skill."

"I have spoken with no one else, Moira, nor shall I. Your night-sky curtains are peerless. The job is yours and yours alone."

"I am flattered, my lord," she said with relief, "but may I ask, if your intent was to hire me at the outset, why broadcast the job announcement on the Clarion Call Network for all to hear?"

Cronus shifted in his chair. He tugged at the gathered toga material impinging on his neck. "That was Gaia's doing. She insists we present ourselves as equitable and fair gods, to show we bestow titles and responsibilities based on skills and effort, not family connections. She claims the future will bring great rewards to so-called 'equal opportunity employers.'" Cronus shook his head petulantly, as if harking back to a private argument on the topic. "She seems to forget we gods are incestuous by nature. Rhea is both wife and sister to me. The entire applicant pool are my children, cousins, and consorts! Gaia says it will not always be so, and we should lay the groundwork for a time when our bloodlines have thinned." Cronus sighed. "I did not pursue it further. Such is the price of domestic tranquility. No matter. You are here. What say you? Will you join us?"

Moira's heart welled with ardor. To be admired and coveted by the king of the gods! "How can I refuse, my lord?"

Cronus looked torn. "You may refuse, if you wish. You are the master of your fate . . . and if you accept, you will become the master of many other fates." He leaned forward and spoke urgently but furtively. "In all frankness, Mother Gaia told me to say that. She warned me not to admit you have us over a barrel, but I much prefer the direct approach to negotiations. What more can I offer you? State your desire. If it is within my power, I shall grant it forthwith."

Moira felt a peculiar strength, as if she'd just downed a tankard of human faith. The shackles of her mother's identity were unlocking and sliding off her limbs. In the heavens, she would have a distinct identity, defined by her, for her. She'd step out of her mother's dour penumbra. Free.

Moira was in a strong bargaining position. Cronus foolishly had admitted as much. Although she didn't wish to alienate her future employer, she couldn't squander the golden opportunity. She had to assert herself unapologetically. Before spinning a single spool of yarn or stringing one warp thread, she had to make it crystal clear that this Moira – the Moira of the heavens – had her own wants and demands and would not be denied.

She fixed a cold stare on Cronus and said in her new intrepid voice, "I require a window."

Cronus nodded deferentially, barely able to contain his relief. He rose from the throne, stepped off the bema, and, with his scythe, cut a large rectangle from the wall. Sunlight streamed in. The brightness dazzled Moira's eyes, inducing another peculiar sensation. Her facial muscles, especially those around her mouth, were stretched and flexed to the point of aching. This ache, however, was good. Very good indeed. The kind of ache that brought a smile to her face.

CHAPTER

FIVE

Livorno, Grand Duchy of Tuscany, 1603

Stasi stood at the base of the Old Fortress, Hermes' hat – the wishing hat – tucked securely under his arm. Behind him loomed construction cranes for the Duomo and the new synagogue. Before him was the crowded inner harbor, where merchants on floating bazaars peddled salted fish, Portuguese pepper, Brazilian sugar, Egyptian linen, cotton from the Levant, and silk from Naples. The Grand Duke's galley ships, with their low profiles and long oars, resembled an armada of seafaring centipedes. The outer harbor was even busier. Treadwheel- and windlass-powered cranes employed complex block and tackle mechanisms to hoist cargo from the holds of moored carracks and caravels. Lighters, barges, and prams transported the bales and crates ashore, where porters wheeled them on carts to the lazaretto for inspection and quarantine.

Stasi set off down the quay. It was slow going with his gout-inflamed feet until a gaggle of rowdy mariners overtook and swallowed him in their current. The sun-cracked men in baggy breeches moved with a swift, pendulous grace, which served them well on roiling seas but proved drunken and desultory on terra firma. The horde carried Stasi past a young mate getting his first tattoo. The mate winced when the grizzled ship's cook pricked his forearm with a knife tip and rubbed gunpowder in the wound. The gaggle passed a narrow alleyway of stacked grain casks. Stasi recognized his old acquaintance's furtive movements in the shadows. Despite her advanced age for a woman in that line of work, she moved as lithely as the night she'd introduced him to the pleasures of the fairer sex on his sixteenth birthday.

A peddler was handing out leaflets touting "Arconum Antiveneral" pills for sale at the Globe and Urinal Apothecary Shoppe on Leather Lane. The "miracle pills" purportedly were good for "those hot, sharp pricking pains when making water, indicative of *morbus gallicus* or the French Pox, as well as scurvy and all other rheumatick aches and pains." Stasi spurned the leaflet. He knew that apothecary all too well – intimately, one might say. Twenty years before, the apothecary had prescribed Stasi a hot tallow enema for a bout of malaise. The apothecary lost track of time during the procedure and had to administer five sea-water clysters to flush out the congealed wax. The next morning, the apothecary deposited a "peace offering" on the Petasos' doorstep. Stasi, who'd gone to Pisa for the day, returned that evening to find Bianca reading by the light of a misshapen candle possessing the precise caliber and length of his rectum.

The mariners veered left, off the quay, spitting Stasi from their midst like a watermelon seed. Stasi followed the porters into the lazaretto. There, merchants perused bills of lading posted in front of piles of bales, boxes, and hogsheads. He stiffened when he spotted the Fasci Sansone inspectors in their signature long-billed caps and brown short-waist doublets embroidered with the image of a bundle of sticks superimposed over an orange sun. He longed for the old days, when the short-staffed Livorno Customs Office regulated shopkeepers and artisans with a light touch, before Sansone de Medici assumed control of the Florentine guilds and expanded their geographic influence. All at once, Sansone assessed dues on the Livornese merchants and imposed arcane guild rules on price and quality.

The Fasci Sansone would not release cargo into the mandatory fifteen-day quarantine until verifying that the merchants claiming the goods belonged to the appropriate guild, were paid up on their dues, and had no outstanding fines. Stasi was in trouble on all three fronts. He owed money to the wool guild and hadn't yet paid a twenty-florin fine for mispricing a turban. On top of that, he was picking up furs and wasn't a member of the fur guild. Fortunately, the inspectors focused on the largest shipments first – the casks of beer, hogsheads of grain, fish and seal oil, and boxes of salt, chalk, and spices. They wouldn't reach the smaller cases of silks, wool, furs, and tanned goods at the back of the warehouse for a while.

Stasi found his bill of lading attached to a lone crate branded with the image of a skeleton key over the words "G. Rabino. Monticello." He pulled a pry bar from his purse and popped off the lid. Inside were the pelts of rabbits, hares, and the wild tabby cats of the Sicilian mountains. "*What the—*" There had to be at least five more pelts than he'd ordered. He shook his head in mock outrage. *Typical, Gennaro. Generous to a fault.* He replaced the lid and returned the pry bar to his purse.

He was ready. He put on the wishing hat, positioned a hand on the crate, and jammed a foot underneath. He formed an image of the cutting room in his mind and exhaled. But before he could make the wish, a hand landed on his shoulder.

Stasi yelped, tore off the wishing hat, and guardedly rotated his head. His torso and legs followed a beat later, lending a theatrical flair to his coiling turn. He was face to face with a twelve or thirteen year-old boy, the typical age of Fasci Sansone inspectors, whom Sansone recruited from Florentine orphanages. The young "incorrigibles" were all too eager to pledge two years of servitude and wear ridiculous uniforms in exchange for room and board and a hundred florins at the end of their term.

"Forgive me for startling you, Maestro," the inspector said while adjusting his doublet. "But you may not open the crates until the Fasci Sansone has cleared them."

Stasi was familiar with the boy. The gawkish inspector had issued him the twenty-florin fine for the mispriced turban. In other circumstances, Stasi might have taken a liking to the boy, who was far less militant than his colleagues. He projected an earnestness, which, no doubt, made him well-suited to apply rigid guild rules, but he wasn't officious. He didn't seem angry at Stasi, rather, genuinely perplexed how anyone could violate such a clear and explicit rule.

"Quite right, my boy. Quite right," Stasi concurred.

Like the other inspectors, the boy carried a string-wrapped graphite stick and a folio listing the merchants' names, guilds, and account statuses. He opened his folio and flipped through the pages until landing on Stasi's name.

"You are Maestro Anastasi Petasos, are you not?"

"Guilty as charged."

"You already have a twenty-florin fine. Now, you have opened a crate prior to clearance from the Fasci Sansone. This warrants another twenty-florin fine."

Stasi didn't protest. "You know the rules to perfection," he said in a complimentary tone.

The boy paused. He cocked his head in a quizzical way. "Why do you flout the rules so?"

"I am swimming in your rules. I spend so much time figuring out the prices for my hats that I have no time to make them. Soon, I will have amassed more fines than hats. Your rules are putting me out of business."

The boy's forehead crinkled. "They are not my rules. They are Padre Sansone's."

"*Padre* Sansone? I wasn't aware he was in the Church."

"Not that kind of father, Maestro."

Maybe Stasi had to rethink his opinion of Sansone. Maybe Sansone's relationship with his inspectors wasn't purely transactional. That might have been a good thing, or it might have been very, very bad.

"What is your name, boy?" Stasi asked.

"Matteo. Matteo Ricci."

"Tell me, Signore Matteo, what will you do with your one hundred florins after your two years are up?"

"Whatever Padre Sansone sees fit for me."

"Surely, you have dreams of your own."

"Well . . ." Matteo shifted his stance and looked cautiously right and left. He leaned in and spoke confidentially. "My uncle is a Jesuit monk. He lives in the Forbidden City. He serves as an adviser to the Imperial Court of the Wanli Emperor. He predicts solar eclipses."

"How fascinating. Would you join your uncle if you could?"

"He is too far away. I cannot afford the passage."

"But if you could, would your uncle have you?"

Matteo shrugged. "His letters often recount his joy in teaching me the movements of the planets."

"You remind me of my son, Andolosia. He, too, has an inquisitive mind. He would prefer a life of science to the family business. I shall tell him about your Uncle Ricci in the Forbidden City. I shall offer to pay his passage there so he may learn about eclipses. Your uncle would be happy for an Italian visitor, would he not?"

The boy bit his lip. Envy oozed from his face. "You would do that for your son?"

"It hadn't occurred to me until I met you. I had planned on leaving Andolosia the hat business, but now, with the Fasci Sansone's rules, I do not think it will be possible. Yes, the Forbidden City sounds like a much better plan. Andolosia will be very excited about it, don't you think?"

"If, as you say, Andolosia is like me, I have no doubt he will."

Stasi stepped close to the boy. "Tell me, Matteo. I've heard the Forbidden City is a large place. If my son were to meet your uncle there, what landmark would make the most sense?"

"Landmark?"

"I wouldn't want them to miss each other among the throng of princes, military generals, and courtesans dressed in their large black hats and embroidered silks. Nor would I want Andolosia to get trampled by the elephants pulling the emperor's royal carriage or distracted by the cherry-lipped prostitutes with peonies in their hair."

The boy blushed.

Stasi went on. "Do you have any suggestions for a specific spot in the Forbidden City, where my son may avoid the elephants and pretty girls' peonies, so he may find your uncle and spend the rest of his days unlocking the secrets of the stars?"

Matteo looked as though a great weight had been set on his shoulders. He replied softly, despairingly. "I suppose . . . I suppose if it were me, I would go to the Gate of Supreme Harmony. My uncle says it is where the Emperor holds morning court."

"Thank you. I will tell Andolosia to go there." He shot Matteo a pitiful look. "Too bad you shall never see the Gate of Supreme Harmony with your own eyes. Then again, why would you trade away the rich life you have here, with your new father, the great Padre Sansone de Medici, for a frivolity like the Gate of Supreme Harmony? You work here is vital."

"It is?" Matteo said dubiously.

"So vital, in fact, I venture that when your two-year term is up, you will choose to stay on with the Fasci Sansone."

"Why would I do that?"

"To oversee the younger inspectors, of course. You will collect their folios at the end of each day and make sure they have applied the rules, tallied the fines, and the florins just so. Each night, you will retire to bed, folios beside your pillow, knowing you have made your father richer. You will do that day after day until you die. A most satisfying life if I've ever heard one!"

Matteo looked ready to jump into the sea and swim to China or die trying. "I love Padre Sansone. I do. He is like a father . . . and yet I wish . . ."

Stasi donned the wishing hat. "And yet you wish what?"

Matteo was on the verge of tears. "And yet I wish I could go to the Gate of Supreme Harmony . . . if only for a moment."

Stasi gave an avuncular smile and rested a comforting hand on Matteo's shoulder. "I wish that too, my boy."

Stasi exhaled, steeled his abdominal muscles, and closed his eyes. With a metallic shriek and a flash of indigo light, he and the boy vanished.

Thirty seconds later, Stasi was back in the lazaretto, next to the crate of furs from Gennaro Rabino. He was holding Matteo's folio and graphite stick, which the boy had dropped while retching his guts at the Gate of Supreme Harmony. Stasi marked his twenty-florin fine as paid, recorded himself as a dues-paying member of the fur guild, and left the folio on a nearby crate. Another inspector would find the folio, but not the inspector who'd lost it. The Fasci Sansone's reach was vast but not as far as the Forbidden City.

CHAPTER

SIX

Mount Othrys, 1600 B.C.E.

Moira modeled her new loom on her former one in Tartarus, substituting wood for iron. She was pleased the wooden version didn't radiate cold or require nearly as much exertion to operate as its ferrous ancestor. Rather than clanging against the frame with a harsh, metallic *clink clunk*, the wooden batten knocked with a muted *thub dup*. The crashing-cymbal sound of her old loom had been superseded by a thumping bass drum. Throw. *Thub dup, thub dup.* Throw. *Thub dup, thub dup.* Her "Loom of Destiny" had a heartbeat.

It was cumbersome to weave with Destiny Thread of varying thicknesses, so Moira segregated and spliced segments of the same thickness into three gauges, wound them onto separate, six-foot-tall spools, and mounted the spools on dowel rods for ease of rotation. She then wove some experimental tapestries. She started with relatively minor, time-limited destinies – a slip and fall accident, a brief tryst, food poisoning from spoiled goat meat. After those proved successful, she graduated to marriages,

Fate Accompli

children, occupations, and deaths. More success. The process was simple, really. She needed only keep the fate's particulars in the forefront of her mind and let her hands translate them into her unique textural language.

"Splendid!" Cronus beamed after Moira informed him of her progress. "Gaia is finishing her preparations with the oracles. We should be ready to launch in earnest quite soon."

Cronus inspected the experimental tapestries hanging on a rack. As he ran his fingers over the fabric, he delighted in the tingling sensation and marveled at Moira's artistry. He turned to several tapestries woven from the thicker threads. Their designs were similar to the others, replete with Moira's inscrutable logograms, but these tapestries were hotter and more magnetic.

"These are especially vibrant," he remarked.

"Because they are for demigods and gods. I discovered their fates require the thickest gauge of thread."

"You weaved a *god's* fate?" Cronus asked in a mortified tone.

"Several, my lord."

Cronus' left eye twitched. "Which gods?"

"Oh, minor, obscure deities."

"Hee hee. Who exactly, Moira?" he pressed, voice shaky.

She gestured to the tapestry before him. "That one there is for Prophasis, the spirit of excuses and pleas. She sounded so querulous, I think, because she lacked self-confidence. I arranged to have her fight and vanquish a giant. Since then, there's not a hint of whininess in her voice, and she speaks with gravitas. Same tired old excuses, but now they're actually persuasive.

"The next tapestry over is for Gelos, the spirit of laughter. I never found Gelos very funny. All puns and scatological humor about the public privy. I arranged it so

70

he'd walk into a tavern with a gorgon, a harpy, and a man-eating giant. The peril dramatically improved Gelos' timing and inspired many new jokes. Good jokes. Everyone was too consumed with laughter to kill each other – at least they were when I left them."

Cronus tugged nervously on his bottom lip. He glanced around the throne room, assessing whether anyone was in earshot. He took Moira by the elbow and escorted her behind the loom.

"Moira," he said urgently, "this is a very grave development."

"It is?"

"Yes. Very grave. Your ability to determine the fates of gods – should it become widely known – could spell disaster. The selfish gods – and there are many, believe me – would pressure you to weave tapestries that further their interests at the expense of the others. Ahem. Why, a mere swatch from your loom could end my reign."

Moira was affronted. "I would never weave such a tapestry, my lord."

"I know you wouldn't. Not willingly. But if you were under duress, you might have no choice but to weave me a fate like my father's." He unconsciously tented his fingers in front of his groin.

Moira smacked her palm on her forehead. "Forgive me, my lord. I had no idea. What should I do?"

"Keep this discovery to yourself. And, heavens forbid, if anyone asks you to make a god's fate tapestry, demur. Say only Gaia – only the Mother Goddess can commission a god's destiny. No one would go up against Mother. Is that clear?"

"Yes, my lord."

"Good. Remove the spool of thickest thread from this room at once. And be discreet."

Moira immediately relocated the spool of god-gauge

71

thread to a utility closet and concealed it behind a curtain woven to resemble the room's marble walls. It would remain there until the gods were able to keep their selfish tendencies at bay – in other words, forever.

CHAPTER

SEVEN

Livorno, Grand Duchy of Tuscany, 1603

Andolosia shook his head in disbelief as he set the letter on the far corner of the cutting table. He regarded the parchment severely, wondering if it could be a forgery or someone's idea of a nasty joke. Part of him desperately wanted the letter to be authentic; part of him did not. He considered tossing it in the ceramic stove and letting the cruel dream turn to ash.

Back to work.

He slid the swatch of mohair in front of him. He cursed Stasi for having drunk so much wine during the felting process. Inebriation and millinery made regrettable bedfellows. The intoxicated Stasi had layered twelve bats of the imported Angora goat hair, instead of the standard four, which, after compression, yielded a sheet of felt-like armor. Due to Stasi's arthritic hands, it befell Andolosia to assemble the fabric into something they could sell. He settled on a beret-crowned hat, which, of all their designs, required the fewest stitches. That, of course, assumed it was possible to stitch the felt. Andolosia hadn't been able to pierce it with any of the standard millinery needles.

With an awl, he made a pin-prick-sized opening for the sewing needle. In his rush, he drove the awl into the flesh of his opposite hand. He was too exhausted to scream, though the injury certainly was scream-worthy. He yanked the awl from the web of skin between his thumb and forefinger. No blood, just a tiny red dot. He sat back in the chair, wiped away the blood droplet, and scrutinized the hole in his hand.

The hole would heal. He wondered why some holes healed and others did not. He recalled his boyhood, when he'd listen to his mother's heart through the physician's ear trumpet and pepper him with incessant questions about the murmur. Dissatisfied with the doctor's dismal prognosis, Andolosia sketched designs for an artificial heart. If the doctor couldn't mend the hole in Bianca's heart and it wouldn't close on its own, then he would replace it with a mechanism as reliable and sturdy as the large clocks springing up around Livorno. Andolosia's artificial heart designs were not crude, puerile drawings but detailed schematics based on mathematics, alchemy, and anatomy texts that Stasi's wealthy clients lent from their private libraries. The designs never got past the conceptual stage before Bianca died.

Andolosia felt torn over his mother's death. As much as he mourned her loss, her sickness had ignited a passion for scientific inquiry that he might not have discovered otherwise. He vowed to continue his work on the mechanical heart, so no other boy would have to lose his mother before her time.

At age eight, he created a hand-held pendulum device for measuring the human pulse. At ten, he developed a water clock with a float valve modeled after an animal heart to regulate the mechanism's motions. In his early teens, he observed the fluid dynamics of rivers and streams, hoping they would inform his understanding of blood flow. He found a river in the hills with a whirlpool and studied its seasonal cycle. In the spring, the vortex was a twirling dancer's skirt of dead leaves and pink oleander petals. In the summer, dry pine needles spun themselves into an aquatic bird's nest. In autumn, orange-red oak leaves and moss-coated river rocks mixed into a polychromatic blur, transforming the vortex into a painter's palette. In the winter, the rotation slowed to a clear, moribund swirl dreaming of spring and the next infusion of pink oleander.

After a decade of such explorations, Andolosia still didn't know how to blend his observations into a coherent design for a mechanical heart. It was as though he'd collected the swatches for a magnificent hat but had no notion of the kind of hat he could make from them. He needed the guidance of an expert tutor.

At nineteen, he wrote to Dottore Galileo Galilei at the University of Padua, explaining that his lack of siblings or a mother to help with the family hat business made full-time enrollment impossible. Nevertheless, he was hoping Dottore Galileo might spare a few days a month for independent study. He mailed the letter and expected that would be the end of it. Surely, Galileo had better things to do than waste time on the tinkerings of a merchant's son.

But Dottore Galileo replied. His letter, which sat on the corner of the cutting table, praised Andolosia's self-directed interest in science. He congratulated the boy for pursuing "direct experience" as the path to scientific knowledge, unlike the devout Aristotelians, who refused to trust what was right in front of their faces. Most stunning of all, Galileo agreed to the proposed arrangement. Given the distance from Livorno, he advised Andolosia to come to Padua for the last Friday and Saturday of every month to assist him with experiments on magnetic loadstones. "The work will be tedious," Galileo wrote, "but that is how the pursuit of knowledge works – drip by drip into the bottomless well of human curiosity. It is an unquenchable thirst, an unfillable emptiness, but maybe you already know this." Galileo concluded with a request. "If it is not too much trouble, might you grace me with a sunhat made of the legendary Livorno straw?"

Andolosia's excitement fizzled when he contemplated the logistics of studying with Galileo. Even with a blazingly fast horse and short rests, Padua was a ten-day round trip. Adding his two days with Dottore Galileo, Andolosia would be gone from the shop twelve days a month, cutting his hat output by more than a third. Profits would suffer, which they couldn't afford due to escalating guild dues. There was also Fate to consider. Straying from the hat business was a precarious proposition.

Andolosia cleaned his wound with vinegar and wrapped it with a scrap of linen. He would leave the felt project for another day. He opened the curtain a crack and peered onto the shop floor. Stasi was speaking to Madonna Vincenzo, a middle-aged, three-time widow with beady, wide-set eyes and an egg-shaped head. Stasi was complimenting her profusely, and unjustifiably, in a shameful attempt to sell her a hat that never should have seen the light of day. Edged with silver clips and trimmed with vulture feathers, the green silk hat evoked the tableau of a rabid bird crashing into a manicured boxwood plant. This was the consequence of millinery under the influence of opium, which Stasi took for gout pain. There was no way to deconstruct the hat and salvage the deep green silk. Foisting it on the lonely and wealthy widow was the best option for recouping the cost of the material.

Andolosia closed the curtain and bit his lip nervously. He dreaded speaking with his father about the Galileo matter, but he couldn't endure another second knowing that studying with the genius was a possibility, albeit an impractical one. He pictured Stasi's face contorting with anguish and hurt. They'd exchange harsh words. Tears would flow. Andolosia would beg Stasi's forgiveness. He would grant it. They'd hug and get back to their work in the hat shop. Andolosia would make hats for the rest of his life.

No! That cannot be my fate. There must be another way.

Andolosia steeled himself, emerged from the cutting room, and strode toward his father. He stopped and hovered in his peripheral vision. Stasi was reassuring Madonna Vincenzo that the feathers' gamy odor would fade after a few hours in the sun. Andolosia roved to the other side of his father, who tracked him out of the corner of his eye. The split second of distraction was sufficient for Madonna Vincenzo to extricate herself from Stasi's pressure sale. She seized a Moorish turban with a long trailing scarf and wandered off, taking with her their best chance of unloading the topiary specimen masquerading as a hat.

Andolosia stepped into the void vacated by Madonna Vincenzo. His fingers nervously crinkled the letter.

"Ah," Stasi said with a knowing nod. "You've received the letter from Dottore Galilei."

Andolosia was flummoxed. "What? How did you know?"

"I read the letter you sent him – quite by accident, I assure you. Do you realize you left it with the Thurn and Taxis Post Office without fronting money for postage?"

"I did?"

"You did. Since the letter was from an 'A. Petasos,' the mail courier assumed I, Anastasius Petasos, had written it, and demanded payment. Our handwriting is very similar, so only after breaking the seal did I realize it was your letter. I re-sealed it and paid the postage."

Andolosia was incredulous. "You read the letter and yet paid the postage anyway? Why?"

"Because letters require postage."

"No, that's not what I—"

"I wrote to Maestro Gamba. You remember him, the fabric merchant in Padua. His niece is having an affair with the good Dottore Galileo. I asked him to pay him a visit."

Andolosia became alarmed. "For what purpose? To threaten Galileo with blackmail?"

"Nothing so sinister. Maestro Gamba vouched for your good character. He also may have relayed my offer for three free bespoke hats."

Andolosia's eyes widened. "You offered Dottore Galileo a bribe?"

"A simple quid pro quo."

"Which, in this context, is a bribe."

"Call it what you will, Andolosia. It worked. Professor Galilei is amenable to taking you on."

"Which you'd know only if you've already read this letter in my hand."

"Yes, well, the dottore's letter was addressed to 'A. Petasos.' Had I known our common initial would cause so much confusion with the post, I would've insisted on a different birth name for you. Your mother wanted Andolosia. I fancied Leonardo. In a way, your mother is responsible for my actions in this matter."

Andolosia relaxed. "No, Father. I am responsible. I should have told you what I was doing. Frankly, it didn't seem necessary because I did not think the professor would respond. Now that I have considered the logistics of travel to Padua, I realize how foolish I was. Selfish, too. We can't afford my absence from the shop."

"You will be with the professor only two days a month."

"Plus ten days of travel, there and back. And that's assuming I don't run into highway robbers or foul weather."

Stasi smiled. "Have you forgotten?"

"About what?"

"About Hermes' hat. You can wish yourself to Padua

and back."

"You've warned me about using the hat."

"I know, but you wouldn't be the first, nor likely the last."

"What are you saying?"

"Well, for instance, my father used the wishing hat, or so he told me. He said he had no choice, that lives were at stake. He never shared the details about the who, the why, and the where. He said it was safer that way."

"Have you used the wishing hat?"

Stasi grimaced and stroked his chin. "Well . . ."

Andolosia crossed his arms. "The load of furs that were here in the morning – you said they were delivered from the port at night. We've never had nighttime deliveries. You wished those furs here, didn't you?"

"It was so much quicker than wrangling a donkey and a cart."

"Have you lost your mind?"

"I did not purloin the furs," Stasi fired back. "We paid Maestro Rabino handsomely for them."

"Yes, but we owed the Fasci Sansone substantial duties for importing them. Also, they weren't due to be released from quarantine for two weeks. Please tell me you at least paid the inspectors."

"The duties were not an issue."

Andolosia's voice went up an octave. "Suddenly, the Fasci Sansone don't care about duties?"

"Let's just say the inspector responsible for our furs was not in a position to care."

"What does that mean?"

"It means he is now roaming the Forbidden City."

"You wished him to China?" he said shrilly.

Andolosia became faint. He steadied himself against the table of ecclesiastical hats.

Stasi shushed him. "Keep your voice down. The boy is

fine. He has an uncle there."

Andolosia squeezed his forehead. "Oh, Father."

"You worry too much. The wishing hat took care of that problem, and now we can use it to take care of your little problem."

"But you've warned me not to use the wishing hat. One wish leads to another wish and another, and soon all you want to do is wish yourself to places."

"That is true. Misuse of the hat can consume a man, but not if used judiciously, in moderation, for a noble purpose. Scientific discovery is just such a purpose."

Andolosia shook his head disapprovingly. "I don't know. Fate doesn't take kindly to Petasos men who leave the hat business."

"You wouldn't be leaving it, not entirely. Millinery would become your part-time endeavor."

"Fate might see part-time millinery as a prelude to total abandonment. She could pluck me off that slippery slope the first time I wish myself to Padua and punish both of us. No, Father. It's too risky."

Stasi gripped his son's shoulders. "There's risk if you squander your brilliant mind making hats. Think how many mothers your mechanical heart might save. Think how much pain your discoveries could spare future sons and husbands. If Fate is opposed to that, to hell with Her."

Andolosia looked upward anxiously. "Do not speak that way. You will invite Her wrath."

"If Fate's wrath is the price for your freedom to make this world a slightly less horrible place, I welcome it." Stasi's voice trembled. "And so would your mother, if she were still alive."

Andolosia wrestled with Stasi's argument. The more he gave into its truth, the more a world of possibility opened to him.

He embraced Stasi. "I love you, Father."

Stasi swallowed the lump in his throat and patted his son's back. He descried Madonna Vincenzo, who was observing the father-son drama from afar. She was beaming with maternal warmth. She also looked ridiculous. She'd tucked her hair inside the tight-fitting turban. Combined with her greenish-brown complexion, the turban made her head resemble a titanic olive.

"We are attracting attention, Andolosia. Come with me."

Stasi brought Andolosia into the cutting room and insured that the curtain was shut. He removed the Hermes portrait. He reached into the nook, pulled out the scaly leather hat, and handed it to Andolosia, who accepted it with great reverence. Andolosia ran his fingers along the wide brim. Stasi nodded, giving him tacit permission to don the hat. Tight at first, the leather expanded to a comfortable fit.

"It is very warm," Andolosia said. "How exactly do I travel with it?"

"Think of a place and ask the hat to take you there. Always in that order."

"Must I form a mental picture of the place I want to go?"

"As long as it is an actual place, the hat will take you there. If it's a city or town, it will drop you in the center. Which is why you must be careful about cities with rivers or sewers running through the middle. You could end up knee-deep in shit. Always best to have a landmark in mind, preferably a secluded one."

"All right. I'm ready," Andolosia said excitedly while closing his eyes. "Sistine Chapel, here I come."

"Oh," Stasi recalled. "I forgot to mention. You have to exhale—"

Andolosia already had formed the wish. He vanished amidst a shriek and a flash of indigo light.

"Oh dear," Stasi lamented to the empty space where his son had been. "I do hope you picked a secluded spot."

Teleportation via wishing hat was hard on the mortal body. It whipsawed the traveler from being to nothingness, then back to being again, leaving his somatic cells quivering with existential shock, especially the epithelial cells along the digestive tract. Exhaling prior to the wish prevented reflexive gastric expulsions – i.e., hurling one's guts – upon arrival. Stasi had little doubt Andolosia was learning this lesson right then.

The curtain parted, and Madonna Vincenzo poked her head in, startling Stasi.

"Maestro, I would like this turban in red."

Stasi gave a slight bow. "As you wish, Madonna."

"But I absolutely must have it by the morning," she insisted. "I am leaving for the festival in Florence, and only red will do."

"I'm afraid there isn't time."

She narrowed her beady eyes to slits. "I will pay double. Make that triple, and that is the end of the matter."

She retracted her head and closed the curtain before Stasi could object. Not that he would've said no to one of his best customers. He gave a resigned sigh, regarded his arthritic hands, and prayed Andolosia would wish himself back soon.

CHAPTER

EIGHT

Mount Othrys, 1600 B.C.E.

Gaia recruited priestesses from floundering temples to deliver her prophecies and tasked Moira with translating them into fate tapestries. Moira figured her job was straightforward until a gryphon-courier deposited the first tapestry order beside the Loom of Destiny. The parchment scroll from the temple in Smyrna pertained to Kados, a goatherd who'd asked the oracle which of two available women he should marry, Dorcas or Enyo. Acting as Gaia's mouthpiece, the priestess prophesied, "When a mule enters the home, the walls will founder."

Moira scratched her head. *What in Hades does that mean?*

Kados scratched himself elsewhere, but he, too, wondered what in Hades it meant. At first, he felt foolish. He should have known better when the priestess had offered the prophecy at such a steep discount. He'd gotten what he'd paid for. But later, as he tended his goats and reflected on the oracle, a meaning began to coalesce. Dorcas' parents were native Smyrneans, whereas Enyo's father hailed from

Fate Accompli

Lydia, Smyrna's sworn enemy. As a Smyrnean-Lydian hybrid, Enyo was, in a metaphorical sense, a mule. (Kados was the rare goatherd who indulged in metaphors.) Enyo also possessed mule-like traits – intelligence, sure-footedness, and extraordinarily long ears – unlike Dorcas, who was dim-witted and clumsy and had tiny, ferret-like ears. The point was, if Kados were to marry Enyo, their offspring would have Lydian blood. Should Lydia invade Smyrna one day, his mixed-blood children might fight for Lydia and cause Smyrna's "walls" to "founder." As a Smyrnean patriot, Kados was obligated to marry the inferior Dorcas. He congratulated himself for deciphering the oracle's cryptic words, resigned himself to his fate, and requested Dorcas' hand in marriage.

There was only one thing missing from Kados' interpretation – any resemblance to reality.

Moira's tapestry ordained that Dorcas would spurn Kados' proposal, leaving Enyo as his only option. Their marital union, moreover, would be totally unrelated to Enyo's kinship with mules, metaphorical or otherwise. Rather, Kados would leave his front door ajar before departing with Enyo on their honeymoon. As the newlyweds frolicked in the Aegean Sea, a mule would wander into Kados' house, chew up the Persian carpet, and saunter through the brittle rear wall, leaving the home in shambles.

And so, Kados' actual fate was opposite to the one he'd expected. Yet he was not the least disappointed. To the contrary, he was thrilled. For one, he preferred Enyo to Dorcas. *Those ears!* For another, the rampaging mule had validated belief in the gods, multiplying his faith a hundredfold and inspiring him to recount his story to his customers, who hurriedly queued at the temple for their own cut-rate prophecies.

In weeks, lines of mortals were winding like thread around temples in Smyrna, Ephesus, and Samos. Othrys'

84

red cloud of faith tripled in size and poured ceaselessly into the funnel. Destiny Thread was accumulating on the pool faster than Moira could fish it out and separate the different thicknesses. Meanwhile, the scrolls were piling up around the Loom of Destiny. The backlog of tapestry orders was getting out of hand. She needed help.

"The faith pool runneth over!" Cronus said cheerily while striding into the throne room. He sniffed the air. "Ah, do you smell that, Moira? Burnt offerings. The mortals sacrificed a hundred goats today. You should be proud of yourself. Word of Kados' 'miracle mule' is spreading like wildfire in Hades."

Moira nodded uncertainly. She was weary, partly from fatigue and partly from an encroaching sense of shame.

"Moira?" Cronus asked with concern. "Whatever is the matter?" He noticed the scrolls – hundreds of them – stacked behind the loom. An eyebrow shot up in alarm. "I trust the gryphons are delivering prophecy transcriptions in a timely manner."

"Yes, my lord. The backlog is my fault. Mother Gaia's prophecies are so vague and ambiguous, half the time I have to guess their meaning. I spend more time scratching my head than weaving."

"You are thinking too much. Do not let perfection be the enemy of the good. For that matter don't let the good be the enemy of the so-so. The tapestries need not be ornate sky-curtains. Just pick one element of the prophecy – a piddly detail – weave it into the tapestry, and move on to the next scroll."

"I know that's what I should do, my lord. It's just . . . it's just I feel badly for the mortals. The prophecies do not seem all that helpful."

Cronus tsk-tsked. "Moira. Moira. Moira. Helpfulness is beside the point. Think of us as farmers. Faith farmers. Think of ambiguity as the fertilizer for our crop. Confusion and bewilderment make the mortals apprehensive, which inspires them to offer us prayers, libations, and sacrifices, which then blossom into faith in my pool. Understand?"

"I do. We are like cows shitting on a farmer's crops. We dump our dung on the mortals' ignorance and then feed off the consequences."

Cronus flashed a look of mild disgust. "I wouldn't put it so crassly, but, yes, that is about the size of it."

"Doesn't that strike you as wrong?"

"*Wrong?*" Cronus scoffed. "You sound like those human philosophers who claim that right and wrong are more real than we gods. Right and wrong exist, if at all, at our pleasure. As king of the Spheres, I decree that our scheme is right. Satisfied?"

Moira harrumphed.

Cronus tipped up his nose and said haughtily, "Unless you'd rather tell the mortal fools nothing whatever about their destinies. Leave them blind and untethered. Would that be preferable?"

Moira opened her mouth, but the words "Maybe it would be" lacked the courage to announce themselves. Cronus and Gaia's deceptive scheme was the only reason she had her cushy weaving job. She wasn't about to abandon the Loom of Destiny out of fidelity to some ill-defined concept of rectitude.

"I suppose not," she conceded.

"And don't forget we are fostering the mortals' belief in a power greater than themselves. In return, we get their faith. All sides benefit, you see? This is just good business. Have I put your mind at ease?"

She nodded.

"Good. Now maybe you can make progress on the backlog."

He tugged his tunic in the crotch region and swung around to leave.

"Wait, my lord. Please."

He turned back around.

"I cannot do this job alone. There is simply too much work. I need assistance."

"I could place an advertisement for a helpmate in the Clarion Calls. But based on our poor response to your job announcement, I would not be optimistic. How about taking on an apprentice?"

"I haven't time to train a neophyte, my lord. And apprentices can be unreliable. We would have to trust her with your secret."

"What secret?"

Moira leaned in. "About the thicker Destiny Threads?"

Cronus stared at her blankly.

Moira continued in an urgent whisper. "Tapestries that control the fates of gods? The secret that poses an existential threat to your reign?"

"Oh! That secret. Ahem. Hee hee. Right. An apprentice is risky. Do you have another idea?"

"Reproduction. Ideally, I would spawn a child with my skills. My mother created me from a piece of herself, but I have no idea how, and we're not exactly on speaking terms these days."

"Is that all?" Cronus was smiling as if eager to reveal a big surprise. "I can create your identical twin by snapping my fingers."

"Really? So easily?"

He snapped his fingers, and Moira's double materialized next to him. She was identical, except her hair wasn't disheveled, nor did she have bags under her eyes.

Moira approached the double and smiled with awe. "Remarkable."

Cronus was pleased with himself.

"Hello," Moira said to the double.

The double didn't respond, maintaining a flat, vapid

smile and vacant eyes.

"Hello," Moira repeated. "Can you hear me?"

The double responded, "Ahem. Hee hee. Ahem."

"Oh dear," Cronus said. "It appears she takes after me. Well, I'm sure her language skills will develop in time. What matters is her weaving."

"Can she weave?"

"Of course." Cronus escorted the double to the loom, sat her down, and extended her arms. He rested her left hand on the batten and placed the shuttle in her right hand. "There we go. Go ahead now. Weave."

"Ahem. Hee hee," the twin responded without affect. She pounded her fist on the batten and threw the shuttle on the floor.

Cronus picked up the shuttle and put it back in the double's hand. "You just need to get the hang of it. Here. Give it another go."

Again, the twin pounded the batten and threw the shuttle on the floor. She howled like a wild animal and shouted, "Ahem! Ahem! Ahem! Heeeeeeeeeee!"

Cronus backed away in horror from the loom.

Moira shook her head pitifully. "It is hopeless, my lord. There is nothing of my essence in her. She does not share a drop of my blood."

"Perhaps under your tutelage, she could—"

"No," Moira interjected.

"No. No, you're right," Cronus agreed. After a pause, he shot Moira a sideways glance. "You say your double must share your blood?"

"It is the only way."

Cronus tugged at his toga, which was constricting his throat. "There is, as you know, the option of . . . the option of insemination."

Moira's eyes widened. She was dumbstruck.

Did he just say what I think he said? Don't answer him.

Perhaps he misspoke.

Cronus rubbed the back of his neck and pressed on with his proposal. "That is to say, if you so desire, I can offer you my seed, as it were. We could create a goddess who would share your blood . . . and mine."

The double head-butted the loom and brayed like a donkey.

"Oh, shut up!" Cronus scolded. He snapped his fingers, and the double vanished.

Moira was becoming faint.

Don't pass out! she told herself. *He'll think you're seducing him. Just let him down easily.*

"Your proposal is most generous, my lord. You honor me, and I . . ."

Cronus' narrow-set eyes widened. A grin was hatching under his rodent-like nose.

Get to the point, Moira! He's getting the wrong idea.

"But," Moira blurted. "But," she repeated with emphasis, practically shouting it, "I have another option I must exhaust before burdening you with . . . with insemi – with your proposal."

"I assure you it is no burden," he said with alacrity. "I am only too—"

"No," she said curtly.

Cronus' rigid spine turned semi-flaccid. "Yes. Yes," he stammered. "Let's keep things professional."

Cronus pretended to hear a distant sound and cupped his ear. "What's that? The gryphons are squawking about another strike? Forgive me, Moira, but I'm needed elsewhere. Mother Gaia is wise in matters of creation. You might try her." He snapped his fingers and vanished.

That was awkward.

Moira breathed easier with Cronus gone. She slipped on sandals and set off for the Earth Mother's mountain retreat. It was a steep hike with many switchbacks, precarious scree, narrow crevasses, and knee-deep streams. She fell three times, twisted both ankles, scraped her ribs on a jagged boulder, and lost a sandal stepping into a huge mud puddle. She wasn't built for this kind of exertion. Her job was sedentary, resulting in spindly legs and poor endurance. She should've hired a gryphon.

Breathless and battered, she hobbled to the trail's terminus at the mouth of a cave. Inside, she spied Gaia, who was inserting various picks and hammers through loops in a waist belt. Gaia's ample bosom strained against her tight leather overalls. The muscles of her burly arms rivaled any of the Titans', and her legs were thicker than the cypress beams holding up Cronus' palace. Her hands were stubby-fingered vices. Moira pitied the boulder that found itself in their grasp. Yet Gaia was no lumbering giant. Her movements were graceful and efficient.

Gaia glanced up at her visitor. Moira gasped. Gaia's face, though plain, exuded an improbable blend of kindness and ferocity. Her eyes sparkled like emeralds, though they were a deeper green, the color of oak leaves in summer. Gaia green. Indigo specks encircled her pupils like tiny moons. Hers was the most beautiful face Moira had ever seen.

Gaia didn't mince words about Moira's ability to reproduce asexually like Nyx had. As Gaia worked a claw hammer into the loop beside her hip, she said coolly, "Even though there's no sex involved, you still need the right kind of womb. Your womb is sorely wanting."

An involuntary, discomfited gasp hiccupped from Moira's throat. "I beg your pardon."

"Your womb isn't up to the task."

Moira felt an improbable urge to defend her womb's honor. "But ... but you know nothing of my womb." Suddenly unsure how much Gaia could see with her oracular vision, Moira asked, "Do you?"

"Only the original Primordial goddesses can conceive

without insemination. You'll have to find yourself a mate. Choose wisely, though. Steer clear of the meeker gods like Crius and Cronus."

She belittles her own sons.

"But Cronus is king, and didn't he sire Hades and Poseidon?" Moira asked.

"So Rhea says."

Moira was unsure what to make of Gaia's cryptic answer. She figured the less she knew about matters of Titanic paternity, the better.

"Is there an option other than insemination? I'm so busy on the loom, and I don't want to take on the responsibilities of child-rearing."

Gaia waved her hand dismissively. "Divine children grow quickly. Takes only a day or two."

"Yes, but the hard part – the mothering – that's eternal. Or at least it should be."

"How quaint you are." Gaia nodded knowingly, as if Moira had just confided with her. "I understand. You have a wretched mother, and you're afraid you'll end up like her."

"I didn't say that."

Gaia wagged her finger devilishly. "Ah. But you're thinking it. I'm not judging. In my view, a child is duty-bound to resent his parent. No intelligent species can flourish without a healthy dose of irreverence. Meek children have their roles to play, but the rebellious ones make the strongest leaders."

"Is this why Cronus leads the heavens?"

Gaia chortled. "Cronus is no rebel. None of my children are. He's the most pliant. I can project my strength through him until a more formidable god comes along."

"Why not a formidable god-*ess*?"

Gaia smirked. "Are you seeking a promotion?"

Moira flushed with embarrassment. "Heavens, no. I'm quite content as a weaver. Frankly, I detest politics. I was thinking of you, Mother Gaia. Why work through others? Take the mantle yourself."

Gaia laughed heartily. "Me? No. No. If I took the throne, I'd have no time to make mountains and rivers. Like you, I live for the work. The gods are different that way. Nothing fires their loins more than imposing order, bossing people about, crushing mortals and insects under their sandals, that kind of thing. They can't help it. The gods are bullies by nature."

"Why?"

"Because men – human men – created the eternal note, and the eternal note created the gods and goddesses."

Moira's face screwed up with confusion. "That's backward, isn't it? The eternal note created the gods and then the gods created men."

"That, my child, is a myth we Primordials concocted to bolster our fragile egos. I know first-hand that humanity preceded divinity by eons. Mortals imagined us into existence, which is why we need their faith to sustain us."

Moira paused, letting the revelation's enormity sink in. She, of all people, understood the power of myth, but still . . .

"Even if that's true," Moira countered, "why would the eternal note, the most beautiful sound since Creation, make men into bullies?"

"When the human race was young, the men sat around the communal fire and conceived an all-powerful, unseen music spirit who plucked his lute and produced the eternal note. It's a lovely story but with one major flaw: the women played no part in these imaginings. They weren't welcome at the fire. They were tending the children and mending the men's furs, preoccupied with 'woman's work.' So, the men dreamed up an eternal note that mostly resounds in their image. Hence, the note's fundamental tone is masculine. You look troubled, Moira."

"Confused. The eternal note doesn't sound masculine or feminine. A note is incorporeal. How can it have a gender?"

"Not just a single gender, Moira. All genders wrapped into one."

"This is not helping."

"The next time you hear a gryphon's call or walk by Oceanus' humming waters, let the eternal note flow through you. It's a beautiful sound, exquisite, as you know. But if you really concentrate, if you let the sound overwhelm you, you'll begin to feel a jagged coldness creeping into your center. That's the fundamental tone, the masculine element. Most people stop there. Don't. There's more. Keep listening until the jaggedness smooths out and warmth floods your insides. Those are the overtones. Those are distinctly female."

"Why would men put female overtones in the eternal note?"

"They had no choice. The masculine cannot exist without the feminine, just as up needs down and a wave needs a crest and a valley." Gaia regarded Moira's glum expression and added, "You look like someone just slaughtered your pet weed-sprite."

"The fundamental tone is stronger than the overtones," Moira said despondently. "We are destined to be the weaker sex."

"Maybe. Maybe not. I believe if the overtones combined, they would equal the fundamental tone. I have dreamed of three sirens standing and singing on three rocks in a river. Their voices meld into a harmonic triad and, suddenly, there is just one siren on a single rock. All the while, there's a drumbeat. *Thub dup Thub dup. Thub dup Thub dup.*" Gaia's lips broke into a mirthful smirk. "I'm certain I've heard this *thub dup-thub dup* before, but I can't quite place it."

"My loom," Moira said with excitement. "That's the sound my loom makes!"

Gaia nodded with mock astonishment. "So it is."

Moira furrowed her brow. "What does the drumbeat mean?"

Gaia shook her head. "I swear, Moira, you can be positively daft when it comes to interpreting signs. The drumming means your Loom of Destiny will give my dream a flesh and blood heartbeat. You will bring it to life."

Moira shook her head vigorously and was about to profess her inadequacy when Gaia silenced her with a stern glance. "Your lack of self-confidence offends me," she scolded. "By doubting yourself, you doubt me. I brought you to Othrys for this reason. This is your fate, Moira. Live with it."

Moira bowed her head. "Forgive me, Mother Gaia, I didn't realize . . . I won't let you down. I—"

"Yes, yes," Gaia said dismissively. "Save the pledges. Just get it done." Gaia clapped her hands, breaking the tension. "Now," she said cheerily, "About your little problem."

"My problem?"

"You're overworked, remember?"

"Right. How silly of me. The whole 'fate of womankind' business threw me for a loop."

"There's a foreign god – not a Primordial or Titan – the god of the Hebrews. He sculpted a clay figure of a man and breathed life into it, or so the rumor goes. It could be another myth. I'm not sure."

Moira waited for more information. None was forthcoming.

"Wait. That's it?" Moira asked. "Did this god use special clay? Did he have enchanted breath? Did he use a spell or potions?"

"All excellent questions – questions for which I have no

answers."

Gaia hoisted her sagging tool belt and strode off.

"Wait, Mother Gaia. Where are you going?

"Mountains aren't going to move without me."

Gaia put two fingers in her mouth and produced a shrieking whistle. Python, her dragon, alighted at the mouth of the cave and exhaled a fiery breath.

As Gaia exited the cave, she said over her shoulder, "I thoroughly enjoyed our little chat, Moira. Let's do it again soon."

Moira let out a frustrated sigh and moseyed down the mountain, back to the palace. The dearth of instructions about creating a double from clay frustrated her. Nevertheless, the idea warranted further investigation, given her only other option was insemination by Cronus, who, although well-intentioned, was a Titanic twit.

Gathering the clay would be simple enough. During her gryphon ride from Tartarus, Moira had spotted red-brown clay lining the banks of the River Oceanus. The breath of life part would be trickier. Moira's breath was pleasant enough, but life-creating? Not so much. But her fingers – yes, her fingers – were quite another matter. They wove fate tapestries that defined every critical detail of a person's life, death, and everything in between. In a way, she breathed life through her fingers. But did the power to define a life encompass the power to create a life in the first instance? She was about to find out.

She wove a very different kind of fate tapestry – forward-looking instead of reflective. The textile didn't delineate her future but memorialized where she had been. It was an autobiography in fabric, a memoir about coming into the world fatherless, daughter to a morose goddess, and escaping a wretched existence by losing herself in her night-sky curtains. It was an honest account. It didn't ignore the persistent solitude that inspired fantasies of leaping into

Chaos. It acknowledged the serendipity of Titans recognizing her talents.

After battening the final row, Moira stepped back from the loom and beheld the tapestry, awestruck. Her weaving had evolved beyond glorified storytelling. With a palate of warps, wefts, and weaves, she'd transformed black yarn into a multi-dimensional collage of textures and patterns corresponding to the majesty and inscrutability of a life – her life. She'd pinched off a piece of her soul.

Either that or I just wasted a lot of time making an attractive doily.

Moira took the small tapestry to Oceanus, bringing along a tree-elf to assist her. The tree-elf had orange hair and was far more genial than the blue-haired grouch who'd "welcomed" her to Othrys. When the hour was right, and the sun shone at the proper angle, she cast her shadow on the clay, which the tree-elf meticulously traced with a stylus. The tree-elf brought Moira buckets of clay, and she built up the shape into the form of a body. As the clay dried, she scraped and shaped the finer features, relying on the tree-elf's scrutiny to confirm that she'd molded an identical facsimile of herself, right down to her stark widow's peak, bell-shaped nose, soft forehead creases, and trapezoidal facial shape. As Moira regarded the sculpture, she wondered if she was beautiful. She considered asking the tree-elf but thought better of it. His opinion would be hopelessly biased by his tree-elf aesthetics, which prized the short, squat, and hairy.

Then came the moment of reckoning. Moira stuffed the tapestry in the sculpture's mouth. By degrees, the clay absorbed the tapestry and transformed into warm flesh. The chest began rising and falling. The mouth gasped. The eyes opened. The helpmate was alive.

"Come," an exhilarated Moira told the helpmate. "I will take you home and introduce you to the loom."

Superficially, the helpmate was Moira's identical twin. She looked and moved like the original Moira. Although she did not speak – or, perhaps, chose not to speak – she understood Moira and seemed to assiduously follow her weaving instructions. Upon closer examination of the helpmate's work, however, Moira noticed beguiling textures and patterns, which took on different aspects depending on the observation point. From one perspective, the weave portended a life of struggle and deprivation, while from another, it signified a rich and carefree life. Other viewing angles altered longevity, occupation, number of children and wives, temperament, and thousands of other elements. As the subject of the tapestry lived her life – as she made choices or choices were thrust upon her – the ability to see different possibilities from alternate perspectives dwindled, until death, when the tapestry assumed a final, fixed design. The helpmate's tapestry was a joint creation of Fate and the fated, both predetermined and indeterminate.

The helpmate's talent made Moira weep. Moira was ashamed of her envy. She'd long prided herself on her weaving skills. Weaving had been her greatness and no one else's. But the thread-stuffed lump of clay had surpassed her.

The helpmate seemed to sense her creator's bruised pride. She cupped Moira's cheeks and telepathically conveyed the central truth of their symbiotic existence: *When you made my life tapestry, you gave me a piece of your soul. I am part of you, and you're a part of me. We are sisters. Forever.*

"Sisters?" the bemused Moira asked, as if sisterhood was a foreign concept. "Sisters," she repeated, this time definitively.

Moira cheered up. She wiped away her tears. "You are very wise, Sister. Wise creatures must have names."

The helpmate nodded.

"Since you have shown me the beauty of weaving chance into the tapestries, I will call you Tyche. How does that suit you?"

The helpmate smiled.

Thereafter, the sisters divided their labors. Moira planned the tapestries' essential life milestones – first words, first love, first loss, successes, illnesses, a tragedy or two, failures, redemptions, cause of death. After Tyche worked through the night, Moira arrived at sunrise to pick up where her sister had left off. Moira imposed only one rule: Tyche's work product had to preserve at least one path to the next milestone. That way, each tapestry remained true to Moira's overarching design without sacrificing the element of randomness accorded by Tyche's kaleidoscopic aesthetic.

They worked in this dialectical fashion down through the ages, synthesizing their antithetical techniques into a novel style with its own living, breathing identity. It was as if weaving in tandem spawned an unseen third sister, a ghostly sibling who was the loom's true master, and her name was Fate.

CHAPTER

NINE

Livorno, Grand Duchy of Tuscany, 1603

While the coach barreled down the sinuous road, Sansone de Medici dipped a powder puff into a tin of ground alabaster and patted the swarthy patches on his pock-marked face. There was a sudden, thunderous thump on the coach's right side. The coach rocked, banked violently, and tipped onto the right wheel. It teetered in precarious equipoise until gravity's hand slammed the left wheel down on the road. A plume of white dust mushroomed in Sansone's face.

Sansone pushed open the door and stumbled onto the road. He wiped his eyes and sneezed four times in quick succession before shouting at his coachman, "Vittorio, you ninnyhammer!" He blew his nose in a handkerchief. "I've warned you about speeding on these provincial roads. How much did you drink this morning?"

Vittorio fingered the bulge in his coat pocket. It was light. Thus, the answer to his master's question was "Quite a lot," which he did not volunteer.

Sansone peered under the carriage. "You probably

broke an axle." He walked around to the other side. "Let it be known, any damage will be coming out of your—" He stopped cold at the severed leg lodged in the right wheel. A second leg, also severed at the knee, hung limply in a nearby laurel tree. A bloody trail behind the carriage lead to an older man lying in the road. The man was still, eyes closed and breathing steadily.

An absurd thought struck Sansone – *Why the Devil is he napping in the road* – which fled his mind upon observing the blood-soaked ends of the man's torn breeches, where legs and feet should have emerged.

"God's Blood," said the shaken Sansone. He batted back his nausea. "Vittorio! You struck this poor man. Fetch him some bandages."

"We've no bandages, Messer," Vittorio answered dismissively, as if reminding his master that his job description didn't include first aid to fool peasants on foot.

"Then improvise some!" Sansone pointed at a dirt-stained, red turban spilling out of a crushed hat box. "Get off your arse and shred that into bandages forthwith."

Vittorio grumbled and descended his perch – drunkenly – and picked up the turban. Sansone sat on the road and rested the injured man's head on his lap. He pulled a white kid leather glove off his right hand, which was considerably darker than his ghostly, powdered face, and began stroking the man's forehead.

"Forgive me, my good gentleman," Sansone said.

The man roused. "I am no gentleman, Messer," he said through gritted teeth. "Just a poor hat merchant who shouldn't have been in the road." He groaned.

"What is your name, Maestro?"

"Stasi. Stasi Petasos."

"We shall take care of you, Maestro Stasi."

Vittorio pulled a cutlass from his waist and poked a hole in the turban's center. He worked his fingers into the rent and ripped the fabric in two. Though slipping into shock, Stasi lamented the destruction of his son's fine work. He'd labored all night to finish Madonna Vincenzo's turban, sick with the aftereffects of hat travel – nausea, headache, and blue-tinged vision. Stasi had decided to deliver the hat himself, swollen ankles and feet be damned, rather than wake his exhausted son.

"Hurry, Vittorio," Sansone commanded.

Vittorio pressed the swatches into each bleeding stump. Stasi winced and arched his back in agony.

"Easy, Vittorio!" Sansone admonished.

Sansone unfastened the silk ribbon securing his bobbed blond hair and bound it snugly to Stasi's right stump. He removed his ruff collar and used it to secure the other bandage.

"Good. We've stanched the bleeding," Sansone said to Vittorio. "We will take him to the physician in Livorno. Help me load him inside."

Sansone stepped into the coach. He gripped Stasi under the arms while Vittorio lifted what was left of Stasi's lower half. As they laid him on the bench, the empty flask fell out of Vittorio's coat pocket and hit the floor with a hollow clink. Vittorio backed away from Sansone's withering stare. Sansone sat on the bench, gingerly raised Stasi's head, and rested it on his lap.

All at once, a severed leg sailed into the coach and thudded at Sansone's feet.

Sansone started. "What on God's green Earth are you doing, Vittorio?"

Vittorio poked his head in. "Fetching the gentleman's leg from the wheel."

"The leg is of no use to him now. Leave it."

"Aye, Messer." Vittoria paused. "What about the leg in the tree?"

Sansone sighed, exasperated. "Surely, if one leg is of no

use, two legs are doubly useless."

Vittorio yanked the leg from the carriage and tossed it to the side of the road. He shut the coach door and headed to his perch.

Sansone noticed Stasi's eyes had closed. He shook his shoulders. "Do not sleep, Maestro," he pleaded.

Stasi opened his eyes halfway. "I am so tired."

"You have lost much blood. If you fall asleep, you may not wake up. Tell me about your hats."

"We make the best in Livorno – my son and I."

"You are a maestro of millinery, then."

"I was," Stasi said weakly. "I fear I have made my last hat."

"Pshaw! You will survive this. I *insist* you survive." Sansone's eyes widened, and he said excitedly, "Indeed, I have a commission for you."

"No need to pity me, Messer."

"This is not pity. I have had the most wonderful inspiration. You will make a hat for my opera."

"What is an opera?"

"A play that is sung. Its title is *Daphne.* Do you know the water nymph's story?"

"Aye. Apollo chased her. She turned into a laurel tree."

"That is the old myth. In my version – the perfected version – Daphne's father transforms into the laurel tree, Apollo catches Daphne, and they unite in love. I have been puzzling over how to stage the transformation, and now Fate literally has thrown the answer in my path. You, Stasi!"

"Me?"

"Oh, I see it so clearly in my mind's eye. Branches and leaves will sprout from the top of the hat. A trunk – perhaps of brown silk – will descend from the brim. I venture the hat will have levers and pulleys and articulating arms. Can you build it?"

"My son, Andolosia, can, but he leaves for Padua today,

and the expense—"

"Clearly, your son will have to delay his trip. And, as far as the expense, I shall pay you two-hundred florins plus the cost of the materials." Sansone counted out twenty florins' worth of gold coins and slipped them in Stasi's purse. "A down payment for the materials." He glanced out the coach window. "Fret not, Maestro Petasos. The physician will clean and cauterize your wounds. Then you will instruct your son to fashion my hat. I can wait a month, but no longer. Can I trust you to honor our arrangement?"

The carriage halted. Stasi swooned. His eyes drifted upward.

"We have arrived at the physician, Maestro," Sansone said urgently. "I must have your answer. Can I trust you to honor our arrangement?" Getting no response, Sansone shook Stasi's shoulders. "What is your answer, Maestro?"

"Aye . . . Aye, Messer."

"And I must have the hat no later than the twenty-first of November."

Stasi gave a woozy half-nod and passed out.

Sansone's eyes glazed over, and he said in a peculiar voice, "At long last, the nymph shall be mine."

* * *

Andolosia postponed his trip to Padua to care for his father. It was touch and go the first week, but a regimen of fastidious wound cleaning and good hydration with a nutritious broth enabled Stasi to stave off infection. He began eating solid food and returned to his loquacious self, even expressing a desire to return to work.

Andolosia pondered how his father would get around once he was out of bed for good. Crutches would have been the obvious choice, had he lost only a single leg. Combining crutches with a wooden leg or two was an option, though cumbersome. A wheeled chair would've been less strenuous but difficult to operate inside a cramped shop and house, let alone up and down stairs and streets. While sketching out the possibilities, Andolosia heard a chiming clock. Inspired, he feverishly designed mechanical legs powered by a coiled spring. In principle, the design was sound. The only way to know for sure was to build it.

Andolosia worked with the clockmaker and goldsmith to machine the custom parts. He assembled the pieces in the cutting room, carried the contraption out front, and cranked the spring to high tension, locking it with a lever. When he released the lever, the legs lurched into an immediate sprint toward the port. Alarmed pedestrians scattered into shops and alleyways. The legs slowed to a brisk walk and then a saunter before petering out. Clearly, the legs needed a serious adjustment, if Andolosia didn't want to give his father severe whiplash and terrorize the citizenry. He incorporated a cone-shaped pulley to moderate the spring's energy release. He also added a brake to slow the pulley's movement and an emergency release that would halt the legs in case the pulley failed.

Stasi recovered enough strength to test the modified contraption. Andolosia ensured the human testing phase would not become a public spectacle. He cleared the shop's floorspace of obstructions. He lifted Stasi from the bed, just as Stasi used to lift him from his bed as a boy. The role reversal disturbed Andolosia. It was unnatural and backward to be handling his father like a child, or worse, like a lifeless bolt of cloth.

Andolosia guided Stasi's legs through the openings in the cushioned seat and fastened him with suspenders and torso straps. As Stasi did before embarking on significant journeys, he exhaled as much air from his lungs as he could. This got a rise out of Andolosia, who smiled for the first time since the accident. Andolosia cranked the spring to one-quarter tension, released the lever, and darted in front of Stasi to shield him from walls and furniture while coaching him how to throttle the spring's tension.

Stasi quickly got the hang of the throttle. Balance was the bigger challenge. His abdominal muscles were so weak, he struggled not to double over. To stabilize him, Andolosia fashioned a torso harness and rigged the harness to a pulley on a bar running the length of the shop. After ten days, Stasi's core muscles had strengthened enough that he no longer needed the harness.

An unexpected feeling stirred in Andolosia after Stasi took his first competent steps with new legs. Pride. Andolosia understood why people wanted children. Parental pride was the opiate that enticed even the most miserable of the human race to propagate. That evening, Andolosia altered a pair of Stasi's breeches and fitted them around the mechanical legs. The sight of his father on two feet again, albeit ersatz feet, filled him with a sense of restoration. Stasi was his father again, and he his son. He wept with relief.

Andolosia had been working on Sansone's hat in tandem with the mechanical legs. The projects complemented each other because levers and springs were integral to both, though they served vastly different purposes. From the outside, Sansone's hat was a top hat of felted beaver fur with a tall, moderately-trapezoidal crown. Inside was a complicated network of gears, miniature pulleys, and springs that, if all went well, transformed its wearer into a laurel tree.

He labored through the night, embroidering the brim, and finished around noon the following day. After the final touch – a blue silk ribbon around the crown – he rested his forehead on the cutting table and closed his eyes for what he promised would be only thirty seconds. He fell asleep. Thirty seconds stretched into thirty minutes, ample time for the recurring nightmare to unfold.

Once again, he was on a mountain, before a doorway leading into a massive stone edifice. Scents of olive oil and cloves wafted from the darkness. He was afraid to go inside, but curiosity impelled him. At first, he descried only two oil lamps flickering on the far wall. When his eyes adjusted, he saw an enormous nautilus hovering in mid-air. Her beauty melted his heart. *Her? Yes, her.* The creature with the curved shell and indigo stripes was definitely female. How did Andolosia know? Certainly not based on his paltry knowledge of molluscan anatomy. He knew in his bones. Her pin-hole eyes exuded an enticing, emerald green glow. She beckoned him with her undulating golden tentacles. He stepped closer. The scent of cloves intoxicated him. Her tentacles caressed his cheeks, and she sang to him, though she had no mouth – none he could discern anyway. Her song induced a pleasant warmth in his head. Heat radiated to his extremities. The song had a complex melody, but its words were simple and few. To Andolosia's consternation, he never recalled them upon awakening.

There was a creak and a deep groan behind the wall, followed by a grating, metal-on-metal squeal. The nautilus' tentacles were trembling. They seized Andolosia's face and throat in an iron grip. Unable to breathe, Andolosia mouthed a soundless ".Why?" She answered with a waterfall. A cylindrical organ near the bottom of her shell's opening unleashed a deluge. Water blasted him through the doorway and carried him down the mountain, thrashing him on boulders and trees along the way.

Andolosia shot awake with a sore neck and a long black thread dangling from his perspiring forehead. Bleary-eyed, he puzzled over why the nautilus always turned on him. He struggled to recall the words of her song. As usual, he came up empty. He stood stiffly and shuffled to the kitchen. He stuffed a hunk of stale Monticello bread in his mouth and gave his jaws a workout. He splashed water on his face and toweled his neck, underarms, groin, and buttocks. He fetched a clean shirt and fresh – well, fresh enough – underwear. The bread in his mouth had softened sufficiently that he could swallow.

After packing Sansone's hat in a carrying box, he had forty-five minutes before the pre-arranged, three-o'clock meeting at the Florentine palazzo. Any other hatter would've despaired about getting to Florence in time. Any other hatter didn't have a divine teleportation hat. He retrieved the hat from behind Hermes' portrait and put it on. Since he was the last person to have worn it, the leather already conformed perfectly to his skull. Its preternatural warmth bled through his head and down his spine, a sensation both blissful and terrifying. He reached down and picked up two hat boxes, one containing Sansone's hat, the other to store the wishing hat upon his arrival in Florence.

He was ready. He exhaled every sip of air from his lungs. He wasn't about to repeat his first experience with hat travel – arriving under the glorious ceiling of the Sistine Chapel only to projectile-vomit on the back of a cardinal's blood-red cloak. Stasi called it the "Immaculate Projection" and joked that Andolosia likely would spend the afterlife in a pit of infernal stomach acid.

Andolosia closed his eyes and pictured a secluded spot along the Arno River in the shadow of the Duomo. He steeled his guts and thought, *Take me there.*

There was an indigo flash and a brassy squeal, and then just an empty room.

CHAPTER

TEN

Cronus looked terrible in the waning days of his reign due to increasing paranoia and sleep-deprivation. His hair had thinned to a sad smattering of ringlets dangling off his ashen scalp. His face was gaunt, cheeks sunken, eyes weighed down by bulbous, blue-gray bags. He hadn't changed his emerald-green robe in decades, and the accumulated patches of dried ambrosia, mead stains, and dust had dulled the fabric to the color of old snot. His sorry state was Gaia's fault, or, rather, the fault of her prophecy. Her words had been unambiguous and specific, unlike the inscrutable fortunes her priestesses conveyed to mortals: "Your child shall castrate you and assume the throne."

A considerate mother with the gift of forevision might have kept this insight to herself, let the ugly business play out, and left her son blissfully ignorant until his bloody fate was upon him. But Gaia wasn't a considerate mother, not to Cronus anyway. And no matter how many times he pressed her for more details, she didn't say, or wouldn't say, when the vile deed would occur or who among his children would commit it, only that it was inevitable.

Refusing to don an ungainly – not to mention undignified – chastity belt, the desperate Cronus secretly asked Moira to weave him a fate tapestry to subvert the prophecy.

Moira balked. "My lord, you told me never to weave tapestries for gods because it would encourage them to pursue their selfish ends. We would have civil war."

Cronus blinked slowly. A sheen of fatigue and weariness coated his corneas. "I did say that," he said raggedly, "but this tapestry will *prevent* –ahem – will prevent civil war."

"What will happen after the next emergency and the next one after that? You'll demand tapestry after tapestry." Cronus opened his mouth to interject, but Moira didn't allow him. "No. No. Don't deny what you know in your heart to be true."

Cronus' tone turned pleading and childlike. "Please, Moira. No one needs to know our secret."

"Mother Gaia will know as soon as her prophecy is thwarted. And once the secret is out, the other gods will demand their own tapestries with competing fates. I won't be able to reconcile them. Please don't make me party to the heavens' downfall. You're a better god than that."

Moira didn't actually believe that, but she figured that stroking his ego would put an end to the matter. It did.

"Of course. You are right, Moira. Forgive my . . . forgive my moment of weakness. I commend your commitment to principle. It is most admirable. It doesn't comfort my testicles any, but it is admirable nonetheless." He added a lifeless "hee hee" and left her be.

Moira felt ashamed. She wasn't principled at all. In truth, Gaia previously had warned her that Cronus would approach her and ask for a fate tapestry. She claimed she'd had a vision of the conversation as well as the great tragedy that would befall Moira should she weave the tapestry: "A sister of Fate will return to the mud from which she had sprung." Moira wasn't certain if Gaia was trying to manipulate her with a false prophecy, but she wouldn't risk Tyche's life to preserve Cronus' manhood.

Cronus grew more desperate. Since he didn't know which child would betray him, he consumed them, assuming they couldn't castrate him from the inside. It wasn't as grotesque as it sounds. He didn't eat them, *per se*. There was no chewing or digestion involved. Cronus simply unhinged his jaw and swallowed them whole, seriatim. First was Hestia, followed by Demeter, Hera, Hades, and Poseidon. As for the sixth child, the infant Zeus, Cronus failed to notice that Rhea had disguised a baby-sized stone in a diaper and bonnet. By the time a half-mad, cannibalistic god reaches in the cupboard for child number six, his palate tends to be far less discriminating.

Cronus held onto power a while longer. Indeed, the five children and the stone in his belly so weighed him down, no rival god could have extricated his bloviated body from the throne. But so isolated and wretched did he become, he eventually resigned himself to his fate, and soon enough, he longed for it.

It happened at daybreak. Moira was tamping the batten, about to throw the shuttle across the shed in the warp, when she heard retching sounds from the bema. Cronus was on all fours, vomiting up his five children and a stone dressed like a baby. The now-mature Zeus was looming over him, scythe in hand. Moira looked away because she knew what was coming. Cronus exclaimed an agonized "Hee Hee!" and something sailed across her peripheral vision and out the window. *A coin purse? A wineskin? No, you know exactly what it is, Moira.* The Titan era was finished.

Zeus invited Moira and Tyche to the gods' new home in

Olympus. He enticed the "Sisters Fate," as he called them, with plans for a grander palace with massive, floor-to-ceiling windows in the throne room. Moira needed no enticements to accept the offer. The alternative was unemployment or the basalt mines of Tartarus.

Zeus was so pleased, he arranged to have the Loom of Destiny and two spools delivered to his throne room in the morning. With his next breath, he gave Moira his first order: at dawn, she would head to Earth and teach his mortal lover Lamia how to weave. Zeus snapped his fingers and vanished before Moira processed the demand, let alone could request a brief postponement.

This could be a problem – a huge problem.

Moving-sprites were notoriously incompetent. If they misdelivered the hidden third spool of god-gauge thread to Zeus' throne room, the consequences would be disastrous. Zeus would commission fate tapestries for the gods. His power would grow unchecked. His ego would push Olympus into another civil war. Testicles would be whizzing across the firmament once again.

What could Moira do? She couldn't count on Tyche to supervise the moving-sprites. Tyche had been working the night shift the entirety of her young existence. She slept through the mornings like the dead – no, like the dirt that covered the dead. Even if Tyche somehow managed to stay awake, would she be lucid enough to supervise the move? Doubtful. Also, she didn't speak a word. She'd have to use hand gestures to communicate with the lunkheaded moving-sprites. It would never work.

Moira took the only precautions she could think of. Before dawn, she visited the head moving-sprite, the fore-sprite, at his hovel. She instructed the disheveled, rheumy-eyed creature to deliver the loom and the spools with the two thinnest-gauged Destiny Threads to the throne room. She impressed that it was critical he transfer the spool hidden in the utility closet – the spool with the thickest thread – to the anteroom off Zeus' mead cellar. She had written the instructions on parchment and drawn a tri-color-coded map corresponding to colored numbers she had painted on the three spools. She handed the fore-sprite the documents and made him repeat the instructions to her multiple times. With each recitation, she backed further from his blasts of mead-tinged breath.

He slurs his words. She dismissed the observation with a, *Well, that must be how moving-sprites speak.*

The following morning, Moira delivered the weaving lesson to Zeus' mortal lover. Because Lamia was a slow learner, Moira didn't arrive back in Olympus until the evening. She didn't wait for the gryphon to touch down before dismounting on the grounds of Zeus' palace. She stumbled in the dirt, got her footing, and raced to the throne room, praying there had been no glitches with the move.

The first thing she noticed was Tyche seated in the Loom of Destiny. That made sense. It was the evening. Tyche was exactly where she should have been at that time of day. But Moira noticed not two, but three, spools of Destiny Thread beside the loom. The spool of divine thread was so fat with yarn, it stood out like an aroused colossus at the public bath. Worst of all, a massive god in a cobalt blue robe was looming over Tyche. Moira's stomach seized.

Zeus!

"Ah, Moira," Zeus said, waving her over. "Perhaps you can shed light on something. Your sister is a goddess of few words – no words, really."

Tyche was feverishly throwing, pushing, and pulling the different parts of the loom. She was staring forward with a soft, sleepwalker's gaze.

"Forgive Tyche, my lord," Moira said. "This is how she works. How may I enlighten you?"

Zeus stroked his cloud-white beard and said, "I recalled there being only two spools in Cronus' palace."

Breathe, Moira. Breathe. Make up an excuse and make it good.

"That's right. That's because . . . because Cronus' throne room was much smaller," she offered. "The third spool is a spare. We stored it elsewhere to avoid clutter."

Zeus squinted as if trying to discern a hidden meaning to the third spool. Moira interposed herself between him and the spool, obstructing his view. Zeus shifted to the right. Moira followed suit. Zeus shifted left, as did Moira.

"Would you stand still?" the irked Zeus said.

"Apologies, my lord. I was trying to get out of your way."

"Really? If I didn't know better—"

Tyche set down the shuttle with a loud clank and slid the batten hard into the lower warp beam. Zeus' attention shifted toward the noise. Tyche slipped out of the loom, approached Zeus, and gazed at him as if he were one of her crazy, kaleidoscopic tapestries. Discomfited, he harrumphed and wandered off. Moira was stunned but relieved Tyche had gotten Zeus to back away.

Two worker-sprites and the fore-sprite entered, the fore-sprite consulting Moira's color-coded map.

"Sorry for the mix-up, miss," the oafish fore-sprite said to Moira. "We had a lick of trouble matching the colors on the map to the numbers on the spools. Probably should've mentioned I'm color-blind."

"You think? I also wrote out the instructions in great detail. I numbered the spools for you."

"Can't read either."

Moira threw up her hands. "You might have mentioned at least one of those things this morning."

"In my defense, I was quite drunk. No worries, miss. We can sort out the spools right here and now."

Moira seethed. "That was precisely what I wished to avoid."

The fore-sprite became pensive. "S'pose it was. Ah.

Don't fret. We'll get that spool in its proper place faster than you can say Bacchus is your uncle."

"Then do it."

Moira fumed as the fore-sprite directed two worker-sprites to lift the spool of mortal Destiny Thread.

"Wrong spool, you idiots!" Moira said in a loud stage whisper. Frantically, she pointed at the spool of god-gauge thread. "That one! That one!"

"You heard the lady," the fore-sprite scolded his workers. "That one."

The workers shifted to the spool of divine thread and lifted it.

Zeus wheeled around from the throne room's doorway. The hem of his flowing robe twisted a half-beat behind. He stormed over to the spools and ran his fingers over the threads on each spool.

"As I suspected," he remarked at the spool of divine thread. "These threads are much thicker and more vibrant than the others."

"Are they?" Moira asked innocently, as if the goddess who'd been harvesting Destiny Thread for eons had never noticed this obvious fact. She touched the divine spool. "Why, I believe you're right," she added with feigned surprise.

"The spool is bursting with the stuff. Have you used any of it?" he asked pointedly.

"The other two spools are more than adequate for human and demigod tapestries," Moira said. "The threads before you are extremely thick and unwieldly. Very difficult to work with."

"But it seems wasteful not to exploit their use."

She scratched her forehead. "What use would that be?"

"It stands to reason the thickest threads are the most potent."

"Greater potency is irrelevant without a more potent

purpose."

The gears were turning in Zeus' mind.

I could throttle those sprites!

Moira shrugged and started to turn away. "Well, if that is all, my lord, my sister and I have much work to do."

Zeus ignored her. "Have you considered whether these threads could make a fate tapestry for a god?"

Moira stammered, "I . . . we . . . we've not attempted such a feat." She fumbled for the excuse Cronus had concocted for this very scenario. "You see, our loom is a conduit . . . a conduit for Gaia's prophecies. Her prophecies are for mortals and the occasional demigod."

"That has been her practice, to be sure. Nothing prohibits you from following a different practice, does it?"

"A different practice? I don't– why would I want a different practice?"

"Because I would like to commission tapestries for my divine brethren."

Moira balked. "We weave mortal fate tapestries because humans are the source of faith. Meddling with gods' destinies would detract from our vital work."

"Then you must redouble your efforts."

"There are only so many hours in a day."

Zeus stepped close to Moira. Her face was practically in his abdomen. She craned her neck upward.

"I shall devise fates for my brethren. You and your sister shall implement them. Prepare your fingers to weave the thickest threads."

True to his word, Zeus designed fate tapestries for his divine brethren, and the Sisters Fate dutifully weaved them. Gaia got wind of the divine tapestries and confronted Zeus, who readily admitted his part. In protest, she birthed a tribe of giants and attempted a coup, personally leading the ill-fated charge atop Python, her dragon. To avoid imprisonment in Tartarus and spare Python, Gaia accepted exile. The civil war was over. Moira and Tyche's troubles were only beginning.

Not long after, Zeus thought he'd try his hand at a mortal tapestry. He was positively giddy as he relayed his idea about a girl named Myrrha who would lust after her own father and trick him into bed. The father would discover Myrrha's deception and try to kill her after she gets pregnant. As a "mercy" – Zeus' word, not Moira's – he would transform Myrrha into a tree. Tragically, the human fetus in Myrrha's pulpy womb would continue gestating, requiring Lucina, the goddess of childbirth, to hack the baby free.

"What say you?" Zeus asked. "Clever no? Far more interesting than Gaia's boring tapestries."

Moira betrayed no emotion. She was too stunned, anyway. After gathering her wits, she calmly demurred. "I am sorry, my lord, but we cannot weave this tapestry."

"Cannot or will not?" he seethed.

"Will not."

Zeus narrowed his eyes. Sparks of rage percolated through his thick, cloud-white hair and beard. "I trust the Sisters Fate understand the consequences of insubordination. Defy me, and you shall be cast to a prison cave in Tartarus. There, you shall weave for all eternity, sustaining yourselves on one-third faith rations."

Moira kept her cool. "May I take a moment to confer with Tyche?"

Zeus nodded, tucked his hands behind his back, and moseyed off.

Moira escorted Tyche to the gap between the loom and the window, out of earshot. She suggested they accede to Zeus' demand but alter his design so that Myrrha lusts after her married tutor instead. Since only Moira and Tyche could read fate tapestries, Zeus wouldn't discover the change until it was a fait accompli. As a precaution, Moira and Tyche would weave fate tapestries that insulated themselves from a Tartarian prison. Tyche nodded eagerly.

"We shall weave ourselves a tolerable fate, Sister. Oh, Zeus will yell and thunder. He will make a big show of being kingly, but he won't send us to Tartarus. No, he'll confine us to our chamber and cut our faith rations to half for a century or two. His fury will fade like a child's temper tantrum."

A lightning bolt struck the loom, cracking the warp beam in two. Startled, Moira turned to see Zeus only a few feet from them.

The cunning god snuck up on us!

The miniature lightning bolts permeating his hair and beard follicles had multiplied ten-fold. His face glowed with a ruddy heat, and the muscles underneath roiled with agitation. The tip of his index finger sparked with blue flames.

Zeus trained his finger on Moira. "Treacherous bitch!"

Moira raised her hands in a protective motion, bracing for excruciating pain. But just before the bolt left Zeus' finger, Tyche stepped in front of her and absorbed the brunt of his electric wrath. After the smoke cleared, only the singed outline of her sandals remained.

Moira keened. She dropped to her knees and stared wide-eyed at the void her sister had occupied only seconds earlier. She brushed her fingers around the smoldering silhouette of footprints. Tears leaked from her eyes and hissed on contact with the hot marble.

Moira's voice trembled. "My sister . . . My sister . . . You killed her." She broke into gasping sobs.

"Pull yourself together," Zeus grumbled. "Tyche isn't dead. She's in Tartarus."

"For how long?"

"Until you've proven your obedience."

"I can't weave fates without her."

"Nonsense. You weaved tapestries for my father before you created Tyche."

"It doesn't matter now. Your bolt shattered the loom's warp beam."

Zeus grunted, snapped his fingers, and vanished. A moment later, he reappeared holding a bow-shaped yoke engraved with the letters iota and omega on both ends. He threw the massive yoke at Moira's feet.

"What is this?" Moira asked.

"It's a cow's yoke. It belonged to Io before I changed her back into a woman."

"I require a straight board of maple."

"What you require, Moira, is a reminder that you are my beast of burden. The yoke is made of sturdy oak, and it is long enough to suit your needs. Make the repair."

Moira mitered the yoke's ends and fit the new beam into the loom's maple frame. After restringing the warp threads, she pulled Destiny Thread from the mortal spool and tied it to the shuttle. As a test, she threw the shuttle across the loom and tamped the row twice. Although the loom was functional again, its altered aesthetics made Moira sick to her stomach. The replacement warp beam was crooked and amber-colored and had a wild woodgrain, unlike the straight, cream-colored maple planks comprising the rest of the loom. Much later, after Moira had recovered from the shock of Tyche's absence, she would mount two halves of a nautilus shell over the unsightly seams where the clashing grains joined.

"Begin," Zeus commanded, firing a bolt from his finger for emphasis.

Moira flinched, gathered herself, and began to weave. Zeus retreated to his throne to observe. He scrutinized each pass of the shuttle and tamp of the batten. Since he couldn't read the tapestry, he shocked Moira with lightning whenever he suspected she might be thinking about sabotaging his design. In due course, Moira weaved Myrrha's abominable fate, fashioning a horrific destiny that desecrated the sanctity of both childhood and motherhood. She cut the tapestry from the loom, laid it at Zeus' feet, and walked away in silence. Had a doorway to Chaos spontaneously opened before her, Moira wouldn't have hesitated to walk right through it.

CHAPTER

ELEVEN

Florence, Grand Duchy of Tuscany, 1603

Andolosia appeared at the Arno's shore with the two hat boxes in hand. He already had been exhausted from sleep deprivation and worry. Thanks to Hermes' hat, he could add ringing ears and a clawing headache to his complaints. At least he hadn't vomited on any clergymen. Actually, he had one additional complaint, this one courtesy of his nose. The air hanging over the Arno was thick with the ferrous stink of fresh blood. Flies swarmed around goat guts and fish entrails lapping against the stone piers, detritus from the butchers and fishmongers who sold their wares on the Ponte Anatole. He stored the wishing hat in its box and began ascending a steep footpath.

Sansone de Medici's palazzo sat high on a hillock, looming over the Arno like a gargantuan gargoyle. Originally a Gothic cathedral, the structure was abandoned in 1483 after the ground subsided, a piece of the dome crushed five parishioners, and the foundation settled at a fifteen-degree tilt. The only occupants until Sansone moved in a century later were invasive vines, opportunistic seedlings, and rodents. Sansone's father was Adriano de Medici, known colloquially as "Adriano the Dark" due to his brown complexion. Officially, Sansone's mother and father succumbed to malaria within minutes of each other. The true cause – the unspoken cause – was the arsenic-laced cask of wine "gifted" by Adriano's pale-faced siblings. They deposited the orphaned Sansone in the decrepit church with an old prostitute-turned-nanny to look after him.

A year before, Sansone began remodeling the church into the semblance of a habitable home. He ordered the creeping ivy torn from the façade, broken windows replaced and reglazed, and mortar joints repointed. He commissioned a circular, stained glass window for the palazzo's second story. The window depicted the Fasci Sansone's symbol of bound wooden staves over an orange sun. None of the aesthetic improvements, however, addressed the structure's fifteen-degree tilt. If anything, tidying up the exterior accentuated its lopsidedness.

Breathless and sweaty, Andolosia crested the hill and ambled toward the palazzo. As he approached the entrance, two sentries in orange and white harlequin uniforms emerged from narrow doors framing the larger main entryway. Each held a caliver gun on his shoulder and carried a sword at his side.

"Halt," the identical twin guards ordered in unison.

"State your business," said the guard on the right.

"I am Maestro Petasos," Andolosia said. "Messer Sansone commissioned a hat for his opera. He is expecting me."

"What is in the boxes?" the guard on the right asked.

"Why, the hat, of course."

The guard on the left leaned his head toward the other and said incredulously, "Two boxes for one hat? Sounds suspicious to me, Brother."

"Aye," the right guard concurred.

Andolosia piped up. "Yes. Well, one box is for the Messer, and the other . . . the other is not."

The left guard fixed a hard stare on Andolosia and nodded to his brother, who nodded back and pushed open the heavy oak door. The guards resumed their sentry posts beside the door and said, in unison, "The Messer is expecting you."

Andolosia was irked that they'd hassled him for no good reason. "That is what I said at the outset."

As he stepped through the open doorway, he caught his toe on the wooden threshold and stumbled forward. He managed not to fall and, after gathering himself, noticed that the floor was level. Evidently, Sansone had constructed a new floor over the pre-existing one to compensate for the tilt, resulting in a precarious initial step inside. Andolosia would have appreciated a warning from the guards. He figured this was how they amused themselves during their otherwise stultifying duties. Of course, leveling the floor had had no impact on the windows, ceilings, and fireplaces in the grand library beyond the foyer. All were off kilter. He thought he might go mad living in that place.

A lanky man with stooped shoulders entered the foyer. Andolosia assumed he was Sansone's manservant. He walked with a slight flexion in his knees, as though expecting the floor to shift at any moment. Unkempt, white-blond hair framed a gaunt, pockmarked face. His eyes were strange. His brown irises were flecked with amber. Set against his powdery moonscape of a complexion, they exuded an animalistic quality, as if plucked from the face of a man-tiger chimera.

The man nodded his head. "You are the milliner's son?"

Andolosia responded with a head bow. "Aye. Maestro Andolosia Petasos for Messer Sansone de Medici. Is the Messer about?"

"I am he."

"Oh, forgive me. I assumed a valet would . . . I thought

the custom . . ."

"Customs be damned," Sansone said dismissively. "You and I agreed by letters sealed with our imprimaturs to meet at this very time, at this very place. Why muddle the matter with superfluous customs of the moneyed class?"

Sansone extended his hand. Andolosia did a quick double-take. Sansone's hand was much darker than his powdered face. Andolosia shook his hand and bowed his head.

"It is a great honor, Messer Sansone."

Sansone's bearing was discomfited. His facial muscles were strained, as though he needed to relieve himself or was trying to prevent it.

"You must be famished after your long journey. I am afraid my humors are out of balance, so I cannot partake. My cook has prepared a feast of roast thrush, tortellini, and beans."

"I hadn't anticipated a lengthy visit, Messer. You needn't have put him to the trouble."

"It was no trouble. Many of my inspectors will be arriving tonight from the far reaches of Tuscany. One extra mouth is no imposition."

Andolosia was famished. He'd eaten only a hunk of stale bread in the last twenty-four hours. Yet he did not want to linger in the strange palazzo. He opted for a lie.

"You are most kind, Messer, but the dry figs and bread I purchased on the Ponte Anatole have sated me."

"Then let us get on with our business."

Andolosia set down the two hat boxes. He removed the lid from Sansone's box, pulled out the dark brown top hat, and offered it to Sansone. Sansone took the hat and ran his fingers over the blue silk ribbon, the rich embroidery on the wide brim, and the solitary pearl affixed at the middle of the crown. Without a word, he took the hat into the library. Unsure, Andolosia followed. Sansone stood in the puddle of orange light from the stained-glass window and inspected the hat from all angles, inside and out, and tested the hat's weight. After a contemplative pause, he shook his head, displeased, and handed the hat back to Andolosia.

"This is not what I commissioned," Sansone said coldly. "The hat I described to your father should have levers and pulleys and mechanical arms. It is my fault. He was in no condition to take my order."

Andolosia stepped closer.

"But Messer, this hat has all of those things and more. Allow me to demonstrate."

Andolosia donned the hat and depressed the pearl on the crown. That action released the tension on a whirring flywheel. The hat's top popped open, and a golden foil trunk emerged. Thin branches shot from the trunk at various angles, while green silk leaves emerged from tiny slits in the branches and unfurled in corkscrew motions. Finally, a delicate golden veil descended from the brim, transforming Andolosia's body into the lower part of the trunk. The flywheel slowed to a quiet whir and stopped.

Sansone's face had a peculiar mien, best described as corrupted. The creamy whites of his eyes appeared to be leaching into the outer rim of his yellow-brown irises. Something was seriously wrong with the man – unnaturally wrong. Fearing Sansone might pounce and tear out his throat, Andolosia stepped back. But Sansone's lips stretched into the semblance of a smile – at least, Andolosia hoped it was a smile.

"It is a work of art," Sansone declared. "Equal to Da Vinci's greatest contrivance."

Andolosia felt relief and pride. That was the highest compliment he'd ever been paid for one of his creations.

Sansone strode to a mahogany wood sideboard. He opened a drawer, removed three velvet pouches, and handed them to Andolosia. By the pouches' weight, Andolosia estimated Sansone had paid him at least four hundred florins.

"Messer, I believe you have made a mistake. This is far more than you bargained for."

Sansone held up his hand. "It was no true bargain. Maestro Stasi was in no position to negotiate. It is a pittance for his suffering."

Andolosia was astonished. "You remembered my father's name."

"Why wouldn't I?"

The question took Andolosia aback. "Well, because . . . because you . . ."

"Because I am a Medici? Because I come from a line of wealthy merchants and your father from hoi polloi? Pshaw! I do not condone such base class distinctions. Do you think a spoiled aristocrat could create a hat such as you've made for me? You, Maestro, are a genius. I should bow to you, not vice versa. Tell me. How does your father fare?"

"His injuries have healed better than expected. He may even walk again."

Sansone's eyes widened into saucers. "God's Blood! Has the old man sprouted new legs?"

"Nothing so magical. I fashioned him mechanical legs. He is still getting used to them."

"Good man. You've put your genius to practical use. A far worthier pursuit than my frivolous opera hat. I trust your mother is assisting him in your absence."

Andolosia felt a twinge in his chest. "My mother is no longer of this world, Messer. She died when I was but a boy."

"I am sorry for your loss."

"Much obliged. I am just thankful Fate spared me the wretchedness of growing up an orphan." Andolosia realized he'd put his foot in his mouth. "Forgive me, Messer Sansone. I meant only that I was blessed with a wonderful father. Certainly, there is no dishonor in being an orphan. Fate played you a cruel hand by infecting both your mother and father with malaria."

"Malaria? Ha! They were murdered."

Andolosia blanched. He didn't know if he should apologize or join in Sansone's amusement.

"Oh, come now, Maestro Andolosia," Sansone warmly chided. "Don't act so scandalized. Everyone in Tuscany knows my uncles and aunts murdered them. But I've moved past that."

Andolosia was impressed Sansone had come to terms with his parents' ugly deaths. He didn't seem weighed down by the injustice Fate had done him.

"Forgive me if this is presumptuous, Messer, but may I ask how you moved past the anger of your loss?"

"I owe it all to Niccolò di Bernardo dei Machiavelli."

"Messer Machiavelli died seventy years ago, did he not?"

"Oh, Signore Machiavelli did not assist me personally. I refer to his writings. Are you acquainted with them?"

"Cardinal Orsini is a client of ours. He lent me *Il Principe*."

"Then you know Machiavelli predicted the demise of the hereditary prince. He said the day will come when the right to lead will depend solely on a man's strength of will, not his name or bloodline. My aunts and uncles murdered my parents because they couldn't stomach the prospect of their mongrel brother becoming the next Grand Duke. Well, they got their wish. But the fools were short-sighted. They did not anticipate the rise of a leader more powerful than the Grand Duke, more powerful than any king, queen, or Pope. They did not foresee the Supreme Prince."

"I do not recall a Supreme Prince from *Il Principe*."

"He is a creature of my own invention, the inevitable extension of Machiavelli's argument."

"How so?"

Sansone's eyes smoldered. "A twig is weak, solitary and

easily snapped. But bind a thousand twigs, and you have an unbreakable bundle. One man's will is but a brittle twig. The collective will – the fasci – is invincible. The Supreme Prince is the tie that binds the fasci."

"Fascinating. The Supreme Prince is nearly god-like."

Sansone's mouth curled up on the right. "For all intents and purposes, he is a god. He plays the part of Supreme Prince as if he were divine. His bearing is regal on purpose. The pomp and ceremony around him reinforce his divinity in the collective imagination."

"Then the Supreme Prince's superiority is an elaborate deception."

Sansone's voice turned shrill. "An elaborate, *noble* deception. Only the Supreme Prince can pull back the veil and expose the truth in its purest, Platonic form."

"What truth is that?"

"The truth we've been discussing," he snapped. "That accidents of birth do not determine a man's nobility. The true nobleman does not covet royal lineage or epidermal purity. He cultivates his wits and directs his will to the benefit of the greater whole."

Sansone was panting. The pulse in his carotid artery throbbed through his skin. Beads of perspiration cut winding troughs down his powdered cheeks. The whites of his eyes appeared to be bleeding into his irises, shrouding them in a hazy sheen. He was shaking, on the verge of some sort of fit. His head fell back, and he swooned. Andolosia seized his arm and eased him into an upholstered chair.

A short, pot-bellied fellow rushed into the room. He was carrying two bowls, one filled with ice, the other containing a thick white paste.

"Perso," Sansone said wearily.

Perso set the bowls on the sideboard, removed a damp rag from the ice bowl, and draped it over Sansone's neck.

"Come, Messer," said Perso, his voice effeminate and

didactic. "You must lie down now."

"I have a guest."

"Messer," Perso urged, "you are in the midst of an episode."

Perso pulled a spoon from his doublet, dipped it in the bowl of paste, and brought it to Sansone's lips. Sansone turned away petulantly.

"Have mercy on me, Perso. No more ground oyster shells."

"Messer, they will slow your heart."

"As well as my bowels. Brunelleschi could've mortared the bricks to his dome with my feces." Sansone patted Andolosia's hand gratefully and stood on his own. "I am feeling better. The heat has abated. Just go, Perso."

Perso grimaced. "Need I remind you, Messer, this is the calm before the storm. The heat will return with a fierce rage. You know I do not exaggerate."

Sansone relented. "How long do I have?"

"Fifteen minutes," Perso said.

"Very well. I shall spend ten minutes with Maestro Petasos. That will leave five minutes to spare to get in the ice bath."

"But you may have only ten minutes," Perso remonstrated. "This is not an exact science."

"Meaning there's just as much chance I have twenty minutes. Let us split the difference."

"Your health is not a negotiation, Messer Sansone."

"Ten minutes, Perso," Sansone insisted.

Perso gave up and exited.

"My personal physician," Sansone explained. "I employ him to be overprotective. Come, Maestro Andolosia. I require your advice in the theater."

"I am not much of a thespian," Andolosia admitted.

Sansone laughed and walked away. "This is more of a behind-the-scenes query."

Andolosia picked up the hat boxes and followed Sansone under the broken dome and into the apse of the former cathedral. Where the altar once stood, a young laurel tree was emerging through the buckled marble floor. The tree was a sapling, suggesting Sansone had planted it recently. Andolosia would've inquired about the oddity, but Sansone already was entering the northern section of the transept. There stood a massive elevated stage.

Sansone turned toward Andolosia with a grand sweeping gesture. "Welcome to my opera, Maestro Andolosia."

Andolosia's jaw slackened. A river of blue silk embedded with iridescent pearls flowed through a miniature forest of ferns, ginkgoes, pines, and pomegranate trees. A golden orb and puffy clouds dangled from rafters, as did sculptures of gryphons and dragons painted in brilliant colors. The backdrop was a painting of Mount Olympus. Greek-style palaces, mountain nymphs, and goats dotted the slopes. The largest palace – Zeus' – sat at the peak. Below the mountain, sprites tended fields of lavender and barley, while wood nymphs hunted in the forest and water nymphs sang near the river.

"Remarkable," said the awestruck Andolosia. "May I ask what inspired this spectacle?"

"Have you ever had a dream that you cannot extricate from your mind? A dream so vivid and true, it feels more real than when you are awake?"

The giant nautilus flashed in Andolosia's mind. "I have."

"So it was with the opera. It played out each night as I slept with such clarity and salience, it was as though I was experiencing it for real. But the dream took a heavy toll on my health. I awakened with a raging fever and speaking in tongues. Thankfully, Perso darkened my door. I have the Romans to thank for that, having banned Jews from the medical arts. Perso's medicines taste like mortar and the ice baths are agonizing, but they stemmed the fevers. The dreams, however, did not relent. I was going mad. I'm ashamed to admit I contemplated suicide. As you see, I did not give in to the darkness. Rather, I gave into the dream. In a flurry of creativity, I wrote a libretto, adapted Jacopo Peri's score, and designed the set and costumes. I haven't suffered the dream since. It's as if my unconscious mind vomited the dream into the waking world. Well, that's putting it crudely. I'm quite proud of my vomit. People would pay good florins to watch my vomit. Tonight is the dress rehearsal. Tomorrow is the show for my inspectors."

They ascended the stage and headed to the wings, where stood a tall spool connected to the blue silk river.

"This is the source of my problem," Sansone said. "The spool is supposed to retract the river during the most critical scene in the opera. My engineers cannot get the blasted thing to work. It pulls a yard or two and stops every time. Perhaps you, Maestro Andolosia, can bring a fresh perspective to the problem."

Andolosia climbed a ladder that was propped against the spool and peered into the mechanism's innards.

"I see the problem," Andolosia said. "You need a governor to regulate the uneven pull of the mainspring."

"Can you fashion such a device?"

Andolosia surveyed a nearby table containing a panoply of levers, weighted balls, wires, and cutting tools. "I believe I can."

"Will you do me the honor?" Sansone asked with the pleading eyes of a starving cat.

"Of course, Messer. It should take me an hour or so."

Sansone smiled. "Here I hire the best engineers in Florence, when I should've hired a hatter! If you get this contraption working, you must come work for me."

"That is very gracious, Messer, but I have obligations in

Livorno."

"Millinery is an honest trade," Sansone conceded, voice growing hoarse, "but wouldn't you agree your talents are better spent elsewhere?"

Andolosia agreed, but he didn't say so. "Fate has imposed certain duties on my family."

Sansone's breathing became labored. "Machiavelli wrote that Fate is a woman, and if you wish to keep her under control it is necessary to beat and ill-use her. She allows herself to be mastered by the adventurous. Be a man, Andolosia, and stand up to Fate."

Sansone was blinking rapidly. Three beads of perspiration traced a milky path down his right cheek. He had a faraway look, as though observing the world through the wrong end of a telescope. Once again, his irises had turned milky.

"I . . . I . . ." Sansone sputtered. He then swooned.

There was no chair to set him in, so Andolosia held him. Andolosia was shocked by Sansone's emaciated condition. He was skin and bones. What strange illness afflicted the poor fellow? Andolosia never imagined he'd pity the man who'd severed his father's legs, but he did.

Perso rushed in. He flung Sansone's arm over his shoulder and walked him down the stage steps.

"It is past time for your bath, Messer," Perso said.

"Yes, Perso," Sansone said lethargically. "Make haste to the bath . . ."

Sansone and Perso exited the transept and headed toward the library. At one point, Andolosia thought he'd heard a third voice, resonant and tinged with a Greek accent. Had someone else joined them? Perhaps an actor from the opera. The voice grew quieter until a heavy door somewhere squeaked open and slammed shut.

Andolosia stood alone at the spooled mouth of the silken river. He felt disoriented. Was he a hatter, an engineer, or something else entirely? He could fix the broken river, so, at that moment, he was a riversmith. With that settled, he got to work.

CHAPTER

TWELVE

Mount Cyllene, 750 B.C.E.

Maia was the loner of her mountain nymph tribe. The other mountain nymphs annoyed her, so she avoided them, especially the young wildlings, who roamed the mountain unsupervised and out of control. It was beyond her how the furry little shits ever grew into functional adults. As far as she could tell, the stinkers spent every waking hour howling, kicking up dust, and throwing unripe plums at each other. Adult mountain nymphs were better behaved but equally insufferable. The females were uninterested in sensible discussion topics like sheep husbandry and diversifying the tribe's diet with leafy greens. Instead, they were preoccupied with gossip about the tribe's eligible bachelors. *Yuck.* The prospect of intimacy with a mountain nymph male disgusted Maia – what, with their open-mouthed chewing, deviated-septum breathing, overabundant body hair, and eye-watering stench. The males operated as if living in the open air at the top of a mountain justified their complete inattention to personal hygiene. For Zeus' sake, the men spent half their days in circles, chewing intoxicating tree bark, honing their hunting blades, and spinning tall tales of unfought battles. Surely, they could have spared a few minutes to shave one another's backs or rinse an armpit or two. No, Maia would never take a mountain nymph mate. Nevertheless, motherhood awaited her.

Maia emerged from the cave, wiped the sleep from her eyes, and cracked her back. She had just started her morning commute down to her flock of curly-coated sheep when an old man with a full white beard wandered onto the escarpment. He looked to be in distress. He staggered on the sedimentary rock, fretfully tugging at his mountain of silver hair. He half-sat, half-stumbled onto a boulder. He was enormous, at least twice Maia's height. He was too short for a Hyperborean giant, yet he was too handsome and in possession of one too many eyeballs for a Cyclops. His cobalt-blue toga embroidered with golden lightning bolts settled the matter. He was an Olympian, the most powerful of his ilk – he used to be, anyway.

What brings Zeus to this desolate mountain? The dotard is supposed to be in seclusion.

Zeus was weeping inconsolably. His prolific tears formed a saltwater river. The river rushed down the escarpment, across the scrubland, and through the dense pine forest. Maia worried the flood would inundate her sheep grazing on the grassy plain below. She approached the bereft god in hopes of stemming his tears.

"My king," she said softly.

Zeus wiped his runny nose and regarded her dubiously. "Why do you call me king?"

"Is that not the proper honorific for the lord of Olympus?"

His tears dwindled to a drip. He dabbed his face with his toga. "It is cruel to tease an old man."

"I speak truly, King Zeus."

"What is your name, nymph?"

"Maia."

"Well, Maia, the Zeus you know is a complete stranger to me. It's as though I have swallowed the River Lethe." He laughed faintly. "Ironic. I can recall the name of an amnesia-inducing river but not my own name."

"What do you remember?"

"Not much. A palace, I think. Yes, I was in a palace. I was staring into a pool of red . . . of red . . . What was that red stuff? Water? No. Wine? Blood? Whatever the liquid was, its level was very low, nearly dried up. And then . . . and then . . . walking . . . wandering . . . and then you."

"My lord, I believe you speak of the pool of mortal faith inside your palace."

"What a strange feature to have in one's home," he mused.

Zeus' stomach growled. Maia opened a purse affixed to her tunic, poured out a palmful of purple pellets, and offered them to him.

"What is this?" he asked.

"Lavender nectar. They stave off hunger."

"They look like the scat of a baby gryphon," he said with mild disgust. "But I am so famished, gryphon scat doesn't sound half bad right now." He swiped the pellets and popped them in his mouth. He chewed, swallowed, and nodded with approval. "Mmmm. Tart. Ooh. I'm buzzing all over. How invigorating."

"Not bad, eh? Some crush the pellets and snort them. I prefer ingestion. It energizes the entire body, not just your head. Would you like more?"

Zeus was going to say yes until he glimpsed inside the pouch. She'd given him three quarters of its contents. "Maybe later."

Maia cinched the purse shut.

"A very strange food," he said.

"It's mostly what we eat these days, owing to the lack of

mortal faith."

"Hold on. You eat faith?"

"You really have forgotten, haven't you," she remarked. "All the demigods and gods eat mortal faith, even you. Especially you. This is why you are not yourself. You are the greatest god, so you need the most faith to survive. Which is why you suffer most when the pool starts drying up."

"We are in some sort of faith drought?"

"We are."

"What is the cause?"

Maia shifted uncomfortably. Her teeth fidgeted with the inside of her lower lip.

"Don't be coy, Maia," Zeus pressed. He patted the boulder. "Come. Sit here. Tell me about the drought."

Guardedly, Maia sat beside Zeus. She ruminated over how to convey Zeus' epic failure in a non-accusatory manner. "Olympus has lost many followers," she said after a sigh. "With fewer followers, there are fewer sacrifices and tributes to feed the red cloud that rains on your palace and fills the pool."

"Where did our followers go?"

"I . . ." Moira demurred. "I live on this isolated mountain. I hear rumors from time to time. I don't have reliable information."

Zeus scanned the barren landscape. "By my estimation, you are the only one around who has any information whatsoever. Tell me the rumors."

"That the gods have been keener on debauchery and tearing each other down than engaging with their followers on Earth. Naturally, the snubbed mortals have turned to other gods, like Yaweh."

Zeus looked to the sky and groaned. "I am to blame. A king worth his salt wouldn't have let this happen." Tears began flowing again.

He was absolutely right. He'd been a terrible king. But

Maia had her sheep to think of. She couldn't let him flood the lowlands with self-pity. She took his hand and looked searchingly into his face. "No. No, my lord," she said in a voice reserved for coaxing reluctant sheep from the pen. "You are in a rough patch, that's all. Happens to the best of us. You will recover your glory. I'm sure of it. Soon, we will have more faith than we know what to do with. A veritable flood. We'll be drowning in the stuff."

Zeus stared warmly into her cavernous black eyes. "At least someone has faith in me." He brushed her cheek with his hand, which was comically large compared to her face.

Maia blushed and shyly bowed her head. She heard a thumping sound. It was Zeus' throbbing heart.

What is happening?

Zeus grazed his index finger along her smooth bronze leg, etching a line of prickly heat from knee to mid-thigh. She shivered. She also had a sensation akin to a bird flapping its wings in her stomach. The sensation intensified when she noticed a bulge growing in Zeus' toga. Spontaneous arousal was a common side effect for nectar pellet first-timers.

Interesting.

Until that moment, sex hadn't held much allure for Maia. Her pool of potential lovers had been limited to other mountain nymphs, sasquatchian charms and all. She might not have held such a dim view of her tribesmen had she been a pure-blood mountain nymph. She was a mongrel – her father, a Titan; her mother, a sea nymph. Sea nymphs were dark-skinned like their mountain nymph cousins, but significantly taller, leaner, and less feral. Like Zeus, Maia was an outsider here. Maybe that explained her affinity toward him, her arousal. It didn't hurt that, even in his dotage, Zeus was a magnificent specimen – powerful, muscle-bound, odorless, and nary a hair poking from his toga.

She met his icy blue eyes and slid her hand onto the

bulge.

Zeus shrunk himself to a more manageable size and disrobed. He conjured a thick wool blanket on the gravel and lay down. She unfastened her suede tunic and straddled him. She was exhilarated that the most powerful god in the history of the spheres was about to deliver her first penis-assisted orgasm.

Only it didn't quite pan out that way. Zeus wasn't a rough or demeaning lover. Nor was he tender. In retrospect, he'd performed precisely as one would expect of a senile god with no sense of his awesome power or memories of past sexual exploits. His modus operandi amounted to satisfying a biological urge with minimal fuss and effort. After five mechanical thrusts, he ejaculated. He groaned, but it sounded more like relief than pleasure. Meanwhile, Maia's insides absorbed a shot of seed that emitted the heat of a thousand suns. She blacked out from the searing pain.

Maia awoke later with her head resting on Zeus' silver-haired chest. Wisps of steam were rising from her crotch. That was disturbing. She was smoldering. She prayed Zeus hadn't caused her lasting injury.

"I remember everything, Maia," he said as her eyes fluttered open. "I anointed Apollo steward of Olympus. I charged him with restoring the flow of mortal faith to the heavens. My poor choice has doomed us all."

His chin quivered under his beard. Tears welled in his eyes.

No. Not again.

Maia propped herself on an elbow and said encouragingly, "Oh, I doubt it's as bad as all that. If Apollo can't cut it, surely another god is up to the task."

He sniffed and wiped his tears. "Pray tell. Who might this savior be?"

"I don't know. I'd have to think about it." Without a pause, she snapped her fingers and announced, "No, I don't.

I know just the god. Apollo's twin sister. Artemis. She has a feisty spirit and is much admired by the demigods. If anyone could rally Olympians and inspire the mortals, Artemis could."

Zeus scoffed. "Tell me you are jesting. A goddess on the throne? Seriously? Do you wish to hasten our demise? At best, a goddess would inspire a weak, womanly faith." He slid from underneath Maia, slipped on his robe, and reverted to his normal, gigantic stature. "Still, you are onto something with Artemis. I erred by giving Apollo a sister. She has not provided him the requisite degree of sibling rivalry. Apollo needs a foil with abilities and ambition that rival his own. I will create a brother who will claw and scheme and connive against him. Apollo will have no choice but to step up his game. Brother versus brother is the alchemy that will transmute his soul of soft gold into hardened lead. Brilliant! And I owe it all to you, Maia."

"What? No." Maia was mortified. "Need they be rivals, my lord? The brothers could work together, cooperate. I reckon their combined talents would carry the force of three gods."

Zeus chortled. "Cooperate? Has the thin mountain air robbed you of reason? Stick to what you know, Maia. Gods are not sheep."

The insult stung, but she rejoined with a veiled barb instead of a sharp riposte. "Like you, I have forgotten myself. Who am I to question the all-wise Zeus in matters of sound leadership?"

The irony was lost on the demented old fool. "Precisely," he concurred.

Arsehole.

"Thank you, Maia, for the nectar pellets and the . . . uh . . . the company."

"My pleasure," she said flatly.

Ha! Hardly.

"Now, while I have my faculties, I must make haste to Mount Olympus and have a word with Apollo."

"What about Apollo's new brother? Shouldn't you create him first?"

Zeus glanced at Maia's bulging, naked belly. "I already have."

* * *

Maia was laying her newborn in the crib when she heard the pained squawk followed by a thudding crash. She ran out of the cave and stopped short at the heartbreaking sight. The gryphon was an old, weathered bag of bones. Feathers patchy, beak scuffed and cracked, talons shredded, the exhausted beast was a victim of the devitalizing Olympian atmosphere. Maia unsheathed her knife and knelt beside its eagle-like head. Piercing eyes regarded her with a look of *Get on with it already*. She nodded and sliced the bulging artery by the gryphon's throat. Purple blood poured from the gash and pooled on the dry mountain clay. The noble beast released a rattling gasp and went still. She thrust the knife below the sternum and heaved. Her arm and back muscles strained. The knife wouldn't budge. She leaned in and pulled harder. This time, the fascia and sinew relented, and the blade tore a yawning rent clear to the abdomen. Peeling back the steaming flesh over the base of the trachea exposed three tympaniform membranes. She excised the hot slabs of scaly flesh and laid them side by side on a boulder.

I really have to pee.

Maia had given birth that morning. Her kidneys were feverishly excreting the divine hormones that had nurtured the god-in-being. The post-partum purge was an uncomfortable process. As if involuntary muscle twitching, a racing heartbeat, and itchy gums weren't bad enough, her urine was infused with a galvanic quality that transformed her pisses into liquid lightning. Still, the accursed piss was not to be squandered, for it teemed with divine vitality. She straddled the tympaniform membranes, squatted, and saturated them. After the blistering sunlight tanned them into leather, she carried the swatches to her cave, where she trimmed and stitched them into a wide-brimmed sunhat – a *petasos* – for Hermes, her son.

Maia set the hat on Hermes' head, careful not to rouse him. Much too large at first, the hat quickly shrunk and conformed to the boy's skull. The inherent warmth of the vibrant gryphon leather melted the tension in his brow. She scooped her son into her arms, brawny from years of scrambling up and down Mount Cyllene, shearing sheep, and toiling in the downcountry.

He's getting heavier. Longer, too. These little gods grow so fast.

Maia unbuttoned her tunic at the shoulder to liberate her engorged breast. Hermes' eager fish lips latched onto the nipple. The hat's broad brim shielded him from Maia's view, but his suckles were loud and distinct. After he drained the one breast, Maia stopped humming and switched him to the other. Before latching on, he looked at her expectantly.

"What is it, my little Olympian?" she asked. "Oh, I see. You liked my humming, is that it?"

Hermes gaped at her.

"Shall I sing a song?"

His eyes widened.

"Mountain nymphs sing a special song while packing dirt on the levees. It's hard work under the hot sun. Singing helps us forget our toils. My mother sang the song to me when I was little, though not so little as you. It was a very sad time."

Hermes' aspect turned quizzical.

"You want to hear about my sadness?" she asked. "Little

ones should not hear sad stories. There will be plenty of time for sadness when you are bigger."

Hermes held his stare.

Maia sighed in a conciliatory manner. "True, you will not be little much longer. Very well."

Hermes latched onto the nipple and listened attentively.

Maia explained that, when she was a young girl, the Olympians condemned her father, Atlas, to hold up the sky. The grieving Maia refused to eat, frightened the Olympians would come for her mother next and leave her orphaned. Desperate to break Maia's depression, her sea-nymph mother whisked her to a grotto on the Argolic Gulf, where millions of horn-shaped mollusk shells had accumulated. Eons of storms and tidal cycles had eroded and molded the shells into a byzantine network of tubes. As the tide surged and ebbed, the formation played the eternal note.

"My mother called it a water organ," Maia said. "She put a hand on my chest and said the eternal note was inside my beating heart. And you know what? She was right. I heard it, and I was no longer sad."

Maia extricated Hermes from her chest. His lips suckled the air for a few moments.

"The water organ inside my heart sustains me in these difficult times," Maia said. She touched Hermes' chest. "The note that began it all is in your heart too." She touched his head. "With this hat, you will be like a gryphon, sounding the eternal note across the spheres."

Hermes gazed drowsily at his mother's loving visage. Warmth cascaded from his head to his heart. He inhaled the intoxicating mixture of spicy perspiration and sweet cedar and tried to make sense of his mother's allure. The geometrical terms she'd taught him were inadequate. Her beauty was more than abstract curves and angles. Her face projected the rugged wonder of Thessaly's granite cliffs. Her cheekbones weren't compact half-spheres but rocky outcroppings sculpted and smoothed by the rains. Her nose, narrow at the bridge and flaring at the nostrils, was the waterfall where the four great rivers merged in the underworld. Hers was not a map of beauty but beauty's living geography.

The boy's lips widened into a gummy smile. He belched. A drop of milk dribbled down his chin.

Maia checked Hermes' linen diaper. It was clean. Of course, it was clean. He wasn't a sheep. Immortals didn't excrete solid waste, only a rarified "divine wind." The diaper was for warmth and modesty. She discarded the diaper, sewed him a tunic of Arachnean flax and embroidered it with silver thread. Like gryphon leather, Arachnean flax fibers maintained their vitality and would grow with her son's rapidly increasing proportions. She wound more flax fibers into thick cords, bound them to soles, and decorated the sandals with unsullied gryphon feathers. She dressed Hermes and laid him back in the crib for a nap. She flipped up his hat's brim and kissed his forehead. She said she was off to tend the sheep but promised to return before he awoke.

CHAPTER

THIRTEEN

Florence, Grand Duchy of Tuscany, 1603

A ndolosia incorporated the governing device into the coiling mechanism and tested the retrofit with a flip of the lever. The silk river retracted and coiled into a tight spiral in fifteen seconds. He didn't know if that was too slow or too fast. He would've asked Sansone, had he any idea if and when Sansone might be returning from his bath. Andolosia fretted that leaving without bidding him farewell would be a terrible faux pas. With the family hat shop under the Fasci Sansone's jurisdiction – and Stasi breaking guild rules with abandon – it was best to remain on the man's good side.

Andolosia meandered from the transept into a narrow hallway with antechambers and branching, dead-end corridors. He knocked on and tried opening every door he passed, to no avail. He called hello. No one answered. The hallway terminated at a winding stairway, which he ascended. The upstairs hallway, with its original floor, was tilted. He compensated for the imbalance by leaning to the right as he walked. More hellos and door knocks ensued.

Again, he was greeted with silence. He felt queasy with hunger. He should've taken up Sansone's offer for roast thrush. His belly emitted a lengthy, lilting growl. At the growl's tail end, he could have sworn he'd heard the words "hungry . . . fool . . . harpy" and the phrase "Shut your mouth." Andolosia was perplexed. His digestive system had "spoken" only twice before, both times in Greek and never an entire phrase.

There was a shout of "Lottie!" from the door at the end of the hall.

Andolosia's urgent knocking went unanswered. Finding the door unlocked, he cracked it open and peered in. The two sentries from earlier were speaking in agitated tones. One, named Gino, called the other Dino. They were arguing about a feral, deranged woman splayed on the floor with her hands bound. Gino dipped a spoon into a bowl of porridge, as Dino restrained the wilding's face. Her hair was an explosion of blonde frizz, sausage curls, and caked porridge.

"Steady yourself, disobedient wench!" Gino warned.

"Shove that gruel up your arse!" she yelled back.

"Take your medicine, you muck-spout," Dino said.

"I'd sooner bite off his bollocks!" she snapped.

The woman pitched forward and sunk her teeth into Gino's inner thigh.

"Ah!!" Gino screamed. "The hellion's got her fangs in me! Help me, Brother."

Dino released the woman's face, fetched a bucket of water, and doused her. After releasing Gino, she spat a swatch of his pants at him.

Gino inspected his thigh. "You've bruised me in a tender spot, Lottie. The wife's going to rain hellfire on me. I promised I'd sworn off whores, especially of the biting variety."

Andolosia couldn't fathom Sansone sanctioning such

145

savage treatment of a woman. He assumed the sentries were torturing this poor creature for sport while their master was incapacitated. He burst through the door.

"What is the meaning of this depravity?"

"Giving Lottie her medicine," Dino said. "Not that it's your concern, Maestro."

"For what ailment?" Andolosia asked.

"Dottore Perso says it's madness from too much yellow bile," Gino said.

"Is Messer Sansone aware of this barbarism?" Andolosia demanded.

"'Tis on his orders," Dino said. "Lottie is his sister. Wild thing, she is, without her medicine."

"Liar!" the woman shouted. "I am not that flaccid worm's sister! He kidnapped me."

Her accent was Sicilian, if Andolosia wasn't mistaken.

Gino roared a laugh. "Such tales Lottie spins."

"My name is Carlotta, not Lottie. Lottie is a dog's name, and a mangy dog at that."

Gino moved close to Carlotta with the bowl of porridge. She snarled rabidly, and he recoiled.

Carlotta turned to Andolosia. "Please, Maestro. You must help me. Sansone is a madman."

"You are mistaken my dear Madonna," Andolosia said gently, "I conversed with Messer Sansone at length not an hour ago. He had his wits about him. He conversed rationally and most eloquently."

"Wait till his face turns crimson and rains sweat," she said. "Wait till his voice changes, and he claims to speak as the god Apollo."

"Of what does she speak?" Andolosia asked Gino and Dino.

Dino and Gino glanced at each other, unsure what to admit.

"Family, she is," Dino said mindlessly, as if drawing

146

upon a set of stock answers. "Sansone's sister."

"I'm not his fucking sister, you arseworm!"

"Come now, Lottie," Gino said. "Take your medicine. It's nearly time for your rehearsal."

"Rehearsal?" Andolosia asked. "For this opera?"

"Aye," Dino said. "Lottie sings the part of Daphne, water nymph of Olympus."

Andolosia turned to Carlotta. "You are a performer?"

"I perform only because they force Perso's foul medicine down my throat. His herbs bewitch me. I cannot control what I say or do. I'm dreaming and awake at the same time."

"The medicine calms her addled mind," Gino said condescendingly.

"It *steals* my mind," she remonstrated.

"Now, now, Lottie," Dino said, kneeling before her. "Be a good girl and take a spoonful."

Carlotta turned contrite. "You win, Dino. Forgive my boorish behavior."

"That's a good little Lottie."

Dino shoveled a spoon of the goopy porridge in her mouth. She accepted it willingly, which made Dino smile. Carlotta reciprocated with a smile of her own, after which she spat the blob in his face.

"Ah!" Dino screamed. "Foul creature! Quickly, Brother. A towel. The wench has blinded me!"

Carlotta gestured for Andolosia to come close. He tentatively knelt beside her. She smelled of sweat, stale milk, and cloves. Coils of her hair brushed against his face. He froze with an overwhelming sense of déjà vu even though none of this was familiar. He'd never visited Sansone's palazzo, and he didn't know this wild woman from Adam. And yet . . .

"Do you have a weapon, Maestro?" she asked in an urgent whisper.

"I am a hatter, not a soldier."

She nodded toward the scissors tucked in Andolosia's belt. "Give me those."

"What good—"

"Stick them in the back of my skirt," she said. "Hurry."

Andolosia balked. "I don't think . . ."

"Do it!" she growled.

Andolosia pulled the scissors from the belt and slipped them between Carlotta's skirt and bodice. Because she wasn't wearing a petticoat, his fingertips grazed the small of her back as he retracted his hand. A cloying heat erupted across his face.

Noticing Andolosia's proximity to Carlotta, Gino asked, "What are you two plotting?"

Abruptly, Andolosia stood. "Nothing. I . . . she asked for help. I refused. That is all."

"You had better be speaking true, Maestro," Gino said while gripping his sword's hilt.

The strums of a stringed instrument sounded in the corridor. As the strums grew louder, the player launched into a sequence of alternating chords and arpeggios. Whoever it was had exquisite fingering, but something was off. The delightful melody was infected with an obnoxious overtone, causing everyone in the room to wince. The door swung open, and in flounced a revitalized Sansone, clad in a toga and holding a lyre. His hair was brushed and tied neatly in the back. His face and hands were caked in light ochre foundation.

Sansone smiled, exposing a rack of pinkish-gray gums. "Ah, Maestro Petasos," he said with delight. "I am so pleased you are still here. I wanted to properly thank you for repairing my river."

"You are most welcome, Messer. And I am pleased you are in better humor."

"Thanks to Dottore Perso's medical skills, I have yet to

miss a rehearsal."

"Do you play a part in the opera?" Andolosia asked.

"But of course. I am the great Apollo," Sansone declared with a theatrical flourish.

"And this woman here . . . she is portraying Daphne?"

"Indeed." Sansone frowned at Carlotta's bestial appearance and cast a withering stare at his guards. "Though she clearly is in no condition to rehearse."

Dino piped up. "Lottie refused her porridge, Messer."

"Is that so, fair sister?" Sansone asked her. "How do you expect to sing if you do not take your medicine?"

"I am not your sister, you moon-faced twit!" she barked. "Let me go!"

Sansone shook his head with pity. "The savage conditions of her confinement pain me, but it is for her own good. There is no telling what she might do if unbound."

"Oh, there's telling, all right," Carlotta threatened. "I'd slice your fucking throat!"

Her profane and vivid remark gave Andolosia a start. This woman was ferocious. He was afraid of her but also intrigued.

Sansone shrugged off the comment. "Obviously, we do not keep sharp objects about either."

Andolosia blanched. "Most prudent," he said weakly, envisioning his shears lodged between the wild woman's skirt and her flesh.

"Are you all right, dear fellow?" Sansone asked Andolosia. "You've gone pale. Perso, fix the man a tonic."

"That is not necessary," Andolosia said. "I hope I am not overstepping the bounds of propriety, but if I may inquire, what is Carlotta's affliction?"

"She was born with a savage temperament and a propensity for wild fits," Sansone said.

"And what of her claims that she is not your sister and that you kidnapped her?"

"She is also delusional," Sansone added.

"No more than you," Carlotta fired back.

Sansone straightened his spine. He turned from Carlotta, strode two steps, and wheeled around with the flamboyance of a lawyer about to impeach a witness.

"Maestro Andolosia, ask the Madonna about the water nymph Daphne – not the one in my opera but the one who lived in Olympus amongst the gods, the one who turned into a laurel tree. Ask her if she claims kinship – an actual blood relation – with this mythical creature. She will deny none of it."

"Is that so?" Andolosia asked her.

"You do not care what I think," Carlotta said, despondent. "No man does."

"Oh," Sansone said, "I neglected to mention she also maintains that the god Apollo is, as we speak, attempting to take over my body."

"He is, you fool," Carlotta said. "How else do you explain your spells and this ridiculous opera?"

Sansone directed his answer to Andolosia. "My spells are from an imbalance in the humors, which Perso is treating. As I explained to you in private, the opera is my divine inspiration."

"Exactly," Carlotta said. "From Apollo surfacing inside you."

Sansone scoffed, but her accusation had unsettled him. "Only a madwoman would insist that Apollo's spirit is possessing me merely because I have cast myself in the role of Apollo."

"Your days are numbered," Carlotta said. "The god is too powerful for your flimsy vessel. Even with Perso's medicine, you will shrivel and die before year's end. You know it to be true."

Sansone's mouth tightened to a slit. "Take her to the cellar," he ordered Gino. "Strap her to the rack. Use the heretic's fork, if you must. Just get that medicine in her and clean her up for rehearsal."

Gino yanked Carlotta to her feet and began dragging her toward the door. The scent of cloves wafted from her as she passed Andolosia. The uncanny sense of familiarity came flooding back. Andolosia's head was swimming in confusion. Who was right, and who was wrong? Sansone was eccentric, but eccentricity didn't necessarily make him a depraved barbarian. If Carlotta truly was Sansone's intractable, mad sister, Andolosia couldn't fault him for the difficult conditions of her confinement. She'd brought them on herself. Also, Carlotta hadn't denied her alleged kinship with an Olympian creature. Surely, that was an objective mark of madness.

Or was it?

The hat box at Andolosia's feet contained a god's stolen property. He knew firsthand that divine connections were possible, though, in his experience, those claiming them were invariably lunatics or clergymen – usually both. Yet Carlotta hadn't struck him as mentally disturbed, just steadfast. Beneath her porridge-smeared skin, beaver's nest hair, and seething demeanor were flawless, emerald green eyes, a long, smooth neck, and more strength and spirit than ten virile men. If only he could have surreptitiously wished her to a quiet place and sorted the matter without distractions.

Gino dragged Carlotta into the corridor and closed the door behind him.

"I apologize for that unpleasantness," Sansone said. "Would you consider staying the night and attending the opera as my special guest tomorrow eve?"

Andolosia demurred. "Regrettably, I must decline. I have my father to tend to."

"Stasi is fortunate to have a devoted son." Sansone offered a subtle, deferential head bow. "I wish you safe travels. Dino, show the gentleman out."

Fate Accompli

Andolosia's stomach churned as Dino escorted him from the palazzo. He fretted over Carlotta's welfare while praying she wouldn't maim or murder someone with his scissors. Regardless of which prayer Fate answered, he was certain of one thing: the way forward was fraught.

CHAPTER

FOURTEEN

Mount Cyllene, 750 B.C.E.

The Clarion Calls had announced Hermes' birth. Apollo thought he'd pay his new brother a visit. When Maia was down the mountain with her sheep, he entered the cave and approached the crib. He brushed the boy's face with his thumb. Though they shared identical bone structure, Hermes' face was sheathed in bronze skin, whereas Apollo's was as white as Carrera marble. Hermes cracked an eyelid, spied his brother, and quickly closed his eye, feigning sleep.

Adorable, Apollo conceded. *But why did Father give him my face?*

Apollo raised a hand in a smiting motion but hesitated. He couldn't smite a fellow immortal. Not truly. At worst, he could consign his brother to the prison realm of Tartarus for a spell. In a lucid moment, Zeus would learn of Hermes' whereabouts, yank him back to the heavens, and punish Apollo harshly – very harshly. The Olympian king's second-greatest joy after sleeping with his own kin was punishing them.

Apollo lowered his hand, dejected, and exited the cave. He mounted his horseless chariot and drove off to formulate a subtler form of fratricide.

Hermes' eyes shot open. He was disappointed Apollo had departed so quickly. He wanted his brother to show him his prized cattle, purportedly the most beautiful and fecund cows in all the spheres. Hermes' stomach growled. He was weak with hunger. He wished he could go to the glade where Apollo's cows grazed and suckle on them. All at once, the gryphon hat emitted a shriek and a blinding purple flash. Hermes vanished from the crib. An instant later, he appeared in Thessaly, on the very glade he'd imagined.

The glade was just as his mother had described it during his breast-feedings. There was a rich carpet of grass with clumps of skinny pine trees standing like sentinels for the three hills beyond. He toddled to the brown and white cows and petted their coats. He crawled underneath and sucked teat after swollen teat, swelling his belly to bursting. The nourishment elongated and fortified his bones and stretched his flesh, until, by final suckle, he was adolescent-sized. So appreciative of the cows was he, he decided to keep them. He led the herd across a sunburnt plain of withered wheat and fields of anemic lavender and around cordoned-off, bottomless sinkholes. His mother had mentioned these too. The Olympian landscape – the "godscape"– was deteriorating from insufficient faith.

Hermes led the herd into a cool grotto for a well-deserved rest. Near the cave's far wall, he stumbled upon a pile of old gryphon bones. As he bent over to inspect a small rib, a cow bumped him from behind, driving his head into the wall. He turned, cursing at the rude bovine. To his dismay, however, he was facing far more than one rude bovine. Hundreds of the stupid cows were filing into the cave. He ordered them to back out, but the cacophony of mooing and flatulence drowned him out. The cattle continued their dull march forward, compressing themselves into each other and Hermes. Soon, they'd pinned him into the wall. In his struggle to extricate himself, the gryphon hat tumbled from his head and disappeared in a sea of clomping hooves.

Unknown to Hermes, the grotto was home to the ancient tortoise, Lyra. When the wizened Lyra poked his head out to investigate the tumult, his cold, leathery pate collided with a dangling udder. The startled cow backed into another cow, startling that one, and so on and so on, triggering a chain reaction of frenzied bovines.

After the dust from the reverse stampede settled, Lyra was dead of a snapped neck. Hermes wailed like an infant, understandable given he'd been one earlier that day. He imagined his mother's voice urging him to stop crying and use the music in his heart to make things better. He stemmed his tears and wiped his snot. He used a shard of obsidian to scrape out the shell's innards. He sized up the rib bones of the long-dead gryphon. He affixed a small rib to each end of the shell to give the lyre arms. He connected the tops of the arms with a longer rib to form a yoke. He did the same to the arms' bases to form a bridge. He stretched four strings of entrails between the yoke and the bridge. When he plucked them, their rich sounds filled his soul with joy. He thought, *This is how Mother's water organ must have sounded.* He would call the instrument a lyre, in honor of the tortoise who'd given his life for music.

About then, Apollo came upon the glade where his cattle normally roamed. Finding them absent, he landed his chariot and dismounted. He went into a panic, certain his cows had broken through the fencing around a sinkhole and fallen into Chaos. But then he noticed unfamiliar foot impressions in the grass. He concluded the prints belonged to a rustler who'd stolen his cows. The footprints were oddly tiny. *A tree-elf rustler?* He followed the prints to a long trail of dung, which eventually led to his cows, which were milling about near the mouth of a grotto. He accounted for all of them, and they appeared in sound condition. That much was a relief. Now, he was furious.

Apollo poked his head in the cave. "There's no using hiding, you thieving knave! Reveal yourself!"

Struck dumb with terror, Hermes groped along the grotto floor for his hat and put it on. With lyre in hand, he wished himself to the most distant place in Olympus he knew – the banks of Oceanus. Once there, he scrambled under the arms of a weeping willow. He plucked the lyre and prayed Apollo would not discover his culpability for the purloined cows. The lyre's unusual timbre, however, drew Apollo's attention. He followed the sounds until he spied Hermes' dung-caked feet poking from the willow's canopy.

"Thief!" Apollo shouted. "When I get my hands on you, I shall plunge you in Oceanus. The indigo waters will absorb your divine powers like a sponge. See how you like that!"

Apollo parted the canopy of branches.

"Aha! Prepare yourself for my wrath," he raged.

Hermes' mind had gone blank with fear. He couldn't think of a specific place to go, and a vague "take me anywhere" was insufficient to trigger the hat's teleportation function. In a panic, he exclaimed, "Help me, Father!"

Before Apollo could grip his brother's neck, a jagged bolt splintered across the clouds over Mount Olympus, and merged into a uniform, blinding ray. When the beam winked out, the willow tree was a smoldering stump.

Apollo and Hermes reappeared in Zeus' throne room. The brothers were now of equal stature and standing side by side at the short end of a rectangular pool. Hermes was in a state of boyish awe. The pool was empty except for a few inches of wine-colored fluid at the bottom. Its white marble liner bore the ancient stains of more prosperous times, when the levels had reached a depth of twenty feet. A thick copper tube extended from the bottom of the pool, forty feet up, and through the palace ceiling. The ceiling coffers were carved in high relief with scenes of Zeus battling giants and communing with centaurs and Amazons. The soffits were painted with red and indigo flowers and white stars. Bronze spears, silver shields, and golden chariot wheels hung high on the walls. Below the metallic adornments hung tapestries bearing abstract, seemingly haphazard, designs. Zeus' massive gold and ivory throne was near the far wall, in the center of a towering colonnade laid out like the letter pi.

Apollo descried a seated figure on the throne and reacted with surprise. "Father? Oh good. You have returned. The sprites said you wandered out of your private chambers. We were worried. Did you go for a stroll and lose your way?"

"I was fucking a nymph," he answered in a booming, gravelly voice.

After recoiling, Apollo responded cheerily, "Oh. I see. Well, that sounds delightful."

"Approach," Zeus commanded. "Both of you."

Hermes advanced along the pool's left side. Apollo went right. Torches mounted on alternate columns licked and hissed at them as they passed. Moira was seated at the Loom of Destiny, weaving in the light from a tall window. After each pass of the wooden shuttle, she pulled the batten toward her twice, producing a *thub dup thub dup* sound. The steady palpitations reminded Hermes of cuddling against his mother's chest. Three man-sized spools stood next to the loom, each wound with shimmery thread of different thicknesses. The spool for the thickest-gauged thread was empty, Moira having weaved it into tapestries for the pantheon.

Hermes and Apollo reunited in the shadow of the throne. Zeus raised his furrowed brow from his palm, eyes colder than a glacial lake, and asked Apollo, "Why do you attack your brother so? You compelled me to expend a bolt to bring you here."

"Hermes purloined my cattle," Apollo said.

Zeus turned to Hermes. "Is this true?"

"It is, Father. I—" Hermes stopped, taken aback by the resonance in his maturated voice. He cleared his throat. "I was playing. Is that not how brothers are supposed to behave?"

Apollo sighed with exasperation. "He stampeded the cows across the glade with abandon." Apollo grabbed Hermes' hand holding the lyre and held it up. "He trampled old Lyra to death. This is what's left of him."

"Wicked, wicked boy!" Zeus thundered at Hermes. "You shall be punished."

"Quite so, Father," Apollo said, stepping forward. "I was about to smite him when—"

"I dispense the punishment."

Apollo stepped back. "Forgive me, Father."

"You both shall be silent as I deliberate."

Zeus rested his forehead in his palm.

Hermes began plucking a hypnotic melody.

Zeus raised his sleepy head and asked dreamily, "What is that instrument?"

"I call it a lyre," Hermes answered. "Lyra lives on through music. Does that not mitigate my punishment?"

"A specious argument," Apollo declared with disdain. "The hunter who fashions a pelt into a coat does not make his prey any less dead."

Hermes fingered the strings in a complex arrangement. Zeus smiled with delight. His big toes tapped along to the melody.

"The music is quite beautiful, my son."

"Thank you, Father," Hermes said.

Apollo glowered.

"What is on your head?" Zeus asked Hermes.

"Mother fashioned this hat from a fallen gryphon,"

Hermes answered. "With a wish, it takes me anywhere."

Zeus stroked his hirsute avalanche of a beard. "My deliberations are complete. You shall give Apollo the gryphon hat as recompense for your theft."

Apollo nodded. "I'd prefer you banish Hermes to Tartarus, but the hat will suffice."

"Father," Hermes remonstrated. "I have owned this hat all my life."

Apollo cackled. "Oh, please. He was born this morning."

"It's been a very long day," Hermes rejoined. "It will break Mother's heart when she sees I have lost her precious gift on my first day of life. She will complain to you. Day after day, she will throw herself at your feet and beg you to reverse your decision. For all eternity, I should think. Maybe longer."

"All right. Enough," Zeus grumbled. "Keep the gryphon hat. Give Apollo the lyre."

"But the lyre is an extension of the music in my heart," Hermes whined. "I can no more give away the lyre than I could hand over a piece of my soul."

"I have passed judgment. Give it to him."

Hermes complied, albeit petulantly. He dropped the lyre before Apollo could grasp it. The instrument smacked the marble floor and resonated with a dissonant jumble of chords.

Apollo knelt to examine the lyre. "You fool!"

Hermes shrugged. "Sorry, Brother," he said flatly. "It slipped."

Apollo ran his fingers over the furrows in the carapace. He flipped the lyre over and plucked each string. "You are lucky. It appears undamaged."

"If that is all, Father," said Hermes, "I shall take my leave."

Hermes closed his eyes, about to wish himself away.

"Wait," Apollo said. "Father, an issue has arisen since you went into seclusion."

Zeus leaned forward. "If you mean your utter failure to fill the pool with faith and the sorry state of the godscape, I am well aware of the issue."

Apollo swallowed hard. "This issue is related to that issue."

"Wonderful," Zeus said sarcastically. "An issue with an issue. Spit it out."

"With the air thinning, the gryphons are suffering a die-off. This has led to a backlog of letters and parcels to and from the other spheres. Also, we are behind in delivering mortal souls to the underworld. Hades is threatening to file suit with Athena."

Zeus glanced at the ceiling and mused, "I leave him in charge for a few measly centuries, and he turns my kingdom to shit." He fixed on Apollo and added, "Funny you should mention Athena. Are you trying to make my head explode?"

"Of course not, my lord. I bring up this issue with the issue because it presents an excellent opportunity for my new brother. With his gryphon hat, he's perfectly suited to pick up the gryphons' duties."

Zeus preened a silver ringlet spilling over his ear. "Hmmm. Not a bad idea. Very well. Hermes, it befalls you to deliver the post and convey the souls. Can I trust you to do your job, unlike your disappointing brother?"

Apollo bit his lip.

Hermes straightened his posture and said in a soldierly tone, "I will not let you down, Father."

"Are we done here?" Zeus asked.

"Almost," Apollo answered. "There's also a vacancy in the patron department. What better way for my new brother to get up to speed on godliness than to wear the mantle of guardian and protector of a virtue or two?"

Hermes smiled. "Oooh. I like the sound of that. Thank you, Brother."

Apollo's eyes sparkled. "You are most welcome."

"What is the vacancy?" Zeus asked.

"Patron of thieves and liars. In light of his performance with my cattle, I can think of no one more qualified for the job."

"No, Father," Hermes protested. "Please. I paid my penance with the lyre."

"Becoming a patron is no penance," Zeus corrected him. "It is a great honor. And to become a patron on the very day you grew out of infancy? Well, that's unprecedented, my son. With your youth and gumption, you will become the greatest liar and cheat to grace these halls. Congratulations."

"Thank you . . . I guess," Hermes stammered. "I . . . I have no doubt it is a great honor. It's just that Mother instilled me with a love of music – *her* love of music. I have forfeited that gift to Apollo. Now I have to assume the title of deceiver-in-chief, too? How low I have fallen, and I haven't lived even a full day. I fear Mother will spit in my horrid face."

Zeus reddened with anger. "You have no face but the one I gave you – mine!"

Apollo plucked the lyre, disconcerted by its atonal twang.

"I am sorry, Father," Hermes responded, voice cracking.

Zeus waved him away. "Leave before I make you patron of beggars and whores as well."

Hermes sniffed and bowed his head. He turned and took three slogging steps before vanishing in a shriek and an indigo flash.

Apollo strummed the lyre's strings with escalating fervor. He plucked them seriatim and in chords. No matter how he played, he could not rid the lyre of its shrill overtones.

Zeus frowned. "You should consult your brother on

how to play it."

"My playing is not the issue. Hermes broke it. Summon him back and punish him properly."

"You've heaped enough on the boy for one day. Leave him be."

Zeus' head tipped toward his chest. He was dozing off. Apollo lingered, mustering the courage to say what was really bothering him. He placed a hand on his father's knee.

"Father?" Apollo inquired softly.

Zeus grunted and raised his head. "Why are you still here?"

"I couldn't help but notice that Hermes' lip curls in one corner. His chin is strong and square. His forehead is broad like the heavens. These are my features, sheathed in brown instead of white."

Zeus cast a withering stare. "Were you not listening? Hermes bears *my* face, not yours. If your face displeases you, say the word, and I shall wipe it clean and make you the no-faced god."

"No. No, I love my face – I mean *your* face." Apollo bowed. "Forgive me."

"Just go."

"There is one other delicate matter."

Zeus rolled his eyes. "What? You don't like your backside either?"

"My backside?" Apollo touched his buttocks uncertainly. "What's wrong with my—" He shook away the self-conscious digression. "What I don't like are the rumors circulating through the lowlands."

"What rumors?"

"Of discontent amongst the demigods. Stirrings that Olympus needs new leadership. That you should step aside for good."

"The demigods mean to overthrow me?" He banged a fist on his knee. "Ha! Let them try. I will shackle them in the flaming pit for all eternity."

"A very sound plan. Meantime, we cannot ignore the work stoppages and strikes, the demands for increased nectar allotments. Should someone come along, make brazen statements and bold predictions, he could rile up the demigods and bring Olympus to a standstill."

"Who would dare?"

"Not sure. All I can say is that the mountain nymphs are abuzz now that one of their own is the twelfth member of our pantheon, a mere heartbeat away from the throne."

"Hermes?" Zeus scoffed. "He is my son and but a babe. He can't lead a rebellion."

"As you noted, he has gumption. His mother gave him a hat that takes him anywhere he wishes. His father just anointed him the patron of thieves and liars. A dangerous combination even for the most loyal and well-intentioned of gods."

Zeus gripped his forehead. "Why are we having this conversation? You are the steward of Olympus, Apollo. Do your job and let me rest."

"As you wish. If I should determine Hermes is conspiring with the mountain nymphs, I shall take care of it."

"You shall do nothing of the kind."

"But you just said—"

Zeus interjected, "If Hermes betrays me, I shall . . . I shall deal with him in my own way." His voice quaked with hurt.

Apollo glanced at Moira and said in a saccharine tone, "Let us pray to Fate you are not compelled to end my brother's existence at such a tender age."

Zeus looked stricken.

Apollo was still staring at Moira. She stopped weaving and stared back at him hard.

"I don't take requests. Not anymore."

She turned to Zeus, who grunted.

"Do not trouble yourself with Hermes," Apollo reassured his father. "I could be totally wrong about him . . . notwithstanding his being sneaky, elusive, and the patron of thieves and liars, that is." Apollo gestured to himself. "Know that this son will never betray you. That should give you great solace."

Zeus' chin slumped to his chest, as his breathing devolved into a sputtering snore.

CHAPTER

FIFTEEN

Livorno, Grand Duchy of Tuscany, 1603

Stasi lay in bed, his leg stumps chafed, red, and warm. Andolosia mixed up a salve of egg yolk, oil of rose, and turpentine and applied it to the inflamed areas.

"You should rest now, Father."

"How can I rest after what you told me about the woman in Florence? Tell me more. She must sing like a bird if Sansone has seen fit to hold her hostage."

"I did not have occasion to hear her, but I'd venture she has an exquisite voice. I'd hazard that her long neck conceals a powerful throat and nimble voice box."

Stasi smiled. "You've taken a fancy to her."

Andolosia's scrunched his brow. "Not in the least. Purely an anatomical observation based on my study of medical texts."

"To be sure," Stasi said, unconvinced. "You are a terrible liar."

Andolosia plopped on the bed beside his father and slumped his shoulders. "I know." He threw up his hands. "Hell, Father! I cannot think straight. Sansone's madness has infected me."

"It's not madness. You are smitten."

Andolosia wrung his hands. "I don't know what to do."

Stasi studied his son for a moment and inquired, "Whatever happened with Adreana?"

"What in God's name does she have to do with Carlotta?"

"Your evening with her should've made you more comfortable with the fairer sex. You quake like a flower in the wind whenever you catch the scent of a pretty girl."

"I do not . . . not every time. Anyway, you wasted your florins on Adreana."

"I paid for an hour, and you spent the entire night. I'd say I got more than my money's worth." Stasi's self-satisfied smile faded as a realization dawned on him. "Wait. You and she didn't—"

"No, we did not," Andolosia shot back. "I wish you hadn't arranged it in the first place. When I set the florins on her bedside table, it felt like . . . I don't know. It felt like I was buying a hunk of pancetta."

"Mmmm. Pancetta," Stasi said dreamily.

"You missed my point, Father."

"What did you two do all night?"

"We talked. She spoke of her father, who worked at the docks. As a girl, she watched the stevedores hoist cargo with the massive block and tackle systems. She'd asked them questions ad nauseum." Andolosia chuckled. "She told me about a john of hers who was so heavy, his valet had to construct a pulley over the bed to hoist him into position. The valet confided in Adreana that the task was inflicting great strain on his shoulders and he feared he'd have to find other employment. Adreana studied the single-pulley system and recommended he modify it into a gun tackle configuration. With two pulleys, she explained – one fixed, the other moving – the valet would have the benefit of two sections of rope supporting his master's weight instead of one. The valet implemented the idea, and it worked to perfection. She cut his workload in half and saved his shoulders and his job!"

Stasi shook his head in disbelief. "Leave it to my inventor-son to waste a perfectly good whore on a discussion about a more efficient pulley."

"Why did you offer Adreana to me in the first place?"

"Because my father bought a whore for me, as did his father. It's a tradition."

Andolosia stood and went to the window. "Perhaps some traditions should be abandoned."

"Oh, pooh. Did you at least lie next to her on the bed?"

Andolosia turned toward him. "Yes, Father. She even kissed my cheek a few times. Does that make you feel better?"

"A bit." Stasi gestured to the decanter of wine on the nightstand. "Pour us each a cup, would you?"

Andolosia filled a pewter cup with wine and handed it to Stasi.

"Where is your cup?" Stasi asked.

"I am not thirsty."

"Thirst is not the issue. 'Tis the last Friday of the month. We drink for Hermes."

"Another pointless tradition."

Stasi shifted uncomfortably. "Tell me, Maestro Da Vinci, what is your brilliant suggestion for summoning Hermes?"

"I don't have one."

Stasi took a gulp of wine and handed the cup to his son. "Then shut up and drink."

Andolosia took a beat before taking an obligatory sip.

He shook his head. "How do we even know that giving the hat back to Hermes will break the curse? There is no Delphic prophecy to guide us, only the baseless assumption of our ancestors. If, by some miracle, Hermes manages to escape Oblivion, he'll probably take back his hat and smite us."

"You worry too much." Stasi patted the bed. "Come. Sit."

Andolosia sat stiffly.

"Now lie down," Stasi added.

Andolosia set down the empty cup and lay on the bed, facing away from Stasi, who gazed at the ceiling and scrutinized the stucco crannies.

"I'm proud of you, Son. You're not afraid to do things your own way, even if it means forsaking the finest prostitute this side of Florence. I couldn't have done it. I'm a born cur. I thank Fate every day for introducing me to your lunatic mother. It took a woman who dressed as a man and made cakes in the middle of the night because she'd dreamt that a queen was coming for a visit to make me an honest man. All I can say is if there's a chance this mad woman of Florence could make you as happy as your mother made me, you must go to her. The madder the woman, the better. If the Fasci Sansone takes revenge on the hat shop, so be it. We've been frugal. We'll survive. We always have. There are other places to sell hats, places he won't find us."

"Where?"

Stasi shrugged. "Your aunt writes that she is flourishing in Schwarz Boden."

"But we do not speak German."

"We'll learn it. You taught yourself Greek in six months, remember?"

"This is true."

"So, there it is, Son. You have nothing to lose."

"Your wisdom follows a very twisted trail, Father."

Stasi tapped the side of his head. "That's because of the giant pulley between my ears. It's got hundreds of blocks and a thousand miles of rope strung between them. It's a tangled cobweb, but it gets the job done. Now kiss my cheek."

Andolosia kissed Stasi. He stood and set the money pouches from Sansone on the bedside table. The florins clattered on the wood.

"I'm going to Florence," Andolosia said. "I promise to be back soon."

"Men!" Stasi said in an effeminate voice. "You have your way with us, deposit your florins, and leave. I feel so cheap."

* * *

Andolosia appeared on the ledge beneath the stained-glass window, thirty feet above the stage, which was illuminated by scores of candles. Hundreds of the young Fasci Sansone inspectors stood shoulder to shoulder in the transept. They'd grouped themselves into nine distinct squares, three across and three deep. A boy at the interior corner of each square held a standard with the emblem of the sun and the bundle of wooden staves. The boys were a diverse group of Tunisian Moors, Bohemian Slavs, Greek Jews, and African blacks. They all wore identical stockings, knickers, duckbilled caps, and doublets emblazoned with the Fasci Sansone emblem.

Carlotta entered stage left. She was dressed in a sleeveless suede doublet, short skirt, and tall buckskin boots. She strolled languidly beside the blue silk river. Her eyes were glassy, and her lids hung heavy. A harpsichord and a lute played two measures before Carlotta broke into a song about joining Artemis' hunting party. Andolosia was thunderstruck by the purity, power, and dexterity of her voice. She syncopated certain notes, and flattened, bent, and melded others. Andolosia felt whipsawed between feelings of happiness and disquiet. One musical phrase climbed and built with such mastery and nuance, he felt inspired enough to leap from the ledge and soar above the stage. He refrained.

Sansone, portraying Apollo, stood stage right. He was looking up at the bough of a tree with a furious expression. At a pause in Carlotta's solo, Eros, portrayed by a thong-wearing dwarf, shot Sansone in the chest with a streamer of golden glitter. Eros rearmed and struck Carlotta with a lead-colored streamer. Sansone staggered, turned, and spotted Carlotta. In a thin and reedy voice, he sang about his new-found love, the water nymph Daphne, and declared his intent to lie with her. Carlotta recoiled in disgust. She fled to the shore of the blue silk river. She raised her arms to the sky and beckoned her father, the god of the river, to save her.

With a wave of his hand, Sansone cued a fat golden sun to descend over the river. The spool in the wings spun rapidly, yanking the silk river offstage in a matter of seconds. Left shivering and naked in the dry riverbed was the river god, portrayed by an emaciated old man. To Andolosia's surprise, the old man was wearing the fur hat he had made for the opera. In Sansone's twisted version of the myth, Daphne's father – not Daphne – would transform into a laurel tree.

The old man pressed the pearl on the hat's crown, and the internal gears and pulleys whirred to life. The top of the hat sprung open. Ersatz branches coiled upward and outward. Laurel leaves unfurled and formed a canopy, while a shimmery fabric trunk descended over the old man's torso and legs. Sansone donned a laurel wreath and raised his arms in victory. The audience gasped in collective awe.

The glazed-eyed Carlotta stood alone and exposed at center stage, bedecked in skimpy water nymph attire. Sansone gave a lascivious grin. The maniacal Medici was poised to pounce on her right then, right there in front of his boy army. Andolosia was mortified. In making the finest hat of his life, he had aided and abetted a public rape.

"At last, Daphne is mine!" Sansone reveled to the crowd. "I have prevailed where even the great god Apollo failed. Now I will lie with the nymph and prove my worthiness as your Supreme Prince."

The audience burst into howling cheers and raucous applause.

As Sansone soaked in their adoration, Andolosia closed his eyes, exhaled, and wished himself on stage. The ensuing flash and squeal silenced the crowd. Andolosia reappeared next to Carlotta and seized her arm. Surprised, Carlotta dropped something metallic from her hand – the shears Andolosia had given her.

Sansone regarded the couple with shock. He lunged for Carlotta and shouted, "No!" But he was too slow. Andolosia already had imagined the place, exhaled, and made the wish. There was another squeal and a blinding flash. They'd vanished.

CHAPTER

SIXTEEN

Olympus, 390 C.E.

For eons, Moira had worked for no pay. A salary would've been absurd, for she had no need to buy anything. Like the other gods, she'd derived all her sustenance from the spigot of faith in her bedchamber. That changed when Zeus went senile, the faith pool dropped to drought levels, and the inhabitants of Olympus were confronting starvation. Apollo's first official act in Zeus' stead was to implement the industrial-scale harvesting and refinement of lavender nectar into pellets, which, when ingested or snorted, ameliorated the debilitating effects of faith deprivation. He also drafted nymphs, minotaurs, gryphons, dragons, and Cyclopes into a massive public works initiative to shore up the degrading godscape, paying them nectar pellets for their labors. Apollo distributed the remaining pellets to the gods. He allocated them according to an undisclosed formula that purportedly correlated with "each god's respective contribution to the divine economy."

At the time, Apollo had promised the pellet system would be a stopgap measure until the gods cultivated new sources of faith. After a thousand years, the stopgap petrified into a permanent fixture of Olympian life.

The gods collected their pellets – colloquially known as "kibble cash," "purple pelf," or "blossom bucks" – at a dispensary in Zeus' palace. One at a time, they slipped behind a blue velvet curtain, where Ploutus, the god of wealth, spewed kibble cash from his mouth. A thousand years of this demeaning work had stained his brilliant white teeth and pushed his upper dentition severely out of alignment. Once renowned as the "gentleman god" and the paragon of erudition, Ploutus not only resembled a buck-toothed simpleton, he'd developed an unfortunate habit of spitting purple saliva when he spoke.

One such payday, Moira was waiting behind Hermes in the dispensary line when the curtain rod dislodged from the degrading stone and crashed to the floor. Hermes stepped over the heap and cupped his hands under Ploutus' mouth. Well more than a hundred pellets poured out. Moira was flabbergasted. She always received seventy pellets. Granted, Hermes was the god of travel and commerce and the patron of thieves and liars, but she wasn't exactly the goddess of chopped liver.

"I'm Fate, dammit!" she argued to Ploutus. "I play a highly influential – nay, determinative – role in events that impact everyone, including Hermes. In a way, that makes me Hermes' boss. And don't forget I'm a Primordial. I have far more seniority than he. So why am I underpaid?"

With a spray of words and spittle, Ploutus professed he had no discretion over pellet allotments; Apollo made those decisions. Moira wiped her nose and made Ploutus an offer. She would alter his fate tapestry to dispense nectar pellets from his shirt sleeve instead of his mouth. In exchange, he would tell Moira how many pellets each of the other gods earned. He flashed her a donkey smile, indicating they had a deal. She asked Ploutus to write the information on parchment, ostensibly because of her poor memory but really to avoid a second shower. Unlike his vocalizations, his penmanship was perfect.

Armed with evidence, Moira headed to council. "Council" was Apollo's snobby term for a staff meeting. He loved his staff meetings because he took Zeus' place at the head of the enormous marble conference table. He was a pitiful sight. Before each council, he'd rub enchanted nectar onto his smooth, naked cheeks, which caused a dense forest of follicles to sprout and swell like a dry sea sponge in water. He'd fluff and primp and prick at the bushy thing to mimic Zeus' glorious beard. The end result was somewhere between unshorn sheep and Angora rabbits locked in frenzied coitus.

Apollo was seated when Moira entered, clad in Zeus' ceremonial blue robe with the white-lightning-bolt lapels. The robe was too large on him. He looked small, especially in the capacious council room. It was the second-largest room in Zeus' palace after the throne room but no less impressive, spanning a hundred by fifty yards and reaching twenty-five yards high. The highly polished black limestone floor was streaked with deep red veins, as if awash in the blood of a recent slaughter. Rows of blue and red fluted columns supported thick wooden ceiling beams. The friezes bore reliefs of gorgons and gryphons. Gold-leafed statues of gods occupied the evenly spaced wall niches. But for all its grandiosity, the council room was impractical for group discussions. The sole light source in the interior room was a chandelier of meager oil lamps, and the cavernous space swallowed voices. Gods shouted to be heard, causing even civil discussions to devolve into heated arguments.

Most irksome was the council room's stink of burnt offerings, though that didn't stem from the architecture.

Incinerating a slaughtered animal was the most effective means for mortals to deliver a prayer to a god. Encased in greasy smoke and lubricated in animal fat, the prayer slipped from the mortal to the divine realm and cut to the head of the intended recipient's prayer queue. After the recipient-god answered the prayer with a "yay," "nay," or "send me another two goats and a cow," the odor vanished. If left unanswered, however, the prayer lingered, cloud-like, about the god. Thus, it was custom, if not common courtesy, for gods to answer prayers immediately. Because Apollo had stopped answering prayers, he was perpetually enshrouded in an invisible, smoldering pyre of barn animals.

Moira took her usual seat by her brother Moros, the god of Doom, whose doleful countenance was true to his name. Apollo consulted a parchment with lines of text written in an elaborate script. He banged his crystal gavel and called the gods to order. Since most did not hear Apollo's voice or the gavel, he repeated these actions twice more before they quieted.

Apollo scanned the scores of faces around the table. "Welcome, my brethren. I trust everyone is well."

The agitated Moira piped up. "I am not well."

"Ah, Moira," Apollo said. "What troubles you?"

"Why do I earn only seventy percent of Hermes' pay?"

Apollo emitted an avuncular chuckle. "There is an order to these proceedings, Moira. We shall address your issue during new business."

"These councils go on so long, we never get to new business," Moira said. "I beseech you to address this matter forthwith. Why am I not paid equitably?"

"Very well, Moira. I shall overlook your procedural breach because we can quickly dispense with this nonsense." His tone oozed with condescension. "As you are aware, Hermes is an Olympian. You are not. Primordials are on a different pay scale." Self-satisfied, Apollo plucked the parchment from the table and flicked it into a state of rigidity. "The first agenda item is—"

Moira interjected. "Why pay Primordials less? Is that any way to treat your progenitors?"

"It is a simple matter of mathematics," Apollo said with irritation. "There are many more Primordials than Olympians. As a group, you receive more nectar pellets than we. Is that fair to my kind? Perhaps the most equitable thing to do is to reduce the Primordials' allotments. Would you prefer a pay cut?"

"Why distinguish the immortals at all?" Moira asked. "Treat everyone equally."

"Because we are not equal," Apollo said, voice rising. "Let me remind you the Olympians overthrew the Titans after the Titans seized control of the godscape from the Primordials? Primordials are twice defeated. Be glad we pay you at all."

Apollo had a point. Wars had consequences. Moira was fortunate the Olympians hadn't locked the Primordials in Tartarus. Yet, she couldn't shake the sense that Apollo was being disingenuous. He was omitting a key fact. She just couldn't put her finger on it. She mulled the information from Ploutus.

Apollo glanced back at the agenda. "The first issue is the unkempt maze hedges. I propose we supply clippers to the mountain nymphs and—"

"Your argument is unsound," Moira interrupted. "Eros, the Primordial god of love, also earns more than I. Obviously, my nature as a Primordial is unrelated to my lower pay."

Upon hearing his name, Eros tittered excitedly and launched himself from his chair. The chubby man-baby flitted above the conference table, feverishly flapping his tiny wings to stay aloft. He dipped and flipped through the ceiling trusses, paused on a beam, and dove toward the conference table. He pulled up short to avoid colliding with the table, performed a barrel roll, and hurtled toward Apollo. Apollo swatted at Eros, missed badly, and caught his hand in his own beard.

"You are wrong, Moira," Apollo said, red-faced, eyes rheumy from the self-inflicted beard tug. "Eros is not a Primordial. He is the son of two Olympians, Aphrodite and Ares."

Aphrodite blushed and exchanged a guilty glance with Ares.

Moira shook her head. "I knew Eros long before the Titan War," she said. "He was flitting about Tartarus when I was a child-god."

Apollo snapped his fingers. A pearl-encrusted ledger book appeared before him, the cover stenciled with the words "Property of Divine Resources." He flipped halfway through the book and dragged his finger down the page until he'd located whatever he was searching for. "Ah. Here we are. Eros' job application identifies him as the son of Aphrodite and Ares."

Apollo slammed the book shut. Aphrodite's cuckolded husband, Hephaestus, groaned.

"Eros clearly lied on his application," Moira said.

"Even if your allegations are true," Apollo said, "you and Eros have vastly different responsibilities."

"But of equal importance," Moira argued. "Indeed, Eros couldn't do his job without me."

"Since when is love dependent on fate?" Apollo asked.

"Without fate, love is a blind, hapless encounter," Moira said in an "isn't it obvious?" tone. "Without fate, no poet would write, 'Our love is written in the stars.' No lover would profess, 'We are meant to be together.' Without fate, love is an accident, a tantalizing pipe dream."

Murmurs of agreement percolated from her brethren around the table. An irked Apollo banged his gavel.

"Plus," Moira added, "Eros is grossly insubordinate. He perpetually violates the dress code. He doesn't wear a shred of clothing. And need I remind everyone of his poor job performance?"

Eros was an inept god of love. Not only did he fire love arrows indiscriminately, his aim was atrocious. He didn't care about improving. He never showed up to remedial archery training with Artemis. Indeed, he insisted on shooting blindfolded. Sadly, his only redeeming quality was the abdominal fat fold that mercifully shielded his infantile genitalia.

Moira had an epiphany about the true reason for her low pay. The reason cut across every divine classification in every sphere. As Gaia had told her, the reason was insidious and so ingrained in the gods' way of life as to be invisible. It was as old as time itself, persisting through the reigns of Uranus, Cronus, and Zeus. It was why Nyx, her mother, had done all the "woman's work" while Erebus was free to sit around, fattening himself on ambrosia and mead.

Moira stood and declared, "It is my female essence."

"What is?" Apollo asked.

"The reason you pay me less than Eros. He is male. I am female."

"Preposterous." Apollo huffed. "The Twelve may discriminate between classes of gods, but within classes we are equals."

"Ha!" Hermes guffawed from the other end of the table. "I am compensated the least of any of the Twelve. What else but invidious discrimination explains the discrepancy?"

"You are the most junior Olympian, dear brother," Apollo explained. "Inexperience is not an invidious distinction."

"I also have the darkest face among us. Is that invidious enough for you?" he said acidly. "If you continue to divide us, Apollo, we are doomed."

"Are you threatening rebellion, Brother?" Apollo

seethed.

"I merely appeal to your good sense, Brother."

"Be careful, Hermes," Apollo seethed. "Father is on to your machinations."

"What machinations? What outrageous lies have you told him?"

"Father dubbed you the master of lies, not I."

Hermes stewed.

Apollo noticed Moira was still standing. "Sit down already."

"I have more to say," she said.

Hermes stood. "I, too, have more to say."

"Not you too." Apollo banged his gavel. "I have the gavel." *Bang.* "And if I say we are moving on . . ." *Bang,* "we are moving on." *Bang.* "Sit, both of you!"

Moira sat. Hermes did not. He donned his gryphon hat.

"What are you doing?" Apollo demanded.

"I have to go."

"I have not adjourned council. Sit down."

"Some among us have actual work to do, Brother. The Pythia has summoned me to your temple in Delphi. She has sacrificed three calves, a dolphin, and two dozen fish in the last hour alone. It smells extremely urgent."

"Oh, the Pythia is always complaining about something," Apollo said in a pooh-poohing tone. "Her stool is uncomfortable, the myrrh sap she smokes gives her a headache, Romans are scaring off the supplicants. Blah. Blah. Blah. Her voice has an annoying drone, have you noticed? And the wench speaks everything in rhyme. So pretentious." He waved his hand. "Ignore her, Brother. The issues in Olympus are far more pressing."

"Like the overgrown hedges?" Hermes asked.

Apollo sneered. "Leave, if you must. This had better not be a ploy to steal my cattle again. The stress of your last kidnapping inflamed their teats and soured their milk," he said with an unconscious stroke of his left pectoral area.

"I gave you the lyre as recompense," Hermes remonstrated.

"A *broken* lyre."

Hermes caught himself mid-simper and wrangled his lips into a grave mien. "Sorry, Brother. The lyre slipped from my hand. I am happy to take it back if you are no longer up to serving as the patron of music."

Apollo snapped, "Just . . . just stay away from my lyre and my cows . . . and anything else that is mine." He made a shooing motion with his hands. "Go."

Hermes shut his eyes and vanished in a frisson of light and sound.

Apollo muttered to himself while fumbling for the agenda. "Where were we?"

"My paycheck," Moira said.

Apollo sighed. "A committee shall study the matter in due course."

Moira opened her mouth to protest.

"*In due course*," Apollo emphasized. "We are behind schedule. Without objection, I shall make an executive decision and direct the mountain nymphs to trim the hedges. Hearing no objection . . ." He banged his gavel and consulted the agenda. "The next item is . . ." His face sagged, as did his voice, if that were possible. "The godscape concern." He quickly added, "All in favor of tabling the item?"

Hands shot up around the table. Apollo began counting them.

Moira stood. "Point of order! We have tabled the godscape concern thrice before. The rules prohibit a fourth tabling."

Apollo grumbled, but he knew she was right. "Your point is well taken, Moira. Rules are rules."

Satisfied, Moira sat down.

Apollo scanned the disinterested faces around the table. "All in favor of suspending the numerical limit on tabling?"

Hands shot up. Apollo began counting.

Moira stood again. "This is outrageous. Shame on all of you. The godscape is coming apart at the seams. Sinkholes. Depleted soil. Buildings crumbling. Eroded levees flooding the demigods in the lowlands, forcing them into refugee camps in the foothills below your posh palaces. The faith pool has been so low for so long I can't remember the last time I scooped out a single Destiny Thread. My stock of mortal-gauge thread is so diminished I've had to splice in demigod thread to make up the difference. It's risky, but what choice do I have if we are to keep our faith-based economy afloat? I've done my part. You all must do yours. Head to Earth and mingle with the mortals. Convince believers to offer more devotions and convert non-believers."

There was a collective groan from the table.

"I get it. Proselytizing hoi polloi is slow, tedious, dirty work. Mortals are loud and unclean, but lest you forget, hoi polloi created us. We owe our existence to those fleshy bags of wind and fluid. The time for blathering at councils is over. Take action or else Olympus will collapse!"

Moira's voice echoed in the capacious room. After a pause to let her words sink in, she took her seat.

Apollo laughed nervously. "Don't you think you're being a tad alarmist, Moira? Why, this council has made tremendous strides on the godscape. We commanded wood-sprites to fell giant oaks and willows and form corduroy roads over the slush. Admittedly, we had to displace the tree-elves who called those trees home, but we paid them fair market value in nectar pellets. What else? Oh, yes. We ordered water nymphs to gather yew branches and weave them into fences to cordon off sinkholes. That cut the number of demigods plummeting into Chaos by forty percent – no, forty-*three* percent. We had the gryphons construct a wall around the unsightly refugee camp you just mentioned. Mountain nymphs are hard at work patching the levees. I could go on."

"All cosmetic fixes, Apollo. They have bought us a little time, time you all should have been out there hustling for followers."

Apollo banged the gavel. "We do not need a Primordial lecturing us on how to behave like gods."

"I beg to differ," Moira rejoined.

Apollo was about to bang his gavel again, when Eros swooped down and knocked it from his hand. The gavel clanked violently on the floor. Apollo picked it up and discovered a deep, sinuous crack in the crystal. "Curse you, Eros!"

Eros zipped out of the council room.

"Meeting adjourned!" Apollo shouted. He summoned his horseless chariot and climbed aboard. "Follow that fat fool!"

Apollo vanished in a streak of yellow light.

Dionysus invited the gods to drink mead, do lines of nectar, and sit in a shvitz fed by the River Lethe. Moira didn't join them, returning to the throne room instead. She couldn't prevent Olympus from falling, but as long as she had hands and a loom, she would do work. Not "woman's work." Just work.

CHAPTER

SEVENTEEN

Livorno, Grand Duchy of Tuscany, 1603

They appeared in back of the hat shop. The green-faced Carlotta wobbled and retched on a beaver pelt sprawled across the cutting table. Andolosia cringed. Beaver pelts didn't come cheap. But he didn't fault the hat-traveling neophyte for her misdirected vomit. He was irked at himself for leaving the pelt out in the first place. He'd used it as a pillow for cat naps during his marathon session on Sansone's hat. Fortunately, Carlotta had soiled just the upper right corner, which he could clean or, at worst, trim off. That was a relief.

Carlotta was the opposite of relieved, as she wiped hot spittle from her lips and moaned. "My head throbs. My ears are buzzing."

Andolosia placed a hand on her shoulder. "It will pass, Madonna," he said gently. "You are safe now."

She whipped her shoulder free.

"Unhand me. I was about to kill him. You ruined everything with your misguided sense of chivalry."

Andolosia was befuddled. He hadn't anticipated her

resentment. Where was the gratitude? The exclamations of joy? The hugs? The token kiss?

"But . . . But I saved you. You were bewitched by Perso's medicine, utterly at Sansone's mercy. He was going to rape you in front of all those boys."

"You fool," she said with venom. "I'd thrown up the porridge in secret and only pretended to be spellbound. I'd rubbed wine in my eyes to make them red and glassy. Do you realize how difficult it was to conceal those shears after Gino and Dino stripped me naked?"

Astonished, Andolosia's imagination ran wild. "You hid the shears on your person? Where exactly—" He waved off the question. "Had you stabbed Sansone in front of a thousand inspectors, they would've seized you. They would have hanged you for murder."

"They would have had to catch me first."

"There were a thousand inspectors and only one of you. Even if you'd escaped, they would've hunted you from the Adriatic to the Tyrrhenian Sea. Admit it, Madonna. You are very fortunate I intervened."

"You merely delayed the inevitable. Sansone won't relent. Nowhere is safe until he's dead, which he would've been had you not—" Carlotta stopped and examined her surroundings. "What exactly did you do? How did we get here? Wherever 'here' is." She fixed a reproachful gaze on him. "And why are you wearing that silly hat?"

He quickly removed the hat.

"We are in my hat shop in Livorno."

"Do you take me for a fool? Livorno is hundreds of miles from Florence."

Andolosia gestured with the hat. "This is how we are here. My Greek ancestor stole this hat from the god Hermes. Hermes used this very hat to travel between Olympus, Earth, and the underworld. He could wish himself here, there, or anywhere. This is a wishing hat."

Carlotta folded her arms. "You are as mad as Sansone."

"How would you explain being in Florence one moment and Livorno the next?"

"You say I'm in Livorno. Is that so, or am I still in Florence? This room could be anywhere. It could be in Sansone's palazzo."

Andolosia scratched his head. She had a good point.

"Don't take my word for it, Madonna. Part the curtain, step through the front door, and see for yourself. My hat shop has an excellent view of the city. Tell me if you do not see the construction cranes for the Duomo and the Jewish synagogue. Tell me if you do not see two harbors, an inner harbor with ten of the Grand Duke's galley ships, and the carracks and caravels moored in the outer harbor. Then explain to me how I managed to transport the landlocked city of Florence to the coast."

Carlotta stiffened. "I accept your challenge, Maestro," she said defiantly.

After she passed through the curtain, Andolosia heard the shop's front door open and close. A minute later, the door reopened and frantic footsteps approached the cutting room. The curtain parted, and in walked Carlotta, breathless and stupefied.

She struggled to form a coherent sentence. "But the wishing . . . the hat . . . it's the stuff of myth. 'Tis not real."

"You might say the same about water nymphs, no?" Andolosia rejoined.

Carlotta stared at him, debating whether she was bothered more by his insinuation about her nonexistence or her inability to cast doubt on her transportation across the Italian peninsula in the blink of an eye. One way or another, a miracle was at play. She had to give him that. She extended her hand toward the hat.

"May I?" she asked. Her fingers glided over the compact scaly leather. "It is so warm," she remarked.

"Gryphon leather. Even postmortem, the flesh exudes

the beast's vitality."

Her eyes widened with wonder.

"Best I put it away for now," he said.

Andolosia stuffed the hat into the wall nook and rehung the portrait.

He sighed and turned around. "You are upset with me, Madonna Carlotta," he said contritely, "and I am sorry I thwarted your carefully-planned homicide."

"Some homicides are justified," she rejoined.

"The legal niceties aren't the issue. I want you to understand I was trying to help."

She unfolded her arms and relented. "I know your intentions were honorable. For weeks, I've been caged and abused like a beast. But that does not excuse my beastly behavior toward you. I apologize, Maestro."

Andolosia's insides warmed. "Oh, there's no need to . . ." He was overcome by a floating sensation, as if he were a moon caught in her orbit. *Snap out of it, Andolosia.* He heard himself say "apologize" and clapped his hands, which broke his trance. "Good. Well, you are safe here for the time being, Madonna. Sansone is a good three days from Livorno."

"Can your hat take me to Sicily?

"It can take you anywhere you wish. But I don't recommend returning home as of yet. Surely, Sansone will seek you there."

"I hope so. I shall be ready for him, and this time I will not be interrupted."

Andolosia ignored the jab. "Is what you said in Sansone's palazzo true? Do you believe the god Apollo has possessed him?"

"I do."

"I understood the gods fell to Oblivion after the Romans sacked the Temple at Delphi."

"That they did, but Apollo figured a way out. He's been

surfacing in mortal men for twelve centuries. Every woman in my family has had to confront him at least once. But until he possessed Sansone, he hadn't survived more than a week in his mortal host. The divine candle burns too bright for the mortal coil. Only Perso's ingenious medicines sustain Sansone."

"All this because you are related to the water nymph Daphne?"

"To Daphne's twin sister, Charis, but yes."

"Fascinating. And here I'd assumed Hermes' hat was the only relic to survive the fall of Olympus."

"Are you calling me a relic? I really must look a fright."

"No. No, Madonna," he sputtered. "I did not mean it that way, although, in defense of relics, they typically are rare and valuable, and many possess unsurpassed beauty." When he realized he'd called her beautiful, he changed the subject. "Anyway," he said with a hitch in his voice, "if Sicily is where you wish to go, I shall take you there."

"I am much obliged to you, Maestro," she said through a yawn.

"Please, Madonna. Call me Andolosia."

"Very well. And you should call me Carlotta." She yawned again and stretched her arms in a feline manner. "I do not think I can withstand another journey with your hat just yet. Let us depart in the morning."

"As you wish, Carlotta."

She fixed her green eyes and severely arched eyebrows on him. "Have you a bed for me to lie upon?"

Andolosia froze, unblinking, the words "bed" and "lie" flailing about in his infatuated brain.

"Andolosia?" she said.

He snapped out of his reverie. "Yes. A bed. Follow me."

He went to the kitchen and pulled a taper from a spill vase on the oven. He opened the oven door and poked around the embers until the taper ignited. He lit a candle for

187

himself and another for her and escorted her upstairs. Only when he put his hand on the doorknob did he realize he had led her to his bed chamber. True, he wouldn't be joining her in the bed, not that evening, probably not ever. Still, she would be lying on the very bed on which he'd lain since boyhood. Her head would sag into the depression he'd made in his pillow. The blanket that had swaddled his body would swaddle hers.

"Why are we standing here?" she asked.

"Sorry."

He opened the door and gestured for her to enter.

Carlotta set the candle on the bedside table. She sat on the bed, pulled off her buckskin boots, and blew out her candle.

"See you in the morning," she said.

After she lay back, Andolosia noted that her shoulders were broader than his, extending nearly the width of the mattress. He reckoned she could take him in a fistfight. Why did that excite him? He also noted her head fit perfectly into the swale in his pillow. Were men and women with similar-sized heads more compatible? He wasn't sure. Women might prefer men with larger craniums than their own, perceiving a big head as a proxy for strength and intelligence. No, that didn't seem right either. He knew of at least two counterexamples. Madonna Vincenzo had a large, ovate head, yet her three successive husbands, and their respective skulls, had gotten progressively smaller. Also, the stevedore Jacopo had a virtual cannon ball for a head. Although slight and dumb as a rock, Jacopo's sexual dalliances were legendary.

How long had he been hovering over Carlotta, engaging in these absurd ruminations? Her eyes were closed. Could she be asleep already? Her breathing was quiet and steady, her face a slumbering blank. Yes, she was sleeping. That was a relief. Time to leave.

He was about to step toward the doorway, when he froze. He had to tread lightly. If he exited clumsily, she could awaken and take him for a predator, and, as mentioned, he didn't like his odds in hand-to-hand combat. But the idea of not moving clumsily made him hyperaware of his body. What he normally did unconsciously – taking four steps out of his bedroom – now demanded his full attention. He would have to concentrate on each individual muscle in his hips, legs, and feet to ensure they tensed, flexed, and relaxed in the appropriate order, with the appropriate degree of force, and in a coordinated manner so that his ambulation would be efficient and soundless. God's Blood! The enormity of the task overwhelmed him.

Andolosia stared at the ceiling and tried to collect himself. He needed to calm down. He took a breath and exhaled. There. He felt better, though he was confused why it suddenly was so dark in the room. Where was his candle? He was holding it. Where was the candle's flame? Blown out by his calming breath. Now what? He'd forgotten which direction he was facing, toward the door or the window. He took a partial step, and his shin bumped the bed. Carlotta stirred but didn't awaken. The pain in his shin hadn't been for naught. If the bed was in front of him, that meant the door was behind him. He turned one-hundred-eighty degrees and took small, shuffling steps with his arms out in front until he reached the wall. He groped along the wall, rejoicing when he felt a closed door. Odd. He didn't recall shutting the door. Carlotta must have closed it. No matter. He opened the door and stepped through, whereupon his face smacked into a rack of cloaks and doublets. He was in the closet. He stepped back, shut the closet door, and groped along the wall three more feet to the right. He exited to the hall and gently shut the door.

Andolosia groped his way down the dark stairs and made his way to the kitchen, which was dimly lighted by the glowing oven. He rested his head in his hands, wallowing in a dispiriting sense of failure. How preposterous for him to have thought Carlotta would fall in love with him after the rescue. Obviously, a rescue didn't entitle him to her affections any more than a drowning woman would become smitten with the rope that had pulled her from the sea. Rescuing was not wooing. He had no idea what wooing was. He had no experience in that domain. He'd spent all his free time studying gears, pulleys, and fluid dynamics, when he should have been mingling with local women at the tavern or on the floating bazaars.

Andolosia re-lit his candle and headed back upstairs. He walked to the end of the hall and entered Stasi's candlelit room. The air reeked of sickness. He called to his father, who answered weakly and unintelligibly. Andolosia pulled back the cloths over the stumps. He was horrified. The redness had returned with a rage, and the suppuration had advanced. He felt Stasi's forehead and chest. He had a high fever, and his heart was racing. Stasi wasn't going to recover.

Andolosia was crying. He couldn't lose his father. He wasn't ready to be all alone.

Stasi roused. "Ah, Andolosia. Did you rescue your mad woman of Florence? I should like to meet your lover."

Andolosia sat on the bed, beside Stasi.

"Father, Carlotta is not . . ." He trailed off. He didn't have the heart to admit the truth.

"She's not what?" Stasi asked. "Not here? Too bad. I so wanted to meet the woman with whom you'll be spending your days after mine have ended."

"She is here, but she is not awake. You can meet her in the morning."

"I haven't another morning in me. Rouse her. Bring her to me."

"Don't be so maudlin, Father. You shall see tomorrow's dawn and many dawns thereafter."

Stasi flashed him a stern glance. "Wake Carlotta. She

will understand."

Andolosia swallowed hard. Surely, it was ignoble to lie to his dying father.

Stasi was overcome by a coughing fit. It was a wet, hacking cough. The infection had reached his lungs. He hadn't much time.

Andolosia rubbed his chin nervously. Ignoble or not, he wouldn't let Stasi depart this life knowing his son was unloved and alone. A taste of hope on his parched, enervated lips, even false hope, was a blessing to the man on death's precipice. Bones moldering beneath the earth were indifferent to prevarication. Lies were the business of the living.

"As you wish, Father."

With a sickening dread in his stomach, Andolosia headed toward his bedroom door – or was it *her* bedroom door now? Suddenly, he was an interloper in his own bed chamber. How was that fair? He cracked open the door and stepped toward the bed. He assumed Carlotta wouldn't take kindly to being awakened, but his father was more important at this moment. He leaned over and spoke her name several times in a progressively louder volume. She remained blissfully asleep. He jostled her shoulder, and her eyes popped open. Her expression morphed from vacant, to confused, to supremely irritated. She pressed her hand squarely into Andolosia's face and pushed him away.

"It is not yet morning. Let me sleep," she groaned.

"Carlotta. I'm sorry. I wouldn't have awakened you unless it was important."

Abruptly, she turned and sat up. "Is Sansone here?"

"What? No, nothing like that."

"Then get the hell out of my room."

Affronted, Andolosia started to say, "Excuse me. This room belongs—" But she pressed her hand in his face before he could complete the sentence. She pounded the pillow and lay back down.

"Listen, Carlotta," he said with urgency. "My father is dying. I fear he has only hours to live. When I mentioned you to him earlier, he got the impression there was something more between you and me. It's absurd, of course, because we barely know one another, but he worries I will be alone after he passes. You're the first woman I've ever brought home. Might I prevail upon you to pretend you have affection for me. I understand if you must refuse. After all, you just escaped a man who demanded something very similar of you. Be assured, however, I am nothing like Sansone. I expect nothing more of you than a brief, noble lie to comfort my dying father. I will still take you to Sicily tomorrow, as promised. I—"

"In which room does your father lie?" she asked.

She swung her legs off the bed and planted her bare feet on the floor. She rose from the bed and stepped into the hallway.

"End of the hall," Andolosia said.

Andolosia regretted not tidying up Stasi's room first. He should have opened the window to air out the putrid odors and placed a sheet over the raw infected stumps. At a minimum, he should have wiped the bits of dried mucus from Stasi's upper lip. Carlotta, however, seemed unperturbed upon entering. Her nostrils didn't flare or flinch. Her eyes didn't goggle at the feverish amputee in pus-soaked bedsheets. She saw only a man. A father. She sat near Stasi's head and took his hand. She held it with such affection and familiarity, Andolosia had to remind himself they weren't actually father and daughter. She was playing her part to perfection. And when Stasi rolled his head toward her, he unwittingly played his part of the ignorant dying man. His eyelids peeled back in excitement. His face broke into the radiant smile he hadn't flashed since Bianca's death. His broad grin stressed his chapped lips, causing tiny, bloodless fissures to erupt. His revitalized cheeks shone like overripe cherry tomatoes.

"Carlotta?" Stasi asked.

She nodded.

Stasi beamed. "I am so happy to meet you. Normally I stand in a lady's presence, but in case you haven't noticed, I have no legs." He laughed at his morbid joke and broke into a coughing fit.

"You remind me of my father," Carlotta said after the coughing abated.

"Oh? Does he make hats too?"

"He is a traveler, an expert in rivers and dikes. He advises cities throughout Europe how to work with the flow of water, instead of against it. He urges compromise and compassion instead of domination and control. He says rivers crave their freedom. No different than people in that regard."

"What a beautiful philosophy," Stasi said. "I believe he and I would've become fast friends."

"Perhaps one day you will."

Stasi hummed a non-committal sound and then changed the subject. "Tell me about your mother. No doubt your beauty derives from her. Where does her expertise lie?"

"Baking. She makes the best mafalda bread in Taormina."

"Ooh. I wish I had a mafalda right this moment." Stasi squeezed her hand. "My son has chosen well, or should I say, you have chosen poorly."

Stasi winked at Andolosia, who felt a wave of moist heat erupt around his collar.

"You are Sicilian, no?" Stasi asked.

"I am."

"Good. That is very good. Listen. Both of you." Stasi nodded to Andolosia. "You should go to Monticello."

"I know this place," Carlotta said. "It is a day's donkey ride from Taormina."

"My good friend Gennaro Rabino lives there," said Stasi. "I have bought deerskins, beaver pelts, and rabbit hides from him for decades, as did my father before me. Gennaro is a good, honest man. He can give you two sanctuary until the Medici threat abates."

"That is most kind, Maestro Petasos," Carlotta said, patting his hand. "After you get well, we shall go together."

"Sweet child, we both know my candle is nearly extinguished. Do not linger here on my account."

"Nonsense," Carlotta chided, voice trembling. "I must return to bed." She cleared her throat, wiped her leaky eye, and headed to the doorway. "Forgive me, Maestro."

"Please," Stasi said. "We are family now. Call me Father."

She fixed an uncompromising gaze on him. "I shall see you in the morning, Father. I expect you to teach me all about hats."

"Andolosia has ten times my skill," Stasi said.

"That is because you have given him ten times the love most fathers give their children."

Carlotta departed, leaving Stasi and Andolosia gaping at the empty doorway.

"Don't lose her, Andolosia. She is a rare find."

Stasi broke into a long, hacking coughing fit. Andolosia propped him with pillows, gave him a handkerchief to stifle the coughs and rubbed his back until the fit subsided.

After his father had settled, Andolosia excused himself to thank Carlotta for her performance. But when he reached her bedroom, he heard muffled sobs on the other side of the door. This had been more than a performance for her. Her grief was genuine. He felt terrible. He wanted to burst in and console her. He wanted to wrap her in his arms and hold her. But he wouldn't intrude again. He returned to his father's deathbed.

Stasi drifted in and out of lucidity the rest of the night.

His lungs filled with mucus while his ability to clear them deteriorated. Labored breaths led to delirium. He began speaking to the empty space beside Andolosia, believing Bianca was there. He laughed at her Barbary pirate get-up – the mustache and beard and the towel wrapped around her head. After incoherent conversation with the specter, his smile faded. He remarked that Bianca's skin was bluer than before. He patted the bed and told her to lie with him. He reached for her apparitional hand and said, "Fate has smiled upon us. The sea is smooth as glass today." Those would be his final words.

At sunrise, Andolosia set a decanter of hot coffee on the kitchen table and took the chair closest to the oven. He rested his chin on his hands and observed the steam curling into nothingness, imagining that his father's essence had dissipated into the same invisible place where steam went to die. Bleary-eyed Carlotta entered the kitchen. She inhaled the scent of the exotic beverage and sat opposite Andolosia. He acknowledged her with a nod and poured her a cup. She took a tentative sip and, after relishing the bitterness and ensuing rush of giddiness, took a gulp.

"He's dead," Andolosia said without affect.

"Oh, Andolosia."

Carlotta put her hand on his. Yesterday, that gesture would've set his heart a-pounding. Today, he felt nothing. Her touch was an expression of sympathy, no more. It was a heartless convention.

"Thank you for going along with the deception last night," he said. "I just realized I failed to consider that you might be betrothed to someone. I imagine that would've made your duplicity all the more difficult. I apologize."

"No need. I am not betrothed."

Andolosia's interest was piqued. "Oh."

"Nor shall I ever be. I have foresworn marriage and children. It is the only way to end our infernal curse."

His interest waned. "Oh. That's logical, I suppose. Still, asking you to perpetuate a deception on a dying man was a lot to ask."

"I wasn't entirely duplicitous. Stasi really does remind me of my father. They have the same bulging, beguiling eyes, that same fixed expression of 'I don't know what's next, but I cannot wait to find out.'"

Andolosia chuckled. "I never noticed that about him, but you're right. Maybe that's where I got my inquisitiveness. I always thought I got that from my mother. The littlest things excited her. A butterfly. Fresh bread. A new codpiece."

"Perhaps you got it from both of them."

He nodded.

After a silence, Carlotta said, "I learned baking from my mother, but, deep down, I wanted to follow my father's path. He took me to his projects when they were close to home. He'd show me his plans for seal walls, dikes, and diversion ponds. He'd ask my opinions. On occasion, he altered his designs based on my input. At least he said he did. As his reputation grew, his work drew him farther from home – eventually, all the way to Denmark. My mother's whole family is in Sicily, also her bakery, so we couldn't go with him. I begged him to take me, but he wouldn't. He said the northern seas were no place to rear his 'delicate flower.' That's what he called me. His 'delicate flower.' I wonder. Might he have been willing to uproot his delicate flower had I been his son?"

She took a slow sip of coffee and then continued.

"He visits every few years. For all we know, he has a whole other family in Copenhagen, a second wife who bore him a brood of sons. A veritable forest of sturdy, Scandinavian evergreens."

"My father asked to be buried on the bluff overlooking the harbor," Andolosia said. "It is not a cemetery, so I must dig the grave myself. There won't be a service. Maybe a few words from his friends. He had many—" His voice caught on his grief. He stood, and as he passed Carlotta, he added, "When I return, I shall take you to Sicily."

Carlotta grasped Andolosia's forearm. "Have you a second shovel?"

* * *

Carlotta rifled through Bianca's closet for something to wear to the funeral other than her skimpy nymph outfit. It was no easy task. She didn't think it appropriate to mourn in the guise of a court jester, pirate, or Capuchin monk. She narrowed her choices to three options: a silken gown with a pomegranate motif popular a century earlier; a gray doublet and breeches with a matching gray mustache; and a similar ensemble in crimson with a matching red beard and codpiece. Since she would be assisting with the grave-digging, she settled on the less formal, crimson doublet and breeches – sans beard and codpiece.

Friends, fellow merchants on the Via Ferdinanda, bureaucrats from the Customs House, professors from the University of Pisa, fabric suppliers, and a smattering of prostitutes gathered at the mulberry tree on the bluff. All wore hats, most of which were Petasos hats. A bird's-eye view revealed a mélange of felted flat caps, woolen berets, velvet bonnets, conical hennin hats, silk turbans, crimson fez, four-peaked biretta, and plaited straw hats. The fanciest hats were accented with ostrich or peacock feathers or adorned with delicate taffeta, damask, or gold-threaded brocade.

Andolosia hadn't planned a formal service, just a gathering for friends and customers. Thus he was surprised to learn that word of Stasi's death had wended its way to the Archbishop of Pisa. When Monsignor Carlo Antonio Dal

Pozzo showed up at the mulberry tree, bedecked in a mitre cap and bejeweled vestments, Andolosia worried the memorial would take on an overly religious bent. It didn't, though.

The Monsignor queued between a professor of mathematics from the University of Pisa and a Livornese prostitute. Once at the graveside, he spoke not as a priest but as a friend. He told a story about meeting Stasi in 1582, just before his consecration as archbishop. Stasi had delivered him two, white silk mitre hats, one plain and unadorned, the other ornamented with gold disks, embroidery, and scores of pearls. The Monsignor recalled telling Stasi that the ostentatious hat reminded him of the Book of Matthew's Parable of the Pearl: "The kingdom of heaven is like unto a merchant man, seeking good pearls: who, when he had found one pearl of great price, went and sold all that he had, and bought it." Stasi told the Monsignor he had bought just such a pearl and it hadn't cost him a single florin, only his soul. The alarmed Monsignor worried Stasi had made a deal with the Devil, until Stasi clarified that his pearl was his wife, Bianca, who would be tickled to know the Archbishop of Pisa considered her the antichrist.

The Monsignor's anecdote inspired laughter, but it tugged at Andolosia's heartstrings. He might have begun weeping had Carlotta's tear ducts not preempted him. Damning his inhibition, he draped an arm around her shoulders. The warmth of her body counterbalanced the sagging weight of his grief. He kept his arm there until the last of the mourners departed.

Andolosia picked up the shovels and handed one to Carlotta. He peered at the pine casket resting at the grave's black bottom. The instructions for the wishing hat popped into his head: *First, think of the place. Then, ask the hat to take you there. Not the other way around.* He hadn't a clue why he'd thought that. His father was dead, and whether his next destination was an afterlife or eternal nothingness, he wouldn't need a wishing hat to get there. So, Andolosia latched onto a different idea, one without instructions, one that didn't require a miracle to be realized: *Farewell, Father.*

* * *

After hiking back to town, they propped the shovels against the cutting room wall, next to Stasi's mechanical legs. Exhausted, Carlotta retired to her bed chamber, and Andolosia retreated to his father's room. Both collapsed on their respective beds and drifted into slumber, which, they'd hoped, would last until morning. It didn't.

In the dead of night, Andolosia awoke to Carlotta standing over him, vigorously jostling his shoulder.

"Wake up!" she said in a panicked whisper. "Wake up!"

"Wha— What is it?"

He gave a fright when he glimpsed her. The moonlight through the window distorted her face in hideous chiaroscuro.

"There's an intruder," she said. "Do you hear?"

Andolosia listened to the silence for thirty seconds.

"I don't hear anything. Go back to sleep."

"Just wait."

Seconds later, there was a thumping and a rustling downstairs, followed by a series of clicks, whirrs, and hums.

Andolosia swung his legs off the bed. "Stay here."

He headed down the hallway and descended the stairs. He found no one in the cutting room. He paused there and listened from behind the heavy velvet curtain. Distinct mechanical sounds – whirring flywheels and cranking pulleys – were coming from the front of the store. He looked for an object to protect himself from whatever was lurking in front. He perused the bolts of cloth, hat blocks, tape measures, pliers, and thimbles. None of those would do. He considered the shears and the iron before deciding those implements would necessitate a close-up confrontation. He settled on the hat stand. It was long, and the iron base would make a serviceable bludgeon. He counted to three and flung open the curtain. The intruder knocked him to the floor and stepped across his chest.

Andolosia wildly swung the hat stand from his prone position. He missed the intruder and caught the curtain instead. The curtain rod broke from its moorings, and the drape smothered him. Andolosia shook the drape from his head. The intruder walked into the tall cabinet of hat blocks, turned, and ploughed into a desk where the accounts were kept. More astonishingly, the intruder didn't back away from the desk. He appeared hell-bent on pushing the desk through the wall.

Carlotta descended the stairs and screamed a litany of vile threats at the intruder, whom she assumed was Sansone, even though he couldn't possibly have arrived in Livorno so soon. One bizarre threat entailed baking Sansone's testicles into a focaccia and force-feeding it through his nose. Andolosia momentarily fixated on the logistics of following through with the threat. Focaccia dough was far too thin to accommodate all but the most abnormally small testicles or abnormally large nostrils.

"For God's sake, Andolosia!" Carlotta shouted. "Get up!"

Andolosia kicked off the drape and stood. The intruder still hadn't turned from the desk. Andolosia was now more curious than afraid. The intruder appeared to have neither torso nor head. Moreover, he was wearing Stasi's shoes and pants. Andolosia glanced at the wall, where they'd propped the shovels. Both lay on the floor. He deduced that one of the shovels had slid into the catch on the legs' spring mechanism, setting them in motion.

"No reason for panic," Andolosia said reassuringly. "Only my dead father's legs."

He flicked the catch on the legs, and they stopped.

"Get the wishing hat," Carlotta demanded, shaking with fear and rage. "Wish us to Sicily immediately. I cannot remain here one second more."

"We should get some more sleep. Sansone is still more than two days away," he protested, "and that's assuming he comes to Livorno first."

"I don't care. I can't sleep here. I refuse to risk another attack from a stray body part, mechanical or otherwise. Either you wish me to Monticello, or I shall start walking."

Andolosia sighed. "As you wish," he said dejectedly.

"Thank you."

Andolosia started toward the stairs.

"Where are you going?" she asked.

"To pack."

"Pack? Why? All you need is the wishing hat."

"If you don't mind, I'd like to bring clothes, maybe a few tools, and some remembrances."

"That hardly seems necessary for a quick wish to Monticello and back."

"I'm not coming back to Livorno, Carlotta. I can't. The Petasos hat business is finished here. When Sansone arrives, he will have me arrested and tortured for your whereabouts."

"Fair enough. But you have the wishing hat. You can go anywhere."

"And I choose Monticello," he insisted.

"Why?"

"As my father said, I have a family friend there. Gennaro Rabino."

"You have family nowhere else?"

"I have an aunt in Prussia. What's with the inquisition? Does my presence so offend you that we cannot even reside in the same town?"

"That's not what I'm saying, Andolosia."

"What are you saying then?"

"That we have our separate lives, and you shouldn't burden yourself with my curse."

"Lest you forget, I, too, am cursed. Regardless, I can't simply drop you in Monticello and leave. You require a proper introduction to Maestro Rabino."

"I suppose you are right."

"Of course I am right," he snapped. "When that is done, then, and only then, shall I consider a different place to settle." He added in a martyr's voice, "Don't worry, Carlotta. You won't have to endure my presence for much longer."

Andolosia wheeled around to head upstairs. She seized his forearm.

"Wait, Andolosia. Just wait."

His red, pouty face oozed hurt.

"You haven't troubled me at all," she said, now contrite. "I have treated you poorly in your time of grief. Please forgive me. Will you forgive me?"

Rheumy-eyed, he nodded. "Can I go now?" He tried extricating his arm, but she wouldn't let go.

"I have one more thing to say. If you truly want to make a new life in Monticello – if you are making that decision of your own free will and not out of some misguided sense of chivalry – I welcome the company. It would be good to have a friend in a strange place."

His face brightened. "It is good to have a friend anywhere."

"Indeed." Carlotta gave him a peck on the cheek. "Go. Pack your things."

Spirits soaring, Andolosia practically floated upstairs.

CHAPTER

EIGHTEEN

Delphi, 390 C.E.

Hermes appeared on the southern slope of Mount Parnassus. A riot was underway at Apollo's Temple. Bemused Roman soldiers stood by as men pulverized the limestone columns, toppled and urinated on statues of Zeus and Poseidon, smashed urns and oil lamps, and denounced "pagan polytheists."

The Pythian priestess approached Hermes, flanked by two toga-wearing priests. She was clad in flowing white robes and adorned with elaborate gold jewelry. A purple veil obscured most of her face. Her crow's feet and wrinkled brow belied her youthful maiden costume.

An animalistic shout came from the temple. A chunk of limestone – the nose from the Zeus statue – sailed over Hermes' head. He ducked and asked with alarm, "What goes on here?"

The Pythia answered in a solemn monotone, her eyes fixed in a state of rapture. "The Roman emperor favors his church. The other gods does he besmirch. Christ, for him, is the only true lord. He is behind this destructive horde."

"What can be done?" Hermes asked.

The Pythia handed him a scroll. "Take it to Apollo with all speed and haste, lest all the gods' temples be reduced to waste."

Hermes unrolled the scroll and read it aloud. "Thy followers have dwindled; they no longer believe. Show thyself now; the Temple closes this eve." He rolled up the scroll, shaking his head. "Apollo won't show. My brother is in complete and utter denial."

"If he does not come, Olympus is done," the priestess said ominously.

Hermes knitted his brow. *I see what Apollo means by her incessant rhyming.*

"What do you expect Apollo to do?"

"Inspire his followers to take up their arms. Spare his best temple from further harm."

Hermes scoffed. "My brother? Inspire? He's the most boring god in the pantheon. He inspires us gods to fall into slumber. He'll put mortals to sleep for nineteen Novumbers."

She has me rhyming now . . . and badly at that.

The Pythia narrowed her eyes. "How else can we keep all the Romans at bay? Please tell us, young Hermes, or be on your way."

Hermes sighed with resignation. "I don't have a better idea. Fine. I shall fetch my brother. I expect he is still blathering away at council."

"Godspeed and good luck," the Pythian intoned.

As she began her second couplet, Hermes formed a mental image of the council room and wished the hat to take him there.

"Should you not find him, we all are—"

Hermes vanished on her last word. An instant later, he reappeared in the council room. Everyone, Apollo included, was gone.

Where in Hades is he?

* * *

A frenzied Hermes burst into the throne room and scanned the space.

"No! Where is he? Where is he?"

He paced back and forth, stopped, paced some more, and stopped again. He groaned in frustration and began humming nervously and fidgeting with the Pythia's scroll.

Moira paused the loom and did a double-take at Hermes. She'd been too distracted during council to notice he had matured into a stunning specimen. He'd cast off his staid tunic in favor of two strategically-placed leather flaps held up by crisscrossing suspenders. The new uniform left little to the imagination. The strap of his shoulder bag angled across his naked sternum, accentuating well-defined pectoralis muscles. His burnished-bronze thighs and partially-exposed buttocks shimmered in the lamplight. Moira felt a sexual thrill, which instantly evaporated when she focused on his face. He had the same bone structure as his father and brother. She imagined Hermes' face straining and contorting as he approached climax, turning ghost white like his brother's, old and drawn like his father's.

Yick.

"Ah, Moira. Have you seen Apollo?" Hermes asked urgently. "He's not in the council room."

"Sorry. I have not."

"Did he say where he went?"

"No. After we adjourned, we all went our separate ways. Can't you wish yourself to him?"

Hermes sighed. "My wishing hat takes me to places, not people. If I don't know where he is, the hat is useless."

Moira gestured toward the throne, where Zeus sat in a slouch, head tipped forward into his unkempt beard. He hadn't moved in ages.

He really needs a thorough dusting. I should speak to the house-sprites.

"Your father might know," Moira said. "He's near omniscient on a good day. Of course, his last good day was a thousand years ago."

Hermes didn't dignify Moira's suggestion with a response. Instead, he swung his satchel to his belly, opened the flap, and fished around inside. He pulled out a set of mantic dice, which consisted of five knucklebones engraved with numbers. He squatted, rolled the dice, and scurried over to them. He picked up each die and added the numbers on the undersides.

"Twenty-eight," he said.

He retrieved a tiny book from his rear flap. Where he'd been storing it in that skimpy costume, Moira hadn't a clue. He flipped to page twenty-eight.

"According to the Oracle Key, twenty-eight means Gaia will give me the ripe fruit of my labors." He shut the book and smacked it on his thigh. "What in Hades does getting fruit from that Primordial bitch goddess have to do with finding Apollo?" He shot Moira an apologetic look. "Sorry. It just came out. Of course, you are not a—"

"A Primordial bitch goddess? You flatter me," she said sarcastically. Moira didn't blame the young, impressionable god too much. No doubt, he was employing the private epithet Zeus and Apollo had given her.

Hermes scooped up the mantic dice and rattled them in his hand. He squeezed them tightly, as if their meaning was juice trapped in a lemon. He made a fed-up groan. "My brother made a great show of gifting these to me. He promised they would give me oracular vision equal to his. Ha! Why does he get all the good powers?"

Hermes did not know that only Gaia possessed the gift of foresight. After Zeus exiled Gaia, Apollo perpetuated the myth that he'd slain her dragon, Python, and deposed her as the brains behind the oracles.

Frustrated, Hermes whipped the dice across the throne room.

"You might check Apollo's palace," Moira suggested.

Hermes grunted derisively. He closed his eyes. The hat emitted a flash and blasted a brassy shriek. He was gone.

Hermes' noisy departure caused Zeus to stir. His eyelids fluttered open as he struggled to shake off the mantle of sleep.

"Ah, Moira," the bleary-eyed Zeus said, his voice dry and weak. "Has Apollo solved the crisis?"

"I'm afraid not, my lord. Unless you Olympians secure new followers, we are destined for Oblivion."

Zeus sat up on the throne, more alert. "How long do we have?"

"At this rate, a century, maybe decades," she said grimly.

"Come now, Moira. You are Fate. Simply weave us a new destiny, one that restores us and the godscape. Shall I provide you the design?"

How many times had the senile Zeus popped awake and made that same suggestion? Countless. It wouldn't be the last either.

She mustered the semblance of a considerate tone and said, "I cannot weave fates for gods without divine Destiny Thread. I depleted that spool crafting tapestries for your brethren. Since then, the faith pool has not produced any more."

Stiffly, Zeus rose from the throne and shambled toward her. At twice her height, he blocked the light from the oil-burning chandelier, thrusting her into a chilly shadow. He lingered behind her. His dusty exhalations buffeted her neck with the reek of the stale honey and spoiled ambrosia trapped in his beard. He grazed her bare shoulder with his fingernail.

"Such a lovely creature, Moira is," he said to no one in particular. Filtered through his ossified vocal cords, the compliment projected all the seductiveness of a rusty gate hinge.

He bent low, moistened his lips, and pressed them to her cheek. The gargantuan kiss felt like the slap of a kraken tentacle. His lips made a suction sound when he peeled them off her cheek. Following that came a whooshing from his backside.

How lovely. First, a kraken kiss. Then, divine flatulence.

Zeus' mitt of a hand pawed at Moira's right breast. Because of the clumsy, brutish character of his grope, she initially assumed he'd lost his balance, propelled by the force of his recent emission. But no, the breast fumble was his demented conception of a romantic gesture.

"If there is insufficient thread for all of Olympus," Zeus said breathily, "then weave your father a new fate and forget about the rest."

The word "father" from Zeus' lips was a vile profanity. She had a stabbing memory of the disgusting Myrrha affair and losing Tyche. She swallowed the acid burbling up to her throat and said, "There is not enough thread on the spool for you."

Mercifully, Zeus backed off and rounded to the side of the loom.

"What about the weft you have weaved so far?"

"My lord, this tapestry is for a mortal hatter. The gauge of thread is far too thin for a god of your stature. I've spliced in some demigod thread to fill in the gaps, but that procedure won't work for a god as great as you."

Zeus descried the rafters, where the gods' tapestries hung. "I see god-gauge thread all around us."

"I do not follow."

"Up there. Fashion me a new fate with thread from my brethren's tapestries."

"Their tapestries are so old, my lord. I fear the threads

will disintegrate if I attempt to untie them. Beyond that, destroying a god's tapestry will have devastating consequences. To be unmoored from one's fate so abruptly, without a replacement fate, will induce madness and despair. There could be mass suicides."

"I share your fear. Nevertheless, their extinction is a worthy sacrifice for their father."

Moira regarded Zeus' craggy face. His mottled skin was etched with rivers of conquest that time had fractured into a million aimless rivulets. She was horrified that a father, even one wracked with dementia, could behave so callously toward his "children."

Zeus added, reassuringly, "They will understand, my child."

"You should call a council and advise them of your plan," Moira said.

"No."

"But Apollo's bylaws call for . . ."

The air electrified. A black cloud gathered overhead, obscuring the Titanic frescoes on the vaulted ceiling. Zeus' shell-white cheeks flushed red. His head quaked. His aquamarine irises turned a deep, empty black.

Moira braced herself. Zeus struck her with the back of his hand. Jagged knuckles impressed her cheek and rattled her teeth. A second slap ejected her ten feet from the loom. She landed with a thud and streaked another twenty feet across the marble floor. If only that had been the extent of his wrathful outburst. In the tumult, a skein of Destiny Thread dislodged from Moira's robe.

Zeus nudged the wad of yarn with his toe. "What is this?" He picked up the skein and answered his own question. "It is Destiny Thread, and the threads are thick enough for a god. Deceiver! You dare keep this from me!"

Moira stood, wobbly. A hurried self-audit confirmed her limbs were still attached and functional.

"My lord, that skein contains the leftover cuttings from the tapestries I wove for your brethren. I didn't mention it because the quantity is insignificant. To weave a tapestry for you, I would need a skein a hundred times larger."

Zeus brought the skein to his mouth, as if about to bite into a tarry black apple.

Is he going to eat my thread? No. That would be ridic—

Zeus bit a hunk out of the skein and gulped it without chewing. He whipped the ravaged skein at Moira, grazing her head. The veins in his forehead were pulsating. She braced herself for another punch that wasn't forthcoming. Instead, Zeus ascended the throne. He raised his arms and fanned his fingers. The blood-red faith at the bottom of the reflecting pool gurgled and sloshed. Ripples morphed into waves, and the waves morphed into a swirl. The current spun itself into a throbbing red vortex around the copper pipe. By degrees, the vortex uncoiled into a teeming braid and rose from the pool like a watery, faceless snake. The braid slithered onto the floor, coiled around Zeus' feet, and corkscrewed around his legs, waist, torso, and neck until he was cocooned in a red, seething skin.

Zeus opened his mouth.

"No, my lord!" Moira pleaded. "You will end us all!"

The faith rushed into his mouth and down his throat, every last drop. He wiped his lips with the back of his hand. His skin incandesced with the red-orange heat of a thousand furnaces. He jutted his chin out with an air of conquest, ignorant that his reinvigoration was ephemeral, the showy death throes of a swelling red giant sun about to consume the worlds it once had nurtured.

"My lord, you must regurgitate the faith or else Oblivion awaits us!"

"Not all of us," Zeus said cavalierly. "Not the king."

"What is a king without a kingdom?"

"Get it through your distaff brain, Moira. I am the

210

kingdom!"

He lowered his right arm and pointed at Moira.

"No!" she yelled.

Moira recoiled from his glowing fingertip. Everything went black. When she roused, her ears were ringing, and spots and streaks muddled her vision. Her robe was in tatters, skin singed. She clambered to her feet and inspected the smoldering loom. Zeus' lightning had crazed the wood's glossy varnish, but it was otherwise intact. She stumbled backward. The palace floor was heaving and buckling. Buttresses and pillars crashed to the floor and sublimated into dust. The copper pipe detached from the ceiling and toppled.

The palace stopped shaking. Zeus lay on the floor by the throne, deathly pale and unconscious.

The fool!

Moira rushed to the window. Black, starless rents had emerged in the daytime sky, as though riven by a galactic-sized claw. The atmosphere was escaping into the void, causing hawks and crows, swallows and hummingbirds, and gryphons and dragons to plummet. Avalanches tumbled down mountain peaks and escarpments. Oaks and pines crumbled into dust piles. Valleys and plains were tearing themselves apart, exposing craggy black canyons and bottomless crevasses. Lowland creatures scurried for stable ground, many falling into the spontaneous voids, others dangling by their fingers. Worst of all, the devitalization of the heavens wasn't confined to its epicenter at Mount Olympus. It was expanding like concentric ripples in a pond. They had days, if not hours, before it reached and breached Oceanus' levees.

Moira pushed away from the window and picked up the skein of Destiny Thread. She wiped Zeus' slobber on her robe and inspected the hunk he'd bitten off.

Curse him!

The skein had contained just enough thread to weave a modest fate for herself and Tyche. She'd already planned the design. They would reign over a sparsely-populated Aegean island of contented, coconut-gathering mortals. No loom, no fates, and absolutely no burnt offerings. Just uninterrupted quiet and clean sea air. But now that fate was out of reach. The Olympian king's fat mouth had seen to that.

Don't despair. Maybe you can salvage it.

She unfurled the skein and laid out the strands in rows. By the looks of it, she was five yards short.

What if . . .

She darted to the Loom of Destiny. She unwound the weft of the incomplete tapestry and severed the knots binding the fragments of mortal and demigod threads. She spliced the mortal fragments into one long strand and did the same to the demigod fragments. She spun the two strands around each other, forming a single thread with the girth of a god-gauge thread. Whether Moira's mongrel thread would function like a true god-gauged thread was an open question. It was also a hypothetical question because she was still two yards shy.

The only option was to borrow thread from the finished tapestries overhead. Well, not "borrow." *Steal* was the operative word, because she did not plan to return it to the donor-gods. Moira was well aware of her hypocrisy. She'd lambasted Zeus for proposing the very same solution. But, unlike Zeus, she required only two measly yards. For the donor-gods, it would be the fate-altering equivalent of a toenail clipping. No one ever went suicidal from a toenail clipping. And, by taking threads from two tapestries, she would cut the already miniscule risk in half.

She grabbed a hooked pole propped against the wall and fished the two tapestries that were directly overhead. She unraveled a yard from each, spliced them together, spliced the purloined threads with the strand she'd cobbled together, and wound the concoction around the empty spool. She tied the free end of the thread to the shuttle. She was ready to weave.

Clipped toenails. They won't notice a thing. Probably.

A massive sinkhole opened in the floor, its lip inches from where Moira stood. Zeus' golden throne plummeted into the void. His thick, white-haired legs hung over the edge. One more quake, and he was on his way to Oblivion. Shrill howls from terrified servant-sprites echoed in distant corridors.

Hands don't fail me now!

Moira threw the shuttle through the shed between the warp threads and tamped the row twice with the batten. *Thub dup. Thub dup.* Faster and faster, she wove. Back and forth. *Thub dup. Thub dup.* To and fro. *Thub dup. Thub dup.* Her feet danced across the treadles as if they were on fire. *Thub dup. Thub dup.* Her hands and arms became a weaving blur. Perspiration cascaded down her forehead. *Thub dup. Thub dup.* She couldn't feel herself throwing the shuttle or pulling the batten, nor her bare feet pressing and releasing the treadles. Yet she had to be doing these things because a tapestry was taking shape. *Thub dup. Thub dup.* But a more insidious doubt crept in. *Thub dup. Thub dup.* Was she following her design? Any design at all? *Thub dup. Thub dup.* Her chest tightened. Her breathing turned rapid and shallow. She was light-headed. *Thub dup. Thub dup.* She saw the loom from above, as though hovering above it and looking down on herself. *Thub dup. Thub dup.* Her perspective narrowed to a funnel. She was on the verge of passing out. She had to—

Stop!

Moira sat back from the loom, panting hard. She wiped her brow with her forearm. She held her crabbed, quivering hands before her, regarding them like foreign objects, as if a sculptor had replaced her real hands with marble facsimiles. Her aching, cramped wrists and fingers gave off a sticky heat. She despaired. Her pain and effort had been for naught. The tapestry was unfinished. Three rows remained. She was so close to completion, but close didn't matter with a fate tapestry. A destiny was either finished or non-existent. There was no such thing as "a little bit fated."

Moira sensed a presence behind her. She turned to see a drawn, haggard reflection of herself. The woman's robe was filthy and tattered. Her sandals were so worn, it was a miracle they clung to her feet.

"Tyche?"

Her long-lost sister smiled wanly.

Moira embraced Tyche. Her heart ached when she felt her sister's uninsulated ribs and hip bones. Oh, how she'd suffered! Moira was about to ask Tyche how she'd escaped her prison when sensations flooded her mind. They were rich with sight and sound, smell and taste. Somehow, she was reliving Tyche's memories. She was lying on a rough stone bench in a grimy cell when the Clarion Call Network announced the coming deluge. The jailers' keys jangled. Cylinders turned in locks. Hundreds of cell doors creaked open. Footsteps shuffled. She exited her cell for the first time in a millennium. She meandered through the basalt catacombs, following stupefied inmates to the central courtyard. Python was there, nostrils purring with idling flames. From the mount, Mother Gaia said, "Ride with me to Olympus. The cosmos needs you. Your sister needs you." She extended a frail arm to the Earth Mother, who hoisted her onto the dragon mount. As they soared from sphere to sphere, Gaia whispered in her ear, describing how to complete the tapestry of interconnected destinies and "plant the seed of the three sisters."

Moira broke from the reverie. "The three sisters? I don't understand, Tyche."

Tyche sat at the loom. She took a deep breath, threw the shuttle through the shed in the warp, and caught it with her opposite hand. Quickly, she fell into a rhythm of throw and catch, while her feet tapped and pressed the treadles. She twisted and knotted and layered the thread, compressing a kaleidoscope of possibilities into a mere three rows of yarn.

Exhausted, Tyche set down the shuttle. She reached for the shears but was too weak to lift them. Moira picked them up for her.

"Let me. You rest now, Sister."

Tyche had a faraway expression. Her pupils were pinpricks. Her skin looked dry and granular, like dried mud.

Moira was filled with horror. "What's happening to you?"

Reddish-brown dust was accumulating at Tyche's disintegrating feet. The erosion had raced up her legs and was encroaching on her neck. Moira was speechless, so Tyche spoke for the both of them.

"Do not grieve, Sister. You wove me from your soul. I will always be part of you, and you will always be part of me."

The word "me" faded to a whisper as the last of Tyche turned to dust.

Grief wasn't an option for Moira. The world was ending. She focused on what she and Tyche had shared – the one and only thing she could control in her final moments in the heavens – the work. She raised the shears. She opened the blades and brought them to the top warp threads. But just as she was about to snip, she hesitated. Something was off. She leaned over the tapestry and scrutinized the final three rows.

No. No, this cannot be my fate. What did Tyche do?

Moira's remote Aegean island? Gone. Her gaggle of contented coconut-gatherers? Gone. Her uninterrupted quiet and clean sea air? Gone and gone. Gaia never should have entrusted Tyche's prison-addled mind to execute her instructions. Clearly, Tyche had made a profound mistake. But there was no time to undo the weft and rework it. The great deluge was nigh. There was only one thing Moira could do.

Amor Fati.

Moira snipped the warp threads, top and bottom, removed the tapestry from the loom, and held it tight to her chest. As she awaited the inevitable fall, an insuppressible laugh tickled the back of her throat.

CHAPTER

NINETEEN

Monticello, Sicily, 1603

They gathered in the cutting room at sunrise with their valises. Carlotta's valise contained two of Bianca's outfits, an ebony hairbrush inlaid with a mother-of-pearl vortex pattern, and some sundries. Andolosia's contained linen chemises, doublets, and breeches; medical and engineering texts; and millinery tools. He'd also tossed in a handful of pearls, a bobbin of silver thread, and a dozen golden brooches. He could barter them, if necessary. He also had several hundred florins in the purse around his neck. Tucked under his arm was a hat box, empty except for an ancient gold coin bearing Hermes' face. The wishing hat was on his head. He took Carlotta's hand and told her to exhale. Stasi's letters from Gennaro Rabino mentioned the Lake Monticello dam, which, at that early hour, seemed as discreet a spot as any to appear out of thin air. Andolosia exhaled.

The base of the Lake Monticello dam.
Take me there.

They arrived at an immense stone wall mortared with

red concrete.

A wobbly Carlotta gasped and exclaimed, "Jesus, Mary, and Joseph!"

Andolosia grasped her elbow to steady her. "You all right?"

She rubbed her throbbing temples. "I feel as though I've been trampled by an elephant, compressed to a grain of sand, pulled and stretched like linguine, and glued back together, but, yes, I am all right."

They craned their necks to see the top of the dam, thirty feet up, and sauntered along its concave, forty-foot span. They passed three equally-spaced sluice gates. The door beside the middle gate gave Andolosia an eerie sense of familiarity. He was certain he'd been there, that he'd stood on that very spot, yet he was equally certain he'd done nothing of the kind. He'd never been to Sicily, let alone Monticello, nor had he visited a dam of this scale, except, of course, in that recurring dream. Unlike the dream, the doorway into this dam was closed. A childlike curiosity urged him to try the door and see if a giant nautilus might be hovering inside. His adult sense of propriety quashed the notion.

The mountain air was clean and sweet, an invigorating respite from the decay-tinged air of Livorno and Florence. Carlotta's headache and residual nausea faded as they descended a half mile of the gently-sloping mountain, traversing patches of yellow wildflowers, purple saffron crocuses, wild thistle, and lavender, and navigating around stands of eucalyptus, dwarf palms, laurels, and olive trees. The only signs of animal life were the partridges overhead and wild boar sleeping on a moss bed under a plane tree.

Carlotta stopped cold when they arrived at a grassy clearing, where stood a lone date palm.

"Oh," she said excitedly. "Dates!"

She dropped her valise and ran to the tree. She rubbed

her hands over the trunk's diamond-shaped leaf scars and scrutinized the pendulous bunch of dates hanging fifteen feet above. She interlocked her hands behind the tree, planted the ball of her right foot on the trunk, and launched herself up with her left foot. She methodically shimmied up the tree and sat on a clump of branches under a canopy of fan-shaped leaves. She reached down and plucked a date from the bunch dangling by her feet. She took a nibble, spat it out, and chucked the date away. She shimmied down the trunk, jumping the final four feet.

Carlotta patted her palms. "Dates need a few more days in the sun."

"That was impressive," Andolosia said. "Did your father teach you to climb?"

Carlotta flashed irritation. "Mothers climb trees too."

"I meant no offense. I just assumed—"

"I know what you assumed. My mother taught me and my sister to climb, run, swim, survive on berries and twigs, and build a fire and shelter. Lux mothers have been teaching these skills to their daughters for centuries, and so far they've kept Apollo's hands off our vaginas."

Andolosia's face got hot. "I beg your— Did you just say vagi . . ." He found he had insufficient air in his lungs to complete the word.

"Look at you," she teased. "You're blushing like a young bride."

"I . . . I was not expecting such crassness from your lips."

The more he thought about it, perhaps he should have. The invective she'd hurled at Gino and Dino and his father's mechanical legs would've curled the short hairs of the most jaded of pirates.

"Vaginas are not crass," she scolded. "You know what is crass? Rape."

"I agree. The *act* of rape is crass. The word rape is, well, it's a word that can be said in polite company."

Carlotta whipped back her coils of blonde hair in a dismissive way. "What a twisted world we live in, where 'vagina' offends, but 'rape' is polite. I hadn't realized you were so prudish, Andolosia. Would you prefer I refer to my nether part as a jam roll?"

He gestured manically. "Why must you tease me so?"

"Because you invite the teasing, and it is great fun."

She sniffed the air and smiled. "You smell that? Bread. Freshly baked."

Andolosia pointed at the mesmerizing whirl of terra cotta roofs below. "The town's not much farther."

"What a strange place Monticello is," Carlotta marveled. "It resembles a giant nautilus shell."

Andolosia shuddered. She was right.

"I understand the town was built around an old well," he said. "It has only one street, Well Street. They've elongated it over the centuries, adding turn upon turn, just as a mariner coils a rope."

Carlotta started running downhill.

"What's the rush?" Andolosia called out.

"The bakery might have fresh jam rolls," she yelled over her shoulder. "I don't want them to sell out." She stopped and looked back at Andolosia. "And just so we're clear, by 'jam rolls' I mean sweet bread stuffed with fruity filling, not vaginas."

* * *

After the mountain slope transitioned into flatland, they came upon a tannery comprised of two stucco buildings. A noxious breeze of stale urine, dung, and rendered flesh prompted them to take a wide berth. On the other side was a compacted road of dirt and gravel that bisected a lemon grove and a field of fennel. The citrus- and licorice-infused air was a relief. Beyond, a farmer drove a donkey and a vegetable cart painted sea blue and carved with pink and yellow mermaids. They followed the slow-moving cart to the mouth of Well Street.

Adjoining two-story buildings bordered the narrow, cobblestone street. They'd been painted in cheerful shades of white, pink, blue, and yellow. The ground floor of each building had two, sometimes three, windows to display the wares of the merchants who worked there. The second stories, where the merchants lived, tended to have only one small window. Every fifth building was topped with a cupola covered in indigo tile. Locals, clip-clopping in wooden clogs, entered and exited the shops of a silversmith, a butcher, and a barber whose sign depicted blood spurting from a man's arms and legs. Other than the clogs, Andolosia's attire did not stand out. Most men were dressed in doublets, sleeved shirts, hose, and mid-thigh breeches. The women wore doublets, skirts, and thin veils of cotton or silk on their heads. Carlotta felt self-conscious without a head-covering and sporting men's breeches.

Beyond a little Greek cruciform church with a red dome was a sign that read, "Pistore." This was the source of the wonderful bread smells floating up Mount Monticello. Carlotta and Andolosia pressed their noses to the glass and hungrily regarded the cannoli, cinnamon biscuits, and crescent rolls. Carlotta's face lit up when she spotted the mafalda – a bread sculpture of a snake coiling around a pole.

They entered the bakery. The proprietor, a sour-faced woman named Paola Crostelli, acknowledged them with a subtle nod. Paola's eyes were like two tilted raisins, and they seemed too far apart for her broad and pasty canvas of a face. She had no chin to speak of and a flattish nose, which exposed an unflattering amount of nostril. Her head scarf came to a severe point in the manner of a steeple.

"Good day, Maestra," Andolosia said to the woman. "A

mafalda, please."

"You are from the North," Paola observed coolly.

"He is with me, Maestra," Carlotta said, hoping her Sicilian dialect would appease the woman's apparent hostility toward outsiders.

"Who are you, Madama?" Paola asked.

"Carlotta Lux. And he is my friend, Maestro Andolosia Petasos."

"What, pray tell, are you a maestro of?" Paola asked, fixing a withering stare on him with her tiny raisin eyes.

"Hats," Andolosia answered.

Paola harrumphed and then asked Carlotta, "You say he is your friend, Madama?" Her question was tinged with disgust, as if Carlotta had said Andolosia was her personal dung carrier.

"Closer to cousins, actually," Andolosia offered.

"Well, which is it?" Paola demanded. "Friends or cousins?"

"Friendly cousins," Andolosia said with a chuckle.

Paola's gray eyes remained fixed on Andolosia as she reached for the mafalda and handed it to Carlotta. Andolosia paid her a florin.

Paola screwed up her mouth. "Have you anything smaller than a florin?"

"Forgive me, Maestra," said Andolosia. "I do not. We have travelled far and could not be weighed down with many coins."

Paola harrumphed again. She pulled a number of onze and tari from her purse.

"I am Paola Crostelli," she said while handing Andolosia his change. "In addition to the town's baker, I am its watchman. Strangers are welcome, unless they intend us harm. If that is your intent, I am afraid things will get . . . difficult."

"I assure you, Maestra Crostelli, we intend no harm,"

Andolosia said. "We are visiting Maestro Rabino. Perhaps you could direct us to his home."

Paola ignored the request. She wasn't finished with her interrogation.

"How did you two get here?"

"We walked," Andolosia answered without thinking.

"Across the Strait?"

Carlotta elbowed Andolosia and then laughed nervously. "Forgive my cousin, Maestra. He can be slow to the uptake. We took a boat across the Strait, of course."

"Which boat?" asked Paola.

"Let me see . . ." Carlotta looked up at the ceiling in a pretend show of contemplation. "The name escapes me." She glanced at Andolosia. "Do you remember, Cousin?"

He shook his head.

"There are three regular ferries," Paola said with exasperation. "Corleone, Piazza, and Cangelosi. Which one was it?"

Carlotta and Andolosia exchanged uncertain glances until inspiration struck.

"I have an uncle in Messina," Carlotta blurted. "He trawls for fish. He gave us a ride on his boat."

"My brother lives in Messina," Paola said. "He, too, is a fisherman. Perhaps they know each other. What is your uncle's name?"

Carlotta hesitated. "Antony."

"And his last name?"

"Uh . . . Pesce."

Paola placed her arms akimbo. "Madama, half the fisherman in Messina are named Antony Pesce."

"And my uncle happens to be one of them," Carlotta said brusquely.

"How did you get from Messina to Monticello?" Paola asked.

"We hopped on a cart hauling casks of wine," Andolosia

said.

"Odd. I spied you two walking down the mountain, carrying your luggage," Paola said suspiciously.

Andolosia swallowed. "We got off at Lake Monticello and walked the rest of the way. We thought we'd take in the glorious view of the town at sunrise."

Paola's raisin eyes shrunk to two capers. She focused on Andolosia with such intensity, he had the sense he'd shrunk to dwarf size.

"No road goes directly to Lake Monticello," Paola insisted. "The lake is surrounded by steep cliffs. So, unless your cart was pulled by a flying donkey, I should say you are either a liar or a moron?"

Carlotta elbowed Andolosia to shut up.

"My cousin is a maestro of hats but is otherwise a moron," Carlotta piped up. "Most definitely a moron. Maestra Crostelli, if you truly must know the tiresome details of our travels, I will tell you. We had to walk from Enna because the donkey cart broke a wheel. We could have spent the night on the road, waiting for the repair, but we elected to walk. We have been on foot for six hours. We are hungry and exhausted, especially my cousin, who carried our heavy bags. This is why he sounds especially moronic, even by his moronic standards. You must not give any credence to what he says until he has eaten and rested. Now, we have paid for our bread. Before we take our leave, we would be most appreciative if you'd direct us to Maestro Rabino."

Carlotta took a hearty, self-satisfied bite out of the mafalda and chewed lustily, awaiting Paola's reply.

At length, Paola nodded and said, "You will find him at Turn Two. Number 1121."

As they turned to leave, Paola said to Carlotta, "Madonna, if you intend to remain in Monticello, put on a veil and a skirt. The fashion in the north country may be to dress as a man, but that is not our way."

* * *

Maestro Gennaro Rabino was an extremely bald man. He hadn't a hair on his head, hands, or neck and, for that matter, nothing sprouting from his nostrils or ears. Short and corpulent, he resembled an oversized baby with the facial wrinkles of a septuagenarian. Even his laugh was puerile. He giggled as if tickled under the chin by an unseen hand. He was laughing because Andolosia had just related their introduction to Paola Crostelli.

"Maestra Crostelli is a wonderful baker but an even more accomplished pain in the arse," Gennaro said. "Understand, though, Monticellans are suspicious of outsiders. We pride ourselves on making things with our hands and feet – candles, pelts, wine, bread. We don't trust anyone until we see the product of his manual labor."

"We passed a church on the way into town," said Andolosia. "Priests aren't exactly known for working with their hands."

"They shouldn't be, anyway," Carlotta said wryly.

"Priests are the exception. We're all church-going Catholics. The Inquisitors made damn sure of that."

The décor suggested Gennaro was devout. Andolosia spied no less than four crucifixes hanging on the walls. Over the hearth hung an icon of the Virgin Mary framed in rich purple silk. A shelf displayed prayer books with gilt covers, a silver goblet inscribed with "Ave Maria," and rosaries made of coral. A small table near the front door held a copper basin of holy water. Not that Gennaro's aesthetic was strictly religious. There were numerous keys on display. A few ornate specimens dangled from the ceiling as decorative mobiles. Some were simple keys for warded locks, while others were skeleton keys with intricate etching on the bows. They ranged in size from a thumbnail clipping to a hulking human leg.

Gennaro gestured to the dining table, a slab of walnut resting on a tripod. "Come. Sit."

Andolosia sat on a bench, and Carlotta sat next to him. Gennaro poured them cups of sweet red wine from a decanter. Without thinking, the thirsty Andolosia gulped half his cup. On his empty stomach – Carlotta had eaten nearly all of the mafalda – the wine went straight to his head. He felt as if his ears were stuffed with warm cotton. His stomach growled, prompting Gennaro to serve a bowl of olives, bread, and olive oil. When Gennaro set down the oil, the charm on his necklace swung into Andolosia's field of vision. Gennaro also served a bowl of *saimi*, a delicacy made from rendered animal fat sautéed and seasoned with saffron, laurel leaves, and pepper. He set down a plate of fig leaves in which to stuff the *saimi*. Again, the neck charm swung in front of Andolosia's face. It was a golden key engraved with three foreign symbols.

Andolosia dug into the food with gusto. In his tippled state, he abandoned decorum and helped himself before offering anything to Carlotta. He scooped *saimi* into a fig leaf and stuffed the wad in his mouth. His lusty lip-smacking and animalistic swallowing earned reproving looks from Carlotta and a chuckle from Gennaro. Andolosia sliced a hunk of bread and, instead of setting the knife back on the table, stabbed it into the loaf. Carlotta smacked his hand and extricated the knife.

Andolosia flashed her a persecuted expression. "Ow."

"What are you? A barbarian?" Carlotta chided, waving the knife in his face.

Andolosia gazed searchingly at Gennaro, oblivious to his *faux pas*.

"We Sicilians revere our bread," Gennaro explained. "Bread is life. We don't turn life upside down, nor do we stab it with knives."

"My apologies."

The "p" in Andolosia's apology dislodged some *saimi* from his mouth. It landed on Carlotta's hand. She fixated on the glob, wide-eyed. Gennaro sat on the opposite bench and shifted the conversation.

"So tell me," he said, "what brings you and your cousin to Monticello?"

"We are in desperate need of sanctuary," Andolosia said while licking a glob of seasoned animal fat from his thumb. "Temporary sanctuary, that is."

"Oh my," Gennaro said with concern. "Are you in danger?"

"Someone is pursuing us," Carlotta said.

"A bill collector?" Gennaro half-joked

Andolosia hesitated. He and Carlotta exchanged grave looks.

"It is somewhat complicated," Andolosia offered.

"Let me assure you," Gennaro said, "I do not care who is after you, unless he is with the Church. The last thing we need here are prelates poking their noses around town. We have lost many good people to the Inquisition."

"Do not fret, Maestro Gennaro," Carlotta reassured him. "This man is not of the Church, though some of his estranged relatives are. Sansone de Medici."

Gennaro nodded. "Stasi mentioned this Sansone character in his recent letters. Guild fees. Oppressive rules."

"That is all true," said Andolosia, "but Sansone's interest in us – in Carlotta, in particular – goes beyond guild matters."

Gennaro shrugged. "Well, say no more. Stay as long as you need. Stasi is a very good man, Andolosia, an honest man, and a very good friend. By the by, I have not gotten a letter from him in two months. He is very regular with his correspondence. Is he travelling?"

Andolosia looked down and rubbed his forehead. He spoke haltingly. "I . . . I am sad to report, Maestro. My father has died. It was unexpected. An errant coach . . . an errant coach struck him on the road. He lost his legs. He pulled through. I thought he was through the worst of it, but he succumbed to infection. I buried him – we buried him – yesterday."

Gennaro was devastated. "I am so sorry to hear this news. What a terrible loss."

The wine had eroded Andolosia's grip on his grief. He felt as if he might start blubbering uncontrollably. He thought of pulleys and gears, Carlotta's blonde ringlets, his mother's codpiece – anything except his father's casket at the bottom of that hole. He poured himself another cup of wine and drank half of it.

"I never met Stasi in person," Gennaro said. "I never saw his face or heard his voice. We knew each other solely by the written word. Yet even with that limitation, I considered him a flesh and blood brother." He wiped his welling tears. "I assume you will be taking over the hat shop."

"Not right away and not in Livorno, in any event, because of Sansone and – are you certain it is not too much of an imposition? We may be a few weeks. I will pay you. I have florins."

Gennaro dismissed the suggestion with a wave. "Your florins are no good here. I am doing this for your father, my brother in spirit."

"Thank you, Maestro Gennaro."

"But perhaps you can compensate me in another way, the Monticellan way, with your hands. I don't make hats, mind you. I just skin the animals, tan the hides and send them off to men like your father. If that sort of work is not beneath you, I would welcome your assistance."

"I am at your service, Maestro Gennaro."

"Please. Gennaro will do." He turned to Carlotta. "And

228

you." He extended his arms toward her and eyeballed her hands. "May I?"

It took Carlotta a moment to gather that he wanted to inspect her hands. "Oh. Of course."

Gennaro ran his pudgy, calloused fingers over hers and nodded approvingly. "Strong fingers." To Carlotta's surprise, Gennaro's inspection didn't end there. He palpated her forearms and then, reaching further across the table, her biceps and triceps. "God's Blood!" he exclaimed. "You have a warrior's muscles."

He sat back on the bench. His necklace swung forward. Andolosia pointed at the key. "Are they letters?"

Gennaro grasped the key and held it out for him to see. "The Hebrew letters *zion*, *bet*, and *yud*. They stand for *Z'mir b'chol yom*. It means 'a song every day.' The key unlocks the dam's sluice gates. The man who designed the dam entrusted this key to me long ago. The Church forbids us to speak his name. Ah, to hell with it. I am among friends. Mosè Indaco. There, I said his name aloud. Let them excommunicate me too."

"Why was Mosè excommunicated?" Carlotta asked.

"His other option was death. He was a Jew, and that was all that concerned the inquisitors from Palermo, those foolish zealots. There wouldn't be a Monticello without Mosè Indaco."

"How so?" Andolosia asked.

"The Monticello River hadn't been more than a babbling stream until 1535. That spring, the heavens opened up like never before. The banks overflowed and flooded the town. Those in the hinterland took the brunt of it. The torrent washed away lemon and olive groves, the farmers who tended them, and all but ten of the farmers' children. On a lark, the children had hiked to the gorge to watch the rising waters. That lark had spared their lives.

"Mosè urged the town council to prepare for future

floods. He proposed a dam in the narrow gorge. The council scoffed. The flood was an anomaly, they said, the first since the town's founding two hundred years earlier. They didn't take Mosè seriously because he was just a millwright. He'd never built a dam or anything close to a structure of that scale. But they didn't know the true Mosè, the one with a keen mind and a brilliant imagination. He had a vast personal library, which he'd read three times over. He was constantly drawing up plans for fantastic machines – a weir that could be raised and lowered with a crank, a waterproof suit with built-in air sacs for swimming underwater, an organ that played music with the ebb and flow of water. Wonderous creations.

"When I was a wee boy, I stayed at Mosè's workshop while my mother worked in the barber shop. My father had passed before I was born, and Mosè had taken pity on her. I watched Mosè draw with protractors, compasses, and corner rulers. He gave me my own quill, ink, and parchment so I could draw too. We sang while we worked. He said it was important to sing every day, to remind us of the music that created the world. I grew to love the man. I took to calling him Papa, and he took to answering to it. At sundown on Fridays, he would say a prayer and drink wine from a special silver goblet. Though I was Catholic, I recited the prayer and drank the wine.

"Mosè didn't give up on the dam. He drew up plans and showed them to the council, but they came up with a new reason to say no: there weren't enough carpenters and masons in Monticello to build a dam. That was true. Mosè, however, required only ten able-bodied men he could teach the relevant skills. At this point, the council got fed up with 'the crazy old Jew's nonsense.' All the able-bodied men in Monticello were gainfully employed, so where, they asked, would Mosè scare up one such man, let alone ten? Able-bodied men were not forest trees that one could harvest as fast as one could swing an axe. Mosè had no response. It turned out he didn't need one, for at that moment, the ten orphaned farm boys, none older than fourteen, entered the council chamber and volunteered their services."

Carlotta smiled. "I know what happened next. The town council came around, right?"

"Wrong," Gennaro answered. "The council remained unimpressed. A dam constructed with child labor? Preposterous! Meeting adjourned."

Carlotta looked crestfallen. "Oh. That's awful."

"Don't despair, Madama. That wasn't the end of it. The orphans' faith in the dam buoyed Mosè's spirits. He took them in, fed them, and trained them to build. Every morning, they walked en masse to the gorge, singing a psalm about the good Lord, who'd spared them from the flood. They worked until sundown, and when they returned to Mosè's home, he paid them from his savings. It was a paltry amount, but he had no choice. Monticellans revere work above all else, the Church included, though no one would ever say that out loud. A corollary of our creed is that failing to pay for honest labor is a sacrilege.

"The boys' labor was honest but not especially productive in the first month. But they learned quickly, and soon the dam was taking shape. They diverted the stream from the gorge. They leveled the land. They laid stone and slathered mortar. No longer could the council dismiss the dam as a crazy old Jew's wild dream. The progress was palpable. They could touch the progress with their hands, and for a Monticellan, the hands do not tell lies. Not only did the council sanction the dam, they commissioned Mosè to pipe fresh water into town. The rains were heavier the following two years, but the dam held, and Monticello stayed dry."

Carlotta smiled. "As I thought, a happy ending."

"I'm afraid not, Madama. As stout as Mosè's dam was,

it was powerless against the human flood of religious zeal washing over the Kingdom of Aragon."

"The Inquisition?" Andolosia asked.

"It brought out the worst in us," Gennaro said. "Too many Monticellans cozied up to the inquisitors, became their familiars. They condemned friends and neighbors for a cut of their forfeited property. Accusations whipped through Well Street. 'She spat at the Virgin Mary. He hung a cross upside down over the hearth. He doesn't eat pork. She works on Sundays.' Good men and women – many devout Catholics – were hung by the *strappado* until they confessed to something – anything – to stop the agony.

"Of course, the inquisitors came for Mosè. He wasn't a crypto-Jew. He didn't take Communion in church, only to spit it out at home. Mosè proudly wore the *rotella rosa* on his doublet. He admitted to working Sundays and drinking wine and lighting candles on Friday nights. An open and shut case. To make an example of him, the inquisitors staged a public spectacle at the well. They read Mosè the Edict of Expulsion, ordered his property confiscated, and ousted him from the realm. Not a single Monticellan raised their voice in protest. Shameful. But the crowd parted, and the ten orphan boys who'd built the dam ascended the dais. One by one, they admitted they were Jews. The inquisitors were dubious, but the boys were adamant. If the Holy Office was going to send Mosè away, they said, the inquisitors would have to send them away too. The crowd stirred with a question: was it just to expel an elderly Jew and ten children merely because Church doctrine demanded it? Surely not, was the consensus opinion. But the inquisitors knew better. It was not for the laity to challenge Church rules. As God's mouthpiece on Earth, the Church was infallible. Thus, the correct answer to the question – the answer that Church and God demanded – was an unequivocal yes.

Gennaro stared at his hands. He was choking up. "They

escorted Mosè and the ten boys out of town. I remember like it was yesterday. I was standing on the road, near where my tannery stands today. Mosè stopped, knelt down, and kissed my forehead. He pressed this key into my palm and whispered, *'Shalom, b'ni.'* Goodbye, my son. He and the boys continued on, climbing Mount Monticello while praising the Lord who'd spared them from the flood. We never saw any of them again."

Gennaro paused. He fidgeted with the key.

"I have worn this key around my neck for more than sixty years," he continued. "Sometimes, on a Friday, as the sun begins setting, it weighs on my chest like a lead ingot and I slip into deep melancholy. Few of us who witnessed those events are still with us, so it befalls me to bear the burden of the town's guilt. It is a small price to pay to keep the memory of those boys and my papa alive."

Gennaro fell into silence, lost in his sad thoughts.

"You said the key unlocks the sluice gates?" Andolosia asked.

"Yes. I release some water from the dam each spring to ensure the gates are in working order. Not much. Just enough to recharge the well in the center of town. People gather there. Don Salvatore, our local priest, says a prayer for the exiled souls and asks God to repair the hole in the center of Monticello. An empty, fruitless ritual, if you ask me." Gennaro closed his shirt over the key and patted it. "Sorry. I didn't mean to get so maudlin. You two must be tired after your long journey. Follow me to your room. There is only one bed. I presume that's not a problem . . . being cousins, that is." He smiled faintly.

"No," Andolosia said. "We sleep together all the time," he added with more enthusiasm than intended.

"Really?" Gennaro asked, intrigued.

"As cousins are wont to do," Andolosia asserted. "I mentioned we are cousins, did I not?"

"That you did. Several times." Gennaro opened the door to a small bedroom with a narrow bed. "Get your rest, cousins. Today, you are outsiders. Tomorrow, you put your hands to work and become Monticellans."

CHAPTER

TWENTY

Delphi, 390 C.E.

Aesop Petasos' hat shop was a cramped granite and stucco hovel shaded by two decrepit olive trees. The store's sales were equally decrepit. Aesop consulted with an Arcadian priest, who advised him to sacrifice a goat to Hermes, the patron god of merchants. But Aesop had only one goat, a nanny named Antigone, and he wasn't about to slaughter his only friend in the world. Antigone asked so little of him and gave so much back in return. She bleated happily when he fed her a twig and patted her head, unlike his wife, who constantly berated him as a poor provider, though she wasn't one to pass up a good twig and head pat. Aesop figured his best chance of reversing his fortunes was to gamble on wrestling matches in the city of Kirra. Since matches were during the day, and Kirra hours away, he needed an attendant to mind the shop for little pay – preferably for no pay whatsoever. He would train this attendant, then set off for Kirra to make his riches.

Aesop's brother Stavros lived in Thermopylae. Stavros was indebted to Aesop for helping him conceal a dalliance with a Pythian priestess. To clear Stavros' debt, Aesop agreed to accept Stavros' son Faustus for two years of indentured servitude. Faustus, who'd been attending the Sextus Empiricus Academy for Skeptics, was dismayed, but being only fourteen years of age, had little choice but to honor his father's wishes.

Uncle Aesop was not a cleanly man, as Faustus quickly learned. His toga reeked of pickled olive juice, lamb grease, and stagnant water from the moribund public bath. Faustus held his nose as Aesop trained him to produce his "special concoction" for restoring weathered hats – a rank admixture of olive oil, essence of laurel, lavender, aloe, hemlock, pomegranate zest, clam juice, and, most importantly, dog urine. Collecting urine from Aesop's dog, a short breed of Alopekis, was the most difficult part of the process. Faustus had to stand the dog on two overturned urns to create clearance for the collection urn. The dog's kinked urethra gave his urine stream an unpredictable trajectory, and his palsy made the stream more of a spray. Nevertheless, Faustus persevered and proved himself an expert urine collector. He made the special concoction and transferred it into hundreds of small terra cotta jars. Aesop decorated the jars with a meander pattern and priced them at one drachma.

One day, Faustus knocked over a jar of the concoction while Aesop was attending to an old woman. The fluid inundated Aesop's hand. Within seconds, his age spots and wrinkles vanished. The astonished old woman bought three jars on the spot. Aesop's eyes lit up with opportunity. He gave the concoction a catchy name that evoked the good fortune with which he'd been blessed and upped the price to ten drachmae to reflect the great fortune awaiting him. Word spread, and soon the road to Delphi was lined with people demanding Uncle Aesop's elixir of youth. So much money was coming in, Aesop abandoned his plan to gamble in Kirra.

The dramatic spike in business was short-lived. Irate customers returned a week later with festering rashes where they had applied the elixir. Aesop refunded every last drachma to stave off a riot. He instructed Faustus to sell the elixir only to travelers, who would be far from Delphi when their skin began sloughing off. Aesop then reverted to his original plan for riches – gambling on wrestling matches in Kirra. He told Faustus he was leaving and Faustus was responsible for the shop. As much as Faustus detested his uncle's poor hygiene and gruffness, he was anxious about running the business on his own. He followed Aesop outside, onto the Delphic Road, and beseeched him not to go.

"You will do fine, Nephew," Aesop said. "I shall be gone only three days. We have many hats in stock, and you know their prices. Should anyone order a bespoke hat, take their measurements, write down the requirements, and say it will be ready next week."

The wind kicked up. Grit from the road blew into Faustus' eyes. Menacing purple clouds were encroaching on the sun.

"There is a storm coming, Uncle. You should wait until it is safer to travel."

"If you would let me get to my donkey, I could get out in front of the weather."

"But . . . but a storm is a bad omen, is it not?" Faustus asked disingenuously.

"Since when do you believe in omens, Nephew? Are you not a skeptic?"

"I am," Faustus conceded. "I meant only that storms can be hazardous."

"That's where you're wrong. Windstorms are a godsend for the likes of us."

"They are?"

Aesop tapped the side of Faustus' head. "Use that educated brain of yours. Wind blows hats off heads. People will need replacements, which you will sell them. Wind embeds dirt in the fibers. Hats will need cleanings, which you will perform."

Aesop rested his hands on Faustus' shoulders. His porcine face stretched into a broad, insincere smile, and his tone shifted to an equally insincere tone of encouragement. "The storm is an omen all right. It is an omen you are about to come into your own as a hatter. Why, I expect in my three-day absence you shall sell more hats than I have sold the past three months. And, when you are not selling, you will be cleaning hat after hat. You will amass so many drachmae, I will have to secure a larger money box!"

Faustus smiled. "You really think so?"

"I am counting on it, Nephew. Do not disappoint me."

Faustus puffed out his chest. "I won't, Uncle."

Three agitated women approached from behind Faustus. Aesop was horrified. Their faces were red and dotted with oozing sores. Each held a jar of his elixir. They were squawking and grousing like angry hens, spouting phrases like "set fire to his toga" and "gouge out his eyeballs." Aesop let go of his nephew, spun the opposite direction, and broke into a trot.

"I'd better hurry if I want to avoid the storm!"

"Farewell, Uncle," Faustus called into the rising wind. "I will make you proud."

As Faustus turned to reenter the shop, he spotted the three angry women with festering faces and elixir jars in their reptilian hands. They wanted more than refunds. They were out for blood. He glanced at the sundial.

Oh, is it break time, already?

He twirled on his heels and strode to the tavern for a fortifying glass of morning mead.

* * *

Hermes hadn't found Apollo at his palace or on the Earthen glade where his cattle roamed. He'd tried Apollo's birthplace on Delos. He'd also teleported to fishing villages, farms, and houses of ill repute. No luck. Exasperated, he returned to Apollo's Temple in Delphi, hoping the Pythian priestess might divine Apollo's location for him. He closed his eyes, made the wish, and vanished. The wishing hat dropped him inside a dust devil on the Delphic Road, miles short of the temple. Dirt, grit, and fierce winds assailed his eyes. He attempted another wish but went nowhere. He inspected the gryphon hat. It was encrusted in road dust. He smacked the hat against his leg, put it back on, and tried another wish. Futile. Fine particles had embedded into the scaly leather's nooks and crannies.

As Fate would have it, Hermes was standing in front of the Petasos hat shop. He pushed open the door, stooped low, and stepped in. Faustus, who'd imbibed multiple glasses of fortifying mead, stood tipsy behind the counter. He marked the customer's unusual height, musculature, and costume, but it didn't cross his mind that the dark, hulking giant in a bizarre leather hat might not be human.

He must be from Africa.

Hermes pulled a large gold coin from his tunic and slapped it on the counter. "It is yours, if you clean my hat forthwith."

Faustus was unfamiliar with the coin's minting, but the gold was genuine. He saw opportunity. Maybe he could try out his sales skills and liberate more gold coins from the scantily-clad traveler. He scanned the shelves holding the jars of Aesop's special concoction.

This man is not a local. I will sell him many jars and make Uncle proud!

"Good sir, I—" Faustus belched. "Good sir, I have

239

something that is sure to restore your skin's youthful glow. It—" He stopped himself. Although dark and dusty, Hermes' skin was as blemish-free as polished bronze. "What I meant to say, good sir, is that I have something that will *maintain* your skin's youthful glow."

"Just take care of the hat," Hermes answered curtly.

As Aesop did, Faustus ignored the customer's initial refusal. He sauntered to the shelf, pulled down four jars, and set them on the counter. In his intoxicated excitement, he knocked one over, spilling rank fluid on Hermes' hand. Faustus was mortified. He seized a rag from under the counter to sop up the mess, but, in his haste, tipped over a second jar, which released its contents onto Hermes' other hand.

"Stop!" Hermes said. "I have an urgent message to deliver. If you are incapable of a simple hat cleaning, I shall take my leave."

Hermes reached for the gold coin, but Faustus' hand got to it first.

"I am more than capable, good sir."

Faustus hiccupped and coolly pocketed the coin. He picked up the hat and headed to the back.

"Wait," Hermes commanded. "Listen well, boy. Under no circumstances are you to wear the hat. That means do not put it on your head. Do you understand?"

Faustus seethed.

Why would I put his soiled, sweaty hat on my head? And why does he think I don't know that wearing a hat means putting it on my head? I'm not a simpleton. I was voted fifth most skeptical in my class at Sextus Empiricus Academy, and they don't just enroll the first five boys off the street. Not this year, anyway.

With false solicitude, Faustus nodded at the traveler and sauntered through the curtain separating the public area from the workroom. After giving the large floppy hat a quick once-over, he swatted it against his apron. Dust plumed into his nose and triggered a sneezing fit. He used a horsehair brush to remove as much grit as possible. He opened a jar of his uncle's special concoction. The biting odor reminded him how much he despised the hat business. He detested being locked inside a stifling shop on that filthy road. He detested his uncle's belching and cursing. Most of all, he detested dog urine.

He dipped a cloth in the viscous solution and rubbed the hat.

If only I could transform into an eagle and fly away! I would venture to foreign lands – the lighthouse of Alexandria, the steps of the Temple of Artemis, the great pyramid at Giza.

Faustus set the cloth and the hat on the cutting table. He peered through the curtain, wondering what far off places the traveler had explored. Jealousy burbled in his soul. He resented the dark giant's petty admonition about wearing his hat. Defiantly, Faustus turned from the curtain, snatched the hat from the table, and put it on. It was very warm. He picked up a polished bronze plate and gazed at his reflection. The hat was preposterously large, probably because its owner was preposterously large. But something very strange happened. The hat began to compress and shrink, conforming to his cranial contours like a bespoke hat.

What strange leather is this?

Faustus fantasized he was a sailor on Odysseus' ship and that the hat's broad brim was shielding him from the harsh Aegean sun. He figured the traveler had sailed the Aegean many times.

If I could travel anywhere at this moment, where would I go?

"Ah, of course," he announced to his reflection, "to the *Sirenum scopuli*, home of the beautiful Sirens. I wish to go there."

All at once, an invisible force squeezed Faustus from every angle, and a tunnel opened before him and yanked him inside. The force stretched his body as thin as a string until he winked out of existence entirely. He seemed to have no dimension, no mass, no feeling but a sense of impossible acceleration. He was a howling wind, devoid of sound and air. He was nothing at all.

Am I dead?

No, not dead. An instant later, Faustus was on his face in the dirt, back to his old corporeal self. Horrible pangs racked his innards, and he vomited. After the nausea relented, he detected a humming, as though someone had plucked a tiny lyre inside his skull.

Faustus surveyed his surroundings. He was no longer in the hat shop. He wasn't even in Delphi. He was standing on a rocky island, waves crashing around him. Two more islands poked from the sea on either side. A skeleton lay at his feet. The bones weren't human, not entirely. The creature's upper half resembled a man's, and its lower half was avian. Similar skeletons lay on the other two islands.

Where am I? How did I get here?

He recalled wishing to visit the sirens' island lair one moment and vanishing from the hat shop and appearing there the next.

These must be the sirens' bones!

The sirens were long dead. How awful. Yet how miraculous that a hat could transport him so! Where else could the hat take him?

Faustus thought of the Hanging Gardens of Babylon and wished to go there. As before, he was pulled into a tunnel, compressed into nothingness, and ejected into new surroundings. Again, he retched. His stomach empty, he produced nothing but dry heaves and hot spittle. As he wiped his lips, he absorbed the strangeness of the place. He was standing on a vast network of enormous platforms, each a different kind of garden – groves of olive and fig trees, vineyards, fields of golden wheat, rows of asparagus, leeks, squash, and pomegranates. The platforms were interconnected with pulleys and gears that guided them through areas for sunlight, irrigation, weeding, and fertilization. The vegetable garden on which he stood was heading toward the weeding area, where hundreds of blades stabbed and gouged the soil at dizzying speed. To avoid being shredded, Faustus thought of snow-capped mountains, steeled himself against the inevitable nausea by exhaling all the air from his lungs, and wished himself there.

Away he went.

CHAPTER

TWENTY-ONE

Monticello, Sicily, 1603

Maestro Gennaro's tannery was located on the town's outskirts for good reason – to wit, the vats of urine (human) and feces (equine and canine) inside two cramped stucco buildings. The reek wafting from the open windows was potent from a hundred yards away, sometimes farther, depending on the prevailing winds. Inside the "piss building," workers soaked the hides of deer, marten, and rabbit in the urine to loosen the hair remaining from the liming and scraping process. They carried the treated skins to the "shit building," where other workers plunged them into vats of excrement and kneaded them into suppleness. The dung-caked hides were rinsed in water and immersed in a caustic compound made from myrtle. The rancidity of the operation infiltrated a tanner's clothes, hair, and skin. Combined with infrequent bathing, tanners were necessarily an insular group. Their marital options were generally limited to other tanners and cleaners of the public privies. Hence, Gennaro's workers bore a striking resemblance to one another.

Gennaro gave Carlotta a knife and assigned her to the piss building, where she would pull hides from a vat of lime and scrape off the hair. He assigned Andolosia to the shit building, where he would knead hides. Carlotta lasted only fifteen minutes. She cleaned one rabbit pelt, walked it to the shit house, handed it to a green-faced Andolosia, and declared her tanning career *finito*. She collared Gennaro, who was inspecting finished leather swatches in the open air. Despite the cool temperature, his cheeks were florid and shiny with perspiration.

"Maestro Gennaro, I cannot thank you enough for opening your home to us," Carlotta said.

"You are most welcome, Madama. I trust you do not find the scraping too taxing."

Carlotta plastered a smile on her face. "This is what I wish to speak about. I fear my manual expertise does not lie in tanning."

"Tosh! With your muscles? You just have to get the hang of it. Why, in no time, I expect to promote you to the piss vats."

Carlotta's smile stretched into a horrified grin. "And as enticing as that sounds, Maestro, I believe my talents are better suited to a kitchen setting, such as a bakery."

"A bakery?"

"Yes. My mother is a baker, and I have learned much from her. If it neither offends you nor leaves you short on skilled labor, I beg leave to put my bread-making skills to use in town."

Pain creeped into Gennaro's countenance. He squeezed his trembling hand.

"Are you unwell, Maestro?" she asked.

"Too much wine last night, that is all. Gave me disturbing dreams. Forgive me, what were we discussing? Ah, yes. Baking." He rubbed the back of his neck in a worrying way. "It's just that . . . Paola Crostelli . . . she is the town baker."

"Surely, she cannot be the only baker in all of Monticello."

"Yes, she is."

Carlotta was astonished. "There must be a thousand souls in this town. One baker cannot feed so many mouths. The people must be clamoring for more bakers."

"Be that as it may, Maestra Paola . . . she is the baker."

"Yes, you have said so, twice now. Is there a law that forbids anyone else to bake for profit?"

"No, Madama."

"Has the town council granted Paola Crostelli an exclusive patent to sell baked goods?"

"No, Madama, but – have you considered candle making? I could provide you endless vats of tallow at no charge. Think of the profits you will reap!"

Frustrated, Carlotta gesticulated sharply. "It makes no sense for me to learn candle making when I already know how to bake."

"Please, Madama. I beg you, for your own good. The last woman to compete with Paola – Madama Sophia – made the most delicious rolls. The townsfolk bought scores of them. Her shop was gutted by fire. A witness reported that Paola had exited Sophia's shop just before the blaze, but two other witnesses claimed Paola was with them at the time. Before Madama Sophia, there was Madama Margherita. She made a delicious eggbread. She sold hundreds of loaves, until the day her tainted yeast sickened half the town. Although Margherita and Paola used the very same yeast, Paola's bread miraculously did not sicken anyone. Before Margherita, there was Madama Francesca. She had the audacity to make her own mafalda. It wasn't even that good. She probably would've gone out of business in short order, but Paola hastened matters by denouncing her to Don Salvatore. Accused her of being a secret Jew and demanded an inquisition. Francesca closed her bakery, Paola withdrew her accusation, and there wasn't an inquisition. Do you really wish to be the next Madama in this long, sad story?"

"I appreciate the warning, Maestro Gennaro, but the competition will be good for Monticello. More variety. Lower prices. Do you disagree?"

"No, but—"

"I must do this for the good of the town."

"It will not be good for *you*."

Carlotta fixed a hard stare on Gennaro. She was not backing down.

"Do you know where I might find an oven?" she asked. "Perhaps one of the previous bakeries?"

Gennaro sighed. "I don't know. Perhaps Madama Francesca. She is at Turn Seven, number forty-eight."

Carlotta clapped her hands in excitement and gave Gennaro a peck on the cheek. His skin was hot and salty.

Gennaro shook his head. "Tomorrow, I fear, Paola will curse me for not insisting you take up candle making."

Carlotta's expression turned severe. "If so, tell her the only use I have for a candle is when I stuff it up—"

"Madama!" Gennaro interjected, scandalized.

Carlotta smirked. "I was merely referring to the candle I will stuff up the lantern outside my bakery."

Gennaro was relieved. "Of course that's what you meant. Forgive me."

Carlotta muttered, "No, I have something much pricklier in mind for Paola's cinched raisin of an arsehole."

* * *

Maestra Paola Crostelli sold an impressive array of breads and rolls. Rather than attempting to cannibalize Paola's customers with alternative versions of the same wares, Carlotta decided she would offer the citizens of

Monticello something unique. Whatever this bread product turned out to be, it would have to evoke the essence of Monticello. Not decadent or rich, but simple and quotidian – something Monticellans would consume as habitually and reflexively as they breathed the air around them. Well, not the air around Maestro Gennaro's tannery.

Carlotta strolled Well Street for inspiration. She considered crafting a bread roll that resembled one of the ubiquitous roof tiles but decided a roof tile was not the optimal metaphor for Monticello. Roof tiles repelled water. To a roof tile, a raindrop was an invader. Monticellans weren't hostile to water. They merely wanted water in its proper place, behind a dam or flowing from the fonts that dotted Well Street. She also considered a candle-shaped breadstick filled with a "wick" of custard, jelly, or cheese. No, that wasn't right either. Monticellans would view a candle-breadstick as a novelty, something they might consume on a whim, not as a daily staple. Also, fillings required perishable ingredients and added to preparation time.

Perhaps she could pay tribute to tanning by baking bread "skins" resembling animal hides. Brushing dough with alternating layers of olive oil and balsamic vinegar would lend the bread a leathery appearance. She could dress the flatbread with shaved coconut or onion strings to represent the animal hair. But the more she thought about it, that was a terrible idea. She envisioned her shelves lined with rows of stale, unsold bread skins resembling beards and merkins. The unappetizing image made her tongue feel hairy.

Carlotta reached Well Street's final turn, which technically was the street's original turn, because that was where the town had begun. The origination point was the well of the eponymous Well Street. It was surrounded by a low wall of thickly mortared stone interspersed with three sluice gates. Carlotta leaned over the wall and uttered huffs, hums, and hoots, expecting to hear echoes, but none came. She dropped a pebble into the void. There was no splash. The well was either extraordinarily deep or utterly dry. There was no bucket and windlass mechanism for hoisting water from the well, nor was there a hand-pump – curious, until she recalled that the well was a vestige from pre-dam times. These days, Monticellans slaked their thirsts from the gravity-fed fonts along Well Street.

According to Gennaro, they flooded the town each spring to recharge the well. That water seeped back into the earth. The annual flooding served no practical purpose. It was pure ceremony, ritual for ritual's sake. Monticellans didn't cherish the well for the water it provided but the water it lacked. The ritual of replenishment was not a response to a literal emptiness at the center of the town but the emptiness within themselves – the hole in their collective soul left by Mosè Indaco and his ten abandoned orphans.

Only one bread embodied Monticello – bread with an empty center.

CHAPTER

TWENTY-TWO

Olympus, 390 C.E.

Glumly, Charis watched her twin sister whoop with joy and scamper into the River Peneus, fist raised in triumph. Yet again, Daphne had swooped in at the last moment and seized the victory. She had won the right to leave home with Artemis' hunting party. Charis had earned second place, which in a two-nymph foot race doomed her to remain in their Olympian backwater. She would spend her prime years laboring for the Twelve, weaving yew branches into fences to contain the ever-multiplying sinkholes. The monotony would be interrupted only by her duty to take a river god mate and squeeze out the next generation of water nymphs. She turned away from the river in disgust.

Charis decided to retrace the steps of her defeat, magically thinking that if she ran the race in reverse, she could reverse its outcome. She trudged up the limestone slope and crossed the marshland until it transitioned into dry savannah. A nanny goat on the plain regarded her stupidly, grass dangling from her vapid, masticating mouth.

The slitted pupils conjured images of stabbing and slicing.

Charis flashed back to the prior spring's goat hunt and felt sick to her stomach.

* * *

"You are not to use a bow and arrow," Chloris had commanded her twin daughters that day. "No spears or slingshots either. Just a blade to the throat."

Chloris had ascended a promontory to observe the hunt. As was her habit, she tilted her head slightly to the right and screwed up her lips, evoking the air of a general scrutinizing her troops. Her muscular, V-shaped torso cut a long, severe shadow. She loomed over both of her daughters like the Colossus of Rhodes.

Charis had reached the nanny goat first. She unsheathed a knife from her thigh holster and crept toward her oblivious prey. But she froze when she saw the nanny's swollen teats and two kids rustling in the tall grass.

Daphne arrived, brandishing her knife. She had approached the goat cautiously, careful not to crunch the grass blades. She knelt beside the animal, stroked her bony head, and sang soothing nonsense. The goat leaned into her abdomen, drowsy from the nymph's halcyon murmurs.

Charis sensed a thrum in her chest and a pounding in her ears. She wasn't sure if she was feeling her own heart and coursing blood or Daphne's, a consequence of their shared river-god essence. Charis' heartbeat spiked. A decision had been made. Not her decision. An intent had formed. Not her intent. A hand was about to move. Not her hand. There was a glint of sunlight, and it was over. Daphne's slice was so quick and efficient, the goat didn't flinch or bleat. The animal languidly folded her legs and lay in the soft grass, gazing peacefully at her kids as though settling down for an afternoon snooze.

Fate Accompli

* * *

Though it had happened months prior, the slaughter remained all too fresh in Charis' mind. She averted her gaze from the bleating goat and looked to the oak forest beyond. There were no goats in there, thank the gods. Still, the forest could be an unpleasant place. It was home to the wood-sprites. Wood-sprites were a cordial species, hard-working and fastidiously clean, the main reasons gods employed them as palace servants, landscapers, and deliverymen. Charis had no problem with wood-sprites. Rather, it was their feral cousins, the weed-sprites, she dreaded. Weed-sprites congregated in a hollow and had a rude habit of grabbing the feet of passers-by to feast on callouses and toe jam. Once they got a hold with their vise-like jaws, there was little to do but wait until the maniacal pedicure concluded. Charis high-stepped through the hollow. Astonishingly, her feet made it to the other side unmolested.

The kermes oak demarcated the end of the forest and the start of a sprawling fluvial deposit – a mix of loose soil, angular sedimentary rock, and lithified hunks of gold ore. It was a major accomplishment to cross the span without stubbing a toe or twisting an ankle. Swarming insects were another hazard. Sure enough, as Charis passed the kermes oak, a cloud of red insects alighted from the crown and hovered around her sweaty neck and shoulders. She smacked at them, bursting scores of the fragile exoskeletons like overripe cherries. Discombobulated by the crimson innards burning her skin, Charis stubbed her right big toe on a hunk of ore. She caught her left foot in a depression and twisted her ankle.

Charis hobbled to Craggy Rock and climbed the right-most of the three gigantic boulders. Eons of wind and rain had etched a pathway of crude ledges and toeholds. Spindly veins of quartzite spilled from the flat crest like flowing hair.

Bilateral undulations along the escarpment resembled cheekbones; exposed basalt in between hinted at a nose. Chloris had said the boulder was the morphed remains of a drowned water nymph, and the two beside it – one a colorfully banded gneiss rock, the other a pink granite tor – her transformed sisters. Chloris often told creepy stories like that.

Charis was relieved when she reached the clearing with the oak stump. She and Daphne had rubbed the stump before the race's start, a superstitious gesture to curry favor with Fate. Charis had lost the race, but the more she thought about it, it had been the right outcome. A nymph who melted at the sight of a docile goat wouldn't have lasted a day in Artemis' hunting party. Charis lacked a hunter's constitution, unlike Daphne, who craved the sight of blood, even her own. Maybe, Charis thought, Fate had looked kindly on her. Maybe a life of domesticity was the better destiny.

Charis considered her marriage prospects, which were limited to river gods and other nymphs. River gods were good providers and fastidiously clean, a far better spousal option than a hairy mountain nymph or a weed-sprite with perpetual foot breath. She just wished she had a better grasp on how river god-water nymph procreation worked. Her mother had volunteered very little on the subject, refusing to acknowledge that her daughters were of age for that sort of thing. Charis' father Peneus – whose name, by the way, did not sound so absurdly phallic in ancient Greek – was even less helpful. River gods were taciturn. They didn't speak with conventional words. Instead, they infused meaning into splashes, drops, and drips. Despite Charis' fluency in her father's "water tongue," he was a man of few drips on any topic, let alone sexuality. The longest sentence he'd ever uttered to her was, "Get out of my water already."

Charis sighed. She'd have her answers in due course. If

nothing else, she expected that sex with a river god would be a cleansing experience.

Maybe Enipeus would ask for her hand. She'd taken many refreshing dips in him. His flirtations were gentle. He'd swirl around her hips and caress her cheek. He didn't force himself on her like Apidanus or Pamisus, both notorious gropers.

A lusty heat filled Charis' belly. The pain in her ankle and toe were distant whispers of discomfort. She felt light and swift. She was running. When had she started running? The heat insinuated between her legs. She felt desperate to reach Enipeus and dive into his cooling waters.

But someone had gotten to Enipeus before her. A naked water nymph lay on a flat boulder in the middle of the Enipeus River, legs oriented upstream and splayed open. She was moaning and writhing in ecstasy. The current divided around the boulder and merged on the downstream side, encasing the nymph in a kind of flickering water-flame. Embarrassed, Charis glanced away. But the spectacle was too enticing to ignore, so she pretended not to see while spying the river through her peripheral vision. The side glance revealed something that was invisible when viewed head on – an amorphous figure in the shape of a man. He was not flesh and blood but liquid and transparent, a self-contained bundle of flow. He was the river god Enipeus. Although Enipeus comprised the entire river, at that moment, he was focused on the boulder and on the nymph lying upon it.

Charis looked directly at the object of the river's lust. When she did so, Enipeus vanished from view. She saw what appeared to be a naked nymph performing an absurd sexual pantomime. The nymph's head fell backward and lolled left and right. On the third loll, she stopped moaning, raised her head, and locked onto Charis. Her libidinous expression shifted to surprise and mortification.

"Mother?" Charis asked.

Chloris rolled into the water and covered her bare breasts. Charis took off running. Chloris yelled after her to come back. Her call went unanswered.

During her sprint home, Charis didn't register the bruises from the jagged rocks or the abrasions from the low-hanging branches that assaulted her. She punted three weed-sprites who'd attempted to latch onto her feet. She blew past the kermes oak. Before she knew it, she was skittering down that final slope and racing to the banks of the River Peneus.

Charis paced on her father's muddy bank, panting heavily and fretting about whether and how to reveal her mother's betrayal. The water was placid, not so much as a ripple. That was about to change.

Where is he?

She scanned the river with side glances. Her father was in a nearby eddy, stooped over, communing with the minnows. When Charis called to him, the indistinct figure straightened and approached the shore. She lamented her inability to discern his face through her side vision. She had no idea what kind of mood he was in.

Does his current mood really matter? His next mood will be rage. Say it quickly and get it over with.

The amorphous silhouette stood at three times her height and kicked off waves of spray. This was his way of asking why Charis had disturbed his work.

"Father, I . . ."

Maybe this isn't a good idea. Maybe I should ask Daphne what to do.

The spray began to swirl around the silhouette and whip Charis' face. Her father was growing impatient.

"I . . . I have seen something. I have seen mother and Enipeus. They were . . . they were . . . intimate."

Charis braced herself for a violent reaction. She

expected her father to thrash against the rocks, shoot spray in the air, and slosh to and fro. But he didn't betray so much as a burble. Instead, he answered her in calm water tongue. Twice, he scooped a handful of water and let it trickle through his fingers like scattered raindrops. He scooped water with both hands and pressed his palms together. In that way, he said he had long known about Chloris' affair with Enipeus. There was no way he could not have known, since all Olympian bodies of water intermingled, either directly, by sharing common headwaters or merging downstream, or indirectly, through the rain cycle. There were no secrets amongst rivers.

Peneus dropped his voice to a steady, matter-of-fact drip and added, "I brought this on myself. My father urged me to stay celibate. He said I should spawn a rivulet, a pure river-god son, who would bear the crystal-clear face of his forefathers. I ignored him. I succumbed to feminine wiles and mated for love. I have stained the face of our waters with duplicitous nymph blood."

The river's glassy smoothness degraded into a jagged riffle, which grew into a surging current.

"Perhaps it is not too late to redeem myself," Peneus bellowed.

"What do you mean, Father?" Charis asked in a panic. "What are you going to do?"

Peneus ignored the questions. A whirlpool yawned open in the middle of the river. Her father's shape strode to the vortex's edge and stood there motionless, as if contemplating the irreversibility of his next action. He raised his arms to the sky and dove into the whirlpool's eye, vanishing within. The river reverted to stillness.

Charis' innards were twisting in knots. She was furious at her father. How could he condemn all water nymphs, including his own daughters? She'd made a huge mistake. She should've kept her mother's secret. She tugged at her long blonde locks and cried in anguish. She feared for her mother. Perhaps she should warn her. No, she feared her mother's wrath more than her father's. She was paralyzed with indecision. She scanned the river and the woods. Daphne would know what to do. She always knew what to do, and even when she didn't, she made Charis believe she did.

CHAPTER

TWENTY-THREE

Monticello, Sicily, 1603

Madama Francesca unshuttered the windows at the vacant building along Turn Seven. Aside from the dust, everything was as she'd left it two years earlier – the thick wooden worktable, cooling racks and shelves, bowls and mixing spoons, an oven, and chopped wood in the corner. She was only too eager to rid herself of the place. She conveyed it to Carlotta for one florin. She wished Carlotta well and exited at the rear in case Paola had been lurking out front.

Carlotta filled a bucket from the nearby font and scrubbed the store's two tables, ten shelves, bowls, and utensils. Andolosia had given her money for flour, sugar, sourdough, eggs, spices, and seeds from the stores Francesca had recommended. She was disappointed the groceries occupied only half a shelf. She grouped items into separate categories and left ample space between them. She inserted a bowl, plate, or large spoon between the groupings, so they didn't look like desolate islands. She also increased the spacing between individual items within groupings. With those adjustments, there were still eight-and-a-half empty shelves. That was fine, Carlotta reassured herself. She'd fill the rest with bread. She loaded wood into the cavity under the oven, lit tinder with the oil lamp, and started a fire. She gathered a bowl, mixing spoon, and the ingredients for her soon-to-be-famous "Monticello Bread." She just had to figure out how the hell to make it.

According to family lore, bakers on her mother's side of the family stretched back to the fourth century. That was when the water nymph Charis fell from Olympus and washed ashore at the River Lux, and an expert baker from Taormina fished her out. Carlotta had faith that the family's centuries-old tradition of bread-making would guide her creation of Monticello Bread. She had a pretty good idea where to start. Her Great-Aunt Ursula made a circular bread called a *bublik*. Like Monticello, the bublik was empty in the center. Bublik was made in the same way as *pane squaratu*. The dough was boiled for baking, which made the bread slightly hard on the outside and chewy on the inside. Carlotta decided "Monticello Bubli" would be a more appropriate name. She molded and baked ten different prototype bubli, varying them by thickness, diameter, and hole size. She settled on the version about the size of a hand with a hole large enough to fit three fingers.

Although the bubli's form adequately represented Monticello's dry well, her creation was incomplete without a reference to the town's unique spiral configuration. She mixed a batch of dark rye flour, rolled out three thin ropes, and weaved them into a tight braid. She laid the braid around the hole, forming an expanding spiral to the bubli's perimeter. She stuck the bubli in the oven and waited ten minutes. After pulling them out, she examined the steaming buns from different angles and elevations to ensure she'd gotten the shape and topography just right.

Then came the most important test – the taste.

Nervously, she knocked her tented fingers against her lips. *It's now or never*, she told herself. She seized the roll and took a healthy bite. *Ooh.* The texture was ideal – crusty at first, and then soft. And the taste – well, the taste was ... *Hmmm.* She took another bite and chewed deliberately. As the bolus formed on her tongue, she awaited the influx of taste that mysteriously had eluded her first bite. She grew despondent. The bubli was as bland as a hemp rope. She choked down the mass, pounding on her sternum to expedite its descent down her gullet.

I can fix this. Yes. Definitely.

She dusted the still-warm bubli with a mixture three parts salt, two parts sugar, and one part cinnamon. She took a bite. Definitely an improvement but still unremarkable. The bubli was missing a critical ingredient, perhaps more than one. Whatever this putative taste was, it shouldn't overwhelm the taste buds. It should reveal itself subtly, emerging briefly from the fractional pauses between chomps and swallows before slipping back into hiding. It would have to be as graceful, spritely, and furtive as ... *as a water nymph.*

As an experiment, she pulverized two parts bay laurel with one part clove. She moistened the tip of her pinky finger, dipped it in the powder, dabbed it on her tongue, and bit into a bubli. She seemed to slip into a dream. She smelled the yews and tasted the sweet water of her ancestors' Olympian home. She also smelled Monticello's piney air and tasted its grass-tinged water.

I've done it!

She pumped her fist in the air and danced in circles but abruptly stopped herself.

Don't celebrate just yet.

She was right. This was no time for self-congratulation. She didn't yet know the correct proportions of spices to mix into the dough. Moisture, yeast, and oven heat surely would alter their ultimate expression on the tongue.

She prepared batches of dough with varying ratios of salt, sugar, cinnamon, laurel, and clove. One by one, she sampled the baked bubli, mindful to cleanse her palate with unseasoned bread between tastings. She ranked them according to taste. Determining the best wasn't difficult, for only one made her laugh and cry at the same time. How pleased Andolosia would've been with her scientific approach. Her heart warmed.

Hmmm. That's a new feeling.

* * *

Carlotta returned to Gennaro Rabino's home around midnight. She flopped into bed, exhausted but exhilarated. She detected hints of olive oil and rendered flesh in the room, no doubt residual odors from the tannery. She rolled over, forgetting about her sleeping companion. Her flailing arm smacked Andolosia in the gut.

"Oof."

She recoiled, heart racing. "Jesus God!" She put a hand on her chest. "Forgive me, Andolosia."

"You . . . are . . . forgiven," he stammered.

Carlotta settled her head on the pillow. "I am not yet accustomed to your nocturnal companionship. How was your day at the tannery?"

"I massaged shit into leather for ten hours. That counts as a successful day in the tannery business. They say I'm a natural."

Carlotta was only half-listening and didn't register his sarcasm.

"I hope Gennaro is not upset with me for quitting," she said. "Did he mention anything to you about it?"

"I have not seen Gennaro since the morning."

"You did not walk home or supp together?"

"No. He left the tannery before the end of the workday."

"Huh." Carlotta bit her lip. "He seemed strange this morning. Sweaty and shaky. I hope he is all right."

"I'm sure he's fine," Andolosia said with a yawn. "So, did you create your Monticello bread?"

"I did," she said with ebullience.

"Tell me about it."

Carlotta's mind raced, searching for the perfect words to describe her creation. The bubli's empty center represented the well, while the coil signified Well Street's nautilus shape. The play between the bubli's tangible and intangible components made it different than anything Paola sold. Because each bite of the chewy bread included a bit of the empty center, eating it was an homage to Creation – an explosion of taste and texture bursting forth from the vast nothingness. Feasting on Monticello Bubli was equivalent to nibbling on God's ear!

That was what Carlotta had wanted to convey to Andolosia. She said none of it, however, because exhilaration and fatigue had scrambled her soaring thoughts into incomprehensibility. All she could muster was, "It's a roll with a hole in it."

"Oh," Andolosia said flatly. "Well, goodnight."

He went to sleep. She could not. She was too energized and giddy. She would have to rise in a few hours anyway. As Andolosia softly snored, she clambered out of bed and returned to the bakery, relit the oven, and baked bubli until dawn.

* * *

The sign outside Carlotta's bakery read, "Free Monticello Bubli." A queue snaked out the door, around Turns Seven and Eight, and beyond Paola Crostelli's shop at Turn Nine. As word spread about the free bread, customers abandoned Paola's bakery and joined the line. When Paola learned that the source of the excitement was Francesca's former bakery, she cut to the front of the line and prepared to warn Francesca that she would re-denounce her to Don Salvatore. Francesca, however, was not handing out the free Monticello Bubli.

Paola nabbed a roll from Carlotta's shop and marched out, avoiding eye contact with the other customers. Back at her empty shop, Paola examined the ridiculous, wheel-shaped bread. She scoffed. The rolls were a gimmick, an edible toy. To be sure, people lined up when the rolls were free, but would anyone be willing to pay for them?

Paola nibbled one end of the still-warm bread. There was barely any taste, just as she'd anticipated. Smugly, she opened her jaw and chomped into the roll. Her teeth broke through the crusty exterior and melted into the softness inside. Saliva flooded her mouth, and her cheeks flushed with heat. Disconcerted, she went stock still. She knew she couldn't stay frozen for long, not unless she wanted a deluge of drool down her chin. Fine, she would chew, but she would chew on her terms. Not with urgency or gluttony, but deliberately and methodically. And that she did. After grinding the bready mass into a paste, she gulped and took a second, more substantial, bite. For a moment, she had the odd sense her eyes were salivating. That was absurd, of course. She was crying. She was shedding tears of joy. As hard as she tried, she couldn't stem them, nor could she stop the warmth in her face from cascading into her bosom and groin. Had she swallowed a piece of the sun?

Paola held the roll away from her like a rotting fish. She could not deny the startling truth: Carlotta's bubli was not merely the most delicious bread she'd ever tasted. It was ecstasy incarnate.

Paola bit her lower lip and arched her back in a histrionic display of petulance.

This is wrong. Do not give in.

A fissure was opening in her soul. She had to seal it off. She had to block the way or else the Devil would slip inside. Maybe he already had. She didn't feel like herself. Her arms and legs were trembling. Also, she was hearing a voice. It had to be the Devil. His serpentine whispers were wending their way into her brain. He was trying to possess her.

Give in, the Devil cajoled. *The Heavenly Father gave you flesh and bones for a reason. To move. Dance, woman! Dance!*

Paola's eyes rolled upward. She raised her hands to the ceiling and snapped her fingers.

Good, the Devil said lecherously. *Now dance!*

Paola danced a mélange of frenzied movements. She shifted her weight between the balls of her feet. She box-stepped. She twirled. She broke into a circular grapevine walk. She swayed while waving her arms. She shook her shoulders, leaning in, then out, then in again. Faster and faster she danced until overcome with dizziness and breathlessness. She came to a halting stop, though the room kept spinning around her.

She heard music between her gasping breaths. Someone, somewhere, was strumming a lute.

I know this song. I've heard it before. But when and where?

The memories came rushing back. It had been four decades before, during the Founder's Day celebration at the well. Paola had been dancing with the candle maker's son. She'd thought the boy was an angel, with his fresh face, easy laugh, and kind eyes. A reprise of the song had played when the boy invited her to watch the moonrise from a secluded meadow. He'd taken her hand between Turns Six and Seven. At the clearing on the mountain, the boy had plucked a date from the tree, split it in two, and given Paola half. He'd leaned in and brushed a splotch of fruit from her upper lip.

His face had been in shadow when he pressed his lips – and then his hardness – into her. She couldn't move, she was so terrified, yet her terror was tinged with delight.

The morning after, Paola resolved that the Devil had slipped inside the boy. Perhaps the Devil had been hiding in the date and the boy had swallowed him. No other explanation made sense. Who but the Devil could have gripped her upper arms so viciously? Who but the Devil could have thrown her to the ground, lay on her, and performed such sinful acts? And when the boy had finished, and the shaken Paola professed her love, who but the Devil could have laughed so callously and threatened to divulge her sin to the town? Not "their" sin, he'd been careful to say. Hers alone.

Paola dabbed her sweaty brow with the apron and glimpsed her reflection in the window. She felt as if she was observing herself through a stranger's eyes – the eyes of the candle maker's son.

Harlot.

The roll fell from Paola's hand and landed on her big toe. The sensation roused her from the nightmarish reverie.

I've been bewitched.

She felt a spiky chill in her belly. Gelid prickles radiated to her extremities. She shivered as the awful truth sunk in.

Madama Carlotta is a witch. She's in league with the Devil. Who but a witch dresses in a man's breeches and fornicates with her cousin? Who but a witch would poison the God-fearing people of Monticello with an edible sacrilege? The others aren't as strong as I am. They won't be able to resist. I must purge Monticello of the witch and her bewitching bread before it's too late. Madama Carlotta must die.

CHAPTER

TWENTY-FOUR

Olympus, 390 C.E.

Charis spotted Daphne in a copse of yews a hundred yards away, cutting a branch for a new stave. What a relief. She opened her mouth to shout Daphne's name, when a hot wind buffeted her back. She turned to see a glowing yellow orb alighting onto a dry creek bed. Frightened, she crouched behind a willow tree. The tiny sun winked out like a snuffed candle, revealing a white chariot. The rider was magnificent, a colossal creature clad in a golden cloak and a leather kilt. Flawless pale skin hugged his sculpted arms and legs. His eyes were a mesmerizing aquamarine. It was none other than—

The great god Apollo!

Apollo stepped off the chariot, staggered two steps and stopped. He was swaying. Drunkenly, he reached into his kilt and fished around for something. He pulled out his hand, squeezed its contents, and opened his palm to a pile of pulverized nectar pellets. He snorted the purple powder up his nose and burst into a wide, crazed smile. He unleashed an ear-piercing sneeze, the violence of which flipped his cloak over his head. He threw the cloak off his face, doddered back to the chariot, and fetched a lyre. He held the instrument at his abdomen and plucked the strings seriatim, each pluck yielding a pleasant note that immediately devolved into grating overtones. Tightening and loosening the strings didn't help. He tried plucking multiple strings together, but that approach merely produced grating chords. He turned the lyre around and played again. Nope. He altered his technique, strumming quickly, then slowly, furiously, then softly. And he tried . . . Nope. There was nothing left to try. Hermes had seen to that.

Apollo shook his fist to the sky. "Hermes, you rogue! What god of music cannot play music?" He lurched forward, besotted with mead, nectar pellets, and self-loathing. "What good is being the god of anything?" he muttered to himself. "You are an utter failure, Apollo." He squeezed his forehead. "Oh, my head aches."

He stumbled to an oak tree and sat on a bed of emerald-green moss. He set the lyre next to him, folded his hands behind his head, and lay back. Before long, he'd drifted into a peaceful snooze. Three snores later, an acorn pinged off his forehead. He shot up and rubbed his smarting brow.

"Ah! Cursèd squirrels! Now is not the time to gather nuts. Return to your nests, or I shall smite you."

Apollo listened for a moment. Hearing no activity from above, he lay back down and closed his eyes. Another acorn struck his forehead.

He shot to his feet and raged at the tree's crown. "How now!"

Eros leaned from a bough and waved down at Apollo with a fat little hand.

"You," Apollo said, disgusted. "Find another tree, little boy, for the great Apollo rests underneath."

"*Little boy?*" Eros said, affronted. He shifted his weight

from one plump buttock to the other, dislodging another acorn. This one bounded off Apollo's nose.

"I said be off, you blubbery little oaf! I require rest."

"A thousand pardons, great Apollo," Eros said in a sycophantic tone, "but I have more pressing business than your slumber."

"What business?"

"Love business." Eros pointed to a tall yew, where Daphne was skinning bark from a branch. "The water nymph Daphne is nigh. She has taken a vow of celibacy for Artemis, her patron." He laughed lecherously and added, "I shall put that vow to the test."

"I do not care a fawn's fart for your frivolous love games," Apollo said. "I demand silence. Find another tree to rattle."

"Shh. Mark well. She approaches."

Apollo took umbrage. "How dare you shush me! At the next council, I shall propose exchanging your quiver with something more appropriate for your puerile nature – a teething ring or maybe a rattle."

Eros sighed with mock resignation. "Perhaps you are right, Apollo. Little boys should not wield arrows. Observe how poor my aim is."

Eros blindfolded himself, stretched a golden arrow across the bowstring, and aimed it at Daphne.

"Put that weapon away," Apollo admonished. "This is my final warning. I am not—"

Eros shifted his aim toward Apollo's voice and let the arrow fly. The missile penetrated the god's ribs as easily as light through shadow and burrowed itself into his heart from tip to fletching.

Eros peeked under his blindfold. "You are not *what*, great Apollo?" Eros asked with a puckish smirk. "Complete your thought."

Apollo's marble-white skin flushed like a pig's bladder

swollen with red wine. He was perspiring, too. "I am not . . . I am not . . ." he stammered.

Daphne snapped a yew branch, and Apollo turned toward her. Upon laying eyes on the nymph, he felt a powerful twinge in his chest, and he began to quake uncontrollably.

"I am not . . . I am not able to say how much I love this creature," Apollo said shakily while staggering toward Daphne.

Apollo's quaking intensified. The front of his kilt was bulging.

"What is your name, fair nymph?" he asked, voice breathy.

Daphne wheeled around, startled. "Oh!"

Apollo took her hands. He stroked her wrists with his sweaty thumbs, leaving behind salty, golden streaks.

She smiled awkwardly. "My name is Daphne."

"A beautiful name to match the most beautiful nymph in Olympus."

Eros retrieved a leaden arrow from his quiver and strung it to the bow. He snuck another peek under the blindfold and fired off a shot. The arrow pierced Daphne's bosom and sunk deep into her heart, triggering a sympathetic jolt in Charis' chest. Revulsion rankled Daphne's insides. Charis' bowels churned and rumbled. Daphne yanked her hands free from Apollo's and covered her mouth, checking the urge to vomit. Charis, too, felt sick. She silently retched a partially-digested fish cake from breakfast.

Apollo bent onto one knee. "I love thee, Daphne. Come lie with me."

Daphne recoiled at the most disgusting suggestion she had ever heard. A union with Apollo would have been ignoble. Beyond ignoble. Profane. Their essences were mutually exclusive. Oil and water. Gold and lead. He was a burning star, she a gelid satellite. He would pluck her from the celestial void and yoke her into his orbit. She'd sooner die than succumb to his gravity.

"I am pledged to Artemis," Daphne said diplomatically, choking back nausea.

"Artemis and I are twins," Apollo asserted. "Therefore, a pledge to Artemis is as good as a pledge to me."

"Your logic seems unsound."

"I am the god of reason, and I declare my logic perfectly sound."

"Is such an analytical manipulation within your power?" Daphne asked.

Apollo leered. "There is no manipulation outside my power."

Daphne studied Apollo's tropical-blue eyes, two vast oceans of divinity. If she didn't bolt, he would drown her. She took off toward the river, racing past the willow tree, where her sister was hidden. Apollo grinned, excited that the nymph was making a game of it. But he did not give chase, not right away. It was more titillating when his prey thought there was a chance of escape. Charis slunk away and ran after her sister.

Daphne reached the river's shore and sprinted upstream to the spot where her father often lingered. Something was different. An unusual evergreen tree with oblong, glabrous leaves stood where there had once been wide open shoreline. Multiple gray trunks angled outward from the thick main trunk, creating a muscular, V-shaped silhouette. The top of the canopy tilted leeward. The tree's conformation seemed so familiar, but Daphne couldn't fathom why.

All at once, the mud swallowed Daphne's feet, and she began sinking.

"Help me, Father," Daphne beseeched the river.

"You are mistaken, nymph," Peneus answered in water

tongue. "I am not your father."

Daphne sunk to her knees.

"Quickly! The muck shall be over my head. Please, Father."

The river roiled. Jets of current careened into boulders, sending shoots of spray high in the air.

"You are no relation of mine," he rumbled.

"Have I offended you?"

"Ask your mother."

Daphne glanced around her. "She is not nigh."

"But she is. She stands beside you."

Daphne gawked at the eerily familiar evergreen. "Is that . . . Mother? But how? What did you do to her?"

"You shall know soon enough, as will your sister."

Charis came upon Daphne, who was immobilized on the shore.

"I am stuck, Sister," Daphne said. "Help me."

Charis grasped Daphne's right leg and pulled, but she couldn't extricate it. She got on her knees and began scooping the mud away.

"Something's happening, Sister," Daphne said ominously.

Charis assumed Daphne was referring to her excavations. "I'll have you free in no time." But Charis stopped digging and regarded her mud-caked hands curiously. "My hands feel peculiar, Daphne."

"Because Father is changing us," Daphne said. "The same way he changed Mother." She pointed to the laurel tree behind her.

"It's merely a tree," Charis said, puzzled.

"No, that's Mother, or what's left of her."

Daphne moaned in agony. Below ground, her flesh and sinew were morphing into roots. The animal essence was draining from her legs and hips, hardening her bones and muscles into heartwood and her skin into bark.

Charis sensed the wrenching reverberations of her sister's transformation. She had to lean against Daphne to keep from fainting. Her limbs felt heavy, as though she was moving through thick, muddy water.

"It's not too late for you, Sister," Daphne said as the transformation crept up her abdomen and rib cage. "Go."

Charis wrapped her arms around Daphne, embracing a body that was now more trunk than torso. "Fight it, Daphne," she urged. "You're stronger than Father's petty curse. Don't leave me."

"Have you forgotten?" Daphne asked. As bark encroached on her lips, she answered her own question. "I cannot leave. I am part of you, and you are part of me. It will be so for all time."

Charis shivered. "I'm cold. I feel as if I've been struck by ice-lightning."

"Run, Sister," Daphne urged, her words stilted and garbled by her petrifying tongue. "Run before his curse takes root in you."

Bark encased Daphne's mouth and nose, and she could speak no more. Her eyes and ears sealed over, becoming inconsequential knots in the bark.

"Stay where you are, Daughter," her father commanded.

Tingles percolated from Charis' feet to her knees. Her skin crawled with what felt like millions of insect legs. She willed her listless legs away from the river. She managed to trudge across the muddy shore, fighting off the invisible hands grasping at her feet. She clambered onto a grassy embankment and hoisted her legs up, one by one. With her feet liberated from the river mud, her strength returned. She tromped into the woods, where she broke into a jog, her pace increasing the farther she got from the river.

As she ran, Charis searched her mind for a sign of her sister – a pain, a beating heart, a breath, anything. She felt nothing but her own terror.

Apollo arrived at the river, lyre in hand, just as Daphne's arms and head had finished swelling into graceful, sweeping branches.

"What is happening to you, my love?" the distraught god asked.

He rested a hand and an ear on the trunk, trying to detect Daphne's heartbeat.

"Peneus, reverse this curse at once," Apollo shouted at the river.

The river did not oblige.

Apollo raised a fist, but that was all he could do. He did not have the strength to smite the river god. What would have been the point anyway? Vengeance would not bring Daphne back.

Apollo wiped his golden tears.

"Take comfort, fair Daphne. You are not what you were, but you are as evergreen as my everlasting affection for you." He gripped his aching breast and spoke to the sky. "Moira, I beseech you. Unwind this twisted fate, so Daphne and I may be together. You so cruelly took Hyacinthus from me. How much more love must I sacrifice? I swear on Styx to pay you equitably if you restore Daphne's water nymph form."

A skiff bobbed at the river's edge. Apollo interpreted its flapping sail as a beckoning motion. He waded into the water and boarded the boat. He tossed off the mooring rope and set himself adrift. The boat joined the swift current and coursed downstream.

He saw her – a water nymph with long golden locks running through the forest.

She has Daphne's face!

"Thank you, Moira," Apollo said to the sky. He shouted at Charis, "I am coming for you, my love!"

Apollo trimmed the sail and navigated the skiff toward shore. His body quivered with sexual excitement. He could barely contain the anticipation of stroking Daphne's silken skin and inhaling her clove-scented musk. But it was not to be. The Clarion Call Network was broadcasting the news about the Olympian apocalypse: "The levees of Oceanus have breached. Prepare for Oblivion."

CHAPTER

TWENTY-FIVE

Monticello, Sicily, 1603

Carlotta was loading a basket with red grapes, bread, and pecorino cheese when Andolosia entered Gennaro's house.

"Your Monticello Bread is quite the sensation," Andolosia said between munches on a bubli. "The talk of the town for two days straight." He pointed to the basket. "Oh, are you going somewhere?"

"*We* are going somewhere. A picnic to celebrate my bubli business. Do you think Gennaro would mind if we take a bottle of his wine?"

"Why not just ask him?

"Gennaro is not here."

"What?" Andolosia asked with alarm. "He didn't come home last night?"

"I don't think so." She glanced over his shoulder into Gennaro's room. "His bed looks undisturbed."

Andolosia knitted his brow. "He wasn't at the tannery yesterday either. Apparently, Giuseppe was the last person to see him, and that was two days ago."

"Who's Giuseppe?"

"The shit vat supervisor."

"Alas, in my brief stint at the tannery, I did not have the pleasure of making the shit vat supervisor's acquaintance. Did Gennaro tell him where he was going?"

"No. Giuseppe saw Gennaro meandering up the mountain."

"Odd. Well, maybe he was heading to Messina to ship a batch of pelts."

"Doubtful. He was carrying four wine bottles and nothing else. Remember how he mentioned his bouts of melancholy? Maybe he's having one now."

"Should we be worried?"

"Giuseppe didn't seem worried. Still. An old man spending two days and nights on the mountain . . . alone . . . drunk. What do you think?"

Carlotta was thinking she was a selfish woman, because what she really cared about at that moment was her picnic, and she didn't want Andolosia fretting about Gennaro the whole time. She needed to minimize Andolosia's concern without sounding dismissive.

She adopted a didactic air. "Giuseppe knows Gennaro's habits far better than we do. Logically, if the shit vat supervisor is not worried, then we should not be worried either."

Andolosia regarded Carlotta dubiously.

"That sounded much more persuasive in my head," Carlotta conceded. "Look, if Gennaro hasn't returned by tomorrow morn, we will commence a search. In the meantime, we should assume he is fine. What do you think?"

Andolosia was thinking he was a selfish man, for he wanted nothing more than to go on Carlotta's picnic. "I think your logic is impeccable, Madama."

Carlotta smiled and turned to the shelf of wine bottles. "Given that Gennaro took four bottles with him, I am sure he won't miss one more."

She nabbed a bottle and stuck it in the basket. The action took a perfunctory two seconds from her perspective, but for Andolosia, it was like watching a tendril of honey drip from the mouth of a beehive. In those two seconds, he noticed the soft flexion of her latissimus dorsi, the deft manner in which her thumb and forefingers grasped the bottleneck, the subtle articulations of her neck and shoulder bones, and the faint shimmer of blonde hair.

"Hello? Andolosia?"

He shook his head. "Huh?"

"Where did you go?"

"Sorry. I was just . . . nothing." He took the basket from Carlotta and gestured to the door. "After you, Madama."

"Oh, we need a blanket."

She tried pushing past him.

"No. No. You go ahead. I'll grab one from the bedroom."

Carlotta stepped outside, while Andolosia went to the bedroom. He peered toward the front door to make sure she wasn't looking and opened the linen chest at the foot of the bed. There it lay, right on top. He'd intended to surprise her that evening, but an intimate picnic on the mountain was a far better backdrop. He wrapped the item in a cloth and slipped it underneath the grapes and cheese. He prayed to Fate that Carlotta wouldn't take one look and think him an idiot.

Meanwhile, Carlotta's leg brushed against a laurel tree sapling that had sprouted through the cobblestones that morning. Laurel trees weren't remarkable in Sicily, but this was no ordinary cultivar. *Wherever we go, a laurel tree grows* went the Lux family saying. One of the sapling's oblong leaves bobbed in the breeze. She salivated. Reflexively, she pinched the leaf between her thumb and forefinger, preparing to rip it off and stuff it in her mouth. She could have gotten away with it, too. Andolosia was still inside, dilly-dallying as usual. She anticipated the piquant oils coating her tongue, sharpening her senses, and setting her spirit aloft. But Andolosia closed the door behind him and flashed her the eager smile of a man with a secret on his tongue. Carlotta let go of the leaf and furtively wiped her fingertips on her chemise. She didn't need a laurel leaf. Her spirit was already soaring.

* * *

They spread the blanket under the date palm in the clearing on Mount Monticello. Carlotta handed Andolosia a bubli and a slice of pecorino. He poured them cups of wine and proposed a toast.

"To the bubli."

They clanked cups and drank. Andolosia chomped on his bubli. Carlotta leaned in and kissed his bread-stuffed cheek. He froze, unsure how to react. He was thrilled, but her display of affection had come out of nowhere. Should he kiss her back? If so, where should he kiss her? On the cheek? A cheek for a cheek? That seemed fair and equitable. Or should he up the ante and kiss her mouth?

"You are a good friend," she said.

Andolosia abandoned the kiss idea. "A good friend," he repeated back in a deliberate manner.

Carlotta hummed while refilling their mugs.

"Pretty melody," he said.

"My father sang it often."

Carlotta began to sing the words. Her notes twisted around him, pulling him toward her. He was afraid but too fascinated to resist. Her inflections and glissandos instilled him with a thrilling sense of careening down a winding road in a driverless coach.

Show me a man who flows like a river,

flows like a river,
flows like a river.
Show me a man who flows like a river,
and I'll show you a man who is free.
Show me a man who swims with the current,
swims with the current,
swims with the current.
Show me a man who swims with the current,
and I'll show you a man who is free.
Blood may spill from shore to shore.
The fish may die more and more.
But the river stays a river as long as it flows,
as long as it flows,
as long as it flows.
The man may be cut from ear to ear.
There may be no clothes for him to wear.
But the man stays a man as long as he is free,
as long as he is free,
as long as he is free.
Come, little boy. Come, little girl.
River shimmers like a magical pearl.
Cold, cold freedom on your toes.
Abandoning all your petty woes.
Accept my gift of flowing water.
For you, my son. For you, my daughter.
Look, little boy. Look, little girl.
Now, you shine like a magical pearl,
like a magical pearl,
like a magical pearl.
Show me a man who flows like a river,
and I'll show you a man who is free.
Show me a man who flows like a river,
and I'll show you a man who is free.

Andolosia was woozy and lightheaded. He fancied that

an updraft might pluck him off the blanket and whisk him to the clouds. He had no cares, no burdens. There was no curse. No wishing hat. No marauding god. There was not even an Andolosia, at least not the Andolosia he was familiar with. He was no longer solid flesh and bone. He was fluid and amorphous. He could flow or trickle or lap or swirl at will, all at once, if he so desired. He was utterly free.

"Thank you for that," he heard himself utter, because some part of him had not yet reconnected with his body. "Perhaps one day you will introduce me to your father."

"I doubt I will see him again. Years have passed without so much as a letter from him. He has forgotten me by now."

"I doubt that."

"Well, I *hope* he has forgotten me. It would hurt more if he hasn't forgotten and simply chooses to ignore me. I hate him. I love him too. I cannot help it. He has infected me with his reverence for water. As much as I enjoy baking by day, at night I dream about water."

"What do you dream?"

"I dream I am seeing through my father's eyes. I am ordering men about as they construct bridges and dams. They are silly dreams. Impractical. I don't know why I torture myself so."

"Perhaps because you want to bring your dreams into the waking world."

"Ha!" she laughed acidly. "That will never happen."

"Surely, you can build actual bridges and dams. Many men do."

"Right. *Men* do it. No one would hire a woman. Besides, my knowledge of bridges and dams derives only from childhood memories with my father. I do not know the mathematical principles. There is too much to learn, too little time, and no one to teach me."

"I can teach you."

She screwed up her face.

"I am serious, Carlotta." He took her hands. "After Sansone is dead, I will teach you mathematics, engineering, and fluid dynamics. I have many books on these subjects back in Livorno. I have to spend the rest of my days as a hatter, but you – you can be anything you want."

"It would take decades for me to learn all I need to know."

"Indeed it would!" he said, unintentionally projecting his heart's deepest desire. He cleared his throat. "I mean to say, your tutelage would take years, but you would become so absorbed in the learning – and I in the teaching – time would lose all meaning."

Carlotta regarded him warmly. "I don't know what to say, Andolosia."

"Just say yes."

She giggled like a child with a new toy. "Yes!" She kissed his cheek. "Thank you. That is the best gift imaginable."

Andolosia recalled the item hidden in the basket. He took her hands and met her eyes.

"I have something else for you," he said hesitantly.

Carlotta blanched. Her mouth went dry. His words portended rash action, a laying bare of the heart. God's Blood! He was about to propose marriage. The fool. She'd made it plain she was in no position to reciprocate love. Not to any man. Not ever. Yet, spurning Andolosia would weigh on their friendship like an anchor dropped on a bed of flowers. She couldn't afford to lose his companionship.

She pulled her hands from his. "What do you mean?" she croaked. "I don't think you should – I really don't want anything."

"This is really going to please you . . . well, I hope it pleases you. I put my heart and soul into it."

Her heart was hammering. Her palms were sweaty. Was she afraid? Not exactly. This was an exquisite terror, the kind that arose from biology and proximity and opportunity. The irresistible kind that she had to resist at all cost.

"Are you ready?" he teased.

"No, Andolosia. Don't do it."

He reached into the picnic basket and pulled out the cloth-wrapped object. Whatever was underneath was not at all ring-shaped. It was large and irregular. She figured he'd set the ring on a stand of some sort. He pinched the cloth, preparing for the big reveal. She thrust her hand on top of his.

"I don't want it," she said.

"Don't be ridiculous. You don't even know what it is."

"I know exactly what it is."

"I don't see how that's possible."

"Your behavior makes it obvious."

He was confused. "Really?"

She removed her hand from his. "I'm not blind, Andolosia."

He shook his head. "I knew it. I picked a stupid hiding place."

"Don't be so hard on yourself. The gesture is very flattering. I'm just not the right woman to receive it. I told you so back in Livorno."

"You did?"

"Hello! I was very explicit the morning after Stasi died. Did you drift off when I was talking? It's really a bad habit of yours."

"Well, I suppose if you won't take it, I'll offer it to Paola Crostelli."

"Good Lord!" she said with horror. "Don't even joke."

"I'm not joking. Aside from you, she's the ideal person to have it."

"How could you even think such a thing?"

"Isn't that obvious?"

Carlotta's ire was up. "I see. I spurn you, so you resort to insults. I have absolutely nothing in common with that pimple of a woman."

"You absolutely do in this matter, and I'd prefer my efforts not go for naught."

Carlotta was practically speechless. "Your efforts? Have you been wooing Paola behind my back?"

Andolosia chortled. "Of course not. How in the world would you get that impression?"

Carlotta was befuddled. She glanced at the cloaked object under Andolosia's hand. "What's under that cloth? Show me."

He yanked off the cloth, revealing a wooden dowel rod attached to a circular base. There was no ring in sight.

She laughed with surprised relief. "Oh. It's just a . . . It's not a . . . What is this exactly?"

"A bubli holder. I noticed you display the bubli in a bin. Rather than piled haphazardly, they should be stacked neatly. It's more aesthetically pleasing." He slipped a bubli over the tip of the dowel. "See how perfectly it fits through the hole. See how smoothly it slides. Up and down. Up and down. Up and . . ." Suddenly mortified by the obscene implications of the demonstration, Andolosia began stacking more bubli on the rod. When the rod was full of bubli, he held them up. "Beautiful, no? A veritable tower of Pisa without the lean. You can stand them flat on shelves or mount them to the wall."

"This is wonderful, Andolosia. Thank you."

"I thought you'd like it. I don't understand why you were so resistant."

"I'm not big on surprises. Anyway, assuming bubli sales go as well as expected, I shall have enough money to move out in a week or two."

Andolosia turned grave. "Why would you move out?"

She sipped her wine. "I can't very well remain in Gennaro's home – we cannot share a bed – indefinitely."

Now Andolosia was befuddled. "I do not understand.

Do I snore?"

"No."

"Do I toss and turn?"

She shrugged. "Not that I've noticed."

"Do I produce noxious emissions?"

"No more than I."

"So, you agree I'm a very good bed partner."

"The best I've ever had . . . which is not to say I have had many. Only my twin sister."

"Then why would you need your own bed?" he asked.

She pointed the cheese knife at him. "It is an imposition on Gennaro and you."

He crossed his arms. "You find me distasteful, don't you?"

"Nothing could be further from the truth. I enjoy your company very much."

"But as a friend," he said definitively.

"A *good* friend," she emphasized.

He looked down at his hands. "It will never be more than that."

She tilted his chin up. "Alas, I cannot think of you that way."

"Because you are incapable of loving me?"

Carlotta brushed his cheek with her hand. "I cannot think of any man that way."

"Why?"

"Love leads to marriage, and marriage to children, and for Luxes, that means daughters. After they come of age, Apollo surfaces and he comes for them. I cannot, in good conscience, subject a daughter to that."

"You said you have a twin sister. Has she taken a vow of celibacy too?"

"No, she is married and has a baby daughter."

Andolosia smacked his knee in frustration. "Apollo will return regardless of what you do, so why deny yourself a

284

companion? And who says you must have a child? There are precautionary measures. A Venetian has written about a linen sheath that the man secures over the tip of his . . ." He tapped the top of the dowel rod with his index finger. "It resembles a miniature hat. A ribbon holds it snug."

"Like a bonnet?"

"Yes, but for a very small head," he answered before quickly adding, "a small head relative to a head on one's shoulders."

Carlotta tried to draw a mental picture of the thing. "How reliable is this 'penis hat' at preventing conception?"

"If properly fitted, I imagine it should prove effective at least seven or eight of ten times."

Carlotta scoffed. "Those are reasonable odds for a game of Basset, not fornication."

"Substituting goat intestine for the linen could improve reliability."

"But it still wouldn't be foolproof. Also, I'm not sure how I feel about making love to a goat intestine."

"Sheep or cow intestine also would work. Whatever the intestine, you name it, and I will make it work."

"You miss my point."

"If you're insisting on absolute certainty, I cannot promise that."

"I also have a selfish reason for avoiding pregnancy. When Luxes become mothers, we can no longer sing. This happened to my sister, mother, and grandmother. I'm told my mother used to sing with the purity of a mourning dove. To hear her now, you'd think a mourning dove is lodged in her throat. Awful."

"What a strange and cruel fate," Andolosia said with resignation. He sighed and lay back on the blanket, resting his head on his hands. He studied a cloud in the process of dividing. He propped himself on an elbow and said excitedly, "We're overlooking the obvious solution. We must break the curse."

Carlotta choked on a grape seed. "What?"

"Break the curse."

She began to cough. She seized her cup and gulped the wine. "How?"

"I don't know. In the days of the gods, we would have consulted the Oracle at Delphi."

"The Oracle is long gone."

Andolosia nodded. "The Temple was destroyed, true, but the Pythian soothsayers scattered after Rome sacked the temple. Their descendants may survive to this day, perhaps biding their time until Apollo reopens the temple. I can wish us there."

"I don't know, Andolosia."

"What don't you know? The worst that happens is we waste a few hours in Delphi."

Carlotta contemplated Andolosia's suggestion. After a lengthy pause, she could come to no other conclusion than he was right. She leaned toward him. Her expression was severe, as though she was about to scold him or snap off his nose. Instead, she pressed her lips to his and allowed that unique terror to seize her heart, if only for the duration of a kiss.

CHAPTER

TWENTY-SIX

Olympus, 390 C.E.

Hours stretched to days as Faustus wished himself from Alpine forests to Persian deserts to the Ganges' cooling waters. He didn't linger at any one place, because the exhilaration of hat travel made him crave the next wish. But after three days of compression and expansion and elongation and exploration, he couldn't ignore the deafening hum in his head or the leaden weariness in his bones. He wished for home, and that was where the hat took him.

Gray-purple clouds hung low in Delphi's afternoon sky. It was raining iridescent droplets, which, oddly, were not at all wet. The hat shop was dry, along with every other building, tree, and goat to the horizon. The odd bluish rain fell on him, too, yet he couldn't feel anything striking his skin. The droplets seemed to pass right through him.

An uprooted laurel tree blocked the hat shop's door. Faustus clambered through the snapped branches and entered the shop, whereupon Uncle Aesop, inflamed with anger, accosted him. Aesop paced the floor, explaining with wild gesticulations that he'd returned from Kirra two days prior without two drachmae to rub together.

"Why were you not minding the shop, and why was our only customer a highly-dissatisfied god?" Aesop demanded.

"God? What god?"

"Hermes! He tasked you with cleaning his hat, and instead you stole it."

"That customer was not a god," Faustus said condescendingly. "At the Academy, I learned that extraordinary claims demand extraordinary proof, and there is no evid—"

"The man was nine feet tall, Faustus. He wore feathered sandals. The name Hermes was emblazoned across the strap of his satchel. For Zeus' sake, he handed you a hat that takes you any place you wish. At what point does your skepticism become willful blindness?"

Faustus scratched his head. "I suppose . . . when you set out the details, one by one . . ." He trailed off.

Aesop grunted with disgust. "Congratulations, Nephew. You have single-handedly brought down Olympus."

"I can make it right, Uncle. I will deliver the hat to Hermes personally."

"Oh, if only that were possible, I would drive you there myself. The problem is, Hermes is in Oblivion with the rest of the gods."

"I don't understand, Uncle."

"Well, prick up your ignorant ears, and I will explain. Hermes told me he was transporting a scroll to Apollo. It contained a critical message from the Pythian priestess. It said the people had lost faith in the gods, and the Romans were ransacking Apollo's temple. The priestess was begging Apollo to show himself and restore faith in him. But without his hat – the hat you stole – Hermes couldn't get to him.

"As we waited for you, there was a deafening crack. I

thought a thunderbolt had split Mount Olympus in two. We rushed outside. Hermes peered at the sky, and his face turned to dread. He groaned, then said, 'This is our end. This is our end. Oblivion awaits.'"

"But it wasn't the end, Uncle. We are still here."

"He meant the end of the gods. Apollo's temple was the last thread of human faith holding Olympus together. When it snapped, the levees of Oceanus crumbled, and washed the gods away. Poor Hermes flailed and tumbled in the ethereal torrent and then vanished. To Oblivion, I presume."

Faustus wept. "I'm so sorry, Uncle. I did not mean to steal the hat. It just happened, and I got so caught up I—"

"Hermes asked you not to put the hat on, did he not? How many times have I told you: always honor the customer's wishes?"

"Many times, Uncle."

"Putting aside the risk of killing gods, that's just good business."

Faustus considered showing Aesop the large gold coin Hermes had given him, but it seemed woefully inadequate recompense for snuffing out the immortals. He absently pulled at the back of his toga.

"Well, don't just stand there, Nephew. As long as people still have heads, they'll need hats to cover them. We have a business to run. Get rid of that laurel tree out front. Blasted thing came roaring in as Hermes washed away. Nearly impaled me."

"I shall remove it forthwith."

Faustus opened the shop door. The laurel tree was too large to drag away on his own, so he borrowed a saw and axe from the carpenter two doors down and cut the trunk and branches into manageable pieces. Although the hard labor made his palms blister and bleed, they didn't hurt. Indeed, the aroma of the crushed laurel leaves lightened his heart, and their oils softened and soothed his cuts. He began to cry, not tears of sadness but, to his astonishment, overwhelming joy. He fell to his knees and buried his face in the leaves. Their piquant scent reminded him of a woman he'd once loved, which was impossible, because Faustus was still a boy and hadn't loved a woman in that way, not yet. Yet he saw her facial contours clearly in his mind, as well as her blonde hair, emerald green eyes, and curved, anguine brows. He heard her voice, too. She was singing a single, pure note. The note morphed into a word. It was a name. Daphne.

Who is she?

Who is she?

Who is she?

Faustus had no idea. All he knew was that the laurel tree was important. No, more than important. Sacred. He plucked the shiny, oblong leaves from the branches and placed them in a terra cotta pot for future use. He dug a hole and buried the fractured limbs. As an avowed skeptic, he wasn't the praying type, and even if he had been, he didn't know any prayers for fallen trees. Besides, praying seemed presumptuous after annihilating the gods. Still, he felt compelled to say something. He spoke the only word that came to mind: "Sorry."

Faustus returned to the hat shop and announced that his work was finished. Aesop agreed and promptly fired him.

"Why, Uncle?"

"The hat business thrives on word of mouth. If people find out I'm employing a kid who not only flouted a customer's express wishes but brought down Olympus, I'll go under."

"I understand, Uncle. That's just good business."

"Exactly, Nephew. I'm glad I was able to teach you something."

Faustus lowered his head and trekked back to his childhood home in Thermopylae. He was disappointed about losing his first job but also excited about resuming his studies. But his optimism proved short-lived. The day he re-matriculated at his former academy, it burned to the ground, requiring him to enroll elsewhere. The subsequent school also burned down on the first day. The third academy he tried collapsed into a sinkhole as he was walking to the front door.

Faustus concluded that an external power – Fate, perhaps – was compelling him to abandon skepticism. Instead of pursuing a different philosophy, however, he thought it safer to avoid academia altogether and pursue gainful employment. But his ensuing job search merely subjected him to a novel string of disasters. His apprenticeship to a metalsmith ended when he mistook his pinky finger for an iron ingot and hammered it so badly the physician had to amputate it at the middle knuckle. He switched to wine-making but quit after emerging from the crushing pit with two fewer toes than when he'd entered. He also had a brief stint as a model for aspiring sculptors. Although not classically handsome and of short stature, he had a large, bulbous nose, which novice sculptors found easier to carve. He lost that position after the hypochondriacal teacher mistook his sudden bout of systemic acne for smallpox.

Destitute, Faustus returned to Delphi and begged Uncle Aesop for his old job. By this time, Aesop's fury had abated, and it was clear his customers couldn't have cared less about the gods' demise. Moreover, business was booming, and Aesop needed experienced help. He rehired Faustus, extending his term of indentured servitude another five years.

Thereafter, Faustus endured no fires, lost no fingers or toes, and contracted no unsightly skin conditions, leading him to conclude that Fate had cursed him to be a hatter for his crime against Hermes. He would've confirmed his hypothesis with a Pythian priestess, had the Pythians not scattered after the Romans sacked Apollo's Temple. Instead, he assumed that returning the wishing hat to its rightful owner would lift the curse. To entice Hermes to return, Faustus piled stones into a cairn in front of the shop and installed a marble phallus at the shop's entryway. He also toasted Hermes on the god's sacred day, the fourth Friday of every month. Hermes, however, did not, or could not, respond to these overtures.

Faustus never figured out why he'd heard the name Daphne while dismembering the laurel tree. He didn't meet the beautiful woman from his vision or hear her voice, nor did he learn why he'd felt compelled to apologize to her. He eventually fell in love with a woman with dark hair and a large nose. Her name was Danuta. It wasn't such a bad life once Faustus embraced his fate. He developed into a master milliner, the best Delphi would ever know. After Uncle Aesop passed, he created a "new and improved" special concoction from the laurel leaves he had harvested on the day Olympus fell. Although the new formulation could restore skin's youthful glow without the festering rashes, it stunk so badly, very few were willing to smear it on their bodies.

Faustus told his sons about his crime and his subsequent string of misfortunes. To avoid Fate's wrath, he warned, they and their progeny would have to run the hat shop until Hermes reclaimed his wishing hat, which likely was forever, given the gods were imprisoned in Oblivion. But should fortunes shift and Hermes find his way to their shop, they were to refund his gold coin immediately, no questions asked. That was just good business.

CHAPTER

TWENTY-SEVEN

Monticello, Sicily, 1603

Andolosia opened the chest at the foot of the bed and retrieved the box containing the wishing hat. He set the box on the mattress and ran his hand over the lid's gold filigree. As he was removing the lid, Carlotta smacked the back of his head.

"Ow! What in Fate's name—"

"Are you insane?"

"Are you?" He gingerly touched a spot on the back of his head. "It really smarts."

"Good." She folded her arms. "Then maybe it'll sink in. A hat on a bed is very bad luck."

Andolosia looked up at her, incredulous. "That's why you struck me? Because of a stupid superstition?"

Carlotta was unapologetic. "A priest throws his hat on the bed before putting on his vestments for Last Rites. A hat on a bed makes for a deathbed."

Andolosia gestured to the hat box. "Technically, the hat isn't touching the bed. It's *inside* the box, you see? Only the box is touching the bed. Is there a rule against hat boxes on beds?"

Carlotta was not up for a debate on the finer points of hat-on-bed proscriptions. Through gritted teeth, she warned, "Remove . . . the . . . box . . . from . . . the bed!"

Andolosia braced for another blow. "All right. All right." He set the box on the floor. "There. It's off the bed." He pointed toward the head of the bed. Now go stand over there, where I can see you."

After she complied, he took off the lid, pulled out the wishing hat, and put it on. The hat's warmth melted away the residual pain from Carlotta's assault. He stored the hat box in the chest and extended his hand to her, which she seized with an iron grip, evidently not quite over the hat-on-bed debacle.

"I have the place in mind, the Temple at Delphi," he said. "Exhale."

They exhaled simultaneously. After a breathless beat, Andolosia closed his eyes, steeled his guts, and thought, *Take us there.* There was a horn-like blast and an indigo flash. And the bedroom was vacant.

They reappeared in Delphi an instant later. Their ears were humming, their vision was tinged blue, and they were nauseated, but neither upchucked a crumb of their lovely picnic. They were standing on a massive rectangular floor surrounded by six broken columns. In the distance, the twin cliffs of Mount Parnassus reached toward the horizon. The only person in sight was a shabbily dressed woman seated behind a small table. A sunhat shaded her wrinkled face, which was fixed in a sneer. Tucked into the corner of her mouth was a wad of smoldering, rolled leaves. A curl of piquant-smelling smoke rose from the tip. She was applying oil to a dusty shoe. More shoes and boots – some dusty, others immaculate – were arranged in rows on the ground next to her.

Andolosia approached the woman tentatively.

"Shoes off. One drachma in the bowl," the woman said

flatly.

Although Andolosia was fluent in written Greek, he was unsure about his conversational Greek.

"Will you take florins?" he asked.

"You are a long way from home, Florentine."

"I hail from Livorno," he said. "Greece is my ancestral home, though. My family ran a hat shop not far from here. Somewhere on the Delphic Road."

The woman nodded at the bowl. "Five florins."

"Five florins is steep for a shoeshine. Is that what you charge everyone?"

"I normally charge Italians ten florins, but, given you hail from Delphi, I'm giving you a discount. Shoes off."

Andolosia peeked at his shoes. He'd begun wearing wooden clogs in the Monticellan fashion. The only part of the shoe that could be shined was the leather toe-piece.

"Actually, my shoes are fine," he said. "I am hoping you can give me information."

"Information costs ten florins."

Andolosia looked at Carlotta. "She wants ten florins."

"Up to you," Carlotta said. "This was your idea. Is it worth ten florins to break a divine curse?"

Andolosia sensed a hint of passive-aggressiveness in her tone. He would've preferred if Carlotta had said, "Pay the old hag."

"Pay the old hag already," said Carlotta.

That was better. He counted out ten coins from his purse and dropped them in the bowl.

The woman sniffed. "I would've accepted two."

Andolosia reached toward the bowl. The woman slapped his hand away. "What goes in the bowl stays in the bowl." She set down her shoe and rag, leaned back in her chair, and removed the cigar from her mouth. "What do you seek?"

"An oracle," Andolosia said.

"You are a thousand years too late. Look around. This

place is in ruins."

She popped the cigar back in her mouth.

"I seek a descendant of the Pythian priestesses of old."

"The Pythians are no more," she said curtly.

"Are you certain?" he pressed.

The woman leaned forward and widened her eyes. "For another five florins, I could be certain."

Andolosia reluctantly dropped five more coins in the bowl.

The woman made an exaggerated show of contemplation. She stroked her chin and rubbed her aged, sun-cracked face. At length, she answered, "Unfortunately, my efforts at certainty have fallen short."

Andolosia reached for the bowl of florins. "This is ridiculous!"

The woman smacked his hand away and said, "But I have heard rumors that the Pythian line continues to this day, that they have kept the traditions alive, that they have passed the secrets of divination down through the generations."

"Why didn't you say so the first time?" Andolosia asked. "How might we find them?"

The gray-eyed woman regarded Andolosia and Carlotta severely. "The Pythians are a secretive people. There are those who would do them harm – convert them to Christianity on pain of death."

"We mean them no harm," Andolosia assured her. "We only seek their guidance."

The woman swallowed hard, causing the tattoo of hooked crosses encircling her neck to bulge in a reptilian way. She picked a florin from the bowl and bit into the gold to confirm the coin's authenticity.

"Very well," said the woman as she stood from behind the table. "I shall take you to someone who may know. You may call me Gelasia."

As they set off down the Delphic Road, Andolosia wondered where the Petasos hat shop had stood in ancient times. Where was the precise spot Faustus Petasos stood when the god of travel and patron saint of commerce and thievery requested a cleaning for his dust-caked wishing hat? What Andolosia wouldn't have given to seize the ghost of Faustus, shake his spectral bones, and demand to know what in Hades he'd been thinking that day. Why hadn't he just cleaned Hermes' hat and given it back? Then Andolosia would've been born uncursed. He would have been free to study with Galileo. On the other hand, absent the curse, he wouldn't have met Carlotta. He felt stupid for feeling that she made the curse worthwhile, but there it was. That was how he felt. Beneath his resentment for Faustus was a profound gratitude. He loved his fate . . . at least for the time being.

In a half mile, Gelasia veered off the road and wandered onto a wooded path. Periodically, she whistled a series of trills, flutters, and warbles. Farther on, where the path wound through a thicket of olive trees, she whistled the same pattern. Both times, Carlotta had remarked that she'd seen movements in the foliage. Both times, Gelasia attributed the movements to foraging deer.

Gelasia stopped inside a circle of ten laurel trees and quickly stepped away. All at once, ten women with menacing expressions came around the trees and closed in on Andolosia and Carlotta. They were armed with a hodgepodge of weapons, including a dagger, a sword, a mace, an axe, and a pitchfork. In a sign that the ambush was impromptu, their other weapons were a crutch, an iron ladle, a large wooden spoon, and two candlestick holders.

Gelasia turned on Andolosia and Carlotta. "You are Church spies," she accused.

"What is happening?" Carlotta asked Andolosia. "What is she saying?"

"She says we are Church spies," he answered. "We are not with the Church," he shouted to the mob. He pointed to Carlotta. "Her ancestor was the water nymph Daphne. Since the fall of your temple, Apollo has been surfacing in mortal men and trying to rape the women in her family. We seek a prophecy to help us lift her divine burden."

"Liar!" Gelasia shot back. "The Church attempts to infiltrate us all the time. We have been jailed and tortured. Only through ruthless vigilance have we kept the Pythian flame alive."

Andolosia gulped. "Exactly how ruthless is your vigilance?"

Gelasia unsheathed a long, curved sword from her side. The circle of women tightened around them. Andolosia donned the wishing hat and took Carlotta's hand.

"Quick!" he said to her. "Exhale!"

The squeal and indigo flash sent the women reeling. Some threw down their ladles and candlesticks and scurried away. Mass confusion reigned as they exchanged panicked shouts of "What happened?" and "Where are they?"

Moments later, Andolosia and Carlotta sauntered into the circle of laurel trees. The women fell into awed silence, their mouths agape. Gelasia sheathed her sword. The others followed her cue and lowered their implements. Gelasia approached Andolosia with great reverence. She raised her hand tentatively toward the wishing hat, tacitly requesting Andolosia's permission to touch it. He nodded his assent.

She pressed her fingertip on the hat. "It is so warm."

"Gryphon leather," he said. "This hat belongs to Hermes. With a wish, you can go anywhere."

"I have heard stories of Hermes' hat, but to actually touch it . . ." Gelasia's throat caught on her words. "It is a miracle."

"What is she saying?" Carlotta asked impatiently. "Can they give us a prophecy or not?"

Andolosia posed Carlotta's question to Gelasia.

"A prophecy has not been attempted in centuries," Gelasia said. "Before the Temple's fall, the Pythia tapped Mother Gaia's oracular stream. But Gaia is in Oblivion. Her stream is out of reach."

Andolosia was confused. "You are mistaken. Apollo is the god of prophecy."

Gelasia scoffed. "In name only. Zeus cast Gaia from Olympus for trying to overthrow him. Apollo staked claim to her oracular stream."

"Does that mean wherever Apollo goes the oracular stream flows?"

"Yes," Gelasia said. "But, like Gaia, Apollo is trapped in Oblivion."

"Not totally. He has found a means of escape. This day, he walks the Earth inside a mortal vessel. He attacked my companion not a week ago. I beg you to help us."

"If what you say is true, a prophecy is possible," Gelasia said. "Return to the temple this eve, when the moon has reached her zenith."

* * *

In the dead of night, Gelasia's assistant escorted Andolosia and Carlotta to what remained of Apollo's Temple. Gelasia was seated on a stool, straddling a crevice between two limestone blocks. A bowl in her lap was filled with herbs, seeds, and myrrh bark. The assistant handed Andolosia a bunch of laurel leaves, which he offered to Gelasia. She placed the leaves in the bowl and ignited the contents. She took three deep breaths of the thick, pungent smoke. The assistant removed the bowl from Gelasia's lap and set it at the foot of the stool. The smoke rose around Gelasia and, in the flickering candlelight, lent her a spectral cast.

Fate Accompli

The assistant set a bowl of water in Gelasia's lap. Gelasia stared into the water and began to hum. Her humming evolved into wordless singing, which morphed into full-throated wailing. She resumed humming. The assistant handed her a small terra cotta jar decorated with a meander pattern and painted with the words "Waters of Tyche." Gelasia removed the jar's top and inhaled its contents. The odor wafted over to Andolosia and Carlotta. Until that moment, neither had thought they would smell anything as foul as Gennaro's tanning factory.

Gelasia spoke in a breathless, sing-songy voice, as the assistant recorded her pronouncement on parchment.

> *A Pythian tasked Hermes with a critical deed—*
> *deliver a message with all haste and speed:*
> *"Apollo, the mortals – they no longer believe.*
> *Show yourself now; the Temple closes this eve."*

> *Before Hermes left, a gale swirled the dust,*
> *coating his hat in thick, grimy crust.*
> *Faustus Petasos was a hat-maker's ward,*
> *a careless young boy, neglected and bored.*
> *He cleaned Hermes' hat, which he wanted to don,*
> *and against the god's wishes, the boy put it on.*
> *While longing to visit all lands of Earth's sphere,*
> *he thought of a place and wished himself there.*
> *He ported to mountains and deserts and sounds,*
> *while Hermes stood hatless, moored to the ground.*

> *Because Hermes' message was never delivered,*
> *Apollo chased Daphne straight to the river.*
> *While avoiding the rape, the nymph changed to a*
> *tree,*
> *legs into roots, and no longer free.*
> *The Temple at Delphi was raided and shut,*

300

the gods' link to man irreparably cut.
With no prayers from the mortals to sustain its
foundation,
Olympus then crumbled into Oblivion's ocean.

Thus is the curse on the kin of Petasos:
Keep the status quo at the time of the theft.
Sell hats through the ages or end up bereft.
Freedom they'll know when Hermes comes back
for the hat that his head doth now sorely lack.

Thus is the curse on the nymph Daphne's kin:
Fate assigns mortals for Apollo to possess,
so the god may awake from Oblivion's rest.
Apollo's rebirth will cause great trepidation
for the Luxes, with whom he seeks consummation.
These nymph-kin may run or put up a fight,
but killing the host won't end the Lux plight,
only pause the pursuit for the briefest duration.
The god will return for the next generation.
Lo, Apollo abstains when a Lux is a mother.
Pre- or post-birth, the nymph is not bothered.

Heed these directions, which Fate doth decree,
and the intertwined scourges will no longer be:

Find sisters of Daphne who are twins by mistake.
The soul that they share only one person makes.

After Apollo doth surface, Hermes will arrive,
for these sons of Zeus live intertwined lives.
Both clever and strong, and dripping with guile,
sharing high cheekbones and wily, broad smiles.
Their eyes emit love when beholding each other,
but also the envy of two jealous brothers.

Give Hermes the hat that doth answer to wishes,
to aid sick Apollo through means expeditious.
Travel they must to Wisdom's great tower,
where the arrows of Eros carry no power.
Among Plato's Forms, Apollo's heart shall be freed,
and his capture of Daphne no longer a need.
The threat from the Twelve at last shall abate,
as Daphne and sisters incorporate,
And transmit the note inside all the people—
an inaudible song from the indigo steeple.

Gelasia drifted into a hum.

Andolosia shot a quizzical glance at the assistant. "That is it? The prophecy contains more questions than answers. Who are Daphne's sisters? Carlotta has a twin sister, but are they twins by mistake? Who can say? Also, how am I to return the wishing hat to Hermes if I do not know whom he will possess?"

Neither Gelasia nor the assistant answered. Gelasia dropped her chin to her chest and listed rightward. The assistant caught her before she toppled off the stool.

Carlotta tugged on Andolosia's hand. "What did she say? How do we break the curse?"

How could he tell Carlotta the awful truth that his ancestor was responsible for her family's curse? Faustus' theft of the wishing hat had prevented Hermes from transporting Apollo to his earthen Temple, abandoning him in Olympus, where Eros shot him with a golden arrow that infected him with a pathological lust for Daphne and her human kin. Like a hidden seam that binds brim to crown, Andolosia's sin against the Luxes was stitched into his constitution. There were not two curses among them, but one, and his ancestor was responsible. Even worse, Andolosia had no idea how to make things right.

He extended his elbow to Carlotta. "I shall read you the prophecy when we return to Monticello. There are many details to discuss."

She looked at him searchingly. "But did she say my curse can be broken? Is it possible?"

He ignored the hopeless words that Despair was whispering in his ear and said, "It is possible."

He felt deceitful and ashamed. Breaking the curse was possible in the same sense it was possible that a purse with a thousand gold florins might fly off a passing chariot and land at his feet. When Carlotta learned the enormity of their task, she would hate him, and he wouldn't fault her for doing so.

Carlotta locked elbows with him. While exhaling, she said with determination, "Then let us not tarry."

"I don't know about you, but I am fatigued," he said. "We should rest and return to Monticello in the morning."

"Where would we sleep?"

Gelasia, who by this time was fully lucid, said, "It would be my honor to host the travelers in my humble home."

"That is very generous, Gelasia," Andolosia said. "We are much obliged."

"I have only one bed, so we all must sleep together," Gelasia said. "You, her, me, and my twelve cats."

Andolosia's smile faltered. "Oh, well, I am sure we can make do."

Gelasia extended her bowl. "That will be ten florins, paid in advance."

As Andolosia reached for his coins, Gelasia looked up at the sky. "Looks like rain. Did I mention the roof leaks over the bed?"

CHAPTER

TWENTY-EIGHT

Monticello, The Following Morning

The black cloak hung loosely on Don Salvatore's shepherd's crook of a frame. Though his stature was sinuous, his priestly mind was straightforward for a man of his ilk. He believed in a God comprised of three people woven into a singular divine bundle. His parents and nearly everyone he knew held the same belief. Yet, if challenged, Don Salvatore would not have conceded that his belief flowed from the inertia of inherited tradition. No, he had solid evidence. Time and again, he'd witnessed a wafer of bread and a sip of wine transform into one of God's personas. This is not to say he'd actually tasted flesh and blood on these occasions. He hadn't. Indeed, his faith would have been shaken if he had. The senses were notoriously unreliable, deceitful even. Tasting flesh and blood would have been proof of self-delusion, no different than a man accepting that Earth is a sphere after sensing its roundness under his feet. The soul was the clear-eyed arbiter of truth, not the tongue or the foot.

Priests were not known to rank the sacraments in order

of preference, and Don Salvatore was no exception. Nevertheless, he devoted considerable thought to the notion that, should he ever to compose such a list, he would place the Sacrament of Penance at the very bottom. He'd come to this conclusion while delivering Last Rites to his elderly predecessor, Don Giovanni. Don Giovanni confessed that he'd breached the sacred seal of confidentiality between priest and penitent ten times. He claimed he'd had no choice. The Holy Office had accused him of ten acts of sodomy with a local tanner and advised him that his best hope of lifting the cloud of suspicion would be to identify ten heretics. The condemnations were simple, logistically speaking. Many Conversos in his congregation had confessed to lighting Sabbath candles, circumcising their boys, and avoiding communion. In fifteen minutes, he wrote ten names on parchment, sealed the letter with wax, and posted it for the courier to Palermo. A year later, he received a letter from the Holy Office absolving his "five" – not ten – instances of violating the sacred oath of confidentiality. Based on the letter's address, Don Giovanni deduced that his absolution letter had gotten mixed up with a similar letter to one Don Alberto of Messina.

The Church's impersonal, misdirected absolution had not eased Don Giovanni's conscience, so he asked Don Salvatore to absolve him, figuring the double absolution might avoid any second-guessing at the heavenly gates. Don Salvatore obliged Don Giovanni, but he was troubled that the dying priest was in no condition to provide meaningful penance for his horrendous sins. His raspy words of contrition would not bring back the men and woman who'd been stripped of their property and whose arms had been dislocated by the inquisitors' *strappado*. Don Giovanni would bequeath Monticello an enormous spiritual debt, which would go unpaid unless someone assumed it. So, after Don Giovanni passed, Don Salvatore knelt in the church and vowed to forfeit his life before breaking the vow of confidentiality. Although he'd sworn his vow to the crucifix, he'd been thinking of his congregants the entire time. The vow was for them. Without it, he couldn't have continued conveying the most important message in the unwritten ecclesiastical handbook: "Trust me. Trust the Church."

For that reason, Don Salvatore was not happy about standing at Turn 7 with Paola Crostelli. She had leveled a grave allegation of heresy against the outsiders. He was dubious, particularly when the accuser was a notorious bully and busybody like Paola. Yet it was his duty to take such allegations seriously or at least make a good show of it.

"Are you certain they are coming?" Don Salvatore asked impatiently.

"When I was on the church dome, I spied them coming down the mountain," said Paola. "I wonder what they were doing up there at such an early hour. Probably, mixing wicked potions in their lair or fornicating. I bet they alternated between mixing wicked potions and fornicating. More fornicating than mixing wicked potions, would be my guess."

"Please stop saying 'fornicating,' Maestra Crostelli. Also, I wish you would not walk on the church dome. It is precarious up there."

"Risks must be taken to ensure the wrong element does not invade this town."

In his peripheral vision, Don Salvatore noticed Paola's squat, pointy-headed shadow spilling onto him. He sidled to the left until the shadowed portion of his frock was back in full sun.

Paola was right about one thing. Carlotta and Andolosia were indeed getting close. They were rounding Turn 8, having just descended Mount Monticello.

* * *

Carlotta was exasperated. "For the third time, Andolosia, I do not blame you for my curse. You did not steal the wishing hat."

"I cannot tell you how relieved I am to hear you say that," Andolosia said.

"For the third time," Carlotta emphasized.

"Yes. For the third time. I am sorry to belabor the issue. I just really feared you were going to hate me."

"I do not hate you, though the day is young. You may yet earn my scorn."

"Seriously?"

"No! Not seriously. Let it go, Andolosia."

"Fine. Fine. I'll let it go. The important thing is figuring out whether and how to break our curses – or should we call it our 'curse'? That's been puzzling me ever since the prophecy. Do we suffer two different, but connected, curses or just a single curse?"

She shot him a withering glare.

"Right. I'll let that go too," Andolosia said. "We must focus on how to break the curse . . . curses . . . curse." He cleared his throat. His voice went up an octave. "By my calculation, three necessary conditions must be met. First, Apollo must surface in a mortal. Obviously, that has happened. Second, Hermes must surface in a mortal. If that has happened, we do not know whom Hermes has possessed or when. I can only presume Fate has designed our curses . . . curse . . . curses to ensure we would cross paths with this man. Third is the timing. We will succeed only if you and your sister, as de facto descendants of Daphne, are 'twins by mistake.'"

"We also have to share a soul. Don't forget that part," said Carlotta. "It is true, my sister and I emerged from the same womb, one after the other. But other than common hair and eye color, our faces and dispositions could not be more dissimilar. One sister is vain, obnoxious, and foul-mouthed. The other dreams of being like her father. She is curious, strong, and a delight to be around."

"You are being unfair to yourself, Carlotta. You are not the least bit vain."

Carlotta sighed. "That was in reference to my sister."

"Oh. Yes. I see that now."

"Then you also should see that we cannot be the prophesied 'twins by mistake.' Our parents intended to conceive us, or so they have said. There was no mistake on their part. Also, my sister and I are not true twins. We are offspring who happen to share a birthday. We never have been of one mind on anything, let alone one soul."

"You make a persuasive case, yet there is a reason prophecies are called Delphic. The Pythia's words have ambiguous meanings, meanings we may not yet conceive. We do not know which meanings Fate intends. It would be premature to abandon hope. But if your supposition proves correct, would it really be so bad? With the wishing hat, I can keep you safe until Apollo burns up his vessel. Then we can return to Livorno or Taormina together. I can restart the hat shop and begin teaching you mathematics, physics, and hydrology."

She took his hand and said warmly, "You, too, make a persuasive case."

They strolled hand in hand, basking in a sense of ease, which proved short-lived. They pulled up short after rounding Turn 7 and came upon a leering Paola Crostelli. Next to her stood a tall, crooked priest. That did not bode well.

Paola smiled sadistically and pointed. "These are the heretics. Seize them, Don Salvatore."

The priest smiled uncomfortably and greeted the couple. "Good day to you both. I have not yet had the pleasure of making your acquaintances. I am Don Salvatore, the head priest of Monticello. You are Maestro Petasos and Madama Lux?"

Andolosia bowed his head. "At your service, Don."

"I am *Maestra* Lux," Carlotta corrected him. "I run a bakery."

"So I have heard," Don Salvatore said with a quick side glance.

"Dispense with pleasantries already," Paola snapped. "They are in league with the Devil."

"I beg your pardon," Carlotta said.

"It is not my pardon you should seek but the Lord God's," Paola remonstrated.

Don Salvatore raised a hand to silence Paola and then spoke. "There has been an accusation. Maestra Crostelli alleges you, Mad – Maestra, are a witch and you use the blood of children in your bread."

"Is this a jest?" Carlotta scoffed.

Paola stepped aside, revealing a small boy who'd been standing behind her. Paola seized the child's bare arm and displayed the bruises running along his forearm.

"These appeared after he ate your so-called bubli," Paola said. "There can be only one cause. The blood of Christian children."

"That is an outrageous accusation," Carlotta protested. "I use only the blood of heathen children, and I always seek the parents' permission first."

"Mock me to your heart's content, Madama," Paola seethed, "but there will be an inquisition."

"Clearly, there is a more plausible explanation for this boy's injuries," Andolosia interjected. "I have seen the children play a game with a paddle and a round gourd. One throws the gourd, and the other tries to hit it. I have witnessed many a boy get struck in the arms with errant pitches." He knelt and asked the boy earnestly, "Do you play this game, young messer?"

The boy nodded.

"And have you been struck with the gourd?"

"Many times, Maestro." The boy scratched his head. "Nearly all the time. It is very hard to hit."

Andolosia stood. "See? There's your plausible explanation."

"A plausible explanation is not proof," Paola argued.

"Nor is an implausible explanation," Andolosia countered. "And even if we accept your hypothesis that consuming children's blood causes bruising, why only bruising along one forearm and nowhere else?"

Paola huffed. "Evil follows its own twisted logic." She turned to the priest. "Are you going to trust the word of these outsiders?"

The boy tugged on Paola's skirt. "When do I get the sweet bread you promised me?"

She swatted his hand away. "Silence, little urchin."

"Maestro Andolosia does make a fair point," Don Salvatore said.

Paola's face reddened. "There is more, Don Salvatore. Mark the maestro's nose. A Jew's nose, if there ever was one. He and this woman claim to be cousins. It is a lie – a conspiracy between a Jew and a witch – to stain Monticello with the sin of adultery."

Don Salvatore wagged his finger at Paola. "Adultery occurs between men and women who are married to other people. What you allege, Maestra, is garden-variety fornication." As an aside to Andolosia and Carlotta, he added, "A common confusion amongst the laity."

Paola's temper ignited. "Call it what you will, Don Salvatore. It is a sin. The Holy Office must be notified."

Don Salvatore balked. The last thing he wanted was a visit from the inquisitors. Once they showed, petty disputes among neighbors would morph into Christ-spurning charges of "crypto-Judaism." The inquisitors would demand he break the seal of confession to unearth the heresy, root and stem.

"Well?" Paola demanded.

"I will consult with Maestro Rabino," the priest said. "He is an honorable man in good standing with the Church. Should he vouch for their chastity, an inquisition will be unnecessary. No sense stirring up the Holy Office over nonexistent sins."

"With all due respect, Don Salvatore," Paola said with extreme condescension, "the Holy Office's inquisitors are experts in these matters. If you will not dispatch a courier to Palermo, then I shall, at my own expense for the good of the Church."

Don Salvatore straightened his crooked spine as much as he could and delivered a stern warning to her. "You shall do nothing of the kind. The decision to summon inquisitors is mine and mine alone."

The priest nodded at Andolosia and Carlotta and turned to leave.

"Where are you going, Don Salvatore?" Paola asked, demoralized.

"To the tannery. To visit Maestro Rabino."

"You first must imprison the witch and her accomplice. Preventative detention is the standard procedure."

The priest wagged his finger at her again. "Which I shall follow, if, and only if, Maestro Rabino does not vouch for them," he insisted. "May I go now?"

"We just walked past the tannery," Andolosia said. "Maestro Rabino is not there. Hasn't been there for days. No one seems to know where he's gone."

"We must conduct a search," the priest said.

Paola cleared her throat loudly. "Shall I notify the Holy Office you have permitted accused heretics to roam free pending a proper inquiry? It would be a shame for a priest with such a promising career to be defrocked over such a trifling error, but rules are rules."

Don Salvatore glowered at Paola and relented. He

gently grasped Carlotta's elbow.

"Forgive me, Maestra Carlotta," the priest said sincerely, "but Maestra Crostelli is correct about church procedure. I would ask you to stay in the rectory until we locate Maestro Rabino. You will have your own room and bed. I am confident your stay will be brief."

Paola pointed at Andolosia. "What about him? He is her equal in sin."

"The rectory is small," the priest said curtly. "I have room only for Maestra Carlotta." He leered at Paola and added, "Or perhaps you would prefer I confine two alleged fornicators under the same roof, in the same bed."

Paola was chastened. "Well, I suppose there is little risk of his flight as long as she is held. But be sure to lock your door, Don Salvatore. Her kind is unaccustomed to sleeping alone."

Andolosia whispered into Carlotta's ear. "Do not fret. I will find Gennaro. He will prove we are not fornicators."

He couldn't help having mixed emotions about that.

CHAPTER

TWENTY-NINE

Mount Monticello, One Hour Later

After three days on his own, Gennaro might have been anywhere within a ten-mile radius. Andolosia couldn't simply wish himself to Gennaro's location. Hermes' hat took him to places, not people. Still, the hat wasn't completely useless. At the very least, it would enable him to cover more ground in his search. He could wish himself to different spots on the mountain, where he'd have broad and varied vantages of the surrounding landscape. Moreover, the hat would be essential if Gennaro was incapacitated and Andolosia had to transport his rotund friend to town.

After surveying the mountain and its environs for two hours, Andolosia wished himself to the dam. He found the door beside the middle sluice gate open and heard a strange, masculine voice spilling out. The voice was resonant and had a thick Greek accent. He heard a second voice – Gennaro's voice – yell, "Leave me be! I am not your vessel."

When Andolosia approached the doorway, a powerful ammonia smell stopped him cold. He held his breath and stepped inside. Empty wine bottles were strewn across the floor, and someone was slumped against the far wall. Gennaro. The section of wall above his head appeared to be undulating. Andolosia discerned hundreds of bats huddled into a black velveteen curtain. He shook his head, bemused. Only a man who'd spent decades in a tannery could've found solace among all that bat guano.

Gennaro moaned. He looked up and raised a hand to shield his eyes from the light. Alarmingly, he began pounding his head against the wall. The golden key around his neck popped out of his chemise with each blow. Andolosia rushed over and cradled Gennaro's head.

"Stay away!" Gennaro shouted.

"It is I, my friend. Andolosia."

"Beast!" Gennaro wailed. After a beat, he recognized his visitor. His fright dissolved into befuddlement. "Andolosia?"

"Yes."

"I am going mad," he said in a dry-throated rasp. "Strange thoughts are swimming in my head. They don't sound like my thoughts. They speak in a different voice."

"What do you mean a different voice?"

"He is fluent in Greek. How is that possible? I don't know any Greek. Yet, I understand the words. Help me, Andolosia. I am bewitched."

A chill raced up Andolosia's spine as he recalled the prophecy's words: *After Apollo doth surface, Hermes will arrive, for these sons of Zeus live intertwined lives.*

"Listen to me, Gennaro. Does this other voice have a name?"

"What does his name matter? By any name, I am mad."

"Indulge me. What is his name?"

Gennaro sighed. "He calls himself Hermes."

"God's Blood!" Andolosia exclaimed. "I was right."

"Right about what?"

"I have witnessed this same phenomenon in the man whom Carlotta and I are fleeing."

"You said that was Sansone de Medici."

"Yes. Sansone suffers the same affliction. Another soul is using him as a vessel. That soul calls himself Apollo. Hermes, his half-brother, is doing the same thing to you."

Gennaro scoffed. "Come now. I may be drunk and insane, but I am no fool. Apollo and Hermes are pure myth."

"I would agree if I did not possess tangible, irrefutable proof to the contrary."

"What proof?"

There was a silence as Andolosia contemplated whether to divulge the family secret.

"Well," Gennaro said impatiently. "Let's have it."

Andolosia recalled his father's admonition not to reveal the wishing hat to anyone outside the family. Yet, if indeed the circumstances were ripe to break the curse, and Gennaro was fated to be Hermes' vessel, then, according to the prophecy, Andolosia would have to give him the hat eventually. He regarded the wishing hat in his hand and made the decision. He donned the wishing hat.

"This is my proof," he said.

Gennaro's eyes widened. He used Andolosia as leverage to pull himself to his feet. He gripped Andolosia's shoulders and pushed him toward the light.

"I know this hat," he said with amazement. "The image is burned into my mind's eye. How is that possible?"

"This hat belongs to Hermes," Andolosia said. "The hat takes the wearer anywhere he wishes. My Greek ancestor stole it long ago, and Hermes wants it back. He is surfacing in you. He is thinking about the hat. That is why you see it in your mind."

Gennaro shook his head petulantly. "No. No, it cannot be. Why do you tease me so?"

Andolosia patted his hand. "Come. I will show you."

Andolosia draped Gennaro's flabby arm over his shoulder and walked him outside.

Andolosia pointed downhill. "Do you spy the date palm?"

"I do."

"How far would you say it is from here? Four hundred yards?"

"Maybe five hundred," said Gennaro.

"Can you stand on your own?"

"I believe so. Yes."

Andolosia released Gennaro and stepped clear of him. He closed his eyes, envisioned the palm tree, and asked the hat to take him there. Gennaro flinched from the loud squeal and flash of purple-blue light. He futilely scanned his surroundings for Andolosia, until he heard someone call his name. He squinted at the palm tree in the distance. A man – Andolosia – was standing and waving at him. Stunned, Gennaro waved back. He saw a purple-blue flash under the palm tree and heard a squeal a second later. Andolosia had vanished. A second later, Gennaro felt a tap on his shoulder. He yelped and turned. Andolosia was back beside him.

"You are no lunatic, my friend," Andolosia said. "You are a player in a divine struggle."

Gennaro gaped at his companion. "What divine struggle?"

"I will explain after we go home and clean you up."

Gennaro chuckled. "I do hope the role I play in this struggle does not end with a death scene."

"I . . . I . . . cannot say," Andolosia stammered. The fact was, he could say. He just did not want to say that Gennaro might not survive his brush with the divine. He answered a different question instead. "The right herbs and cold baths will keep the god at bay."

"Permanently?"

"The permanent cure is for the god to leave your body.

That I have not yet figured out. In the meantime, the sooner you begin treatments the better."

"Let us make haste."

"There is one other matter," Andolosia said. "Paola has denounced Carlotta and me as fornicators. She has demanded an inquisition."

Gennaro shook his head. "That sour old hag."

"Unless you want inquisitors descending on Monticello, you must convince Don Salvatore we are not living in sin."

"Are you living in sin?"

"Of course we aren't," Andolosia rejoined.

"Too bad," Gennaro said. "I always thought maybe —"

Andolosia's voice went up an octave. "You 'always thought maybe' what? I assure you there has been no 'always-thought- maybe-ing' going on in our bed."

"If you say so."

Andolosia turned shrill. "I do say so, because it is so. And you must tell this to Don Salvatore. No hedging. No hesitation. And absolutely no word about this hat on my head or Hermes trying to possess you, unless you want us all burned at the stake."

"Fear not. I will vouch for your and Carlotta's good character. There has been absolutely no fornication under my roof." Gennaro raised a hand as if taking an oath. "I swear it on Styx."

"What does that mean?"

Gennaro cocked his head, confused. "I don't know. I've never said it before, but it seemed appropriate under the circumstances."

Andolosia nodded knowingly. "Hermes."

Gennaro thought for a moment. "Indeed. I can hear his thoughts. He says swearing on Styx is how the gods make solemn oaths."

"Well, I'm confident you will keep your oath. Will

Hermes?"

"Let me search my mind." After a pause, Gennaro gleaned the answer. "Ah. Good news! The patron saint of liars and deception assures me you have nothing to worry about."

Andolosia looked up at the sky and shook his head. Had he really expected a straight answer? He sighed with resignation and extended his hand to Gennaro.

"Listen well, my friend. Breathe out all the air you can. Steel your stomach. This won't be pleasant."

CHAPTER

THIRTY

Gennaro's House, Five Seconds Later

T he instant they appeared in the bed chamber, the green-faced Gennaro dry-heaved twice, lost consciousness, and collapsed on his bed like a felled cypress tree. Andolosia fretted that the journey had killed the old man. He leaned over his exhausted friend, relieved when he detected respiration. But a slumbering Gennaro was as useless as a dead one. Andolosia shook Gennaro's shoulders. He yelled at him to awaken so he could give exculpatory testimony to Don Salvatore. When that failed, Andolosia uttered a prefatory apology and slapped Gennaro twice, hard enough to leave red finger imprints on each cheek. Still, Gennaro did not stir. It was pointless. Exoneration would have to wait until Gennaro finished his nap.

Andolosia slipped off Gennaro's clogs and draped a blanket over him. He removed the wishing hat, quietly backed out of the room, and closed the door.

"What was all that racket?" asked a woman's voice.

Andolosia's heart leaped into his throat. He wheeled around, startled to see a woman snacking on a bowl of olives at the table.

. "Carlotta? How are you here?"

"Paola withdrew her accusation," she answered without affect.

"Just like that?"

"Don Salvatore surmised that Paola would relent if I agreed to stop baking. He made the proposal. I agreed, and she agreed."

"That is very good. I mean, not *very* good. Your baking career is over in Monticello."

"A small sacrifice to avoid the *strappado*."

"Thank you for that."

"You're welcome. Unfortunately, we have a bigger problem." She spat an olive pit into her hand. "Two days ago, before she'd even gone to Don Salvatore, Paola's accusation was delivered to the Holy Office in Palermo. They have dispatched inquisitors."

Andolosia was confused. He took the chair opposite her and considered the situation. "What am I missing here? When the inquisitors come, Paola simply will withdraw her denunciation. The inquisitors will leave, correct?"

"If they were typical inquisitors." She spat another pit in her hand. "The Fasci Sansone will be acting in their stead."

Blankly, Andolosia stared at her. Now he was even more confused. "But Paola's allegation has nothing whatever to do with guilds. And Sicily is a Spanish territory. The Fasci Sansone has no jurisdiction here."

"All I can say is that Don Salvatore received a letter from the tribunal in Palermo informing him that they have deputized Sansone de Medici to conduct our inquisition. The Holy See in Rome made the request on Sansone's behalf. The request came from Pope Leo himself."

"The Pope? Why would he— Oh, of course. Before he was Pope Leo, he was Cardinal Alessandro Ottaviano de

Medici." He pounded the table. "God damn those Medici! They are as ubiquitous as bed bugs." He plucked an olive from the bowl and stuck it in his mouth. "Did the letter state when Sansone arrives in Monticello?"

"Tomorrow."

Andolosia gagged on the olive. "Tomorrow?"

"My guess is Sansone did not go to Livorno after you whisked me from Florence. He went to Taormina, which is only a day's ride from here. His informants in Palermo must have gotten word to him about Paola's accusation. A stroke of good fortune for him. A stroke of gross stupidity for us. Had we just assumed different names in Monticello, he would've been none the wiser."

"I'm sorry I hadn't considered that option," Andolosia said sheepishly. "I just did not expect the Spanish Inquisition to come crashing down on us."

"No one ever does," Carlotta agreed.

He brightened. "Yet there might be a silver lining."

"Did you hear what I said, Andolosia? Sansone is coming with his army of inspectors."

"Precisely!" Andolosia glanced at Gennaro's bedroom and back at Carlotta. "Wait. You don't know. I haven't told you yet."

"Told me what?"

Andolosia gestured with his thumb toward Gennaro's bedroom. "About Gennaro. I found him at the dam. He looked terrible. Perspiring and enfeebled. Before I got there, I overheard him speaking in a different voice, in Greek." He paused for dramatic effect. "Gennaro does not know Greek. Another mind is surfacing in his head. Gennaro told me this other mind thinks about the wishing hat and calls himself Hermes. Gennaro is Hermes' vessel. And now Sansone is coming with Apollo. The prophecy is coalescing here in Monticello!"

Carlotta tamped down her momentary excitement. "We still do not know if I'm a 'twin by mistake.' There is much uncertainty."

"I agree. Much is uncertain." Andolosia stood and began pacing. "But I defy you to convince me that inaction is the best response to uncertainty. If there is even a remote chance you are this twin by mistake, we would be fools to hide and do nothing. What is the worst that could happen?"

Carlotta made an insincere show of contemplation. "Let me see. First, you forfeit the wishing hat to Hermes. Second, Hermes kills you. Third, Apollo rapes me. Fourth, we lose all hope of ever breaking the curses . . . curse . . . curses. Whatever. Other than that, you make a fair point."

Andolosia tugged at his chin whiskers. "Granted, it sounds rather dire when you spell it out like that. But imagine if we succeed. Our families will be free. I can stop making hats and study full-time with Galileo. You can come with me to Padua and learn from a truly great mind. Don't we owe it to ourselves and our children to take the risk?"

Carlotta laughed. "Our children?"

Andolosia blushed. "My children . . . your children," he stammered. "Not necessarily the same children."

Carlotta shook her head. "Sansone has an army. How can we fight him?"

"We have the wishing hat and the element of surprise. All we need is a fool-proof plan."

"Oh, is that all," said Carlotta ironically. "You will have to give Hermes the wishing hat and convince him to transport Apollo to the Forms. According to legend, Hermes is the patron of thieves and liars. He is likely to wish himself away, and that's assuming he does not smite you first."

Andolosia's face sagged as if he were about to be sick to his stomach. Was it possible to concoct a fool-proof plan, he wondered, or just a plan that would prove him a fool?

A groan came from Gennaro's bed chamber. "Wine!" a voice shouted in a strange Greek accent. "Bring me wine!"

Andolosia stiffened. "He's awake."

"Gennaro sounds different," Carlotta said.

"It is Hermes' voice," Andolosia said. He moved toward their bedroom. "I must store the wishing hat before he – before Hermes – sees it."

Andolosia scurried to their bedroom and stored it back in the hat box inside the chest. He returned to the front room to find Gennaro standing slumped against the door frame of his bedroom, his face florid and sweaty.

"Are you deaf, knave?" Gennaro asked. "I gave a command." His voice was preternaturally resonant, as though his breath emanated from the depths of Oblivion.

Andolosia exchanged a confidential glance with Carlotta and calmly proceeded to the table, where he filled a mug with wine. Hermes seized the mug, gulped its contents, belched, and gestured for a refill. After downing a second mugful, he gestured for another. Andolosia hesitated.

"Do not tarry, boy," Hermes said.

"My apologies, great god Hermes, but excess wine is ill-advised on your vessel's empty stomach."

"I am the god of metes and bounds. I have traversed Earth's continents, across the spheres, from Olympus to Tartarus. Do you insinuate that a flabby mortal stomach can stand in my way?"

Hermes grabbed the decanter and filled his mug. He took two large gulps and wiped his lips with the back of his hand.

"This thirst is unbearable," Hermes continued. "I have been treading Oblivion's briny waters for centuries without refuge or rest. Meanwhile, selfish Apollo remains dry because Fate saw fit to bestow him a boat. You would think my dear brother would have hoisted me aboard, let me dry out for a spell. But no. Scores of times I have beseeched him, 'Brother, luff your sail. Cast me a line! Reel me in.' Each time, he pretended not to hear and sailed toward the island of doors. Well, I showed him. This last time, I didn't call to him. I dove under water and stayed there until he passed overhead. I seized a rope dangling from the stern and held fast until he reached shore. The fool had no idea!

"I spied him walking up the beach. He was holding a lyre. My lyre! He stopped to chat with Moira and proceeded toward the doors. I strode ashore, intending to accost him from behind and seize the lyre. As I was closing in, he stopped at a door and opened it. He was going to step through. I had to hurry. Alas, the door closed behind him before I got there, and as hard as I pulled, I could not open it. I entered the next door over, hoping it would take me close to wherever he'd gone. All at once, I was deep under water. It wasn't Oblivion's sea, though. This was different water. Tasteless and . . . and, well, it didn't feel wet. Yet I was buoyant, floating in a kind of viscous light. I swam toward a brightness above me and surfaced in this vessel – first, in his dream, then, into his waking mind."

Hermes took a deep breath and exhaled. "Ah, it is invigorating to have real lungs that breathe real air and a real belly – a real *blubbery* belly – and fill it with real wine." He set down the mug. He examined his hands and legs and ran his fingertips over the creases on his face, the flesh hanging below his chin, and his bald pate and fat neck. "Great God Zeus! I have surfaced inside a massive cherub." Hermes did a double-take at Andolosia. "Wait a moment. I know your face. I never forget a nose. You are that boy I entrusted with my hat."

Andolosia stepped back.

Hermes continued in an accusatory tone. "I was on the Delphic Road. I needed to get to Olympus. My hat was caked with dust and would not transport me. I paid a clumsy boy with a nose such as yours to clean it. I warned him not to wear the hat. He ignored me and vanished."

Andolosia bowed his head. "It was my ancestor, Faustus. The nose is a family trait. I offer my sincerest apologies."

"Your sincerest apologies," Hermes repeated, and added in a saccharine tone, "Well, as long as you are sorry, that fixes everything." He became furious. "Where in Hades is my hat?"

"In a safe place," Andolosia said.

"Return it at once!" Hermes raged.

"On one condition," Andolosia said meekly.

"You dare steal my hat and then condition its return?"

"It is not my condition, but Fate's."

"How would you, an insignificant mortal, know Moira's mind? Only she can read her tapestry."

"Moira?" Andolosia asked.

"Fate's true name. Moira has weaved the fates of gods and men into a tapestry. She has it with her in Oblivion."

"Well, we consulted a Pythian priestess named Gelasia, who tapped into a – How did she put it? Oh yes – she tapped into an 'oracular stream.' She said Apollo is infected with Eros' golden arrow. To cure him, you, great Hermes, must wish him to the Forms."

"Ha! Why would I cure my gryphon turd of a brother of so much as a hangnail?"

"Because . . ."

Andolosia's mind raced. He looked to Carlotta for suggestions. Her face was a blank.

Andolosia rambled on. "Because . . . and, again, these are the Pythia's words, not my own . . . Because if you help your brother in his time of need, you will prove that you are the superior god, that notwithstanding Apollo's sleights and skullduggery, you chose the noble course."

Carlotta's eyes widened like saucers. What was Andolosia talking about?

"And why would I care one whit about proving that?" Hermes asked.

Andolosia scoured his brain for a semi-plausible

response. "The Pythia addressed that. She said . . . She said . . ." He shot Carlotta a pleading glance. "What did she say, Madama?"

Carlotta felt the jolt of being put on the spot. She snapped her fingers and fiddled with her lip, struggling to think of what to say. "She said . . . She said Fate will . . . Ah, I remember. She said she will liberate you and your brethren from Oblivion. Uh-huh. Absolutely. If you take Apollo to the Forms, she will set the gods free. Those were her words. Exactly." And she added, "Pretty much exactly. More or less."

Andolosia beamed at her.

"Do you both speak true?" Hermes asked.

Andolosia raised a hand in a swearing motion. He nodded at Carlotta to do the same.

"I swear it on Styx," Andolosia said.

"Go ahead, Carlotta," pressed Andolosia, "take your oath of truth."

She tentatively raised her right hand. "I swear it on Styx" she said, her voice lilting up, turning her vow into a question.

Andolosia was dubious that the oath bound mortals, but he figured the best lies demanded the prevaricator's complete commitment. He punctuated their Olympic-sized fib with a quick, "there you have it" head bob.

It worked. Hermes was mollified. The god shifted to a more matter of fact tone. "You say I need only take Apollo on a brief journey to the Forms?"

"The briefest," Andolosia said.

"And that will liberate my father, brothers, and sisters?"

"Oh, yes," Carlotta answered, vigorously nodding her head. "Absolutely." She paused "Pretty much absolutely." Another pause. "More or less absolutely."

As Hermes came around to the idea, he raised his chin

and assumed an air of majesty. "They will hail me as their savior. They will hold me above Apollo. Little brother will become big brother and take big brother's seat at the head of the council table." Hermes lowered his chin and turned to Andolosia. "I am most agreeable to Fate's terms."

"You will not regret this, my lord," Carlotta said. "We expect Apollo's arrival on the morrow."

Hermes swooned. "I don't feel . . ." He collapsed into Andolosia's arms, asleep again.

"God's Buttocks, he is heavy," Andolosia said with strain. "Help me carry him to the bedroom."

Carlotta draped Gennaro's chubby arm over her shoulder, and together they half-walked-half-dragged the corpulent slumberer to his bed chamber. They heaved him onto the bed, which popped and creaked from the sudden onslaught of mass.

Carlotta conducted Andolosia to the corner of the room. In a hushed tone, she asked, "Do you think it was wise to lie to Hermes?"

"No, but what was the alternative? I couldn't very well admit that his act of brotherly benevolence will seal the gods in Oblivion for good. I'm sorry. That was the best I could come up with on the fly. Thank you for stepping in there. You were perfect."

"Oh," she said, flattered.

She looked so beautiful. Andolosia wanted to kiss her. No, he wanted to make love to her. But the idea of doing so next to Gennaro's supine body killed his desire.

"We should have a backup plan in case we're discovered, and the gods turn their wrath on us," he said.

"Fleeing won't be an option," she said. "You won't have the wishing hat at that point. We would have to fight. We could probably handle Hermes, but Apollo would have Sansone's army behind him. We would need a flood of hellfire to defeat them."

Andolosia fixated on the golden key around Gennaro's neck.

"Then a flood it shall be," he announced with a burst of inspiration.

CHAPTER

THIRTY-ONE

The Monticello Dam, One Hour Later

Andolosia and Carlotta hiked to the door at the foot of the dam. From a satchel, Andolosia pulled a candle as well as a gourd in which he'd stored hot coals from Gennaro's stove. He ignited a taper and lit the candle. When he opened the door, a powerful ammonia odor assaulted them.

Carlotta scrunched her face. "Ew. It reeks worse than the tannery."

"From the bat droppings," Andolosia said. "They roost on the far wall."

"Remind me again what we are looking for?"

"The mechanism that controls the sluice gates." Andolosia swept the candlelight across the walls, ceiling, and floor. "Where could it be?"

Carlotta pointed to the wall of bats. "We should ask our winged friends."

"Excellent deduction, Carlotta."

He brought the flame close to the bats – close enough to singe them – but none alighted.

"Careful not to burn them," Carlotta admonished.

"How else am I to clear the wall?"

"I don't know, but I doubt Gennaro incinerates hundreds of bats every time he needs to raise the sluice gates." She stepped toward the wall. "Aw. Look at them. They have such sweet little faces." She leaned in closer. "Though, with their wings folded around themselves," she added with mild disgust, "they resemble blackened horse scrotums." She stepped back and smiled pleasantly. "Aw, but those faces . . ."

"I fail to comprehend how a grotesque, cross-species comparison of animal anatomy informs our strategy for clearing the wall."

"Just use your arm to brush them aside," she said impatiently.

"What a splendid idea." He gave her a deferential hand gesture. "Of course, as the author of this splendid idea, you are best suited to implement it."

"Normally, I'd agree with you. It has occurred to me, however, that I have thwarted your chivalrous gestures at every turn. I would be remiss if I didn't make it up to you. This is the least I can do." She returned the deferential hand gesture. "Good sir."

Andolosia sighed. Using his forearm, he tentatively brushed at the bats. But as he'd clear one small area, the surrounding bats would fill in the empty space.

"Wait," said Carlotta. "I have an idea. Give me the key."

Andolosia removed the key from his neck and gave it to her. She examined it in the candlelight.

"Gennaro said the Hebrew letters mean 'a song every day.' Why those words?"

Andolosia shrugged. "Probably an old prayer or a psalm."

"This is large for a key and look here. What is this hole at the blade's end?"

Andolosia examined the key. "I don't know."

Carlotta clinked the key against the wall. "It's hollow all the way through."

"That is odd. Let me see." He took the key and examined it. "A tiny hinge connects the bow to the blade," Andolosia observed. "I wonder what would happen if I—" He applied gentle torque to the bow, and it folded open. "Hello." He peered inside the shaft. It had a vortex-shaped bore. "A whistle?" he asked rhetorically. He put the key to his lips and blew. Only the sound of his breath escaped. "Apparently not."

Carlotta took the key from him. "You're holding it backward."

She put the other end to her lips. When she blew, the key emitted a high-pitched B-flat. The bats screeched and took off en masse.

"Brace yourself!" Andolosia warned while crouching down.

He and Carlotta cowered against the torrent of flapping creatures. When the last of the bats had flown, Carlotta's hypothesis was confirmed. The bats had been concealing a five-by-five-foot door – a panel really – with a golden keyhole. Carlotta snapped the bow in place, inserted the key in the hole, and unlocked the panel. Inside was a crank. The crank connected to a worm screw mounted against the grooves of a toothed gear wheel.

"You are a brilliant woman!"

Carlotta turned her head toward the compliment, and all at once their faces were inches apart. A ring of heat encircled his neck. She brushed a tangle of hair off his forehead. An invisible tether seemed to be tugging his head toward hers. He wanted to kiss her but resisted the urge. Was she amenable? Was that business with his hair an invitation or had she acted reflexively – out of an innate sense of order – to adjust his coiffure? It was befuddling that a gesture could have multiple meanings, depending on the intention behind it. He shifted his gaze to the sluice levers. At least levers operated by predictable physical laws. He didn't need to know what they were thinking.

"Astounding," Andolosia said. "The bats did not settle here by accident. Mosè Indaco purposefully integrated them into the dam's design as a layer of security. I hazard he experimented with hundreds of sounds before discovering that a B-flat would prompt them to fly off."

"Or maybe he raised a brood from birth and trained them with the whistle."

"That is an even better hypothesis."

Could he kiss her now? No, he decided. She might think he had flattered her only to steal an affection. She would have been right.

"Hopefully, we will not need to open the gates," Andolosia said, "but if we do, Sansone won't stand a chance."

"What about the townspeople?"

"If all goes according to plan, Sansone will be halfway up the mountain. We require only a small deluge to drown him. By the time the water reaches town, it will be a trickle." He closed the panel door and locked it. "We should go." He slipped the key back around his neck.

They stepped outside. As Andolosia was closing the sluice gate door, the bats, which had been roosting in a laurel tree, swooped inside and blanketed the panel in the wall. He shut the door.

Andolosia was quiet as they descended the mountain, steeped in regret. He'd passed up two good opportunities to kiss Carlotta. What was it he'd said to her that very day? *I defy you to convince me that inaction is the best response to uncertainty?* What a hypocrite. He could've punched himself in the face. Indeed, he decided he would punch himself in the face. Right then and there. Not so hard as to knock himself unconscious or so demonstrative as to draw attention to his self-flagellation. He'd keep it simple. He'd rap his forehead with the knuckles of his right hand, hard enough to hurt without bruising. He'd press and prod the sore spot the rest of the day. But something was preventing him from raising his right hand. Carlotta's hand was gripping it. At some point during his tortured reverie, he'd taken her hand or she his. He sensed no resistance or reluctance in her grip, only flesh on flesh, with no empty space between. That cheered him up a bit. Hand-holding wasn't a kiss, but it wasn't a dunk in the piss vat either.

Carlotta let go Andolosia's hand when they reached the clearing. She shimmied up the trunk of the date palm as spryly as before, climbed on a bough, and reached down to squeeze the fruits.

"Ripe for the plucking," she announced.

She pulled a small knife from her purse and cut the bunch from the branch. The dates crashed at Andolosia's feet.

"What are we going to do with all these dates?" he asked, as Carlotta shimmied back down.

She jumped the last four feet, patted her hands, and said, "Bake."

* * *

Herodotus wrote that, before the Battle of Thermopylae, the Spartan warriors didn't fret over their inevitable defeat. They didn't weep or worry or make elaborate devotions to the gods. They behaved as if it were any other day. They breakfasted on cheese, onions, and bloody pig broth. They dusted their cloaks, watered their horses, shined their spear tips, and brushed their hair. Likewise, Andolosia and Carlotta's battle was imminent, and their odds of success poor, if not hopeless. But they would not spend the final hours lamenting mistakes or beseeching an unfamiliar god for spiritual salvation. Like the Spartans of old, they would embrace the prosaic and the tangible. They would bake. They would honor their guts with a devotion of sweet pastries.

Andolosia pitted, chopped, and ground the dates into a jam, while Carlotta prepared a light, buttery dough and divided it into small circles. He stuffed the circles with jam as the oven heated and Carlotta prepared more dough. Over six hours, they mixed, kneaded, shaped, stuffed, and baked five hundred pastries. When the shelves, tables, and windowsills could no longer contain the cooling pastries, they stacked them six-high on planks covering most of the floor. By the end, they had only a three-by-five-foot area to stand in, which, after they ate a dozen-and-a-half of the warm pastries, expanded to three-by-six.

Their feast concluded, they lay on the floor on their sides. They were face to face, enclosed in a fortress of fresh sweet rolls. Never had Andolosia felt so happy. Why, then, did the image of Stasi's coffin at his grave's black bottom pop into his mind?

"Why are you crying?" Carlotta asked.

"I didn't realize I was."

She propped herself on an elbow and wiped away his tear. She wiped a smudge of jam from the corner of his mouth. Her face hovered over his for a moment. What was she doing? Inspecting him? And it happened. She kissed him. He inhaled her intoxicating water nymph scent, a piquant mixture of cloves and cut timber. He kissed her back. She broke from him and stood. She began to undress. Andolosia stood and did the same.

When he'd envisioned this moment – and he had many times – his fantasy was always colored with ecstasy, panic, or some combination of the two. But now that the moment was upon him for real, he was surprisingly calm. He was standing in a hurricane's eye, in awe of, not afraid of, the maelstrom whipping around him. He seemed to know that whatever he did or didn't do next would be as it was meant to be, as if he'd sneaked a peak at Fate's tapestry. Stasi flashed in his mind again. This time, though, he was alive and vibrant and singing the words *Amor Fati*.

For her part, Carlotta's mood was equally measured, though for a more practical reason. The integrity of the stacks of sweet rolls demanded strict corporeal discipline.

Thus, for reasons profound and practical, they didn't rip their clothes off with abandon. They moved methodically and deliberately, with the same manner and decorum as their pastry preparation. They folded and piled their trousers, skirt, and doublets into two neat stacks, side by side. Carlotta lay on the floor and rested her head on her stack. Andolosia then draped himself on her. Her flesh was as warm as the wishing hat. The sensation of his hardness against her abdomen excited him further. He reached for his purse. He uncinched the top and removed a small flat jar. He unscrewed the jar's lid, revealing what appeared to be a deflated jumble of skin immersed in olive oil. He shook off the excess oil and rolled to his side.

"Is that what I think it is?" she asked with a devilish grin. "A penis hat?"

"It is."

He began affixing it to himself.

She kissed his neck. "Did you settle on goat or cow intestine?"

"Given the town's dearth of cows and goats, I resorted to what I could catch in the wild."

He kissed her bosom.

"Did my big strong man slaughter a wild boar with his bare hands?"

"Something like that."

"You felled a deer with an arrow?"

Fate Accompli

"The animal is irrelevant. What matters is the high quality of the intestine, and on that front, you will not be disappointed."

She interrupted their intimacy and regarded him seriously. "Why must you be so coy? If this penis hat is going inside me, I'd like to know its source."

Andolosia dropped his head to his chest. "If you must know, the animal I got it from was quite old. He was also missing a front leg, so he had trouble walking. I went after him with a rock. He fled – well, more like he hobbled and stumbled and tumbled. His heart gave out before I got to him. Poor fellow."

"A tortoise intestine?"

"Don't be silly. There are no tortoises in Monticello. He was a porcupine."

Carlotta became alarmed. "You're slipping a porcupine onto your—?"

"Porcupines aren't spiky on the inside," he interjected and secured the sheath to the base of his shaft with two thin ties. "It's a very thin cross-section of the intestine. Feel for yourself. It's incredibly sheer and smooth. The olive oil kept it supple."

Carlotta reached down to verify Andolosia's claim. He was right. She kissed him. He got on top of her.

"Wait." She gently pushed on his chest. "When did you find time to hunt a porcupine and make penis hats?"

"While you were off creating bubli, I was stalking the elderly, enfeebled creature. It takes a while to dry intestines and make them into tiny hats. That's why I was awake when you came in at the wee hours. Do you have more questions? Because I would like to think the porcupine did not sacrifice his life and his intestines in vain."

"He did it for the best of reasons," she said furtively. "He did it for science."

"For science," Andolosia concurred.

336

She gripped his back and pulled him into her.

* * *

After the lovemaking, a drowsy Andolosia gazed into the jam-filled center of a pastry that had fallen off its stack. The black jam reminded him of Stasi's grave. He saw no coffin at the black bottom, however. He imagined diving into the darkness and swimming down to find his father.

It was daytime. He wasn't sure whether it was dawn or dusk because the sky was sunless. He was standing at the dam. The scents of cooked dates and cloves billowed from the open door beside the center sluice gate. He stepped inside. Candlelight illuminated the giant nautilus. But it wasn't the same nautilus as before. She was in profile and looked inanimate. Indeed, she was a facsimile carved from wood and painted to resemble a nautilus. A seam ran along the shell's outer circumference and was hinged on the left. There was a leaden knob on the right front. He tugged at the knob, and the shell's front half swung open.

All at once, he was in the cutting room of the Petasos hat shop. A man in a chair by the table was struggling to thread a needle. A fat, one-eyed black cat loomed from the top of a tall cabinet, mewing with frustration. The man glanced up from the needlework and regarded Andolosia. One of his eye sockets was a black void. He wore a monocle over the other. He bore a striking resemblance to Stasi. He greeted Andolosia by a different name, which Andolosia understood to be his true name. The man pointed over Andolosia's shoulder and said, "She is here too."

Andolosia turned, and he was on the bluff in Livorno where Stasi was buried. Carlotta was kneeling, shovel at her side, patting earth around a freshly planted sapling. He didn't want to disturb her work, so he turned back to the man.

337

Andolosia became disoriented, for he was now on his knees, staring at the bottom of a grave. There, the one-eyed man lay with the one-eyed cat on his chest.

The man called up to Andolosia. "Between the two of us, we should be able to find the way to black bottom."

Andolosia was confused. Wasn't the man already in the black bottom?

"No," the man answered. "Not yet." He told Andolosia to close the lid, once again calling him that different name.

Andolosia closed the lid.

Carlotta exclaimed, "Ouch."

She was holding her hand, wincing from the large splinter stuck in the tip of her index finger. He pulled it out, and she bled a spot of date jam. He licked the jam from her finger and was surprised by its bitterness. Her eyes were glowing indigo. Had they always done so? Why hadn't he noticed before?

"It is time to water the tree," she said, calling him by that different name. "The tree cannot grow without water."

"Don't you think I know that?" he snapped.

A torrent washed over them.

In the morning, when Andolosia awoke for real, he recalled every detail of the dream, save that different name.

CHAPTER

THIRTY-TWO

Monticello, The Following Morning

Carlotta and Andolosia laid dozens of wooden planks end to end, forming a curvilinear platform down Well Street. After setting the date rolls on the planks, they exchanged a farewell kiss. She headed out of town. He went to Gennaro's house.

Gennaro was awake, and, at the moment anyway, he was Gennaro. He looked unwell. His face was red with fever, and he was perspiring heavily. He also complained of a headache caused by Hermes' mental tantrum. The god was frustrated that Gennaro was still resisting possession. Andolosia brewed a tea infused with extracts of valerian and poppy. By the second cup, Gennaro's color had moderated and he'd stopped sweating. His headache also had abated. Hermes' tantrum had settled to a low, murmuring pout.

Andolosia was encouraged by the tea's sedating effect. The plan's success depended on Gennaro maintaining control of his body until the appointed time. Too much sedation would put Gennaro and Hermes out of commission; too little, and Hermes might be intractable.

Andolosia lamented manipulating Gennaro's biology, even though the plan was his best hope of long-term survival. If all went well, Hermes would leave Gennaro's body and return to Oblivion. Andolosia advised the torpid Gennaro to lie down and rest.

Meanwhile, Monticello was awakening to the scent of warm, fruit-filled rolls. Every turn bustled with oohs and ahs, swinging doors, salivating mouths, and chomping teeth. Sweetness washed over palates and infiltrated blood and brains. To many in this devout town, their giddiness felt carnal so early in the morning. They fretted over whether eating the rolls was unlawful or sinful. Not that their reservations precluded them from partaking. In fact, they helped themselves to more rolls when they saw Don Salvatore holding one in each hand.

There was, however, one unhappy Monticellan. Paola was fuming. She kicked over the planks outside her shop, scattering sweet rolls onto the dusty street. That garnered outraged glances from Madamas Margherita and Francesca, who approached Paola menacingly. She backpedaled, bracing for a violent molestation, until a sonorous peal rattled everyone's bones and shook the shutters along Well Street. It was a strange sound – melodic, yet piercing; poignant, yet hollow and metallic. The sound of stomping boots followed.

Andolosia slipped on a hooded robe and stepped outside to investigate the clamor. Four young men were marching shoulder to shoulder around Turn Eight. They were dressed in brown uniforms and long-billed hats. Two carried standards emblazoned with the Fasci Sansone emblem. The other two held unusual silver horns with an oval-shaped main tube bisected near the mouthpiece by three smaller tubes with plungers. The two boys played a loud, crisp fanfare and stood at attention, horns held vertically in front of them. A platoon of inspectors approached from behind in tight formation. They, too, halted and stood at attention.

A tall, wispy figure rounded the turn with the same horn in gold tucked under his arm. The man moved gingerly, mincing, as though conserving energy. He proceeded to the front of the parade. His doublet and breeches matched the dun color of the boy-inspectors' doublets and shorts. Whereas the inspectors' uniforms were unadorned, his was trimmed in orange silk and his collar was brocaded with the stick bundle and sun insignia. He also wore flesh-colored boots with insignia on each upper. His gloves were fashioned of the same leather and bore the Fasci Sansone insignia. He was Sansone de Medici, of course. His unpowdered, pock-marked face was the color of sienna clay.

Sansone forced a wan smile, which morphed into a leer because he no longer had complete command over his withering facial muscles.

"Where is Don Salvatore?" he shouted to the gathering crowd.

The priest stepped forward, chewing a sweet roll. "I am he, Messer." He wiped a splotch of jam from his cheek.

Sansone parted his blue-gray lips, exposing yellowed teeth and blackened gums. "I am Messer Sansone de Medici." He reached into his vest pocket and extracted a letter, which he handed to the priest. "As you see, the tribunal in Palermo, acting under the authority of the Council of the Suprema, has deputized me to conduct the inquisition of one Madama Carlotta Lux and one Maestro Andolosia Petasos on counts of witchcraft and fornication."

Don Salvatore flashed pique at Paola, who was cowering behind Margherita and Francesca. He read the letter carefully. At one point, he took a bite of sweet roll, and a blob of jam landed on Sansone's name. He wiped off the jam, smearing away the last three letters. He looked at Sansone apologetically. Whatever irritation Sansone was expressing was subsumed in his wraith-like sneer. Don Salvatore handed the letter back to him.

"I am afraid, Messer Sansone, that you have made the journey for no reason," Don Salvatore said, "Maestra Crostelli has since recanted."

Paola squeezed between Margherita and Francesca. "I have not."

"You withdrew it yesterday," the priest insisted. "We reached an understanding."

"That was yesterday's understanding." Paola gestured to the priest's sweet roll. "Today is a new day."

Don Salvatore regarded the standards, cornets, and platoon of uniformed young men behind Sansone. "I am not familiar with these symbols and the dress of these men, nor do I understand why the Church has dispatched a Tuscan guild enforcer and a legion of inspectors to conduct a simple inquisition."

"Firstly, it is not your place, Don Salvatore, to question the tribunal's wisdom," Sansone said curtly. "You saw the Council of the Suprema's seal on the letter. You read the unambiguous words vesting me with authority over this matter. Secondly, there are no simple inquisitions. Often, what lies at the surface is merely the tip of an underground mountain of evil. So I ask you, Don Salvatore, where are Madama Carlotta Lux and Maestro Andolosia Petasos?"

The priest shifted his feet. "Maestro Gennaro Rabino is the key witness here. The accused have been living under his roof. He would know of any untoward behavior."

"And I shall speak to Maestro Gennaro in due course," Sansone said. "But first I wish to interrogate the accused. Bring them to me."

Don Salvatore glanced right. "I do not know their whereabouts."

Sansone turned to the crowd and announced, "Whoever knows the location of Madama Lux or Maestro

Petasos, the Church demands you step forward."

The crowd murmured. No one came forward.

"Be forewarned," Sansone continued, "any interference or harboring of the accused shall be treated as a heresy punishable by the *strappado*."

The crowd rumbled with worry, but, again, no one stepped forward.

"Very well," Sansone said to the priest. "I shall begin with Maestro Rabino. Take me to him."

Andolosia raced to Gennaro's house. He burst through the door and rushed to his bedside. He jostled Gennaro's shoulder vigorously.

"Sansone has arrived with his army," Andolosia said urgently. "He will be here any moment to take your testimony."

Gennaro rubbed his eyes. "Help me to my feet, boy. Bring me to the dining table."

Andolosia did so – no easy task in Gennaro's weakened, leaden condition.

He set Gennaro on a bench and asked, "Are you strong enough for his questions?"

"I believe so."

"Is Hermes still quiet?"

"Barely a whisper. The tea is working."

There was a rapping at the door. Andolosia released a nervous sigh and went to the door and opened it.

"Well, well, Maestro Andolosia," Sansone said with insincere congeniality. "I was told this is the home of Maestro Rabino. How convenient to find you here. I trust Madonna Carlotta is with you?"

"She is not."

"Where might I find her?"

"I cannot say."

"But you *will* say, if you value your life," he said imperiously.

"I suggest you interrogate Maestro Rabino first. His life is more tenuous than mine at the moment. After that, we shall have a palaver, and you may do with me what you wish."

"You are either a fool or madly in love. Judging by your demeanor, I'd hazard both."

Andolosia did not reply.

Sansone sighed. "Seeing I still owe you a debt for your father, I shall grant your request."

Andolosia bowed slightly and gestured Sansone inside. Sansone proceeded to the table and stood opposite Gennaro. Don Salvatore and Paola flanked Sansone. Andolosia lurked behind them, where he could keep an eye on Gennaro.

"You are Maestro Gennaro Rabino?" Sansone asked.

"I am," Gennaro answered wearily.

"I am Messer Sansone de Medici. The inquisitorial tribunal in Palermo has authorized me to investigate charges of witchcraft and fornication against Maestro Andolosia and Madama Carlotta."

"So I have been told Messer," Gennaro said, his voice thin and raspy.

"Are you unwell, Maestro?" Sansone asked.

"A chill has caught me."

Sansone narrowed his eyes. "Is that a Sicilian expression? Do you mean you have caught a chill?"

Gennaro laughed weakly. "Something like that."

"Ask him if he's been poisoned by the blood of children," Paola urged.

"You will be silent, Maestra," Sansone admonished. "Still, it is a reasonable question. What say you, Maestro Gennaro? Does the blood of children ail you?"

"No, Messer," Gennaro said. "Just too much wine and too little confession."

A mien of recognition passed over Sansone's face. "You have a familiar countenance. Are we acquainted?"

"I do not believe so." Gennaro began perspiring. He wiped his forehead with his hand. "Perhaps we were brothers in another life," he added with a snicker.

Sansone sniffed. "I doubt that very much."

"May I ask, Messer, that instrument under your arm – it intrigues me. What is it?"

"A horn of my own design," Sansone answered.

"You are an engineer?"

"Not as such. The design came to me in a dream. I sketched it on parchment and handed it to my engineers, who fashioned it." Sansone pointed to the valves. "These here allow for much better sound control than today's common horns."

"Can you play it as exquisitely as you designed it?" Gennaro asked.

"The Muses have seen fit to bless me with great ability," Sansone boasted.

Gennaro grimaced with jealousy. Andolosia fretted that the tea was wearing off, and Hermes was assuming control. Although Gennaro's voice still sounded like Gennaro's, the content and tone of his speech was distressingly Hermes-like. Andolosia poured tea from the kettle into a mug and set it before Gennaro.

"You should drink this," Andolosia advised.

Gennaro drank the tea. Andolosia prayed it would take effect quickly.

Gennaro belched loudly, startling Sansone.

"I would be honored if you would demonstrate your masterful ability with the horn," Gennaro said.

"Perhaps later, after the inquisition."

Gennaro reached for the horn. "May I hold it?"

Sansone hesitated and relinquished the horn.

Gennaro's eyes widened with fascination. He traced a finger along the opening of the bell, around the valves, and down the main pipe. "I believe I know from whence your inspiration came," he said at length. "Not the Muses, but the god Hermes."

"Hermes?" Sansone scoffed. "Apollo is the god of music."

"In title only. Hermes created the lyre from a tortoise and gryphon bones. It was the very first musical instrument. Every instrument since is but a shadow of the original."

Andolosia felt nervous sweat dripping down his armpits. This was bad. Very bad. He filled Gennaro's mug with the remaining tea and held it under Gennaro's lips. Gennaro took the mug and drank its contents.

Sansone turned indignant. "Hermes forfeited the lyre to Apollo as punishment for purloining his cattle. Hermes has no rightful claim to that instrument or any other." Sansone swiped the horn from Gennaro and secured it under his arm.

Andolosia interjected. "Perhaps, Messer Sansone, you should move on to the matter at hand."

"Indeed." Turning back to Gennaro, the discomfited Sansone asked, "What do you have to say about fornication?"

"I say I am not in the mood, Messer, but maybe after some wine—"

A blushing Sansone interjected, "I am inquiring about the charge against Madama Lux and Maestro Petasos!"

Andolosia regarded Gennaro with trepidation. His eyelids were sagging, and his head was nodding forward.

Gennaro perked up. "There is no truth to it. They are cousins." He pointed to the two bedrooms. "My room abuts theirs, and I am a light sleeper. Nothing but snores have I heard from them."

Andolosia sighed with relief.

Gennaro yawned. "I am very fatigued. I must rest." He gestured to Andolosia for assistance. Andolosia helped him to his feet.

"There you have it, Messer Sansone," Don Salvatore said. "The accusation has been disproved. You and your men can now leave Monticello."

"This inquisition is incomplete," Sansone insisted. "I must take Madama Lux's testimony about the witchcraft allegation. I fear she has fled Monticello."

He eyed Andolosia suspiciously. Andolosia returned a hard stare.

"The whore cannot have gone far," Paola said. "She made those sweet rolls outside, and they are quite fresh."

"Ah, yes, the transcendent odor that greeted my arrival," Sansone said. "It is imperative I sample one . . . for investigational purposes, of course."

Sansone exited Gennaro's home with Don Salvatore and Paola Crostelli. After settling Gennaro in his bed, Andolosia joined them outside. Sansone plucked a date roll off the plank. He sniffed it and took a nibble. His right eyebrow rose. He took a second, more substantial bite. Surviving mostly on Perso's concoctions, Sansone hadn't enjoyed the taste of food in months.

"This tiresome Church business has left me famished," Sansone remarked.

"Messer Sansone," Paola said, "it would be a great honor to serve you my mafalda bread, the finest in all of Monticello."

Sansone took another bite. His eyes rolled upward in delight.

"No mafalda could hold a candle to these sweet rolls," he said.

Paola was affronted. "Use caution, Messer. They may be laced with children's blood. The heretic made them."

Sansone reproved her. "Let us not rush to judgment. What better way to determine whether they are bewitched than to sample them? If they contain children's blood, surely a mouth among us will taste the truth." He raised his voice to address the company of inspectors. "Hear me, boys of the Fasci Sansone. Fortify yourselves with these sweet rolls and commence a house to house search for the nym – for

Madonna Lux."

The inspectors broke ranks, helped themselves to sweet rolls, and fanned out. Sansone took two more rolls and stepped toward Gennaro's front door.

Andolosia ran ahead to block his path. "Where are you going, Messer?"

"It is time for our palaver, Maestro Andolosia."

"We can palaver here on Well Street. I wouldn't want us to disturb Maestro Gennaro."

Sansone waved off the suggestion. "We best discuss this matter in private, lest the good people of Monticello get the wrong impression about my purpose here." He pointed over Andolosia's shoulder. "We will speak softly so as not to disturb the Maestro."

Resigned, Andolosia turned and entered the open doorway. He took two steps and abruptly stopped. Gennaro was seated at the table instead of asleep in bed. He was drinking with his left hand, while his right hand gripped the wine decanter's handle. His eyes were clouded and his cheeks flush and dewy. Andolosia didn't know what to do. There was no more sedating tea and no time to brew more. The question was, who was seated at the table, Gennaro or Hermes?

Gennaro slammed his mug on the table and bellowed a command in the god's resonant, ancient voice. "Mortal, I require mead and ambrosia."

Andolosia had his answer.

"Why have you stopped?" Sansone asked from behind. "Is someone else here? Let me pass."

Andolosia wheeled around, intending to shoo Sansone outside, but Sansone already was pushing past him. Andolosia's shoulder swung into Sansone's back, causing the pastry to fly from Sansone's hand. When Sansone lunged to catch it, the horn slipped from under his armpit and thudded on the floor. He fumbled the pastry, which thudded next to the horn. Hermes ogled the shiny instrument.

"Heavens!" Sansone scolded. "Must you be so clumsy!" He knelt and examined the horn's mouthpiece, coiled tube, and bell. "Fortunately, it is intact." He stood, set the horn on its bell at the edge of the table, and picked the pastry off the floor. "My sweet roll, however, is befouled." He plucked strands and flecks from the sticky roll and nibbled it. "Mmm. Delicious. Maestro Rabino, have you sampled a roll?"

"I'm more of an ambrosia man myself," Hermes quipped.

"Your voice sounds different, Maestro. I hadn't detected the accent when we spoke previously."

Andolosia attempted to interject with an excuse he hadn't yet concocted. "That is because—"

"Too much wine," Hermes interrupted. "Makes my tongue forget itself. I slip into the old ways of speaking."

"You are not a native of Monticello?" Sansone asked.

"I hail from Olym—"

"Delphi!" Andolosia blurted. "Maestro Rabino was born in Delphi. Moved away as a young boy, isn't that right?"

Hermes grunted an affirmation. "A great flood washed our home away."

"A pity," Sansone said. "Forgive the further imposition, Maestro, but Maestro Andolosia and I have unfinished business."

"By all means," Hermes said. "Please. Sit."

Sansone sat on the opposite bench. Hermes got up, came around to Sansone's side, and filled a mug with wine. He set the mug far enough to Sansone's right that he had to lean to reach it. In that instant, Hermes purloined the horn, breezed into the bed chamber, and shut the door behind him. Unaware of the stolen instrument, Sansone sipped his wine and scrutinized Andolosia.

"Let us not mince words, Maestro Petasos. Where is

she?"

"Answer me this first. Who is it that addresses me? Messer Sansone de Medici or the god Apollo?"

"The former. Given my vessel's fragile state, Apollo remains just beneath the surface of my mind. He has agreed to hold off until the water nymph appears. After he has had his way with her, he will vacate my body for good."

"And you trust him to fulfill his promise?"

"He has sworn it on Styx."

Andolosia studied Sansone's swarthy, careworn face and remarked, "I am not accustomed to your unpowdered visage."

Sansone's eyes glistened. "Today is a special occasion. The day of the great unveiling. The day that accidents of birth and blood no longer determine one's social station. The day we crush the myth of inferiority perpetuated by the old guard. The day my children and I cease viewing ourselves through the eyes of our oppressors. The day of revolution."

"You've quite the busy day planned," Andolosia said dryly. "Your florid language almost makes your objective sound noble. Almost. You speak of unveiling. Ha. Your words are just another veil, and a thin, moth-eaten veil at that. But no veil, no matter how obscuring, can conceal your vile means. A revolution born of depravity necessarily yields a depraved end."

"We shall put that proposition to the test."

"Your boy-inspectors are young and soft-hearted. This spectacle will repulse and horrify them. They will turn their backs on you."

Sansone shook his head and spoke in a didactic tone. "You still do not understand, Maestro Andolosia. To those boys, I am their benevolent father, the father who loves them despite their low status and sullied bloodlines. Unlike their natural fathers, I didn't abandon them to the ravages

350

of poverty or, worse, sell them to their enslavers. They are incapable of seeing me – their loving father – commit something so heinous as a rape."

"Will you bewitch them with Perso's medicine?"

Sansone's lips curled into a pitiable smile. "You are a genius with machines but quite the neophyte when it comes to the machinations of the mind. The most potent hypnotic derives not from a plant or the alchemist's laboratory but the myths in which we are steeped. My children will witness what they expect to witness, what I have been promising they will witness – the arrival of a supreme prince more powerful than any god of old."

"You speak of yourself, no doubt."

"No doubt," Sansone rejoined. "I will succeed where Apollo was thwarted. I will bed the water nymph before she becomes a tree. In this new myth, she will not transform. I will. I will become the supreme prince."

"But it will not be your triumph," Andolosia argued. "The god Apollo will violate her through you. Your transformation will be premised on a lie."

"That is your truth. My boys will know a different truth. Tomorrow, they will begin spreading a gospel from Taormina to Turin, from Sicily to Sardinia. They will tell the people about the great miracle on Mount Monticello, how they witnessed a supreme prince descend from the sky on a horseless chariot and lie with the water nymph, a feat not even the great god Apollo could accomplish. Desperate for a new order, desperate to be liberated from the despotism of the aristocracy and the Church, the people will come to believe this story, for the alternative is their withering existence under the status quo. The ranks of the Fasci Sansone will swell with zealous followers."

"They will swell with zealous imbeciles, I should say."

"I agree, for as you know, we live in a world of imbeciles. My despicable forefathers proved that fact many times over.

For centuries, they soaked the masses for every last florin to build a gilded city in God's name. And how did they do this? By perpetuating a myth of their own, by promising hoi polloi a rich afterlife in exchange for the 'blessing' of earthly poverty. You see, the masses are always taken by what a thing seems to be. Few really know what you are. Even fewer try to make that truth known, and those who do, do so at their peril."

Sansone stared at Andolosia, unblinking. He looked exhausted and frail, except for his eyes, which smoldered with determination and ruthlessness. Andolosia had a mind to leap across the table and seize the man's throat. He reckoned it wouldn't require much force to snap his reed-thin neck. But Andolosia's arms felt leaden. He hadn't been in a physical altercation before, let alone killed a man with his bare hands. Even his porcupine hunt ended before it began. It was just as well. Killing Sansone at that moment would have squandered their best chance of breaking the curses and landed Andolosia on the gallows for murder. He would stick to the plan.

The bedroom door flung open and Hermes began blasting sounds on Sansone's horn. He paraded into the front room, playing an improvised tune rife with glissandos, portamentos, and arpeggios.

Sansone was mortified. He bolted upright, knocking into the table and spilling his mug of wine. "Stop that! Remove those fat lips from my horn at once!"

Hermes handed the instrument back to Sansone, who promptly wiped the mouthpiece on his velvet doublet.

"My deepest apologies, Messer," Hermes said with a bow. "I could not resist. Truly, you have created a miracle. Even I, a humble neophyte, can make music with ease. To be sure, my playing must pale next to yours."

"To be sure," Sansone said indignantly.

"I know you said after the inquisition, but might you grace us with a recital right here and now?" Hermes asked like a sycophant.

"Maestro Rabino, please!" Andolosia admonished. He flicked his head in a get-the-hell-out-of-here motion.

Sansone waved off Andolosia's irritation. "We are Maestro Gennaro's guests, after all. I can indulge him with a brief ditty."

Sansone brought the horn to his lips and played a series of pure, crisp notes, investing each one with a precise measure of volume and time. Although pleasant and intricate, the song was mechanical and devoid of feeling. Hollow through and through.

"Delightful," Hermes said disingenuously. "May I beg your indulgence for one more opportunity to play? If I can approximate even a hundredth of your genius, I will count myself richer than Ploutus. I promise to leave you be. No more interruptions to your parley."

"Very well." Hesitantly, Sansone handed the horn to Hermes. "Strive to keep your spittle to a minimum."

Hermes played back Sansone's tune with absolute fidelity. He played it again, this time stretching certain notes and playing others percussively. He alternated between clean notes and glissandos. His rendition was dynamic and exhilarating. Sansone's original version had sounded simple and childish by comparison.

Hermes wiped the mouthpiece on his shirt and returned the cornet. "As I feared," he said with false humility, "my skills are limited. You are clearly the instrument's true master."

Hermes' lip curled puckishly in one corner, triggering a glimmer of recognition in Sansone.

"Let us return to the parley," Andolosia said insistently. "Maestro Gennaro will enjoy a sweet roll *outside*."

Hermes grunted at Andolosia and exited.

"Peculiar fellow," Sansone remarked. "I feel I know him, but . . ." He abandoned the thought and turned to

Andolosia with a severe expression. "I tire of parlay, Maestro Petasos. Where the devil is Carlotta?"

"Nearby."

"Will she surrender without a struggle?"

"Would you prefer a battle, Messer?"

"No. I just assumed you would make a futile attempt to kill me or wish Carlotta away with that stolen hat of yours."

"Carlotta is tired of running, tired of peering over her shoulder. She wants the Daphne Curse to end. If that means a pitiful act of public coitus, so be it."

"Wise decision. I require one hour for Perso's medicines to wear off. If Carlotta does not show herself to Apollo – if she should suddenly be wished to the other side of the world – my inspectors are under order to destroy Monticello. Is that clear?"

"As water. There is a date palm in the clearing on the mountain. She awaits you there."

CHAPTER

THIRTY-THREE

Mount Monticello, One Hour Later

Andolosia removed the wishing hat and reluctantly handed it to Hermes. He'd been taught from childhood that returning the hat to its rightful owner would redeem the Petasos name and liberate them from indentured millinery. He should have felt a sense of triumph. He was that much closer to pursuing a life of scientific inquiry. Instead, his heart ached with melancholy and nostalgia. He felt as if he were severing an invisible thread binding him to his milliner forefathers. He was daunted by the enormity of rethreading the intergenerational needle with a new purpose and stitching together a future without a predetermined design.

"At long last," Hermes marveled. He brought the warm, fleshy hat to his nose and sniffed. "Just as I remember."

He placed the hat on his head. The leather contracted in some places and expanded in others, until it perfectly conformed to his skull. His lip curled up on the right.

"I almost forgot," Andolosia said. He reached into his purse, pulled out the ancient gold coin, and offered it to

Hermes. "For the hat cleaning you did not receive."

Hermes chuckled. "You are an honorable businessman. Keep it. I have no need for gold. I have my hat, and soon I will have my lyre too."

Andolosia bowed his head and returned the coin to his purse. He surveyed the slope. Sansone was ascending the mountain with a horn tucked in his armpit. He was not alone. He had an inspector in tow, the youngest, by the looks of him.

"Your brother approaches," Andolosia said. "You know what must be done. I shall take my leave and observe from afar."

Andolosia staked out a secluded position behind a shrub twenty yards uphill from the palm tree. He hadn't been settled for more than ten seconds, when Hermes deviated from the plan. Instead of remaining at the tree, he traipsed behind a myrtle bush.

"Where are you going?" Andolosia yelled after him.

Hermes didn't answer.

Is he relieving himself?

"Hello?"

When a minute passed without a sound or signal from Hermes, Andolosia feared the worst.

He betrayed us. He wished himself away.

But Hermes emerged from behind the bush and returned to the palm tree. He was no longer wearing the hat. He was holding it in front of himself in a peculiar way, one hand underneath the crown and the other on top.

What is that about?

Sansone was approaching, his gait languid and unsteady. He was perspiring heavily, and his eyes were as murky as leaded glass. His florid face contorted when he caught sight of Hermes.

"What is this trickery?" he demanded in Apollo's magnificent voice. "You are not the water nymph!"

"Salutations, dear brother," Hermes said.

"Broth—"

Apollo's mouth fixed in surprise.

"It is I, Hermes." He gestured to the boy inspector standing behind Apollo. "Who is your diminutive companion?"

"My mortal vessel requested a witness. The boy-prophet will recount these solemn events to the mortals. A Homer of the modern age or some such nonsense. Tell me, Brother. How did you escape Oblivion?"

"Just as you did. Through a door on the shore."

"You made it to shore?" Apollo asked, impressed.

"No thanks to you. I called from the water, but you sailed right by . . . fifty times at least."

"Really? Fifty times?" Apollo remarked disingenuously.

"At least," Hermes emphasized.

"Forgive me, Brother. The sail luffs so loudly, I can hardly hear myself think."

Hermes raised a skeptical eyebrow. "Fortunately, you left a rope dangling from the stern. I grabbed it and held on."

"How careless of me," Apollo answered without thinking. "That is to say, how fortunate for you."

"Indeed." Hermes was seething. "I followed you ashore, but you were too far ahead. I entered a door next to the one you entered. I awoke in this vessel."

Apollo glanced at the hat in Hermes' hands. "Ah, I see you have reclaimed the gryphon hat. Excellent. Please wish yourself far away. I have business here."

"So I gather, Brother. I shall take my leave but not with this hat. I want you to have it."

Andolosia was alarmed.

What in Hades?

Hermes wasn't supposed to give Apollo the hat, only use it to teleport him to the Forms.

Apollo regarded the hat warily.

Hermes went on. "I have spent eons reflecting on my abysmal behavior toward you. I now understand why you have refused to fish me from Oblivion's sea. I am not worthy. I have not paid you the respect you deserve. Stealing your cattle and giving you a broken lyre as recompense – shame on me."

"Then you admit to breaking the lyre?"

"I confess. I was an immature infant-god. It took a millennium in Oblivion for me to realize my folly, but I mean to make amends with this."

"That . . . that is a profound gesture, Hermes. I am deeply moved. At the risk of sounding presumptuous, might I also prevail on you to repair the lyre?"

"You have the lyre with you?" Hermes asked excitedly.

"The lyre is in Oblivion with everything else from Olympus. Everything except your hat, that is. But when we return, I shall keep a lookout for you and pull you aboard, where you can make the fix."

"To be sure," Hermes said, disappointed. "I will make the repair in Oblivion." His lip curled up, and he added. "In the meantime, take the hat as partial compensation?"

"I am at a loss for words, Brother." His eyes became rheumy. "I accept."

"Grant me the honor of placing my most treasured possession on your head."

Apollo bowed his head. "It shall be my honor to receive it."

Hermes maintained his hand under the crown as he set the hat on Apollo's bowed head. He quickly extricated his hand and patted the top of the crown to make the hat snug.

"Wear it in good health, Brother."

Apollo raised his head. His nostrils flared. "The hat is odiferous."

"It has been in the grubby mortals' possession too long. One wish should blow the stench right off."

"How does it work?"

"Simple. Close your eyes, think of a place, and ask the hat to take you there."

Andolosia bit the knuckle of his index finger to stanch his anguish. Hermes was going about it all wrong. He should've been wearing the hat, not Apollo. If Apollo were to vanish with the wishing hat – if he didn't go to the Forms and purge the love arrow from his heart – Andolosia and Carlotta were doomed.

Apollo closed his eyes. "The hat is so warm."

Hermes sniggered. "Such is the nature of gryphon leather."

"And moist, too."

Apollo's face fixed in intense concentration. Hermes was struggling to contain his laughter. After a few moments, Apollo still hadn't gone anywhere, which was a relief to Andolosia but also a source of bewilderment. Apollo opened his eyes. He blinked and scanned his surroundings, vexed.

"The hat does not work for me, Hermes."

"To the contrary, Brother. It works to perfection!"

Discomfited by Hermes' bemusement, Apollo removed the hat. There was a brown, sloppy mass on his scalp. He touched the lump tentatively. He brought down his hand and regarded his fingertips with horrified fascination. He waved his fingers under his nose and recoiled.

"What is the meaning of this?" Apollo fumed.

Hermes cackled. "It is a warm welcome from your precious cattle. They miss you." He burst into rollicking laughter. "Oh, Brother, if only you could see yourself."

Apollo was stone-faced as manure oozed onto his brow.

Hermes' laughter abated. "All right, then. Enough hijinks. There is a serious matter we must attend to involving your nymph-addled spirit. The mortals have reported a proph—" Hermes did a double-take at Apollo. "Oh dear. You've got a spot on your upper lip." He retrieved a kerchief from his doublet and made a move to wipe it off.

Apollo swatted Hermes' hand. The horn fell from under his arm. He tossed the manure-filled hat away, and it smacked into the palm tree. He approached Hermes menacingly.

Hermes cowered. "Please, Brother. It was just a joke. I meant no harm."

But Apollo was not in a forgiving mood. He seized Hermes' throat. Hermes gasped for air and flailed his arms. His face transitioned from crimson, to blue, and, finally, to purple. He evacuated his bowels, and his arms and legs went limp. Apollo released Hermes' vessel. Gennaro dropped to his knees and toppled forward, dead.

Andolosia was enraged. Hermes' puerile prank had led directly – and predictably – to Gennaro's murder at Apollo's hands. Worse, he'd foiled the plan.

Apollo retrieved his horn and shouted up the mountain. "Come to me now, fair nymph, or the blood of a thousand mortals will be on your hands! One blast from this horn, and Sansone's army shall commence executions, starting with the children. I give you to the count of one hundred."

It was time for the backup plan, time to flood the mountain. But Andolosia hadn't counted on Sansone sending a boy up with Apollo. The boy was no older than ten or eleven. Drowning Apollo meant killing a boy who was years away from his first whisker. Who was Andolosia to consign him to death? This boy might grow into a great man who would do great things, in which case his premature death would cost the world dearly. Then again, the boy could do terrible things, in which case his demise would be an anticipatory mercy. In all likelihood, the boy would do nothing of lasting significance in his life – such was most men's fate, to be an inconspicuous stitch in Fate's great tapestry.

Is the boy's life – this undeveloped and inchoate bundle

of orphaned potential – worth more or less than Carlotta's freedom from divine rape? How do I make this calculation? I can't. It would be a fraud. My love for Carlotta skews everything.

He would have to go with his gut. His gut said, although Andolosia Petasos' conscience might adapt to the death of an innocent boy, he definitely could not exist in a world where Carlotta Lux's soul was defiled.

His death will be quick. He won't suffer.

Apollo swooned. He shakily lowered himself to the ground and leaned his back against Gennaro's corpse for support. Sansone's body was petering out.

"One!" Apollo shouted wearily.

Andolosia had to get to Carlotta. The wishing hat would have been the quickest mode, but Hermes had hidden it in the myrtle or on his person. There was no time to conduct a stealthy search with Apollo right there. He would have to transport himself the old-fashioned way. He sprinted up the mountain.

"Five!" Apollo yelled.

* * *

Carlotta paced outside the door beside the sluice gate, nervously fingering the golden key around her neck. Andolosia stumbled toward her, panting and wheezing, legs enervated. He doubled over.

"What's happening?" she asked. "Why are you running? Where's the wishing hat?"

"No . . . time . . . to explain," he said between gasps and huffs. "Hermes . . . betrayed us."

"Why is Apollo shouting numbers?"

"Counting. If . . . if you do not go to him by the count of one hundred . . . he will blow his horn. Sansone's army will start killing . . . killing children. Must open the floodgates.

361

Hurry."

Carlotta darted into the chamber, removed the key from her neck, and folded the bow open. She brought the small golden tube to her lips and blew, prompting the bats to abandon the wall and fly outside. She unlocked the panel concealing the worm-drive. She gripped the massive crank and pulled. She couldn't get it to budge, even after leaning back with all her weight.

"Help me, Andolosia! It's stuck."

Andolosia shambled into the chamber, grabbed ahold of the crank, and pulled with her. His added strength and weight did nothing.

"Sixty!" Apollo yelled up the slope.

"Christ!" Andolosia exclaimed. He plucked the candle from the sconce and inspected the gear. "God's Blood! The worm shaft is jammed with rust. How stupid of me for not noticing this before." He spotted a small basket in the corner. "What's in there?"

"The remnants of my lunch," Carlotta said. "A crust of bread, a few grapes, olive oil."

"Give me the oil. Quickly!"

Carlotta fished an earthenware flask from the basket and handed it to him. He poured the oil around the shaft openings in the gear and worked it into the rust.

"Seventy!" Apollo shouted.

Andolosia pulled on the crank. The gear moved a little. He poured more oil into the mechanism and worked it into the rust.

"We're running out of time," Carlotta said. "I have to go to him. It will give you time to loosen the crank."

"I won't open the gates with you down there. You'll drown."

"Eighty!" Apollo shouted.

Carlotta put a hand on Andolosia's shoulder. "I will lure Apollo away from the palm tree and give a signal. When I sing aloud, when you hear the song I sang you, open the gates. How long will it take for the deluge to reach the tree?"

"Twenty-five seconds from when the gates are fully open."

"I will count to fifteen and climb the tree. I can do it in five, so I'll have time to spare."

"But that volume of water might uproot the tree and you with it. I cannot be certain without doing the proper calculations."

"Ninety!" Apollo shouted.

"A wise man once told that inaction is not the best response to uncertainty," Carlotta said.

"Damn him. There has to be another way."

"There isn't, and you know it. We owe it to Monticello. We brought Sansone here."

"Go," he said begrudgingly. "There is a young boy down there. Sansone brought him as a witness. Your well-being takes precedence, but if there's any way to help him . . ." He choked up at the impossible situation.

Carlotta kissed him tenderly. "I propose we take a meandering route to Padua and explore every bakery along the way. Think of all the strange and delicious jam rolls that await us."

Andolosia sniffed. "I already know my favorite."

"One-hundred!" Apollo shouted. "I am going to sound the horn!"

Carlotta darted from the chamber. "Coming, great Apollo!"

Andolosia returned to the crank. He worked the oil into the mechanism and pushed and pulled the handle to loosen the oxidation. Carlotta was right. Only the deluge would end the crisis and save the town. But there would be a cost. There would be death at the palm tree. That was inevitable.

Andolosia alternately pulled the crank and worked in the olive oil. It budged a quarter turn. With a few more tugs, it moved halfway around. He bore down and gave it a ferocious yank. His palms screamed in agony. His chest muscles and back quaked. His neck veins swelled to bursting. Finally, the gear relented and completed a full rotation. The sluice gates rose an inch, releasing a brief, shallow torrent. He quickly cranked the gear counterclockwise, sealing the gates.

Andolosia caught his breath and awaited Carlotta's signal. He figured she was at the palm tree by then. He tried to envision what was transpiring. He imagined Apollo brushing Carlotta's shoulder with his vessel's pallid, spindly fingers, while his devitalized blue lips beckoned for a kiss. Would she permit it? She'd have to, but she wouldn't make it easy. She'd bob and weave, feigning a lover's game of hard to get. She couldn't put him off for long, though. She'd permit him one kiss, hoping that would sate him. It wouldn't. The kiss would intensify his cravings. He'd move in for another, deeper kiss. She'd push him back with a coquettish admonishment to savor their union. Apollo, however, would succumb to his heart's throbbing twinge and dispense with all pretense of manners and propriety. He'd seize her, throw her to the ground, and tug on her skirt – shedding his last thread of divinity and dignity. Would Carlotta be strong enough to fend him off at that point? True, Apollo was a diminished god inside a depleted body, but his will was formidable. Over the centuries, his obscene, single-minded purpose had petrified into a leaden monomania. Carlotta would have to summon every last ounce of her water-nymph determination.

Andolosia squeezed the crank. His knuckles whitened as he choked the imaginary scene from his mind.

"Come on, Carlotta," he said under his breath. "Give the signal."

Her song began filtering up the mountain.

"Show me a man who flows like a river, flows like a

river, flows like . . ."

Andolosia furiously cranked the worm screw. Its gear clicked tooth to tooth, gradually turning the massive pulleys inside the dam's walls.

"And I'll show you a man who is free."

The chamber rumbled as the rising torrent raced under the sluice gates.

"Show me a man who swims with the current, and I'll show you a man who is free."

The rumble grew into a deafening roar, which drowned out Carlotta's voice. The chamber shook so violently, he feared the walls might crash on top of him. Only after he could crank no further, and the gates were fully open, did the vibrations cease, overtaken by a whoosh not heard since the great River Oceanus broke containment in Olympus.

He began to count. *One.* By his calculation, a twenty-second flow at the fully open position would rise to an eight-foot wall of water at the palm tree, diminishing to an eighteen-inch-deep stream at the mouth of Well Street. *Seven.* Monticellans would incur little more than damp shoes. *Ten.* Andolosia fought the urge to accelerate the count. *Fifteen.* He felt a tickle in his belly. *Twenty is so close. Just five more numbers. Sixteen. Now, only four more!* He adjusted his grip on the crank. *Seventeen.* He positioned one leg slightly behind the other and bent his knees. *Eighteen.* He inhaled and held his breath. *Nineteen.* He exhaled. *Pull!* The lubricated gear moved smoothly and quickly. With four blurry gyrations of the crank, he shut the sluice gates.

Thank you, Mosè Indaco, for designing such an elegant dam.

It had become unsettlingly quiet. No whoosh – he'd expected that – but nor were there twittering partridges or buzzing insects or ruffling leaves. Nothing except his own halting breaths and the thrum of blood coursing behind his ear drums. A gelid thought seeped through a crack in his consciousness. *Everyone is dead.* He flushed the intrusive thought from his mind.

He bolted from the chamber and sprinted downhill. The thicket of laurels between the dam and the clearing had been reduced to a denuded tract of mud, stumps, and snapped branches. The palm tree was gone. He scoured the desolate landscape for survivors. Sansone's corpse was face-down. His broken index finger clung to the horn's grip at an obtuse, grievous angle. The instrument's bell was warped, and its main tube was kinked like a worm struck by a gravedigger's shovel. Farther on, Gennaro's trouserless body was draped over a rocky outcropping. His lip was curled in a puckish mien, a psychic boot print from the god who'd snuffed out the flame of his life. The corner of the wishing hat – the *real* wishing hat – peeked from his torn doublet. Andolosia took the hat, cursed Hermes' name, and draped brush over his dead friend's exposed lower half.

A vulture was picking at something tan and floppy in the distance. It was the boy-inspector's long-billed cap. Stuck to a protruding branch was a tan shirt embroidered with the Fasci Sansone symbol of the sun surrounded by bound staves. The shirt was as small as the lone boot partially submerged in a nearby mud puddle. The boy himself was nowhere in sight.

But there she was.

Carlotta leaned against an escarpment. Her face displayed a nonchalant, almost bored, affect. Her hands were at her chest, surrounding a fist-thick cylinder of wood. At first glance, the harried Andolosia took her to be holding a windlass, as if raising a bucket from a well. A lengthier perusal disabused him of the prosaic image. There was no well, of course, not on a mountain slope. The cylinder in Carlotta's hands was too rough and asymmetrical to be a windlass. It was a bald tree branch, which the deluge had severed from its mother trunk and stripped raw.

He cleared the brush and leaves accumulated around

her torso. She was alert and breathing, though her respiration was shallow and ragged.

"Did we kill him?" she asked.

"Yes," he answered. "Can you move?"

"I'm very tired."

His fingers probed around the spot where the bough pressed against her chest.

"You're really jammed against the rock. I'll have to retrieve an axe to relieve the pressure. Does it hurt much?"

"I am just so tired."

Andolosia retracted his fingers. For a delirious second, he wondered why they were covered in date jam. He peeled Carlotta's hands from the branch. They, too, were blood-soaked. When he spied blood seeping from around the bough's point of impact, he turned brittle inside. He delicately repositioned her hands around the bough, back into the banal tableau he'd thought he'd seen a minute earlier. He leaned beside her against the escarpment.

"We saved the town," she said.

"You saved them," he said absently. "You saved everyone."

"I wonder what my father would think of our solution, using water as a weapon. Blasphemous."

"We saved more lives than we took. I hazard your father would be proud we let the river run free, even if only for a minute."

"I have a strange feeling in my heart."

Andolosia choked up.

"It is so full," she continued. "What a wonderful sensation. It is so full, I fear it will burst."

He wept, unable to speak.

"I forgot to ask," she said. "Do you think Professor Galilei will take on a female apprentice?"

He cleared his throat. "I shall insist."

He stroked her forehead as tears spilled down his face

and dripped on her cheeks.

"They tickle," she said.

"There are many more where those came from."

She gave a faint laugh. "Come closer. I must tell you something before I forget. It is very important."

Andolosia couldn't see much through the saltwater prism distorting his vision, so he leaned down until he felt her fading breath on his ear. After whispering her wisdom, she giggled herself into silence.

He wiped his tears and kissed her cold blue lips. He exhaled for what seemed like a minute before leaning back and marveling at the daytime moon. Though it wasn't uncommon for the emblems of day and night to share the same sky, he couldn't help interpreting the astronomical occurrence as a paradox. The mind was funny that way. The brain's reflex was to draw stark distinctions, categorize and segregate, separate light from dark, and, in general, resist the fundamental truth about which experience continuously reminded us: life was lived in the gray. This was how Andolosia could feel both love and hate, exhilaration and grief. Black Tartarus and gleaming Olympus occupied the same space inside his gray heart.

The gibbous moon has a kind face, Andolosia thought.

A fast-moving cloud soon eclipsed it. He closed his eyes and envisioned a curtain like the one that had divided the front and back of the Petasos hat shop. The curtain hung between who he was at that moment and whoever he would become thereafter. He yanked it good and shut.

CHAPTER

THIRTY-FOUR

Monticello, That Evening

Sansone had not, in fact, commanded his inspectors to assassinate townspeople or their children at the blast of his horn. Rather, while Andolosia and Carlotta had been waiting on the mountain, Sansone had gathered the inspectors and rallied them for the imminent "miracle on the mountain."

"The hour of the supreme prince is nigh," Sansone had told them in a quavering voice before ascending Mount Monticello. "Behold his face, the face of your father, for it is also your face. You are one through me, and I am one through you." In a different voice, he added, "It is time." A hazy sheen infiltrated his eyes. He straightened his spine, pulled back his shoulders, and puffed out his chest. "At last," he proclaimed in a booming voice, accented in ancient Greek. He marched toward the mountain with his youngest and smallest inspector, Jabril.

While two gods and a water nymph grappled on the mountain, Sansone's boy-inspectors loitered on Well Street, munching on jam rolls and exchanging pleasantries with the locals. Soon, to everyone's surprise, water began trickling down Well Street. The trickle grew into a stream, inundating shoes and upsetting planters, carts of root vegetables, and the boards with Carlotta's sweet rolls. It wasn't spring, nor was it raining. The alarmed townspeople feared the worst – a breach in the dam.

They sounded the call to evacuate. They frenetically pounded on doors and grasped the hands of the very young and the very old. They filtered out from homes and shops and coalesced into a single, teeming organism and waded to the mouth of Well Street like a gargantuan amoeba. That was where they got their first glimpse of the miracle. Jabril was floating toward them, clinging to a bundle of palm fronds, as naked and exposed as a frog on a lily pad. The amoeba sensed in its collective mind that it should make way for him. The boy had a natural course, whether or not predetermined, and it would be sinful to divert it, or worse, cut it short. The amoeba parted, closing ranks after the boy had completed his passage. The awe-struck organism followed Jabril around each turn, contracting and swelling to accommodate the diversity of people, animals, and objects, absorbing 999 inspectors of the Fasci Sansone in the process. Jabril's palm-frond raft floated to the town's center and stopped at the wall surrounding the defunct well.

Don Salvatore stepped onto the wall and raised his hand to quiet the throng's excited susurrations. "Years ago," the priest declaimed, "darkness descended upon this village. With the Church's misguided blessing, neighbor turned on neighbor, and we cast out a respected elder and ten orphan boys. The emptiness from their absence has haunted us ever since, which is why we pray for their souls before opening the floodgates each spring. Today's flood is no mere accident of nature or failure of human engineering. I believe the Lord has declared an end to our penance and rewarded us with one hundred new souls for each one we abandoned." He gestured to Jabril and added, "Let us now hear from God's prophet."

The 999 boys of the Fasci Sansone gave beseeching looks to their naked comrade. Jabril blanched. Who was he to speak on the lofty topic of miracles? He wasn't sure what had occurred on the mountain, let alone that he'd witnessed events worthy of a prophet's telling. He recalled foggy bits and pieces – men speaking in strange voices, a hat full of cow shit, a strangulation, and the beautiful woman who'd found him in the torrent and stuffed a wad of palm fronds into his chest. It was all so absurd, he thought, it couldn't have really happened. He must have struck his head on a log and dreamed it.

All Jabril really knew was that the pale-faced Medici who'd plucked him and his brothers from poverty was dead, and they surely would perish without the care of the good people of Monticello. He regarded the multitude of expectant faces clamoring for him to say something, anything, that would add flesh and blood to Don Salvatore's religious reverie.

Jabril stood, concealing his modesty with a palm frond. His was a dual modesty. One aspect was natural shyness. The other was gender, for there was one amongst Sansone's boy inspectors who was not in fact a boy. Jabril wouldn't unveil his true self this day, not while his brethren still viewed his kind as "the weaker sex." Time was of the essence, and unraveling that myth would take years, perhaps lifetimes. Besides, the occasion didn't demand absolute truth. To the contrary. Jabril's self-preserving imperative required him to pull a veil over the people's eyes and weave the myth of the Miracle on Mount Monticello.

Jabril took a deep breath and projected his testimony to the assembled throng. It came to him in a rush, and he let it pass through his lips in a high-pitched and tender torrent. He said Lake Monticello had swallowed him in darkness. He couldn't breathe or see as the current thrashed him about.

But the waters became quiet and calm. He surfaced in warm, brilliant light. Heaven's light! There, he spied God on His throne! Jabril could practically touch His golden sandal. But just as Jabril extended his hand, a wave whisked him away. He was wet and cold again, floating down the mountain, naked as the day of his birth. A voice spoke to him. It was the water's voice. It told him to deliver a message to the town. "For centuries, I have sustained the good people of Monticello. I now give you Jabril, my child. Cherish him and his brothers as you would your own kin."

The locals celebrated Jabril's testimony with cheers and warm embraces. One by one, the 999 boys of the former Fasci Sansone tossed their billed caps into the well. With a thousand brothers and thousands of new parents, they didn't bewail the loss of one father.

In the evening, Monticellans gathered at the well for Maestro Rabino's memorial service. Following Don Salvatore's benediction, a raucous discussion ensued. The people concluded that Sansone de Medici had murdered their beloved Gennaro. True blame, however, rested with Paola Crostelli, for she'd summoned Sansone with false, scurrilous allegations against the two northerners, who also appeared to have perished on the mountain. One person shouted that Paola should be tried for murder and strung up by her neck. Another suggested abandoning the trial and proceeding straight to the hanging.

Don Salvatore waited patiently while his flock vented their spleens. When their exhortations tapered off, he soberly declared, "Paola is no longer one of us. That is justice enough."

On that, there was universal agreement. For a Monticellan, exile was a fate worse than death.

The following morning, the townspeople crowded in front of Paola's bakery and prevented her from entering. She protested vociferously. She shouted futile, red-faced threats to complain to the Holy Office. The people remained steadfast. The merchants refused to sell Paola olive oil and flour, the farmers refused to deliver her milk, and the apothecary would not provide her the roots she took for indigestion. Monticellans guarded the town's fonts, denying Paola access to the town's lifeblood. A day later, she packed her things on a donkey cart and departed her ancestral home for good.

Paola's bakery didn't remain dormant long. It began churning out mafalda under the new management of Maestra Francesca and Maestra Margherita. Within two months, three more bakeries would open, each competing on price, quality, and variety. For the first time in its history, Monticello knew full and free competition, and, Lord, did it taste sweet.

CHAPTER

THIRTY-FIVE

Borough of Schwarz Boden, Berlin, 1661

L orenz Mützenmacher married his assistant, Astrid, two years after delivering Carlotta's corpse, an apology, and a copy of the prophecy to the Lux family in Taormina. Astrid liked to sing while she stitched in the cutting room. She had a good singing voice, great even, though she lacked Carlotta's range and enigmatic ability to intertwine notes. Like the water nymph, Astrid was an excellent baker. But while Astrid's bread loaves were crusty on the outside and soft inside, they lacked a peculiar herbal flavor Lorenz recalled with fondness. Perhaps water made the difference. The Spree River was no substitute for the mountain-fed fonts of Monticello.

On the other hand, Astrid was the Sicilian's equal in bawdiness – no small feat. She exhibited a streak of nonconformity, which, as with the Sicilian, Lorenz found irresistibly arousing. After the hat business was well-entrenched in Schwarz Boden, Astrid would occasionally dress in Lorenz's clothes, don a false beard, and engage certain officious clients – the stodgy priest, the over-decorated military officer, the corpulent baron of middling status – in absurd discussions about the "inferiority of the gentler sex." Lorenz would eavesdrop from the cutting room, biting his fist to muffle his convulsive laughter. Afterward, Astrid would lock the door and slip through the curtain separating the cutting room from the rest of the shop, having removed all her clothing in transit. The spirit gum she used for the beard was not readily removed, so it always remained. Unsettled by the beard at first, Lorenz came to appreciate how the whiskers tickled his clavicle as she huffed and puffed her way to orgasm.

Few children can claim direct matrilineal descent from a bearded mother. Lambert was one of the few or, rather, he would have been one of the few had his parents informed him of the salacious fact. There was, however, a different fact that could not be withheld, a fact that would require him and his progeny to carry on the hat business due to an accident of their patrilineal descent.

Near the end of Lorenz's days, he labored longer and longer in the hat shop. Lambert urged his father to reduce his toils, reminding him of his old age and the headaches, which had been increasing in frequency and intensity. Surely, insufficient sleep and eye strain were making his condition worse. Lambert entreated Lorenz to spend time with his grandson, not cloistered in the dim cutting room amongst the lifeless fabric swatches. Lorenz did not dispute his son's arguments. He promised to abide the advice as soon as he finished the alligator leather hat on the cutting table. So went their conversation on the night before Lorenz finished his final hat.

Lorenz was done just before dawn. With the press of a button hidden in the brim, ostrich plumes folded forward from the crown to form a feathery sunshade. He wanted to show Astrid his masterpiece, but that was impossible and had been for many years. He pulled down the front of his doublet, opened his shirt, and stroked his clavicle with a spare ostrich plume. It was no false whisker, but he laughed anyway.

Enough whimsy. He set the hat in the shop window, fetched a quill, ink, and parchment, and turned to the solemn task he'd postponed for too long. He took a deep breath, closed his eyes, and mustered the fortitude to fling open a curtain in his soul he'd long ago closed. He wrote for an hour. After the ink dried, he slipped the parchment into a case of indigo silk and stuck it in the wall safe with the wishing hat, the prophecy, and Hermes' gold coin. His head throbbed miserably.

Lorenz exited the shop at sunrise. The scent of sweet pastries was wafting up Mauer Street. He strode past bakery after bakery in search of the source, only to find every bakery in Schwarz Boden dormant. Yet the scent persisted, intensifying the closer he got to the Spree River. He knelt at the bank and scooped a handful of the cool river water. He drank. Astounding! The river water tasted like date jam.

Lorenz felt a stirring of that exploratory urge from his youth, from when he went by a different name. He waded into the water. He invited the cold into his shoes, breeches, and doublet. He gazed at the moon, which seemed to be smiling upon him with his mother's face. She was more beautiful than he'd remembered. She was shimmering like a magical pearl.

A jagged pain sliced through his skull. He winced. He licked his lips and drank in the river's sweetness. He heard singing from a great distance. He strained to discern the words and the tune. He concentrated until his head ached unbearably. All at once, the pressure released like pent-up steam, and the song flooded his ears.

> *Show me a man who flows like a river,*
> *flows like a river,*

flows like a river.
Show me a man who flows like a river,
and I'll show you a man who is free.
Show me a man who swims with the current,
swims with the current,
swims with the current.
Show me a man who swims with the current,
and I'll show you a man who is free.

He lay back in the river and dissolved into the flow, no longer Lorenz Mützenmacher or the former Andolosia Petasos, no longer cursed, no longer a father of a cursed son and grandson, no longer a hatter with dashed dreams of scientific inquiry, no longer a creature of flesh and bone. Whatever he had become, he was utterly free.

The End

ACKNOWLEDGEMENTS

I would like to thank my wife, Laura Fentonmiller, for her love, encouragement, and insightful feedback on all my writing projects. I also owe a debt of gratitude to friends and colleagues who have provided constructive feedback on *The Water Nymph Gospels* literary universe:

Will Ducklow, Christine Lee Delorme, Tom Kane, Jennifer Hawkes, my fellow writers in Meg Wolitzer's workshop at the Stony Brook Southampton Writers Conference, Shanna McNair and Scott Wolven of The Writers Hotel, and editors Blair Thornburgh and Julie Miesionczek. I also am eternally grateful to Maer Wilson of Ellysian Press for her editorial wisdom and hard work in getting *Fate Accompli* fit to print.

Finally, I give profound thanks to the exemplary women who have inspired me and many others to be better human beings: Diana Nyad, Simone de Beauvoir, Catharine MacKinnon, Gloria Steinem, and Ruth Bader Ginsburg, to name just a few. Oh, and my mother.

ABOUT THE AUTHOR

 Keith R. Fentonmiller's debut novel, Kasper Mützenmacher's Cursed Hat (Curiosity Quills, 2017), was a Foreword Indies Book of the Year Finalist. He has published short stories with the Stone Coast Review (Pushcart-nominated) and Running Wild Press, and humor pieces with The Satirist and Defenestration. He is a consumer protection attorney for the U.S. Federal Trade Commission. Before graduating from the University of Michigan Law School, he toured with a professional comedy troupe, writing and performing sketch comedy. He lives in Kensington, Maryland with his wife, Laura. They have two grown children, Stoney and Bay. You can find out more about Keith and his writing at keithfentonmiller.com.

A Humble Request

Thank you for purchasing my book. I hope you enjoyed your reading experience. As an author, I depend on reader reviews to survive in the publishing ecosystem, so I would greatly appreciate it if you left a short review on Amazon. A sentence or two and an honest opinion is all I ask.

Also, please visit keithfentonmiller.com and sign up for my mailing list to stay apprised of publishing updates, including about Book 2 of The Water Nymph Gospels series.

ALSO FROM ELLYSIAN PRESS

The Clockwork Detective from R.A. McCandless at Amazon

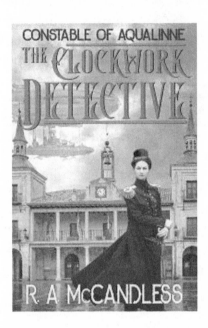

Aubrey Hartmann left the Imperial battlefields with a pocketful of medals, a fearsome reputation, and a clockwork leg.

The Imperium diverts her trip home to investigate the murder of a young *druwyd* in a strange town. She is ordered to not only find the killer but prevent a full-scale war with the dreaded Fae.

Meanwhile, the arrival of a sinister secret policeman threatens to dig up Aubrey's own secrets – ones that could ruin her career.

It soon becomes clear that Aubrey has powerful enemies with plans to stop her before she gets started. Determined to solve the mystery, Aubrey must survive centaurs, thugs and a monster of pure destruction.

"This is my kind of book: a wonderful, fully realized, utterly plausible Steampunk world with a dynamite plot, great characters, and the best dirigibles this side of anywhere. I hope there's more to come."— From James P. Blaylock, World Fantasy Award-Winning Author, Co-Founder of the Modern Steampunk Genre

Moonflowers by David A. Gray at Amazon

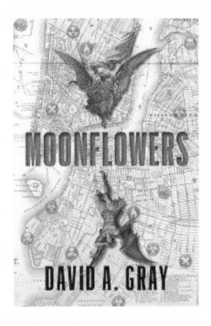

I'm not like those other freaks. The kids who can look inside your head and bring your nightmares to life.

The weirdos who can steal your luck or make a thing true just by wishing it. The outliers born from the mess that followed Armageddon.

The ones you call Moonflowers, half mockingly and half afraid. They're the mistakes that humanity hates – and needs.

I'm not like them. I'm worse. And I'm the only thing standing between you and the legions of heaven and hell.

—Petal – The Armageddon-Lite Archives

A Forgotten Past by Tiffany Lafleur at Amazon

Beast Whisperer – that was Lily's special talent. Useful but not as flashy as some.

Or so she thought.

When she was a child, Lily had washed up on the riverbank near Basolt, with no memory of who she was. Taken in by the couple who found her, she was raised as their own, alongside their new baby.

Years later she does something extraordinary. And word spreads of a new Spirit Hopper, someone who can enter into and control not only beasts, but people. Someone who can change the land of Sapeiro. Someone who had supposedly died years before.

The rumors catch the attention of those who would control her power. Those who would use Lily for their own purposes, no matter how many lives it cost. They set their plots to capture her in motion.

Fate Accompli

But Lily discovers there is at least one group who might

hold the key to her real identity. One group who would protect her. But trust does not come easily for Lily. And her would-be saviors have secrets of their own.

ABOUT ELLYSIAN PRESS

Ellysian Press has been bringing high-quality, award-winning books in the Speculative Fiction genres since 2014.

To find other Ellysian Press books, please visit our website: (http://www.ellysianpress.com/).

You can find our complete list of novels here. They include:

Beneath a Fearful Moon by R.A. McCandless

Time to Die by Jordan Elizabeth

A Forgotten Past by Tiffany Lafleur

Aethereal by Kerry Reed

The Soft Fall by Marissa Byfield

Motley Education by S.A. Larsen

Moonflowers by David A. Gray

The Clockwork Detective by R.A. McCandless

Progenie by Mack Little

Time to Live by Jordan Elizabeth

The Moonlight Herders by Stefani Chaney

Before Dawn by Elizabeth Arroyo

Redemption by Mike Schlossberg

Kālong by Carol Holland March

Marked Beauty by S.A. Larsen

Dreamscape by Kerry Reed

The Rending by Carol Holland March

A Deal in the Darkness by Allan B. Anderson

The Tyro by Carol Holland March

Muse Unexpected by VC Birlidis

The Devil's Triangle by Toni De Palma

Premonition by Agnes Jayne

Relics by Maer Wilson

A Shadow of Time by Louann Carroll

Idyllic Avenue by Chad Ganske

Portals by Maer Wilson

Innocent Blood by Louann Carroll

Magics by Maer Wilson

The **Ellysian Press Catalog** has a complete list of current and forthcoming books.